LORD MISERY

Beastly Lords Book Five

SYDNEY JANE BAILY

cat whisker press
Massachusetts

ISBN: 978-1-938732-39-3
Published by cat whisker press
Imprint of JAMES-YORK PRESS

Cover: cat whisker studio
In conjunction with Philip Ré
Book Design: cat whisker studio

DEDICATION

To my mom, Beryl Baily

You are the original and constant source of love in my life.

All I can say is thank you!

OTHER WORKS
by
SYDNEY JANE BAILY

THE RARE CONFECTIONERY
Series

The Duchess of Chocolate
The Toffee Heiress
My Lady Marzipan

THE DEFIANT HEARTS
Series

An Improper Situation
An Irresistible Temptation
An Inescapable Attraction
An Inconceivable Deception
An Intriguing Proposition
An Impassioned Redemption

THE BEASTLY LORDS
Series

Lord Despair
Lord Anguish
Lord Vile
Lord Darkness
Lord Misery
Lord Wrath
Eleanor

PRESENTING LADY GUS

A Georgian-Era Novella

ACKNOWLEDGMENTS

I want to offer a hearty thanks to my editor, Violetta Rand, for knowing when to give me a pep talk, and to Perry, my best friend, for simply being himself — always happy despite an unfair world.

CHAPTER ONE

1851, Jonling Hall
Sheffield, England

Jameson heard the tapping at his wife's door and ignored it. No doubt one of the maids again wanting to freshen something or try to take away the dead flowers. He lay stretched out upon her bed, having removed his boots because he knew it would bother her if he had his Hessians on the satin counterpane.

The drapes were pulled closed although it was mid-day. It was peaceful, cool, quiet. *Like a morgue or a cemetery.*

No! He mustn't allow his thoughts to go down that road. Not again, not today on her birthday. A blessed day for a gorgeous woman. His perfect wife.

Tap-tap.

He wanted to shout something vulgar and make the intruder go away. But that wasn't his manner. Even after everything that had happened. Besides, he didn't have to let anyone in, nor did he have to go out. That was the beauty of owning one's own home. Truly, like a lord of the manor.

He grimaced at the notion. No one ever mentioned a *bastard of the manor*, but, in truth, that was what he was. And no amount of spit and polish—or having his cousin, the Earl of Lindsey, generously bestow the family's title of viscount upon him—was going to change that fact.

Any more than one could bring back the dead.

Tap-tap.

He threw his arm over his face. Then he let himself imagine it was his Esmera on the other side of the door, wanting to come in. Her silky hair, like rich, black ink flowing between his fingers, her dark, shiny eyes with intriguing thoughts flashing behind them, and her full lips bespeaking her exotic parentage, always warm and kissable—all turned to dust.

"Enter," he said loudly enough so the maid could hear.

The door made a slight creak when it opened. Jameson remembered he had intended to oil the hinges himself, despite her never having said it bothered her. Now, like everything, it was too late.

Too damn late!

"My lord?" came a deep voice.

Not the maid, it was his butler. Mr. Wynn was a superb butler, but he took no notice of Jameson's constant reminder to call him "sir" or "Mr. Turner." He hadn't been born a lord, nor even a legitimate son, and would never feel like one. The only thing the title of viscount had ever done for him was gain him Esmera. Her parents would never have allowed their union otherwise.

"Yes?"

"You have a visitor, my lord."

"No, Mr. Wynn, I do not. That isn't possible when I am not seeing anyone."

Frankly, he didn't care if he ever saw anyone again. He didn't even see himself these days, as he'd had the mirrors covered. However, by the feel of his overly long beard and hair, he knew what a disheveled appearance he presented to the world.

"Nevertheless, my lord," Mr. Wynn persisted, "you do have one."

"Is it Lord Lindsey or his wife?" Jameson could hardly stand to think of a man so fortunate as to still have his wife, but his beloved cousin, Simon Devere, Earl of Lindsey, was the only person with whom he'd allowed himself to grieve while still in Town. Simon, along with sweet Jenny Devere, Lady Lindsey, had arrived in London mere days after the tragedy, and they had stayed with him through the horrors that followed.

A purgatory of black clothing and crape, of funeral and burial, of shock and disbelief that still hadn't quite left him. It had been seven months and a week.

A few years earlier, Simon was the first person Jameson had ever told of his shadowy parentage. Jameson was the illicit result of a coupling between a chambermaid and his father, who was Simon's uncle, Lord James Devere.

So trite. So careless. His father in a nutshell!

He and Simon had become fast friends after he had finally disclosed who his father was. In some ways, Jameson was similar to his half brother, the cousin Simon had grown up with, the one Simon had loved and gone to war with, and whom he'd seen slaughtered before his eyes in a cell in the Burmese jungle. Tobias Devere was the legitimate issue of his father, and Jameson regretted never getting the chance to meet him.

Simon's residence, Belton Manor, was just down the lane from Jameson's own Jonling Hall. In fact, Lady Lindsey had gone into labor in Jameson's own dining room right after he'd bought the place and invited his neighbors over to tell them he was actually kin. That was a mere three years earlier.

When times were happier, it had not been unusual for his cousin to drop in unannounced. However, since the time of Jameson's despairing and hopeless return from London as a widower, he'd declined all of Simon and Jenny's attempts to make him return to society.

They meant well, but their own happiness was painful to him. The blessings of their children reminded Jameson of what would never be for him and Esmera. He was a selfish, miserable nuisance, who could barely stand himself, but such was the way of it.

"My lord, it is a young woman, Miss Darrow, who has come to call."

Jameson lifted his arm from his face and opened his eyes, staring at the blue canopy overhead. How many nights had he and Esmera laid here? *Not enough. Not nearly enough.*

"My lord, what should I tell her?"

Mr. Wynn should have told the woman his master wasn't seeing anyone. That was the standing order, after all.

"What did you say her name was?"

"Miss Darrow, my lord."

Darrow. Darrow? His brain was not as sharp as it once was. He was often light-headed from lack of sleep and food.

"You're not eating enough," his housekeeper, Mrs. Williams, said whenever she caught a glimpse of him, which was why he remained out of sight. He ate a few bites occasionally, but it all tasted like chalk, and sometimes, he even felt guilty that he could still eat while Esmera could not.

His mind often meandered along pathways of thoughts that made little sense, but sent him into emotional despondency again as if the accident had only happened yesterday. He knew if he ate more and regained his strength, his sharp mind would return. A few years ago, he'd been able to count cards with the best gamblers in London. Now, he could barely recall his own age, but he was certain he must be at least a hundred years old.

"My lord, what should I tell her?"

"Why didn't you tell her immediately I was not receiving visitors?"

"I did, my lord, to no avail."

Jameson let that process for a moment. Then he asked, "What do you mean 'to no avail'?"

"I mean, my lord, Miss Darrow will not leave. She is in the drawing room and said she will stay in the drawing room until she speaks with you."

"The devil take her! What cheek!" Then he considered a moment. *Was she a friend of his wife's?* Perhaps she had some nice story to tell him about Esmera.

On the one hand, he wanted to retain every ounce of his wife's essence, including other people's memories of her. On the other, he wasn't convinced he could tolerate listening to tales of happier times.

Groaning with the effort to move, he swung his legs off the bed, sitting up in one smooth movement. Momentarily, he felt dizzy. Without doubt, he'd been lying there too long in what he considered to be his wife's room. They had shared it during the nights when she didn't have a megrim, which struck her too often, causing her need for absolute silence and darkness. During those times, he went to what he considered his own bedroom, containing his clothing and his toiletries.

He hadn't slept a night in it since his return from London. He hadn't really slept an entire night at all anywhere, but whatever rest he did get, he found in her room where he still tried to catch the scent of her opulent musky perfume. Sometimes, it seemed to waft from the pillows. Other times, he couldn't smell her at all.

Glancing up, he looked straight into the pitying gaze of his butler. He'd forgotten the man was standing there. *Why was he there? Oh, yes, Miss Darrow.*

"We could send Mrs. Williams to scare her off."

The housekeeper was a fearsome woman, able to leave housemaids and tradesmen alike quaking in their shoes if she felt a modicum of displeasure at their behavior or their wares. Esmera had hired her and then left everything to do with the running of Jonling Hall to the capable, middle-aged housekeeper. Thus, his wife was the only person in the household, including himself, who had never experienced Mrs. Williams's displeasure.

After a pause, Mr. Wynn confessed, "I did, my lord."

"And?" Jameson tried to imagine the awful scene.

"Miss Darrow said she would not leave without seeing you. Then she turned her back on Mrs. Williams."

"Incredible!" Now he had a sliver of curiosity to meet this woman who could beard a lion in its den apparently.

"Do I still have a valet?" He hadn't seen the man for ages.

"No, my lord, you let him go months ago."

"Right. I cared for myself well enough for years. I certainly don't need someone fussing at me."

Ignoring the way his butler's gaze flitted over him, obviously seeing every out-of-place detail, Jameson stood slowly. Glancing around, he spied his wife's hairbrush still on the bureau. Strands of her black hair remained in it, for he'd ordered it to be left uncleaned.

"I will see her," he said stiffly.

"If your lordship would care to go down the hall to your own room," Mr. Wynn proposed, "I shall be happy to . . . *uh,* tidy you."

Jameson lifted his hands to his wild hair and ran fingers through it, once, twice, thrice. Then he smoothed his hands along his scraggly facial hair.

There! He was as tidy as he cared to be.

Without any shoes or a coat, he would see this woman.

"No need, Winnie. I'm ready to meet Miss Darrow."

MAISIE DIDN'T MIND WAITING. She literally had nothing else to do the entire day. Visiting her aunt, Anne Blackwood, as well as two of her cousins—Jenny, who had married the Earl of Lindsey and lived in Belton Manor, and Eleanor, the one Blackwood sister remaining unmarried—Maisie's stay with them was usually uneventful and relaxing. In a word, blissful.

Apart from Jenny, now Lady Lindsey, Maisie's Blackwood relations lived in a cottage just outside the modern village of Sheffield. She found it a welcome change from the noise, bustle, filth, and smoke of London. And it was not so different from her family home in Dumfries, Scotland, only a couple hours by steady horse from the English border and the infamous Gretna Green.

Being raised in the extreme south of Scotland, Maisie could put on her brogue if she wished or tamp it down and sound like any other English miss, which was her preference, especially when in London.

After a rather shaky, even frightening past Season, this peaceful break was perfectly to her liking. While she loved the music, the dazzling ballrooms, and the highly polished dance floors, not to mention the dapper gentlemen, she had got into a bit of trouble toward the end of the social calendar and was relieved when it came to an end.

Some men were not as upstanding or chivalrous as they appeared to be.

Rather than traveling up to Dumfries first and then returning south to visit Eleanor, Maisie had traveled with her aunt and cousin from London to Sheffield. Eleanor had also been happy to see the end of another busy Season, as the environment of Town did not agree with her love for the natural world or afford her the quiet hours she liked to spend reading and drawing.

Maisie didn't mind being the more outgoing of the two of them, as they formed a nice balance in Town. She only wished she'd listened to her cousin on one night in particular and stayed by her side instead of venturing down the hallway with an unscrupulous lord.

Luckily, that was all behind her.

Upon arrival in Sheffield, Maisie had discovered the once-affable Lord Turner was now considered a veritable hermit, a widower suffering from extreme melancholy as he had for the entire recent Season.

In the past, when Maisie had come to visit the Blackwood branch of her family, there were great parties at Belton Manor, which was only a mile from the Blackwood cottage. Naturally, Jenny, the countess and oldest Blackwood sister, invited all her family, including Maisie, her cousin. At more than one dinner gathering, the viscount, Lord Turner, and his lovely wife, then newlyweds, had been in attendance. What's more, his lordship had taken the time to chat with her and Eleanor about the most interesting topics, such as London's gambling halls, something no one else would tell them.

Also, he described the gentleman's clubs, making them laugh until their sides hurt with tales of men wagering on everything from the color of their dinner companions' socks to the size of the next baked potato that came out from the kitchen, losing fortunes in the blink of an eye.

She still recalled some of his painfully absurd jokes.

"When is a clock on the stairs dangerous? When it runs down and strikes one."

"Why would a compliment from a chicken be an insult? Because it would be fowl language."

Maisie had been in London when Lady Turner died. So shocking, so unexpected. It was all anyone talked about for a month. Jenny and her husband, Lord Lindsey, had arrived in London, as the earl was cousin to the bereaving viscount.

After a while, perhaps it had been two weeks, the Lindseys and Lord Turner had left for Sheffield.

Since arriving in the village, Maisie had tried twice already to pay her respects at Jonling Hall, and twice been refused. She knew about grief, having lost her mother five years prior when she was barely thirteen. True, a parent was not the same as one's spouse, but still, it had shaken her to her core. She feared Lord Turner had not stopped shaking.

Lady Turner, Esmera by name, which Maisie thought a positively lovely name, was the most striking woman ever to grace a London ballroom. She meant no disrespect to her own cousin, Maggie Blackwood, now the Countess of

Cambrey, who was widely considered stunningly beautiful in the classic English tradition. Nevertheless, Esmera had the appeal of the foreign and exotic.

In point of fact, Esmera was everything Maisie was not. Tall, raven-haired, olive-skinned, extremely shapely. In a word, *irresistible*. Maisie was average height, very blond, pale, and apt to blush pink spots on her cheeks.

Naturally, the men hadn't been able to keep their eyes off Esmera, and Maisie had felt similarly drawn to the alluring woman, simply to stare at her unique appearance and mannerisms, and listen to her pretty voice.

And the couple together were a sight to behold. The Turners were obviously very much in love.

The poor man!

Maisie only wanted to express her condolences and, if possible, to tell him how life went on. It seemed cruel perhaps, but the absolute truth of it was everything continued regardless of one's personal sorrow. It was as though grief caused one to stand stock still in the midst of a quick-moving river, while everyone else continued floating downstream.

At some point, however, one had to plunge back in and continue floating along. There was no other option. Definitely not the one Lord Turner had taken, trying to remain alone on the riverbank. As Shakespeare said, *"Screw your courage to the sticking-place and we'll not fail."*

Thus, Maisie waited for his lordship to descend the stairs. Aunt Anne and cousin Eleanor were at Belton Manor with Jenny for the day. Maisie would walk over there eventually, after she'd seen Lord Turner.

And she was determined she would.

In the meantime, she'd wandered every inch of the darkened drawing room, with its heavy drapes pulled decidedly closed against the world outside. She'd looked at a landscape painting above the fire until she could describe it with her eyes shut and watched the minute hand on a grandfather clock grind round and round before finally settling on a comfy chair, resting her head on the winged back, and nodding off.

"Miss Darrow!" She jumped at the voice speaking her name.

At last, there was Lord Turner glaring down at her. Or, at least, she thought it was he, although except for a passing resemblance of chestnut-brown hair and blue-gray eyes, he didn't look like the viscount she recalled.

This man looked as if he'd come *hot from hell*, as Shakespeare wrote of Caesar. Or, at the very least, he'd forgotten all manner of good grooming.

Her heart went out to him instantly.

Rising to her feet, she could only hope she hadn't been snoring softly as her brother Ned used to tease her about. Worse would be if her mouth had been open and—*God forbid! Had she been drooling, even slightly?*

Hating to draw attention to the potential issue, she pretended to raise her hand to touch her gloved fingers to her hair, but actually ran them over her cheek.

Dry, she thought with satisfaction.

"Lord Turner," she greeted with a small curtsey.

He frowned. "Are you a friend of my wife's?"

"No, my lord. I am—"

Before she could finish, he turned away, giving her a view of his hair nearly half-way down his back like a Highland warrior of olden days. He was at the open door before she found her voice.

"My lord, where are you going?"

"Whence I came," he said without turning.

"Will you come back?"

"No." And he left the room without even a "good day."

She hurried after him. He'd already crossed the marble foyer and had one foot on the first step of the staircase when she called out to him.

"*Everyone can master a grief but he that has it.*"

He halted and gripped the railing tightly. This time he did turn, fixing her with a baleful glare.

"What are you babbling about?"

"The Bard, my lord, he said—"

Lord Turner interrupted her. "Are you quoting Shakespeare to me?"

He might look like a barbarian at that particular moment, but obviously, he wasn't.

Maisie would entice him gently back to the drawing room so they could have a chat. It would do him a world of good to socialize a little, even if his sorrow was too personal to express to a stranger.

"I am. I only wish to—"

"Well don't," he snapped. "It's tedious."

With that, Lord Turner continued up the stairs and disappeared from her view.

"*Hm*," she murmured to herself. He would be a hard nut to crack, indeed. Unquestionably a walnut.

Still, she'd had a victory, albeit a small one. She had got him downstairs briefly and, as Shakespeare said . . .

When no relevant words came to mind, Maisie settled for her own personal refrain: *Everything seemed better with jelly*.

To that end, as the butler arrived to see her out, she returned to the entrance hall and found her little basket still sitting on a tufted ottoman. Retrieving it, she turned and handed it to Lord Turner's man.

"A jar of thistle blossom jelly. That's from my home in Dumfries," she told him. "And a jar of strawberry jam, made right here in Sheffield."

The butler stared down at what was now in his hands, his expression aghast as if she'd handed him a basket of snakes.

"Please give these to his lordship with my condolences. I hope he enjoys them. I shall return soon," she promised.

At these words, the butler's eyebrows shot up. She knew he was dying to warn her off.

"Yes, miss," he said, his voice choked.

And Maisie headed out into the brilliant sunshine of a country afternoon.

CHAPTER TWO

Feeling a little disappointed, Maisie strolled down the road to find her cousins. Both Eleanor and Jenny were in the extensive gardens behind Belton Manor. Their mother, Aunt Anne, was there, too.

Jenny, Lady Lindsey, was a gracious hostess, and whenever Maisie was down from Dumfries or up from London staying at the cottage, she was often invited to the estate. She found Eleanor seated on the grass with her head down and practically in the flowers, sketching what was in front of her. Her youngest cousin's Season had not been much better in terms of results than Maisie's own. No suitor gained for Eleanor, either, but her cousin, at least, hadn't experienced the seedier side of London's ballrooms, nor a frightening scoundrel who'd nearly been Maisie's undoing.

Jenny and Aunt Anne were seated on a stone bench out of the sun. A nanny tended to the small Lindsey heir and his younger, twin siblings. All seemed right with the world, except for the suffering of Lord Turner in his gloomy Jonling Hall on such a gorgeous day. It wouldn't be so terrible except Maisie could recall the viscount's former humor and ready smile.

"How was your walk?" Jenny asked as she approached.

"Perfectly lovely." *Should she mention her ill-advised visit?* She had done nothing wrong, so she added, "I stopped at the hall to see Lord Turner."

Her aunt shook her head. "Poor man."

Eleanor looked up from her drawing. "Maybe Jonling Hall is cursed. First, Sir Tobias died so young, then his brother moves into the home, and his wife dies tragically."

"You read too many Gothic novels, dear sister," Jenny remarked. "Tobias died far away in a war, so while a terrible occurrence, not exactly something by which one might point and say 'curse.' As for Lady Turner, sadly, there are far too many such accidents."

"It's true," Aunt Anne agreed. "Train travel is not perfectly safe, although when one considers the number of them running and the many miles traveled each day, it's a wonder there aren't more derailments."

"Be that as it may," Eleanor insisted, "it's still tragic, and I think Lord Turner must feel cursed, losing a half brother he never got to know and then the wife he barely had time to love."

"*Lovers ever run before the clock,*" Maisie reminded them.

"You and your Shakespeare," Jenny said. "Aptly stated, nonetheless. It doesn't matter how long we have, it will not be enough for me with Simon."

"Nor me with your father," Anne added, yet Maisie wondered how her long-widowed aunt could still hold onto such a sentiment after the baron gambled away their fortune. But that was the power of love. And for her part, she longed to experience it.

Indeed, Maisie had believed she was going to do exactly that earlier in the year during the Season, but she'd been mistaken. *Love surfeits not, lust like a glutton dies. Love is all truth, lust full of forged lies.* It had been lust, scary and raw, which she'd encountered in London.

When they went in for the midday meal, Simon Devere, Lord Lindsey, joined them in the lofty dining room, giving his wife perhaps an overly passionate greeting for mixed company. It made Maisie, along with the rest of Jenny's family, smile. However, after the roast chicken and potatoes had been cleared away, when she mentioned Lord Turner, the mood turned somber.

"I shall stop over there myself later," Simon offered. "Jameson has rebuffed my attempts at drawing him back into society each time I've tried, but I shouldn't let estate matters keep me so busy I forget how my cousin is suffering next door."

"Do you think he might come to dinner?" Jenny asked her husband.

"I will try to encourage him. He looked a little lean last time I saw him."

"He did," Maisie agreed. All eyes turned to her. She shrugged. "I do recall him as a sturdy, strong man, cutting a fine figure with his wife on the dance floor or out riding. He is much thinner now, gaunt even, and his eyes look so deep set and sad."

Jenny shook her head. "We must do something."

"You cannot force someone out of grief," Simon said. "Only recall the state I was in when Toby died."

"That makes you the perfect person to help him," Jenny countered. "You understand only too well."

JAMESON SHOULD HAVE EXPECTED another visit so quickly on the heels of the last one. Unwanted things always happened in twos. *Or was it threes?*

He couldn't recall, as he headed downstairs into his parlor to greet his cousin, Lord Lindsey.

"Simon," he said with a nod.

"By God, man, you are wasting away. Jenny will kill me if I don't get you over to our home for a hearty meal. We'll do seven courses, shall we?"

He shook his head. "That is beyond my capacity at the moment."

"All right," Simon agreed. "Only five."

"No, I don't mean the amount of food, I mean going to your home. Please give your lovely . . . wife my apologies, but I cannot venture out."

The word *wife* had nearly choked him. *Dammit! Why wouldn't everyone simply leave him alone?*

"Do you know Miss Darrow?" he asked Simon.

"Yes. She's my wife's cousin."

"What the devil did she mean coming to my home, bothering a man in mourning?"

Simon frowned. "I'm sure she meant no harm. Don't you remember her? You've met her on more than one occasion at my home."

Jameson shrugged, looking into gray-blue eyes like his own. "I don't know. Maybe. I simply wasn't expecting her here, I suppose. Tell her not to come again."

Against all odds, his cousin smiled. "I don't control what any lady does. You've been married. Surely, you appreciate that."

Jameson winced. The way Simon said it was as if he'd had a pair of painful shoes once and now recalled what it felt like for them to pinch his toes.

"I am *still* married, and Esmera is my wife. I just happen to be a widower."

Without asking, Simon walked to the sideboard and poured them each a glass of brandy. Jameson had not indulged except for a single, tear-filled night in London when he'd hoped he could drink himself into oblivion and not wake up at all.

Unfortunately, he'd awakened feeling wretched and still miserable as hell. Sadness and anger—those were the only emotions he ever felt anymore. Except fear. Fear of something else terrible happening, even to Simon or Jenny. *For who else did he have left?* His mother was gone, and he was entirely estranged from his unpleasant father.

He took the glass Simon offered and drank an unseemly gulp, glad to feel the burning sensation.

"Let's look at this another way, then," his cousin said, sitting on the sofa opposite. "Your wife can no longer be annoyed at you. So, why don't you help me? Jenny would be thrilled if you came to dinner tomorrow night, and if you don't, she'll blame me for not trying hard enough. It's a small favor to ask."

Jameson couldn't contain the growl of dissatisfaction.

"You're trapping me, and we both know Jenny is the sweetest person on earth who would never blame you for anything."

"Not true. Every time one of our children scrapes a knee, somehow, it's my fault. The other day, I ended up on hands and knees setting cushions around one of the coffee tables in case little Lionel took a tumble. Two minutes later, he was literally rolling down the main staircase and thoroughly enjoying himself!"

Jameson couldn't help smiling, although it felt strange. In fact, his cheek muscles protested at the new movement, not having used them for such a purpose in so long. He liked Simon's boys and his adorable little girl, but he didn't want to see them, or their happy parents.

"Please come," Simon urged.

"I'm sorry, I cannot. But tell Lady Lindsey, I shall try to eat more. And tell her not to worry."

His cousin sighed. "Is there anything I can do? Anything to help ease your grief? We all liked Esmera very much, and we know she would want you to live your life as well as you did before you met her."

Jameson gripped the glass so hard he thought he might crush it. Hearing her name on Simon's lips caused him renewed sadness. He wanted to call out to his wife over his shoulder and have her enter the room, sit on the arm of the sofa or, better yet, on his lap, laugh, chat with Simon, agree to go to Belton Manor that very evening for a delightful dinner and maybe charades with Jenny afterward.

Not that she'd always wanted to socialize with the Lindseys when she was alive, at least, not in the country.

Sheffield was not his wife's favorite environment, but she usually tolerated it with good grace, while counting the days until they could go to London or Bath or even Edinburgh. The quiet darkness of the countryside unnerved her after growing up in lively Madrid. The turmoil of Spain in the 1830s sent Esmera's parents, Señor and Señora Maradona, and their two young children on a path of constant movement, first to the great cities of Europe and then later to Britain.

When she died, Jameson had hoped for the first time in his life that Heaven was real, for he wanted her soul to be up in the sky with the brilliant sunlight or with the stars sparkling like a thousand candles in a ballroom. He dreaded the idea of her spirit remaining in the ground, in the silent darkness of the Brompton Cemetery on the outskirts of western London where she was interred.

Moreover, he couldn't recall a single conversation in which they discussed the quality of his life before her or ever contemplated what it could be like after. There was not supposed to be an *after* Esmera. Their married life was always about them, as a couple, and what they would do next, where they would go.

If he had been with her when she died . . . then, perhaps things would have turned out differently.

Jumping to his feet at that thought—one he tormented himself with almost daily—he didn't know where to go, except to the brandy decanter. He freshened his drink, and then turned to see Simon staring at him.

"A little more?"

"No, I'll be leaving shortly. I'm sorry if I upset you."

"You didn't. I can't possibly be more upset than I already am." He paused. Sarcasm was all he had left for humor, and it wasn't pleasant or social. He ought to be alone.

Simon stood, too. "After Tobias died and after my captivity, you know I had some sort of nervous prostration, a mental derangement of some sort. Those are not my words, but those of a smart man in Germany who helped me. I spent too much time alone in my room for months after returning from Burma. Grief and fear were my only companions."

"I know." Jameson also knew what Simon would tell him next, but he let him speak all the same.

"I fear if someone hadn't insisted I leave my room, I would be there still."

"Not merely someone," Jameson reminded him. "Your wife."

"Jenny wasn't my wife then, just another person whom I wanted to push away, but she wouldn't let me languish. It's true, she was a decidedly pretty lady coercing me to do pleasant things, like take a walk with her. And I know I'm not nearly as attractive—"

They both smiled wryly at each other.

Two smiles in one day, Jameson thought. *His face might very well break.*

"But I am going to hound you daily to come to take lunch with us or dinner," Simon continued. "Or we could simply go for a ride. Your favorite horse is probably growing fat, as you are getting thinner."

Jameson downed his second drink in one swallow, then choked.

When he finished coughing, he set his glass down. "I will ride with you sometime. Eating in company seems too social, even disrespectful to Esmera."

"It isn't, but I understand." Simon went to the door, then turned. "Tomorrow, then. I'll be here after breakfast, and we'll ride like the devil himself is after us."

TRUE TO HIS WORD, Simon appeared at Jonling Hall the next day, and Jameson had no choice but to let him in.

"I considered not coming downstairs."

"I don't doubt it," his cousin said. "Have you eaten anything? I don't want you to fall off your horse and get dragged around the estate. It wouldn't look good at all."

Jameson considered. "Actually, no. I don't think I've had anything since the brandy."

Simon made a tut-tutting sound like a prim, old busybody, and then produced a basket from behind his back.

"Jenny insisted."

Jameson could smell the sweet spiced buns before Simon even lifted the cloth. All at once, his mouth watered and his stomach panged with hunger. Snatching one, feeling it was still warm from the Belton Manor kitchen, he devoured it, right then and there in the entry hall.

"I guess my wife chose correctly."

There was that word again, *wife*, but Jenny was a friend, too, so Jameson ignored the pain of it and nodded his thanks.

"I don't suppose you have coffee behind your back, too."

"No," Simon said. "Shall we have some before we go?"

"Never mind. If we linger, I'll change my mind, I promise you." Jameson took the basket, set it on the ottoman, and took another sugary bun. "Let us ride."

Stepping out into the sunshine felt like a chore. For a moment, he stood on his front step, blinking, feeling disoriented.

"Come along," Simon urged. "I stopped at the stables first." He gestured toward the two horses. "Your mount is ready."

Wearing his favorite riding boots gave Jameson a small measure of joy, as did seeing his roan gelding saddled and ready. The joy was followed quickly by a wave of strong guilt, which he struggled to tamp down, at the same time, stuffing the soft baked treat into his mouth.

His self-reproach was irrational. He knew that, but felt it anyway, just as he couldn't help thinking he shouldn't enjoy anything while Esmera no longer could.

"Are you coming?"

Simon was already a few yards ahead, and Jameson hesitated. He could go forward, or he could dash back inside as he wanted to do and slam the door closed.

He thought of his dead half brother who would never have the chance to ride again. He tried not to think of his dead wife who might frown at him for looking forward to a good ride in the sunshine.

And then he moved. In a few steps, he was at his horse's side, his foot in the stirrup, and then he was in the well-worn saddle.

Breathing a sigh of relief, he looked over to see Simon, also mounted, studying him.

"You made it, cousin. That was the hard part. Believe me, I know." And then Simon urged his horse into movement with heels to its ribs and a quiet, "Go."

Jameson did the same and, as soon as they were in the meadow behind the hall, they increased their pace. As he hoped, they galloped, running full out for stretches before bring their horses back to cantering, and then going faster again.

No need for words between them or with their horses. It was an old, familiar exercise bringing peace to his tormented brain.

They rode for an hour, most of it while still on Devere land. Making a vast circle, they came back by way of the village, going through its bustling center, before heading toward home.

"Looks as if someone's home at the Blackwood cottage," Simon remarked as they passed a moderate-sized, white-painted home of two stories with window boxes.

Jameson knew of it but had never been inside. "Is that where Jenny grew up?"

"Yes, with her sisters, although they spent most of each year in London. After Baron Blackwood died, they had to sell their townhouse. Maggie lives in Bedfordshire, you may recall, with my good friend, the Earl of Cambrey."

"I remember." At least, he remembered the gorgeous countess and her husband if not precisely where they lived.

He had dined with them when the middle Blackwood sister came to visit her family. He tried not to think of that dinner party because Esmera had given him a hot and buzzing earful when they got home. She thought Maggie had been disrespectful and assumed it was jealousy, despite Jameson having witnessed no signs of it.

Esmera also imagined Lord Cambrey might have been staring at her too long. Jameson could believe that of nearly any man where Esmera was concerned, and wouldn't blame him one bit. However, Lady Margaret Cambrey was stunningly beautiful, the toast of London before Esmera came along, and the earl was obviously head-over-heels in love with his wife.

When Jameson had pointed that out, Esmera had flown into a rage, accusing him of preferring Maggie. He'd had a delightful evening of passionate lovemaking, convincing her otherwise.

"And Miss Darrow, is she at Belton with you and Jenny?" He couldn't imagine why she had popped into his head, or why that question had come, unbidden from his lips.

"No, she's at the cottage with Lady Blackwood and Eleanor," Simon informed him as they left it behind.

Since Jameson actually didn't care where she was residing, he asked nothing more about the strange young woman who had pushed her way into his home, refusing to leave and quoting Shakespeare to him.

As if conjuring her, suddenly, he heard her voice. She was speaking loudly, as though talking to someone a distance away, then she laughed.

It was a pleasant, full laugh.

He and Simon looked at each other, as she seemed to be up ahead of them in an area sloping gently to gully. It was a place for fishing in the shallows of the river running through it, shaded by large oaks growing near its banks. A lovely spot.

Then he heard her shriek, and his heart began to race, even as he kicked his horse into a run, heading in the direction of her distress.

CHAPTER THREE

Maisie shrieked as Eleanor tossed an acorn down onto her head. And then she laughed again.

"You stop that, naughty wench. And make sure you don't drop any bugs into my hair, either."

Eleanor, who had climbed a massively thick oak, with branches that hung out over the River Don, was laughing uproariously and had a fishing line dangling into the river.

"I can actually see the carp from here," Eleanor said with delight. "Do you want to dig a few more worms for me?"

"You know I don't!"

Suddenly, the sound of horses' hooves heralded two riders.

"It's Simon," Eleanor said. "But who is that with him?"

Maisie knew instantly, for her brief encounter with the owner of Jonling Hall the day before had prepared her for his unkempt beard and hair.

"Lord Turner," she said.

"Really?" Eleanor said, before she gave a yell of surprise.

Maisie jumped up. "Are you all right?"

Then she seemed surrounded by horses, even though it was only two circling her.

"What's happening here?" Lord Turner demanded. "Are you hurt?"

"I am not, thank you, but . . . ," she trailed off as a fishing pole landed beside her, a fish still on the hook, startling both horses. Then Eleanor climbed down, dropping the last few feet to the ground.

Simon laughed. "I should have known you were up there, you little monkey."

Maisie was still staring at the viscount, whose mouth was a tight-lipped line of disapproval.

"We heard screams," Lord Turner insisted, sounding angry.

"Eleanor dropped an acorn on me."

"My sister-in-law is a little wild," Simon pointed out.

"She's only having a bit of fun," Maisie defended her cousin. *Why did Lord Turner appear to be furious?*

"I was," Eleanor agreed, then she twisted in a circle, looking behind her, and gasped. "Oh, dear, I tore a hole in my skirt. Mummy will be most displeased. I slipped at the last branch and nearly fell out of the tree."

"You what?" Jameson's tone grew more furious. "Do you realize you could have been killed if you'd fallen on your head? Or at the very least, severely injured."

Eleanor's eyes rounded. "I've climbed many times, my lord, without injury."

"How thoughtless of you," he insisted. "Simon, you should put a stop to this."

Eleanor looked bewildered, and even the earl seemed a little taken aback.

Maisie stepped toward the viscount's horse. "It is not for Lord Lindsey to stop my cousin, in my opinion. Eleanor is not his wife, nor did she do anything wrong."

"Then you are a fool not to see the danger of a woman in a tree high above the ground, especially with skirts which could become tangled and cause incident. As nearly happened."

Maisie fell into silence. She supposed it was up to Eleanor to defend her practice of tree-climbing. Or perhaps Lord Lindsey should restrain his friend. For her to say more would be seen as rude and presumptuous. Yet . . .

"Is it that she is a female climbing or anyone climbing at all that bothers you? Would it be better if she wore pantaloons? Or should absolutely everyone keep their feet firmly planted on the ground? Did you never climb a tree when you were younger, my lord?"

Simon coughed, and Maisie thought he was covering up a chuckle.

"Perhaps Lord Turner is correct in that you should show a little more caution, Eleanor," Simon agreed. "Only imagine how it would upset your family if anything happened to you."

Eleanor gave her brother-in-law a wounded look. "Nothing will happen."

"No one ever thinks anything will happen," Lord Turner bit out harshly. "I bid you good day." With that, he kicked his horse and rode away.

Simon didn't follow, perhaps since his cousin was close to the hall and their ride was over. Maisie felt a little chagrined.

"My apologies," she said to Simon. "I shouldn't have said anything." The man was obviously fearful of anything happening to those around him.

"It's fine," Eleanor said before her brother-in-law could speak. "I appreciate your standing up for me. In any case, I will not curtail all my fun with the worry of what may happen. That is positively no way to live." Eleanor snatched up her pole. "In any case, his wife was doing something perfectly ordinary, riding a train, not anything dangerous."

"This was his first outing," Simon pointed out. "I don't think he expected to hear a woman scream or see another dropping from a tree."

Again, Maisie felt a pang of guilt. She should have held her tongue in front of the widower.

"I should apologize to him."

"You have nothing to be sorry about," Eleanor said.

"Nor would he want you to intrude upon him," the earl added. "He is not the most sociable of fellows right now."

"Yes, I found that out." Maisie had been surprised to see Lord Turner out riding. She didn't know why it mattered to her, nor why she should feel a modicum of happiness on his behalf, but she did. However, being the cause of him fleeing back to the sanctuary of his home bothered her to no end.

Eleanor added her latest catch to her pail of fish. "I'm ready to leave and face Mummy's wrath over my torn skirt."

"Good day, then, ladies," Lord Lindsey said and departed.

"I think I will stop at Jonling Hall and apologize on my way back."

Eleanor stared at her a moment, adjusting her straw hat. "But it's not on the way back."

"I will feel better if I do," she insisted.

"I know you like everyone to be happy as you are," Eleanor said. "It's a very sweet trait. Do whatever you wish, and I'll see you back in time for tea."

"Knowing how prickly Lord Turner is, I'm sure I'll be at home well before then."

JAMESON WAS IN HIS study, the only other room he frequented besides Esmera's bedroom. Occasionally, he looked at correspondence, handled his payments and accounts, or read one of the newspapers piling up on a chair. Mostly, he sat and stared at nothing, as he found himself doing at that moment when a knock interrupted his reverie.

"Come."

Mr. Wynn appeared. "Miss Darrow is in the drawing room, my lord."

"Don't call me that!" he snapped, jumping to his feet at once. This intrusion was going to stop. Today!

Striding past his startled butler, he strode down the passageway to his front room, the spacious drawing room, which still held decorations from his dead half brother.

There she was, not curled up asleep in a chair this time as he'd discovered her on her previous visit. Instead, she was standing, facing him, hands behind her back, eyes firmly closed. On second thought, perhaps she was sleeping.

"What on earth are you doing?"

Her eyelids fluttered open, and he was caught by her eyes. Some might call them brown, but they had a distinct golden lightness flecked amongst the darker brown color. *Topaz eyes*, some fanciful idiot might call them. Luckily, he was neither fanciful nor an idiot.

But when she also flashed a winsome smile at him, he would have to say she was quite beautiful, even if he didn't wish to see beauty anywhere else than in the memory of his wife. Thinking of Esmera, he realized Miss Darrow's beauty was a watery comparison to her dark and exotic looks, steeling himself to any softening toward the living woman before him.

"You came very swiftly this time, my lord. Unexpectedly so. I was testing my memory of the lovely landscape."

"Testing your memory?" *What game was she playing? Why not simply turn around and look at the damn painting?*

"Yes, I was here so long yesterday, I vowed to commit it to memory. On the left are some very leafy trees, looking almost fluffy, and a few Grecian looking people and a statue. Everyone is in flowing robes. In the far distance are some purplish-gray mountains. There's a structure, perhaps a temple, back there, too, and in the foreground, there's a river coming from a waterfall, but it's very still, like a pool with people and cattle in it. I love the colors and the sunlight hitting the trees and the grass."

He'd let his gaze drift to the painting behind her as she'd spoken. He continued to stare at it, a work of art left there by his half brother, although he recalled his father saying it was there even before Toby, and had been purchased by the previous Earl of Lindsey, Simon's father. Yet, he'd never looked closely at it before, and was positive neither he nor Esmera would have been able to say any more about it than it was an Italian landscape.

"How did I do?" Miss Darrow asked him.

Feeling annoyed by her presence, by her knowing a painting more intimately than his wife would ever have the chance to, he said, "You missed a main element."

She laughed, a pleasant sound, further annoying him. It was disrespectful to laugh around someone in mourning.

"I couldn't say it all in one breath," she said. "There's also a tidy stone bridge with very thick, block footings, if that's the right word. And in the far distance, in the middle of one part of the river, there's another structure, maybe a bridge, but with tall towers. I think the artist left it for the viewer to decide quite what it is. Do you know the artist?"

He supposed if he looked closely, he might see a name inscribed across it. "Some Italian perhaps."

"Oh no," she contradicted him, whirling around to study the painting again. "I believe its French. A classic Arcadian scene by a French painter."

That did it! "Do you enjoy being contrary and forward and intrusive, like a cat among pigeons?"

Her face clouded over. Then she groaned, a startling, earthy sound.

"Oh, no, my lord, not at all. In fact, I came to offer my apology. I shouldn't have said what I did by the river."

He couldn't recall precisely what she'd said, only that she'd contradicted him about safety and proper behavior.

"You seem to think it acceptable for your cousin to be in danger."

She shook her head. "My thoughts on Eleanor aside, which differ from yours, I do not think it acceptable to rile up a grieving man, especially regarding danger to women, or to have you hear my shriek and become concerned."

He opened his mouth, then closed it. *What could he say to her reasonable statement?*

"I wouldn't want you worrying about either of us for an instant," she concluded.

If he admitted to an ounce of worry, then he would have to admit to caring, which he didn't. Not for her, that was certain.

"I expressed normal concern for your cousin, especially as she is related to my cousin, and simply because she is a fellow human being. But I don't actually care about either one of you, not personally. In short, I don't give a fig about you, Miss Darrow. You may scream and shriek to your heart's content, as long as I don't have to listen."

There, that put the stopper to her jug. Her mouth remained firmly shut as she blinked at him, although he might be detecting a little grinding of her teeth. Her delicate nostrils at the end of her small, straight nose flared and her full bosom rose and fell. She seemed to be trying admirably to refrain from responding.

He crossed his arms over his chest. Baiting her was the first amusement he'd had in months, except for the ride with Simon. Now, he could walk away and back to his study and leave her standing in his drawing room. It would be the perfect cut direct.

However, he had a tiny measure of curiosity, which would never be satisfied if he walked away at that moment. He truly wanted to know what she would say next.

After a long few moments, she said, "No, *I will be the pattern of all patience. I will say nothing.*" Moreover, she said it so quietly, he was sure she was speaking to herself.

"What are you muttering, Miss Darrow? Am I trying your patience?"

"No, my lord. That was *King Lear.* If he can bear the atrocities perpetrated upon him, then I can handle your frank words. Will you ring for tea? It's still pleasant out. We could sit on your back terrace."

It was his turn to grind his teeth and breathe deeply.

"You wish to have tea with me?" He wanted to ask, *Are you mad as a march hare?*

She produced another beatific smile, and something inside him shifted, like ice cracking on a frozen pond during the first warm day of spring. He didn't like it one bit. It physically hurt.

In fact, he wondered if he was having some sort of visceral episode, an attack of dyspepsia, perhaps.

"I think you should leave," he said.

Her smile faltered. "Honestly, I do not believe you should spend day after day alone."

"I haven't asked for your opinion," he reminded her.

As if she hadn't heard him, she continued, "Not that I can pretend to know what it is like to lose a spouse. However, I do know what it feels like to lose a loved one, and eventually, after time spent grieving, I re-entered society, while still clad in black, of course, for a year, since I had just entered my teen years."

She frowned, perhaps realizing he wasn't wearing anything black, but rather gray trousers, a white shirt, and a gray jacket. He had worn all black every day in the beginning, but it felt like a costume. Moreover, it seemed he was wearing his emotions on the outside for everyone to see, giving them leave to offer condolences, which he had come to hate.

Then he'd worn simply the customary black arm band, and even black gloves, but once he'd retired to Sheffield, both had seemed a showy, ineffectual way to experience his grief. Besides, he was alone. *Why have any display at all?*

In another five months, as a widower, he would be considered out of mourning. And even before then, tradition allowed him to take a wife whenever he wished. How odd to think a new wife would be thrust into black bombazine and crape, but that was also the etiquette of his generation.

What would Miss Darrow look like in black? That would put a crimp in her sunny disposition, he had no doubt.

"Will you leave now?"

"How about we take tea first," she proposed again. "Did you try my jam? You may serve it with a scone, bread, or even a slice of plain cake."

She must be mad after all, prattling on about jam and cake.

"I haven't the foggiest notion to what you are referring."

She sighed. "I left a basket with preserves for you yesterday. Did you not receive it? Is it possible your butler has a sweet tooth?"

The notion of austere Mr. Wynn absconding with a pot of jam tickled him, but he tamped down his good humor, rubbed the side of his forehead, and closed his eyes.

"Do you have a headache, my lord?"

He wanted to ask her to stop calling him such, but feared the slight difference in their social status was the only thing keeping her from ordering him about at her whim.

"No, but if you stay, I am likely as not to get a severe headache quite soon." He paused, then added, begrudgingly, "However unwanted, I thank you for the jam. I am sure it is around here somewhere. If it were in this very room, I would give it back to you on the spot."

"But you must find it and taste it. Truly, it's delicious. The thistle blossom jelly is my mother's recipe, and I brought merely a few jars with me from Dumfries—"

"Your mother can have it back for all I care." He knew he was being rude but couldn't stop himself.

This young woman before him was an easy target for his pent-up anger, and the more she insisted on remaining where she wasn't wanted and talking about mundane things like her mother and godforsaken Dumfries and jelly made from a weed while Esmera lay in the ground, the more he wanted to lash out at her.

How dare she!

Moreover, he had an irrational desire to weep. It washed over him sometime between Miss Darrow wanting to have tea with him and once again thinking of his wife's grave. If he were alone, he would sink to the Persian rug underfoot and sob.

"My mother," she began, but he held up his hand.

"You think you can come to my home and somehow cheer me up, as if I've merely misplaced something or perhaps lost my dog. I want you to listen to me and try to understand the depth of my misery. Mine is not the story of a man who loved a woman who wasn't right for him. Mine is the story of a man who had the perfect wife. I loved her with all her flaws, if she had any, although I cannot, at this moment, recall a single one."

"I didn't mean to——"

"On the day of my wife's funeral, her parents and her brother cried so hard, I feared for them. I could not cry that day. I had no more tears left."

Putting his vibrant Esmera in the ground had been the hardest thing he had ever done.

"Cold," he muttered. "English women are usually cold-blooded like the fish your cousin was catching, and cold-hearted, too. Frosty, passionless creatures." He looked her in the eyes. "Every one of you."

He'd never experienced the white-hot, almost violent passion with any woman other than Esmera. They'd had greedy, ravenous lovemaking that left them both exhausted, utterly spent. Sometimes, he'd almost been frightened with the intensity, and always drained yet satisfied.

"My cousin tells me we've met before, you and I. Yet you are a wan, lifeless, insipid English girl, probably simpering, and without spark. It is no wonder I don't recall ever meeting you."

She stared silently at him, her pretty brown eyes the size of dinner plates, her face grown even paler at his harsh words. And he didn't care. She still had more color in her cheeks than his dead wife had when he'd viewed her at the London morgue.

And then, Miss Darrow's eyes narrowed. Her shocked face reddened, and he wondered if he'd gone too far.

CHAPTER FOUR

Miss Darrow took a step toward him and, from the sheer animosity flashing in her eyes, Jameson flinched, almost taking a step back before managing to hold his ground. He wasn't about to be cowed by a slip of a woman.

"You are a beast! You look like a beast. Frankly, you smell like one, too," she ranted. "And you speak like I imagine a coarse, uncivilized animal of the field would speak if it could form words. It's a pity you can do so, for I have no doubt more polite, pleasant speech would come from any cow or pig."

She walked to the drawing room door, and he thought her rather magnificent in her anger, absolutely giving the lie to his words about cold, passionless English women. In the doorway, she turned.

"*Men in rage strike those that wish them best,*" she sputtered. "No, wait. That doesn't apply, for *I* am the one who is angry, and you certainly do not wish me best or even wish me well."

He watched Miss Darrow breathing heavily, a perfect image of outrage, her eyes boring into his, while her mind obviously searched for the right words.

"*Ah ha,*" she said at last, raising a pointed hand to the heavens. "*Too much sadness hath congealed your blood, and melancholy is the nurse of frenzy.* Act II, scene two from *The Taming of the Shrew.*"

"Are you the shrew in this case?" Jameson shot back, hoping to keep her boiling mad, for then she might stay and continue talking. Her voice resonated as if she were on the stage. Her presence, pushed to anger, filled the room with liveliness long missing.

Missing for a reason, because his wife was dead.

He had no business enjoying the company of another woman, not even if his enjoyment was in prodding her temper.

Realizing he did want her to stay, he took a step back after all, surprised by his own weakness.

Dammit all! Fisting his hands, he vowed to remain silent and speak with her no more. She must leave at once so he could . . . be alone, as necessary.

He simply uncrossed his arms, attempting to look relaxed and unmoved by her, and waited.

"You, my lord, are in a frenzy of hostility against me and English women in general, due to your wallowing in sadness. I hope, for your sake, you find a way out of your deep melancholia. I had hoped to be of assistance, but I can see you are beyond my meager abilities to bring cheer. Good day."

MAISIE FELT LIKE AN absolute failure as she strode home to the Blackwood cottage. She should never have tried to help the man. At least, she had been able to offer her apology for riling him earlier.

Right before she yelled at him and called him a beast.

Groaning, she slowed her steps. She was a meddling fool. If only it wasn't so easy for her to recall Jameson Turner as he was previously, the happy, funny, dashing man with a gorgeous smile.

She sighed. He had lifted her spirits whenever she'd been in his company, no matter how peripherally, and she'd probably spent too much time watching him surreptitiously from across whatever room in which she had encountered him.

She could admit, if only to herself, she'd been a bit smitten, but he'd gone to London and married, and when she'd later met his beautiful bride and seen how happy they appeared, she'd been truly glad for him. In truth, she remembered hoping for a similarly blessed match.

Jenny had told her how Lord Turner felt somehow to blame for his wife's death, even though he hadn't even been on the train when it derailed. His sadness, thus, was twofold and laced with bitterness and self-recrimination.

She considered her own situation with her mother. Fortunately, she had never had to experience the terrible burden of guilt, for her saintly mother died of influenza. However, she had two friends who lived in Dumfries, each whose mother died while giving them life, a common enough occurrence. Each of these girls felt a measure of fear for their own future when they would, in turn, give birth. Yet, they also experienced guilt for having caused their mothers' deaths.

Still, they were luckier than the guilt-ridden London girl who made the newspapers the previous summer for taking her own life in the Thames. Her father faulted her directly for her mother's passing during the delivery, and had kept up the blame for fourteen years until the wretched young woman could stand it no longer and walked into the river.

Poor Jameson Turner.

What if he were to save a life instead?

The notion popped into Maisie's head, as if whispered to her by some divine spirit or perhaps a fairy such as from Shakespeare's imagination in *A Midsummer Night's Dream*.

She could see the wisdom in it, but how would she go about engineering such an occurrence? *Should she mention it to Eleanor?* She didn't want her noble idea to become a lark, a joke between friends, as that was decidedly not her intent.

Maisie spent the rest of the day considering how she could bring about this healing event, and by the time she lay her head upon her pillow, she had come up with a plan, taking her inspiration from the unfortunate London girl.

"ARE YOU GOING TO Belton Manor today?" Maisie asked Eleanor at breakfast.

"I had no plans to but certainly could. Why?"

"No reason in particular. Just a destination for a walk." She hoped she could run into Lord Lindsey and either urge him to go riding again with Lord Turner or find out when such an occurrence might be happening.

"I have a book for you to return to Jenny's library, if you girls decide to go," Lady Blackwood said, rattling her papers.

"Then it's settled," Eleanor agreed.

Maisie needed two things for her plan to work—time alone next to the River Don and Lord Turner out riding again close by. *But how was she to ensure Lord Lindsey didn't save her, himself?*

She hoped further inspiration would come to her, but when it didn't, she knew she would have to let Eleanor in on her plan.

Thus, as they walked toward Jenny's stately manor house, Maisie told Eleanor what she'd been thinking. Then she asked her, "Don't you think saving someone's life would do Lord Turner a world of good?"

Eleanor's brows furrowed. "I understand why you would think so. However, I am not positive saving someone he doesn't particularly know or care about will do anything to assuage his unreasonable guilt over Lady Turner's death."

"It is worth trying though, don't you think?"

"I suppose." Eleanor, who famously loved Gothic novels, got an excited look upon her lovely face. "I could push you out of a window on the highest floor of Belton Manor. Lord Turner could catch you when you fell."

Maisie's insides quivered with the idea of falling and, more precisely, smashing her bones upon the ground.

"No, I was not thinking of anything quite so dangerous, just in case Lord Turner is not where we want him when the time comes."

"True. Do you have an idea for where the great rescue should occur?"

"I do in fact. If we can determine when next Lord Lindsey is going to go riding with him, then I believe my plan will work. For once they are upon horseback, you can approach them with a message from Jenny to return to the manor. Then Lord Turner will be alone."

"What message? I cannot worry my brother-in-law with a false message. Nor will Jenny condone such a thing if we tell her."

"No, we mustn't tell your practical sister. She'll dissuade us, I'm sure." Maisie considered. "Why can't it be something pleasant that draws him away, like one of the children doing something for the first time. Mothers and fathers love that sort of thing, don't you think?"

Eleanor clapped her hands. "Simon does dote on his children. With any luck, one of them will do or say something, and I'll charge out on my horse to tell him to come back home at once."

"If it works, it works," Maisie said. "If not, no harm done." Except she might get a little wet, but that was a risk she would take.

JAMESON KNEW VERY WELL what Simon was doing by coming over two days in a row. His cousin feared if he didn't get him in the habit of going out daily, even if only riding, then he would put his Hessians away and return to isolation.

In a word, the man was going to be his *nanny*. And probably Jenny had put him up to it.

Strangely, Jameson was grateful. When he heard Simon had arrived, he was dressed for riding and downstairs, standing next to their horses in under ten minutes.

"No sweet rolls?" he asked Simon as they mounted.

"Sorry, no, only an invitation to dinner, where there will be heavenly food far beyond the sticky buns. Will you come tonight? Jenny would love to see you, but she won't come over here and intrude like I do."

"Or like Miss Darrow."

"Did Maisie stop by again? I apologize. I'll have a word with her later. A man has a right to his privacy." Then Simon paused. "Except from his only cousin, of course, when riding is concerned."

Maisie? Jameson didn't think he'd known her given name before, or hadn't recalled knowing it. It was a light, flowery, sunny name, and fit her perfectly. Until the moment she practically shimmered with outrage in his drawing room.

"No, I believe I have already dissuaded her from boldly overstepping, at least regarding dropping in on me uninvited."

They were trotting companionably along the fence line.

"What did you do?" Simon asked, sounding a little worried.

"What did *I* do? You should be asking, *what did she do?*"

Simon did ask. "Well, what did she do?"

"She came to my home after our brief encounter at the river yesterday to—" Jameson broke off when he recalled her describing his painting and then . . .

"Actually, I believe she came to apologize."

"The nerve!" Simon declared, then started to laugh. "Perhaps we should call in the sheriff. Oh, wait, I'm actually considered the local law in Sheffield proper. I shall arrest her myself."

"So droll," Jameson remarked and kicked his horse to gallop away from his cousin, whose laughter sounded like the braying of a donkey. He decided not to bring up his own bad behavior of the day before. He'd insulted Miss Darrow, along with basically all the flowering womanhood of Britain. He'd been beyond rude and wasn't even sure why, and he would definitely have to apologize when next he saw her.

They'd been out about forty minutes, circling the estate, following the same route as they had done previously. They were riding along the river when the youngest Blackwood girl approached on horseback. Jameson knew a moment's anxiety seeing her high upon a horse, but she looked to be firmly seated in the saddle.

"Greetings," she called out, sounding positively medieval in her salutation.

Simon drew his horse to a standstill. "Eleanor, no fishing today?"

"No, I was sketching at Belton when little Pamela did the cutest thing. You must come see at once." Then, as if only just noticing him, she added, "Good day, Lord Turner." Then she turned back to Simon. "Do come now and see."

"What did she do?" the earl asked.

"Oh, I cannot explain it. You shall have to see." With that, she turned and galloped off.

Too quickly, Jameson thought, *for safety's sake*. She could be thrown as easily as not. She must be a fast rider all the time, for he could swear her horse's legs were wet, drenched with perspiration.

Simon looked at him and shrugged. "She seems to expect me to follow. Do you mind?"

"Not at all. I can make my way home from here, *Nanny Devere*."

"*Ha!* I'll see you later for dinner. About seven." And his cousin urged his horse to a run.

"I didn't say I would come," Jameson called after him, but Simon had already begun to gallop, and either couldn't hear or pretended not to.

Sighing, Jameson continued on the same path along the River Don. What on earth could Pamela, age less than one—*or perhaps she was already nearly two*—have done that warranted her father being fetched to see her? He could find out later if he went to dinner. If he cared.

At the notion, every sentiment in him reared up in denial. He did not wish to go. *What would the emotional toll on him be?*

He could easily imagine being seated in Lord and Lady Lindsey's expansive dining room, the chair beside him painfully empty, Simon and Jenny taking turns filling in the silences as good hosts, and him wishing all the while he were home. He would undoubtedly count the minutes until he could lie once more upon the bed in the dark and think of Esmera.

He couldn't go to dinner, couldn't bear the—

A scream rent the peaceful country silence and dispersed his thoughts. Exactly like the day before, and sounding as through it came from the same lips—Maisie Darrow. Only this time, Jameson knew Eleanor Blackwood could not be the cause.

Something was very wrong beyond acorns. He urged his horse faster, and then she screamed again, and he saw her.

How on earth had she got into such a predicament?

While not life-threatening, clearly, she was in distress, for she was in a small row boat, leaning precariously to one side, clinging to a rock about fifteen yards out in the river. The current wasn't particularly fast, but the water was too high for her to simply wade back to shore should she fall out of the boat.

"Miss Darrow," he called out, dismounting quickly and tethering his horse to a branch. "What are you doing?"

Even though she was not in immediate danger, his pulse had begun to race, and he could easily imagine at any moment she might fall in the river, slip beneath the surface of the silvery Don, and disappear from his sight.

"I've lost my oar," she called out. "I have only one." She started to release the rock, perhaps to show him her remaining oar, and then shrieked again as the boat nearly tipped.

The sound of a woman shrieking froze his blood, making him go cold from head to toe.

"You shouldn't be leaning so far over." *Dammit!* He would have to swim out to her. *And then what?* He could no more row with one oar or pull the boat in than fly.

"I'm scared to let go. It's quite shallow in truth. There's a high ridge of mud or something, but still . . . ," she trailed off unhelpfully.

"I'm coming, Miss Darrow." Since there seemed to be no imminent threat, he stopped to remove his riding boots, roll up his pants, and even take off his stockings. He would thank himself later when—

"Blast it all!" Miss Darrow's voice reached him as he stood. She had lost her grip on the top of the craggy rock and was now spinning and drifting down the river with no control of the boat.

"Use the oar to turn the boat," he commanded, shrugging out of his jacket and tossing it down, he also drew his shirt over his head, hurling it behind him before wading into the river at its pebbly edge.

She was right. It was not very deep at first, and he could walk in up to his knees for a few yards, but she was moving farther away from him. Moreover, she appeared to be struggling to do as he said, putting the oar in and using it to make the nose of the boat turn hither and yon.

Then she stood up, leaning with the oar nearly flat out, trying to make the boat bend to her will.

"Sit down!" he ordered.

At the same time, the muddy bottom fell away, and he went in up to his waist. Cool but not frigid, Jameson didn't mind the water, although a naked swim was preferable to one with clinging clothing.

Far worse, of course, for a woman.

Then, as if reading his mind and deciding to prove his thoughts true, Miss Darrow lost her balance from stretching her arms out too far and went overboard, seemingly slowly in an arc before his eyes.

In short, she fell in.

Splash!

At that instant, she disappeared as he'd feared. Then she reappeared a moment later, thrashing about, screaming loudly enough to scare the fishes.

Instantly, Jameson struck out, swimming toward her, even as she went under again. She came up once more, this time without screaming, merely her hands slapping at the water, and offering a panicky gasp or two, and then nothing.

He had only a few yards more to go, and he swam them underwater, hoping he was aiming in the right direction. The River Don was deeper there, well over his head, and she had predictably sunk like a stone, a heavy, cloth-covered stone.

Diving down and thrusting his legs, his lungs threatening to burst, at last, he reached her. He didn't know what part of her he first discovered, but as soon as his hands touched something soft, he sunk his fingers in and held on with all his might as he tugged and pulled and yanked.

Kicking hard with his feet, he knew he had to get to the shallows before he could get her above the water. Desperately, he needed air, too, but stayed under as long as she did.

They would either survive together, or he would lose consciousness before sinking to the silty bottom to drown in the river with the impossibly irritating Maisie Darrow.

CHAPTER FIVE

As Jameson swam, he felt her start to stretch her arms and kick her legs. *By God, Miss Darrow was swimming with him, not a helpless weight after all!*

Within moments, his feet touched the river bottom, and finally, he could get a firm hold on her waist and move more quickly. As his head broke the water's surface, he thrust her upward and ahead of him so she, too, could breathe.

In the next instant, they stood together, still waist deep. While he was sucking in great lungfuls of air, she was coughing forcefully. It sounded as if it hurt, but at least he knew she was breathing. His arms were around her, afraid to let her go. When she left off coughing and started to gasp instead, he knew she would recover.

Still, Jameson was amazed he hadn't had to bend her over and try to void her lungs of inhaled water, or press on her slender frame to squeeze from her stomach half the contents of the river he feared she'd swallowed.

"You held your breath very well," he said when he could finally speak.

All she did was nod, unable yet to say anything. Her fingers were splayed across his bare chest, actually threaded through the smattering of hair growing there, and as his panic subsided, he was becoming more aware of her intimate touch.

His arms were still wrapped around her, holding on with an unbreakable grip.

Almost like a lovers' embrace, he thought, *except with terror.*

Moreover, her pretty eyes were closed rather than gazing up at him adoringly as a lover might. Trying to get his mind back on the mundane, he considered the state of her. Her hat, for instance. He believed she'd been wearing one when he'd first seen her, but she had lost it. And apparently, by the feel of her grasping fingers—causing shivers to run down his spine—she'd lost her gloves, as well.

Was she tracing a pattern on his chest?

He supposed his next worry should be whether she might go into shock or catch a chill, neither of which did he want to occur while still in the water. Taking another deep breath, he hefted her into his arms, causing her to shriek again, this time with surprise, he assumed, as her eyes flew open, her golden-brown gaze locking on his.

Good Lord! With her soaking skirts and petticoats and frilly underthings and her stockings and jacket and shirtwaist, she had a surprising weight to her.

Staggering up the slanted riverbed to the edge of the water, the muscles in his arms and legs burning, he ripped the sole of his foot open trying to clear the rocks and the smaller smoother pebbles in order to get to the softer ground ahead.

Nearly dropping her on her bottom, he managed to set her awkwardly on her feet before dragging her down with him to the grassy bank as he slid to his knees, gasping again for breath.

To hell with it; he had to lie down. Stretching out on his back, he looked up at the leafy branches overhead. If he'd taken better care of himself, or even eaten a few more meals the past year, he would have been able to perform that heroic act without practically passing out. After all, he'd carried his share of clothed women from door to bed and never before felt as if he might die while doing so.

Wheezing, seeing stars, he closed his eyes a moment to recover, letting her remain on her knees beside him.

"Are you all right, Lord Turner?" she asked him, as if they had merely taken a stroll along Pall Mall, and he'd become a little winded.

She sounded remarkably hale for having endured capsizing and near drowning.

He opened his eyes to see her staring down at him. Her mass of hair, much darker when wet, hung loose all around her pale face in a bedraggled curtain, reaching even to his chest as she leaned over, looking concerned. Bits of river weed were caught in the tangled skeins. Her eyes were mirrors of concern, and her lips were the merest hint of purple. Despite probably freezing, she looked hauntingly beautiful.

That thought irritated him to no end.

"Will you stop! You're dripping. It's as pleasant as having a half-drowned rat perched on my chest or a wet dog leaning over me."

She flinched and sat back.

Good, he thought. He needed a little distance between them. *Nuisance of a woman!*

Jameson imagined he could lie there all day, resting, listening to the sounds of the river, which were very few now that she had stopped screaming. However, he felt it was his duty to get her home.

Sighing, he rolled over and pushed to his feet before holding out his hand to her. She hesitated, then placed hers in his open palm, allowing him to draw her slowly to her feet. Wordlessly, he tucked her arm in his, acutely aware of his inappropriately shirtless state, and headed back to his horse, aware of pain throbbing in the sole of his left foot.

Miss Darrow was walking oddly, too, and when he looked down, he realized she'd lost a shoe. A small leather ankle boot, to be precise. Since he assumed she was aware of the fact, he didn't mention it.

Soon, they'd reached his tethered horse. Only then did he think of her row boat.

"Whose boat was it?" he asked.

"Lady Blackwood's. Only Eleanor uses it, however."

"Why were you in it, then?"

She hesitated. "That is a good question, my lord."

She said nothing more for a moment, then added, "I knew the views would be lovely from the river."

"The views of what?" he asked.

"Why, the river of course."

He couldn't imagine her, or anyone for that matter, waking up and deciding to row down the river to see the same views she could see from the safety and dryness of the riverbank.

"And were they?" he asked.

"Were they what?" Miss Darrow looked up at him, her arm still held tightly in his, despite how they were now standing on perfectly safe, soft grass. Her other hand was running up and down his bare arm absently.

"Lovely," he uttered. "I mean, the views of the river, were they lovely?"

She shrugged. "I suppose so." Then she offered him a broad smile, lighting up her face, despite the muddy water smears and bits of grass stuck to her cheek. "You saved my life, Lord Turner. I am eternally grateful. If not for you, I would be . . . ," she stopped speaking as she looked past him to the Don.

Then she made a strange sound, like a hiccup, and he realized she was crying.

"There, there, Miss Darrow. I have no doubt you would have found a way to save yourself."

Actually, because of her heavy layers, he could think of no way she could have done so. They both knew perfectly well she would have died if he hadn't been there when she fell in.

"Perhaps you should invest in one of those bathing dresses ladies use at the seaside if you intend to go boating again. In any case, you shouldn't be on a boat alone."

She sniffed and raised her free hand to dash at her tears. He had a handkerchief in his pants pocket and drew it out, soaking wet. Releasing her arm, he made a great show of ringing it out, then shaking it, before giving it to her.

She giggled as he'd intended, and the color returned to her cheeks.

"Thank you," she said, her voice a little wobbly.

The experience had frightened her, which was a good thing in his estimation. It had thoroughly scared him.

"Hopefully, Miss Blackwood will be able to retrieve the boat."

"I'm certain of it. She said there's a place where it will always catch in the shallows, at the upcoming bend." She gestured behind her.

"Really?" It seemed a strange thing for the ladies to have discussed. "Can you ride?"

"Oh, I wouldn't ruin the end of your ride," she said, her gaze now fixed on his bare chest. "I can walk from here."

Ruin the rest of his ride? He looked at his clothing still strewn about, then he glanced at her.

Had she any idea the state she was in? He couldn't let her walk unaccompanied back to the Blackwoods' cottage. Someone might pick her up as an escaped inmate from Bedlam. Besides, she only had one boot.

"What I mean to ask, Miss Darrow, is whether you are a capable rider?" He started to dress, realizing she was watching his every movement—*the minx*—as he pulled his shirt on before donning his jacket. He was warmer already and intended to get her home quickly to undress her.

Or rather, so she could undress herself. And take a bath. Not with him, of course. Alone. In the Blackwoods' home.

Quickly, he wrested his thoughts away from her undressing and bathing. Pulling his boots on, he winced from the cut, then stuffed his stockings into his pocket. Feeling in control once more, he turned to face her.

"There is no question but that you shall go home on horseback. The only question is whether I need worry you shall fall off."

"If you insist on my riding, my lord, then, I am pleased to inform you I am an experienced rider. Shall we both fit upon your saddle?"

"No," he answered quickly. The last thing he intended was riding around Sheffield with his arms wrapped around a single young lady, or having her mounted behind him with her arms around him. "You ride. I shall walk."

Cupping his hands, he waited for her to put her foot onto his palms.

"That feels strange," she said as she did so.

His sentiments exactly. How very strange indeed to have Miss Darrow's toes poking through her torn stockings and touching his skin. Adeptly, she lifted her other leg over the saddle, prepared to ride astride.

And as he stood, his eyes came level with her exposed knee, clad in what was left of her stocking, and, above that, bare thigh.

Something inside him roared to life as she hastily tried to pull her skirts down. He swallowed. He would help her, but touching her at that moment seemed an incredibly stupid idea.

Turning away, he untied his horse from the branch and began the trek to the Blackwood cottage, luckily very close indeed.

AS THEY WALKED TOWARD the cottage, Maisie decided she should break the strained silence.

"Again, I thank you for saving me. It was a brave and chivalrous thing to do."

Leading the horse, his back to her, Lord Turner's only reaction was to shrug. She stared at his broad shoulders as he did so.

Gracious! She could hardly think of anything except his torso after seeing him bare-chested.

Why, she'd actually touched him, her hands drifting near his flat nipples. And then she'd been unable to help herself from stroking his well-defined arm.

He was magnificent, albeit admittedly, a little thin. Nothing some chops and a few roasted potatoes wouldn't alter.

"Only think," she added more loudly, "without you, I wouldn't be here this very moment."

At that, he seemed to stiffen, but still, he said nothing, simply continued steadfastly walking toward Norman's Corner and the delightful little home Maisie preferred nearly to everywhere else except perhaps her father's in Dumfries.

The escapade had gone badly, she admitted. She'd hoped only to remain in the boat, clinging for dear life while Lord Turner easily saved her by walking his horse from river's edge to the rock as Eleanor had done when she'd left her there. She would have handed him the rope tied to its bow and let him lead her to safety, professing her eternal gratitude.

Instead, she'd lost her grip on the cursed rock, and then everything had gone wrong. Quickly, she had drifted too far away for Lord Turner to walk his horse. He hadn't even tried it anyway. He'd plunged in to rescue her—shirtless!

And she hadn't had to fake nearly drowning, for it had almost happened. She couldn't quite fathom how it had turned from play-acting to deadly reality, but it had. One moment, she was perfectly safe in the little boat, and the next, the water was soaking through layer upon layer of her clothing and tugging her down.

She'd found herself absolutely helpless to stop from going under. Not only that, she couldn't touch the bottom, although that was the direction she had been heading. She supposed, eventually, she would have landed on the river bottom and then tried to push herself back up, but whether she would have been able to break the surface before her garments dragged her down again, she truly doubted.

She had almost drowned!

Tears welled up again at her own stupidity, and she started to shiver. Only think how Eleanor would have felt if anything dreadful had come about, having been her accomplice in setting up the ruse. And her brother, Ned, annoying dolt that he was, would also have been upset.

Dear God! What an idiotic plan. So much could have gone wrong. In fact, so much had. And she could hardly imagine the distress it would have caused Lord Turner if she'd perished before his eyes. Whether he cared a whit about her or not, he would have felt responsible, seeing her take her last breath.

She would be more careful in the future, and try taking a different path to helping him.

If she could think of one.

"I'm sorry," he said unexpectedly.

Sorry for saving her?

"I beg your pardon?" she said, hoping that wasn't what he'd meant. They'd come to a halt now before the cottage, and he looked up at her.

"I'm sorry I insulted you yesterday and called you names. It is not a habit of mine to be rude to anyone. Nor did I speak the truth. I do remember meeting you."

And that was that. He said no more and didn't even seem to care if she accepted his apology or not. Besides, now he'd saved her life, a few insulting words the day before were hardly important.

Maisie let him help her down, noticing how his gaze lingered on her legs when she slid down the side of the horse into Lord Turner's waiting arms. When her feet touched the ground, her skirts fell back into place, and his glance snapped up to her face.

"You're truly shivering now. You must be chilled through. Is someone here to help you?" he asked.

"Help me?" They were still standing close, and his hands were on her upper arms. She wished he would wrap his arms around her again and warm her. For he was correct. She felt as if her limbs were made of ice.

Instead, he backed away. "Yes, is someone home to run a bath and see you are taken care of?"

She thought her aunt was home, but probably not Eleanor, who couldn't have made it back from Belton Manor yet. In any case, even with limited staff, they had a servant to help boil water for a bath.

"I'll be fine. Thank you."

She stared at him a moment longer, and he returned her gaze as if there was something else he wished to say.

Had she accomplished anything beyond nearly killing herself?

She supposed she had, for he wasn't saying anything beastly, insulting her on purpose to make her leave, nor was he walking away from her.

"To climb steep hills requires a slow pace at first," she told him.

"I beg your pardon?" He cocked his handsome head. "I don't think a slow pace would have done you any good today."

"True, my lord. I was referring to our blossoming friendship." Her teeth chattered on the last word, and it came out as a mumble.

His eyes widened, and he clenched his jaw.

She saw at once she had made a mistake.

"We are *not* friends, Miss Darrow. Nothing of the sort. Good day."

With that, he mounted his horse and rode away.

Sighing, Maisie entered the cottage, lifting and dragging her wet skirts, which flapped around her ankles, more than ready to get out of them and into a tub.

JAMESON FOUND HIMSELF SADDLING his horse again that evening. It would be rude not to show up for dinner. Unlike Maisie Darrow, Simon and Jenny truly were his good friends as well as family.

Moreover, he hadn't been to Belton Manor in many months. In fact, the last time he had, Esmera had been on his arm. True, she had grumbled a little at the quiet, country dinner party, so tame compared to a London fête, but she had gone for his sake.

After all, he recalled reminding her, any party was better than staying at home at Jonling Hall, which she used to say smothered her in its stillness.

Like a suffocating blanket.

It was probably the only bone of contention between them, her love of the boisterous, frenetic life in London and his enjoyment of the peaceful tranquility of his Sheffield country home.

They agreed to divide their time, though often, his wife won him over by batting her thick, dark lashes, and he would find himself in London again. He didn't mind really. It was simply he'd spent so many unhappy years there, in the gambling clubs, which were noisy, all the while feeling rootless, shiftless, aimless, unloved, transient—an unwanted bastard son who couldn't find his place in the world.

Already his father's minion, Jameson had secretly gambled on Lord Devere's behalf, trying desperately to win enough to pay off the old man's debts, but ultimately failing, as his father never let up his own losing streak. Then after his half brother had died while fighting in Burma, and his father had caved in on himself like an underdone cake, Jameson started over.

And then he'd met Simon and Jenny, and found a family for the first time in his life. After coming into his inheritance as the new Earl of Lindsey, Simon had sorted it all out, taking care of his uncle's debts and forgiving Jameson, his newly discovered cousin, for his deception.

Jameson had never felt more at home than he had at Jonling Hall. And then, one spectacular night, he'd laid eyes on Esmera Maradona, the most exquisite woman he'd ever had the good fortune to meet.

Regardless of his love for his country home, he'd given up a month here or two months there to live in the fast-paced world his wife loved. He could understand why she loved it, too. She was the darling of the *haute ton* with her exotic appearance and perfectly spoken, yet smoothly accented English. She told stories of Spain to her hosts and the other guests, and even showed some of their more adventurous chefs how to cook the food of her homeland.

When she and Jameson entertained, it was with Spanish delicacies brought over at great cost. Surrounded by the social elite, her sparkle far outshone any of theirs. Her eyes would flash merrily, and her rich voice sounded loudly through the room.

To him, everyone else paled in comparison, and he could never begrudge her such happiness. He would give anything to be able to share an evening with her again.

Jameson rode his gelding slowly to Belton Manor that night. He had made an effort, even simply to dine with Jenny and Simon, having tied his hair back like an eighteenth-century nobleman and allowing Mr. Wynn to shave his face clean. Admittedly, he felt a little more civilized already.

Entering through the main door, Jameson nodded his thanks to the butler, Mr. Binkley, who took his hat and coat with a short bow. Then, he made his own way into the smaller drawing room where he knew they would have drinks before dining.

When he took in the occupants of the room, however, he froze in the doorway, of half a mind to turn and run.

CHAPTER SIX

All eyes were upon him, including Jenny and Simon's, as well as Lady Blackwood, Miss Blackwood, and Miss Darrow's. The walls seemed to rush toward him, shrinking the room to the size of a broom closet.

What could he do to escape with some measure of civility intact? His brain was frantically considering options. Cough loudly while backing out of the room as if having a fit of croup. Or . . .

"Good evening, Lord Turner," Jenny said, already approaching and taking hold of his arm as if she knew he was about to bolt. "I am ever so grateful you agreed to grace us with your presence. We had, as you see, an odd number for dinner, which is vexing for dining, as I'm certain you know."

Yes, he knew. Everyone knew how numbers mattered for dinner parties. But in the country, it wasn't usually so strictly enforced. When he'd first had Jenny and Simon over to Jonling Hall, he'd still been a bachelor. With Lady Lindsey heavy with child at the time, he supposed the baby, who turned out to be their first son, counted as a fourth at the table.

Unfortunately, his thought went to how the quantity would still be odd if Esmera were yet living, and someone else would have to be added or subtracted from the party.

"I know you have a head for numbers," Jameson said, which was the next thing that came to mind.

Jenny, eldest daughter of Baron Blackwood, had been a bookkeeper, her identity carefully hidden, working for those in the village and for Belton Manor when she met Simon.

"Would you like a drink?" she asked, smoothly leading him into the group.

Everyone was standing still, so probably had only just arrived.

"Yes, please." His voice croaked on the last word.

"I'll pour you some wine." Simon stood next to the sideboard with a full glass in his hand, which he promptly handed to Lady Blackwood.

"Why don't you all sit?" Jenny said. "No introductions are necessary, which is nice."

Jameson swallowed and finally let his gaze settle upon each person in turn. He greeted the widow, Lady Blackwood, and Eleanor, before turning to Maisie Darrow.

Considering his last glimpse of her had been of a bedraggled, soaked woman with river mud and bits of grass stuck to her, her transformation in a few hours was nearly miraculous.

"Miss Darrow," he said, nodding to her. "You look much improved."

Lady Blackwood made a tut-tutting sound, and Eleanor had the poor sense to laugh. Apparently, she was unaware of the seriousness of the incident.

"As do you, Lord Turner," Miss Darrow said, tapping her own chin, referring to the absence of his beard. "Much improved." Her brown eyes were friendly and her expression, approving.

To thwart her unwanted approval, he almost wished he'd left himself as he was.

Simon handed out more drinks, including one to Jameson, as Jenny asked, "What improvements were necessary to our Maisie?"

Watching her closely, Jameson saw her cheeks turn a rosy hue. That was something he hadn't witnessed with Esmera. Her blush, and thus sometimes her emotions, were hidden by her perfect, olive complexion.

"I fell into the Don today."

"What?" Jenny exclaimed. "How? Why?"

Those questions brought a small laugh from Miss Darrow's lips, which Jameson was pleased to see had lost all traces of purple coloring and now appeared healthy and pink. Also, her lower lip had a fullness where it bowed, which he hadn't noticed before, making her mouth very pretty to look at.

"I was rowing near the bend, just outside the village."

"Whyever for?" Simon asked, sitting beside his wife.

Jameson sipped his drink, waiting for the ridiculous answer. When it came, it still sounded silly.

"For the view from the river."

Even Jenny laughed. "I'm sure they are no better than from the bank."

"Not worth the effort, surely," Simon added.

"Oh, you're both wrong," Eleanor said. "You can sketch the most perfect scene from upon the river which you cannot see at all from the bank."

"Were you sketching?" Simon asked Maisie.

"No. Just looking."

"And how did you end up in the water?" Jenny asked.

"I only had one paddle, you see. And I was holding onto a rock, when luckily, Lord Turner happened by."

Jameson exchanged a glance with Simon. His cousin's expression held more than one question.

"But why did you leave the other paddle at home?" Lady Blackwood asked.

What? Jameson was sure the older lady had the wrong end of the walking stick. He decided to sum up the incident.

"Miss Darrow rowed some distance, then the paddle slipped from her hand, leaving her only one. She had the good sense to anchor herself to a rock but unfortunately, lost both her hold on the rock and her balance. I told her not to stand in the small boat."

Jameson couldn't help giving Miss Darrow an admonishing shake of his head.

"That makes no sense," Lady Blackwood said.

"Of course it does, Mummy," Jenny said. "No one should stand in a row boat."

"I know that, dear. I meant about the paddle. For there was definitely one paddle leaning by the shed when I went outside, but no boat. Later, after Eleanor and George went to retrieve the boat with the wagon, there were two paddles."

Jameson didn't know what to make of any of that. "Who is George?"

"Our help," Lady Blackwood said. "The cook's son. I believe we'll lose him soon as he needs a better job and more skills."

Jameson let the Blackwood women, including Jenny, all discuss young George's merits and where he ought to go next, until Simon interrupted.

"So, how did you row with only one oar?" he asked Maisie, who was exchanging some sort of look with Eleanor.

"I'm sure you're mistaken, Mummy," the youngest Blackwood said.

"I'm sure I'm not," her mother said.

Jenny stepped in as a good hostess to smooth the familial battle. "Why don't you tell us what happened next, Maisie dear?"

However, Miss Darrow looked a little hesitant, even troubled, so Jameson continued the story.

"Two paddles or not, when I found her, she had one, which I suggested she use to help steer her rudderless boat.

Miss Darrow leaned over too far, fell in, and I dragged her out of the murky drink."

Her gaze flew to his. "Lord Turner is being far too modest. I had well and truly sunk and was in grave difficulty making any headway either above the surface or toward the bank."

"Maisie," Jenny asked, sitting up straighter and leaning forward. "Are you saying you were drowning?"

She hesitated. Jameson assumed she didn't want to worry her family overmuch. Eventually, she said only, "Yes."

"What?" exclaimed Lady Blackwood and Eleanor at the same time. "You didn't tell me that before," the older woman insisted. "You came in and had a bath as if you'd simply fallen in."

"Are you sure?" Eleanor asked, and strangely, she was looking at him.

"Yes, Miss Blackwood. I can assure you Miss Darrow had gone down thrice and was not coming up again."

Eleanor paled and threw her arms around her cousin.

Eventually, after much back-patting, they broke apart and Maisie reached for her wine glass, downing it in one swallow. Then she caught him watching her and blushed again.

Something strange was going on. Of that he was certain. However, it seemed as if the entire incident was bringing nothing but distress, as brushes with the grim reaper often did.

"Let's not dwell on it," he heard himself saying, against all odds. "Miss Darrow is perfectly dry and healthy."

"And you are well?" Simon added, a questioning smile playing about his mouth. It must be because he'd shaved his beard.

"Yes, thank you. I am, too. Perhaps we should suspend all boating for at least the foreseeable future."

Jenny nodded. "Did anyone else happen to read in the papers about the Hundred Guinea Cup yacht race coming up? They've made a course for it around the Isle of Wight?"

Eleanor clapped her hands. "I wish I could go see it. The Royal Yacht Squadron against the New York Yacht Club, and one hundred pounds sterling as the prize." She whistled in a most unladylike fashion, which gave Jameson a distinct feeling of amusement.

Jameson thought it a good change in topic, except for it being about boats and water. He sat back with his drink, letting Simon refill it when needed. No one minded when he spoke little.

For his part, he tried not to keep thinking of what the evening would have been like if Esmera were at his side. However, in trying not to think of such, he kept dredging her up in his memory.

She liked the winged chair Lady Blackwood had taken, and she always asked for red wine. When not asked a question about herself, she usually fell silent, tending to appear as if her mind were elsewhere. She didn't play the pianoforte, although she had a fair singing voice if asked. And she ended nearly every evening with a megrim right about the time of the dessert course, so they left directly after dinner.

That only occurred to him at that moment. Tonight, he wished Esmera were there along with her headache so he could rush away with her after dinner, to make fierce love in their bedroom.

His gaze settled on Miss Darrow, who had become subdued after the boating discussion. She looked surprisingly well considering her ordeal. Many people, men or women, when having such a close brush with mortality, might feel exhausted, or at the very least, not wish to go out to dinner the very same evening.

She had obviously had her bath, washed her golden hair, and managed to dry it, before dressing it in a becoming style.

With curiosity getting the better of him, Jameson had to know something. Leaning closer, so only she could hear, he asked, "How did you manage to dry all your hair?"

She looked startled, then she smiled, and the simple sweetness of it made something inside him spark.

"Lady Blackwood has three daughters, my lord. Can you imagine everyone trying to get ready for an event without having learned all the tricks? She used the bellows on me, and my hair was dry in no time."

"Ingenious," he said.

"I assume you know how ringlets are created," she said.

"Yes." His wife had been fond of them, having her maid create smaller ones all around her temples as well as larger curls, too, that hung halfway down her back.

"So, you know the secret of wrapping each hair around a corkscrew and waiting."

"What?" His gaze had drifted as he thought of Esmera and now latched onto Maisie's again. That was when he realized she was teasing him. He chuckled.

"That would take a long time indeed. Perhaps I should introduce you to the wonderful invention of the curling tong."

She tapped the edge of her wine glass against his as if they'd shared a moment.

Had they? He frowned. *Was he already flirting with another woman so soon after Esmera's death?*

What an unbelievable cad he was, as if his vow on his wedding day had meant nothing.

"Excuse me," he said, standing, not entirely sure what he was doing but determined to remove himself from the room.

Simon stood as well. "Dinner is served," he said, as if Jameson had answered some silent summons.

Jenny glanced at her husband who gestured with a nod of his head to Jameson, who stared at them both, miserably frozen in place.

Should he plead with them to release him from this torture?

"I'm sure it is ready," Jenny agreed, standing.

"I shall escort Lady Lindsey," Simon declared. "Lady Blackwood may walk with Miss Blackwood, and Lord Turner may escort Miss Maisie. You will not be disappointed in the meal."

"We never are," Lady Blackwood insisted as she and Eleanor followed their hosts.

Jameson was well and truly trapped. Obviously, his cousin was not going to offer him an opportunity to leave, and he couldn't simply walk out. He would have to escort Maisie Darrow to the dining room.

As she rose, he took her arm, recalling doing the same hours earlier.

"We are in a better state than the last time I escorted you," he pointed out.

"Indeed," she agreed. "I have two shoes, and you are wearing a shirt."

He couldn't help it. He laughed.

MAISIE ADORED THE SOUND of his laughter. In truth, she preferred Lord Jameson Turner with a bare chest, and imagining him as such, there in the Lindseys' drawing room, made her smile. His warmth as he walked beside her into their dining room was a welcome sensation, since she hadn't been able to completely rid herself of the chill of being soaking wet, even after a hot bath.

In truth, something inside her felt a little scared at the seriousness of what had occurred, when she had never contemplated an early death before.

It was sobering. *What had Lady Turner's last thought been when the train derailed and overturned? Had she been happy right up until the terrible moment?* Maisie hoped so.

Her own last thought had been how Lord Turner was coming to save her and what a decent human being he was, right before she leaned out too far and fell in the river.

"I still am a little overwhelmed by what happened today. So abrupt, as it was."

"I understand," he said, pulling out her chair.

"We are not man, woman, man, woman, tonight," Jenny said as they were all seated in their assigned seats, "but Eleanor often acts quite masculine with her tree climbing and archery and whatnot, so she will sit in the man's place."

"How rude!" Eleanor exclaimed, but she was grinning. "Women have done archery since the time of the Athenians, and I can ride a horse as well as any man. Even into water, and you know how hard it is to get a horse to tread willingly into a river."

"Why would you take your horse into the river anyway?" Jenny asked.

Maisie looked at Eleanor sharply, hoping she wouldn't blurt out their entire ill-conceived undertaking, for without her cousin dragging the tiny boat to the rock behind her horse, none of Maisie's plan would have happened.

Her cousin simply shrugged delicately. "One never knows when one will find it necessary to ford a stream or even a puddle."

"Can one ford a puddle?" Lord Lindsey asked.

"Your horse's legs were very wet today, Miss Blackwood," Lord Turner pointed out. "Were you in the river?"

Blast! Maisie wanted to end that line of questioning and could think of only one way.

Reaching for a steaming dinner roll, she interrupted anything Eleanor was about to say with a question, "Why are hot rolls like caterpillars?"

The entire table fell silent, until Eleanor dutifully asked, "Why?"

"Because they make the butter fly," Maisie told her, slicing open her roll while adding a pat of butter to its warm, soft center.

No one laughed, except her youngest cousin, bless her heart, who gave a small chuckle.

So much for a light jest. "What are we having for dinner?" Maisie asked Jenny, keeping firm hold of the conversation, even if she had to ask a slightly rude question.

"Even I, who am barely out in society these days, wouldn't ask such a thing," Lord Turner said, although he sounded amused.

Maisie tilted her head. "We are all family here, so no one minds."

And it was true. She knew he was estranged from his father, Lord James Devere, who lived a distance away in South Wingfield with his second wife, Lettie. Yet, she hoped Lord Turner felt comfort in knowing those he dined with that very night cared about him. Lord Lindsey seemed to treat him as a brother.

"We have onion soup to start, then trout, then chicken," Jenny began, "then beef in pastry. I know Cook has made salad and all sorts of vegetables, too."

Now what should she ask? To push the boundaries any further and question the pudding course was beyond her. To ask Lord Turner about practically anything at all would only remind him of his life without Lady Turner.

Then, surprising her, he asked, "Why are fishmongers never generous?"

Again, the table's occupants fell silent. This time, Maisie asked, "Why?"

Lord Turner picked up his wine glass and took a sip before answering, "Because their business makes them sell-fish."

His joke, unlike hers, received a smattering of laughter.

"Is this a challenge?" Lord Lindsey asked.

"Ask Miss Darrow," Lord Turner replied.

Eleanor clapped twice, getting everyone's attention. "I have one. Ready?"

"Yes," Jenny said, then sat back as her soup was set before her.

"Why is grass like a mouse?"

"Why?" Lady Blackwood asked, sounding as if she'd heard it before.

Maisie bit her lip. She certainly had heard it but wouldn't spoil it for Eleanor, not after all her cousin had done for her.

Quickly, before anyone could spoil her joke, Eleanor said, "Because the cat'll eat it. Do you understand? *Cattle* and *cat will?*"

Then she laughed at her own joke, which made Lord Lindsey start to laugh, too, perhaps at the silliness around his table. Maisie considered the contrast of the entirely formal, exquisitely appointed room, which was, in fact, cavernous, with three elegantly sparkling chandeliers overhead and an overly large painting of the previous earl behind Lord Lindsey's head.

The table, now covered with cloth, and with most of its leaves removed, was nearly large enough to waltz upon. She'd seen twenty-two people seated comfortably at it when fully extended, but was very glad for the intimate party that night.

The Lindseys were a loving, kind couple, and Maisie couldn't be happier for her eldest cousin to have found such a perfect marriage.

"I will give it a go," Lady Blackwood said. "A garrulous fop who had annoyed his lady partner in the ballroom asked if she had ever had her ears pierced. Do you know what she replied?"

"No, what?" Jenny asked her mother.

"She replied, 'No, but I have had them bored.'"

Maisie considered this a moment as the others did. Then Lord Turner leaned toward her, "There is bored, as in, droning on, and as in boring a hole."

"I see." She glanced over at her aunt. "Well done."

Lady Blackwood shrugged and went back to her onion soup.

"My turn," Jenny said. "I'm not very good with jokes."

"Not the way she is with numbers," her husband agreed.

"But I'll try," she insisted. "Why is salve for one's lips like a good chaperone?"

"Why?" Eleanor asked.

Jenny started to laugh before she could speak, obviously tickled by her own joke.

"Come along, dear one," Lord Lindsey urged her. "Tell us so we all can laugh. Maybe you should start over."

"All right, I will. Why is . . . ?" she trailed off and started to snicker, then took a breath and tried again. "Why is lip salve like a good chaperone?"

When she dissolved in laughter again, Simon filled in the answer: "Because it will keep the *chaps* away."

Jenny stopped laughing at once. "How could you?"

They all burst into laughter.

"It was a delightful joke, Lady Lindsey," Lord Turner said. "Even if your husband ruined it."

Jenny beamed at him. "It's quite all right. It's no different really to how we finish each other's sentences. When you've been married long enough—" she broke off abruptly, looking mortified at her faux pas.

Lord Turner stopped moving, his soup soon halfway to his lips.

CHAPTER SEVEN

Maisie bit back a gasp, fearing the man at her elbow might simply rise and leave.

Instead, he looked down at his nearly empty bowl, setting down his spoon upon it with a clatter.

"I am so sorry, Jameson," Jenny said. "That was ill-spoken of me."

Reaching beneath the table, knowing with the cloth being covered by all the candles, glassware, and vases with flowers from the Lindsey gardens, no one could see her movement, Maisie touched Lord Turner's leg, boldly giving it a comforting squeeze.

She felt him jump under her fingers. Then with the slightest of nods, which she thought was meant for her, he looked up, directly at Jenny.

"No need to apologize," he said. "I have recalled another joke, which Miss Darrow will particularly enjoy."

Maisie glanced around the table as everyone relaxed.

"Please tell us, my lord," she said as she surreptitiously pulled her hand away.

"Very well. Who is the greatest chicken-killer in Shakespeare?"

She couldn't help laughing even before she heard its conclusion, for the question alone was humorous.

"I have no idea. Who?"

He turned to her, and his blue-gray eyes seemed to see into her heart, which was overflowing with concerned affection for him at that moment.

"Macbeth," he said, "because he did murder most fowl."

"Most fowl!" she repeated, and laughed harder until tears came to her eyes.

"I think Lord Turner has won the round," Lord Lindsey declared.

JAMESON WISHED HE DIDN'T have a butler so he could close the front door, hard and loud. Having Mr. Wynn open it for him when he returned and then gently close it behind him did not help his mood. Jameson wanted to slam it!

The dinner party had been horrendous from start to finish. At least, he'd thought it was going to be as soon as he saw more people beyond Jenny and Simon. Entirely unprepared for the company of the Blackwoods and Miss Darrow, he'd imagined an excruciating evening.

In truth, it hadn't been as bad as he'd feared, but it had caused him to keenly feel the loss of his wife at more than one instance. However, realizing Lady Blackwood had also lost her husband and Miss Darrow and Miss Blackwood had never yet had spouses, sometime around the pudding of warm apple Charlotte, Jameson had accepted the blissful state of matrimony was both rare and fleeting.

Instead of begrudging Jenny and Simon, by the evening's end, he had feared for them. Jenny had successfully born three children, so that worry could be set aside for the time being.

And there had been no cholera outbreaks or plague in Sheffield for decades.

His brain imagined other potential perils, and, frankly, the future was fraught with danger and death. There was little one could do to both keep healthy and protect one's heart from further pain except stay indoors, live alone, and pray.

Despite having already had brandy in Simon's study, when the two of them had taken time after dinner to smoke cigars, Jameson went directly to his own and gave himself a decent pour.

Removing his jacket, he considered sitting at his desk, but after the light and laughter at Belton Manor, his dark room held no appeal. Instead, he took his drink and went upstairs, still feeling the slight pain in his foot from his earlier endeavor, although he'd drenched the cut in whiskey for want of a better cleanser.

He hesitated in the hallway. Then, for the first time in a long time, he went into his own bedroom and lit the lamps.

He liked this room, and had upon first view, especially knowing it had been his half brother's. The decor had suited him perfectly, and Jameson had changed very little. Now, he could see it needed fresh paint, and maybe a new rug. Much of the house, in fact, probably needed updating or repair, but he'd been so thrilled to have a home when he'd first bought it, he'd done nothing except enjoy it as it was.

Then his new bride had shown absolutely no interest in Jonling Hall. Instead, she had worked tirelessly on the public rooms of their small but elegant townhouse on Princes Street in London, making sure it was *à la mode* for entertaining.

Thus, his country house remained basically as it was when he purchased it.

Almost as if he didn't exist.

A strange thought! It had been a strange night, however, capping a strange day, for that matter. When he'd awakened that morning, how could he possibly have supposed he would save a drowning woman only to dine with her later?

Not to mention have her cheer him with ridiculous jokes and then put her hand on his leg.

What had she been thinking? In his younger days, before Esmera, he would have taken that as an invitation to do more. He might have tried to get her alone sometime in the evening and kiss her pretty mouth with its luscious lower lip. He might have taken her soft hand and placed it somewhere more exciting than his thigh.

In truth, however, that small touch, the briefest squeeze, had been extremely stimulating, in all likelihood because he was out of practice. Or more specifically, because he was in mourning and devoid of any desire to be with a woman. He wasn't an animal, after all. He was a widower.

Sipping his drink, he recalled Maisie Darrow's lovely laugh, as well as her curves soaking wet and pressed against him when he was still hardly able to believe she was alive, gasping air, and standing in the shallows with him. And then he'd seen her thigh, exposed to him as she rode his horse. His loins stirred.

The devil! He was not a green youth to grow randy for the first woman whose close company he'd allowed himself in seven months. She was *not* Esmera. No one could ever be Esmera. And that was all that mattered.

He finished the brandy. He needed to find a purpose. He was shiftless and restless with no claims on his time. He could go back to London and gamble with his old companions at Crocky's or White's. Or he could ask Simon if he had any tasks he needed doing, but Simon had the ever-capable Jenny at his side. Wife, mother, accountant, the perfect helpmate.

Esmera had not been that, Jameson thought, as he undressed, but he hadn't valued her any less for being more decorative than supportive. She was like a sparkling jewel to be admired. And if sometimes she was as hard as a diamond, that had been a small annoyance he'd been willing to overlook for every other exceptional part of her.

Undoubtedly, Maisie Darrow had a hundred more flaws, including terrible balance. She did have a good sense of humor, however, and a remarkable memory for quoted material. Moreover, she'd been exceptionally kind to him, barging into his home and telling jokes, not to mention showing him her leg.

Dammit all! He was back to thinking of her beautiful flesh.

At least, he had been jarred out of the stupor in which he'd been residing for so long. And the Lindsey cook had filled his stomach for the first time in . . . he couldn't remember how long. In fact, his stomach ached a little, probably too much, too soon.

Stretching out upon the bed, he pondered tomorrow, also something he hadn't done in a long time. *What would he do in the morning? What would the next day bring?*

He drifted off thinking of Maisie Darrow.

MAISIE DECIDED TO STRIKE whilst the iron was hot as Hades. Lord Turner had not bolted the night before upon seeing a gathering, nor had he been surly and reserved, both of which Jenny and Lord Lindsey had feared, warning them before he arrived.

If Lord Turner was left alone, though, she was certain he would retreat once more into his grief and isolation.

Eleanor, who'd already been out for her usual early morning walk, met her on the stairs of the cottage as she went down to breakfast.

"Did you nearly drown yesterday?"

"Yes," she admitted. "It went wrong, but ended up all right."

"I would have been responsible for your death," Eleanor hissed.

"Don't be so dramatic, cousin. I didn't die." They went into the small, sunny dining room.

"And no more plans to put yourself in peril?"

Maisie helped herself to eggs and bacon from the platters in the center of the table.

"No, I promise. I accomplished my purpose, and I believe it worked. I may walk over to Jonling Hall today and thank him again for his courage."

"I should accompany you, then. Mummy already grumbled to me about letting you spend too much time alone, and in particular, she didn't like you dropping in on an unmarried man."

"Why didn't she say something to me herself?" Maisie had assumed her aunt found it acceptable since the man was in mourning, seemingly off-limits to any improperly romantic notions and, thus, immune to social reprimand, too.

"Mummy didn't think it was her place, but wanted me, as your closest cousin, to warn you off the inappropriate behavior."

Maisie nodded. "Then, we shall go together."

In truth, she'd been unsure of the etiquette, as it seemed people were a little freer in the country. At least, they were in Dumfries. However, she wasn't a girl anymore. She was a woman who'd had a Season, and as such, the rules had changed. She knew her brother would have frowned, but Ned was a sourpuss anyway, so she wouldn't have paid him any mind. Yet to think Lady Blackwood thought ill of her, how disturbing!

Maisie keenly felt the loss of her mother at that moment. It happened when she made a misstep in a social situation. Or when she'd been shopping for gowns for her Season, or even when she simply wanted to have her hair brushed by someone who loved her.

In fact, she often longed for her mother, and the feeling hadn't lessened with the years.

Tears pricked her eyes, and she stuffed a bite of coddled egg into her mouth.

Undeniably, Lady Blackwood had always treated her with kindness, but there was a stark difference between the love the baroness felt for her three daughters and the fond affection she reserved for her niece. The difference between having a mother's love and not, Maisie supposed.

It was always easier to focus on doing something or going somewhere, or even rereading the endlessly fascinating Shakespeare, than it was to contemplate what she could not change and what she missed.

"Let's take Lord Turner something delicious to eat."

Eleanor nodded, munching on toast. "He positively devoured every course last night, yet he looks thinner than he ever did before. He is definitely mourning in earnest."

"I don't think his continued melancholy is good for him."

"My mother did not grieve similarly, but the circumstances were vastly different," Eleanor pointed out. "Mummy was preoccupied with selling our home in London and all our nice things. I don't think she had time to truly feel sad until months after my father passed. Perhaps it was easier on her, also the fact she was angry as a wet cat over him lying about the state of our financial affairs."

They set off after their breakfast for Jonling Hall, with Cook's meat and potato pasties and some shortbread biscuits. Maisie was still considering the difference of having the wealth, time, and freedom to wallow in one's misery, which was what Lord Turner had done. If he and his wife had had a child for him to worry over, or if he'd been scrambling to keep a roof over his loved ones' heads, as her aunt had done, then he couldn't have languished in his cocoon of sadness all these many months.

Perhaps, instead of him saving her life—while she'd much appreciated it—he should be taken to task for the sheer indulgence of his long, self-indulgent grief.

However, she didn't think she was the one to give him a dressing down over it. That would have to come from his family, either his father or, perhaps, Simon.

The same dour butler let them in, and they waited in the drawing room.

"Such a pretty home, don't you think?" Maisie remarked.

Eleanor nodded. "Strangely, it looked precisely this way *before* Lord Turner got married. In fact, it has always looked this way, or at least as far as I can recall."

"We may have a long wait," Maisie told her cousin, "depending on his humor, be it good or ill today."

Eleanor shrugged. "That's fine. Later, I plan on a walk up to the Smithson orchards. Have I taken you there before? The trees are all gnarled and overgrown. I'm taking my sketchpad and a picnic, and you, of course."

Maisie hoped Eleanor wasn't dragging her along because of Aunt Anne, when surely solitude was desired for sketching, but she would go nonetheless. "Why don't we take the carriage?"

Before Eleanor could answer, footsteps heralded the arrival of Lord Turner. Although his hair was still too long, with his beard entirely shaved off from the previous night, he reminded her more and more of his prior self. What's more, he was dressed as if he knew company had been coming. *Shoes and a coat!*

He nodded to each of them, unsmiling but not scowling. "To what do I owe this visit?"

Maisie noted he didn't say "this pleasure."

"We brought you some food." She gestured to the full basket she'd placed on the low table in front of the sofa.

He looked at it, and then he looked at each of them in turn, and then he frowned and addressed Maisie.

"Why?"

She could hardly insult him by mentioning his appearance. "It is the neighborly thing to do," she assured him. She wanted to add "particularly when visiting a starving widower," but instead added, "especially when you seemed to appreciate a good meal last night."

He nodded. "At the risk of insulting my cook, I thank you. It smells good."

He hesitated and then said, "Well, I won't keep you. I'm sure you ladies have plans for your day."

"Yes," Eleanor said, while Maisie said, "No."

She glared at her cousin. "We hoped we could visit with you for a little while and discuss . . . ," Maisie trailed off. *What could they discuss?*

"Since we only just had some lengthy discussions last night," Lord Turner pointed out, "I am sure I could not come up with anything to entertain you ladies."

Oh dear! He was going to give them the boot, and she'd accomplished nothing.

"Eleanor reads Gothic novels," she blurted, having seen one on the breakfast table that morning. "Do you have an interest in them?"

At least her cousin perked up at the hope of a discussion of dark castles and inexplicable noises.

His lordship didn't look impressed. "I don't actually. I have found life to be grim enough without reading gloomy stories."

"Understandably so," Maisie said, although Eleanor looked as if she might be going to argue the merits of the genre.

"We are going to an orchard today," Maisie informed him. Perhaps she could interest him in going, too. Indeed, his entire being seemed to perk up when he heard.

"Do you have a chaperone?" he fired back.

Eleanor laughed. "We have each other, unless Miss Darrow doesn't go with me, and then I will have only myself."

The look he gave her cousin might have withered fruit on the vine.

"You would consider going alone?"

"Consider, yes, and have done so," Eleanor informed him. "I'm not trekking to Egypt. Only walking to the Smithson's orchard."

"But there are no Smithsons in residence," he pointed out. "The farmhouse burned down long ago. The trees are rotten and overgrown."

Maybe Lord Turner had given the orchard his alarmingly disapproving glare, Maisie thought.

"I wasn't going for the apples or pears, my lord."

"You shouldn't go at all," he insisted. "It's dangerous, with or without Miss Darrow as your companion. Probably more so with her."

She wanted to laugh at his quip even though he was being insulting.

"I assure you," Eleanor argued, "it is not."

"The walk alone is fraught with potential hazards."

"Perhaps we should take the wagon, after all," Maisie said, hoping to quell Lord Turner's growing agitation and Eleanor's burgeoning argumentative nature.

His lordship's glance snapped to her. "What if you roll the wagon? There are some steep inclines on the way. You both could be crushed or thrown."

Eleanor laughed again, which didn't help. Maisie could see he was getting annoyed.

"Or you might lose a wheel," he continued. "There are many ruts in the road. I wonder if I should speak to Simon about repairing them. In any case, if a wheel broke, you'd be stranded there for who knows how long. At the mercy of not only the elements but also any nefarious types who happened along. Pickpockets and charlatans. Men with knives or hunters with guns who mistook you for game."

Maisie could only stare at him as he continued his litany of what could happen and the dangers he foresaw. She was certain her expression mirrored Eleanor's, who had stopped laughing or even smiling, to look perplexed, her mouth a little open in wonder at how Lord Turner's mind worked.

Gracious! It was a wonder he ever set foot outside his home if he truly feared all of that at any given moment.

"None of that will happen," Eleanor protested. "None of those events have ever happened to me in all my years in Sheffield."

"Something terrible has to happen only once," he pointed out. "Once is enough. Look at what occurred yesterday to Miss Darrow. A simple rowing trip became a death trap."

Maisie shot Eleanor a glance, hoping she didn't say anything as to how they'd engineered that fiasco.

"Are these fears the reason you've stayed indoors so long?" Eleanor asked, looking at him now as a curiosity, as if she'd discovered a new species of bug on a leaf.

"What?" Lord Turner exclaimed. "Of course not. I'm a man. None of that would bother me."

"Then why have you stayed indoors like a recluse?" Eleanor asked.

Maisie wanted to slap her own forehead in dismay. *Why was her cousin poking at the poor man?*

"Miss Blackwood," he said, picking up the basket and shoving it into her hands so she had to grasp the handle or let it drop, "my life is none of your business. Good day!"

He glanced once at Maisie and then he turned to leave.

This hadn't gone well at all. She didn't want him to go away insulted and in a huff. She didn't want him to go away at all.

"Please, my lord," she asked, "won't you accompany us to the orchard? *One touch of nature makes the whole world kin.*"

CHAPTER EIGHT

Jameson had made it to the door, almost escaping these annoying young ladies. Then Miss Darrow had quoted Shakespeare, or at least, he assumed it was.

"Please, Lord Turner," Miss Darrow's reasonable yet cajoling tone reached him.

He sighed and turned, immediately caught by her soft gold and brown gaze.

"I see how we might need a companion," she admitted, "if not a chaperone. While Eleanor sketches, I could get up to mischief or even into danger."

Her words nearly made him laugh. She was trying so damnably hard. And why? *Why did she care a fig whether he stayed inside all day alone or got out into the world?*

Her cousin, however, looked as though she wasn't the least bit happy about him joining their party. That bothered him not at all.

Moreover, he'd had a good night's sleep in his own bed, and he'd awakened with the desire to do something. He might as well make himself useful.

"I shall accompany you. When are you leaving?"

"Directly," Miss Blackwood said. "We have only to return home for supplies."

"I shall pick you up in an hour." He took the basket back from her and lifted the cloth to look inside. "It appears I have some picnic supplies already, enough for an army or, at least, for three hungry people."

"You cannot pick us up in a fancy carriage," Miss Blackwood protested. "Either we walk, or we need a sturdy wagon."

"Understood," he agreed.

"I'll get lemonade," Maisie promised, "while Eleanor gets her sketching materials, and a blanket to sit upon. What else might we need?"

And then the ladies left, and Jameson couldn't imagine how a few softly spoken words from Miss Darrow had turned the tide, causing him to agree to go on a picnic. Moreover, he was looking forward to it.

"Mr. Wynn," he called, knowing the man would be lurking within earshot. After all, Jonling Hall wasn't Belton Manor. It was scaled for comfort, and despite having a bell pull in every room, he had always been able to summon staff with a few well-annunciated words.

Esmera had liked the formality of the bell pulls, he recalled. Another thing he missed, teasing her about giving the thick ribbon a tug when a servant was a few feet away on the other side of the wall. She would roll her eyes at him and tug again with a mischievous smile.

Mr. Wynn appeared at once. "I am going to take you up on your offer."

"My lord?"

"You may tidy me up, specifically, you may trim my hair."

Then he looked at the man's own neatly cropped style. "Who cuts *your* hair?"

"Mrs. Williams."

Apparently, his housekeeper had many talents besides intimidating everyone and keeping Jonling Hall orderly.

"Ask her to grab her shears and . . . no, it won't do for her to come to my bedroom or even the bathroom. I guess I'll sit outside on the terrace, and she can cut it there."

In a very few minutes, he had a new haircut, not as short as Mr. Wynn's, but no longer did he look like a bloody pirate. Then he had Cook add a few goodies to another basket, including a bottle of wine. *Lemonade be damned!*

Going to the stables, he examined the old wagon to see if it was in good repair, which it was. Everything ran smoothly at Jonling Hall despite his negligence. He should give everyone a bonus for having to deal with a ghost-of-a-master.

On the other hand, he'd probably made life easy on them with no demands until recently. Setting his two baskets in the back of the wagon, he eschewed the stable boy and hitched the horse himself. One should be enough for this excursion.

Patting the horse's neck, he realized he was looking forward to this outing.

Then, his heart sank. In fact, it twinged, and he would swear he felt physical pain. Esmera was dead, and he was preparing for an outing with two ladies. Not only preparing but happily doing so with a glimmer of anticipation for their company.

Dropping his arms to his side, he stared ahead, thinking of her final moments as he often did. For him, his thoughts were a certain path to misery and regret, one which he let himself dally upon willingly on a daily basis. It brought him closer to her, kept her fresh in his mind, and brought him as much pain as he could handle.

Esmera was traveling from London to Bath on the Great Western Railway with one of her closest friends. The train had barely got underway ten minutes earlier when it derailed between Paddington Station and Drayton, and everything he loved had ended.

She hadn't even had a chance to stop for lunch at Goring, something she loved to do on a journey. Easily, he pictured her seated by the window, Lady Canton-Serise opposite. They would have been remarking on the quality of their upcoming meal and looking forward to taking the waters at Bath. More importantly, as far as Esmera was concerned, by early evening, she would be walking the town, remarking on who was staying on the Crescent, and attending an event at the Assembly Rooms.

Tickets for a dinner party that night and a ball the next day had been in her luggage, which was returned to him after he claimed her body.

All of it, her trunk and her leather bags, he'd set in her bedroom next to his, untouched since his return from London.

And he was going on a picnic? A selfish, frivolous day trip!

Like a man without a care.

Not at all like a widower whose wife's neck had snapped instantly.

Swallowing the emotion causing a lump in his throat, Jameson didn't know how to proceed. He was torn, thinking of Miss Darrow and Miss Blackwood awaiting him, while also thinking of the quiet torment of Esmera's room and the penance of remaining in it for many hours every day, thinking of her, going over every aspect of their life together, and trying to change the days, hours, and even the minutes leading up to her being without him on the train to Bath.

They could as easily have been together in his comfortable carriage. If he'd been going with her, they would most definitely have been. Instead, as it grew closer to the day of departure, he'd received a missive from his father with more than one task to which he needed to attend. Combining that with his own business interests, Jameson had stayed in London, taking her to Paddington Station and boarding with her to get her situated. He took the baggage ticket from the porter and tucked it into her reticule.

"You always take such good care of me," Esmera had said with a smile of gratitude.

He closed his eyes, leaning against his bridled horse, thankful he'd kissed her despite being in public, a long, sweet, lingering goodbye kiss.

Lady Canton-Serise, who had survived the wreck with a broken arm and nearly blind in one eye, had turned her head away to give them privacy, a smile on her lips. Everyone smiled when they saw how much Jameson and Esmera loved one another.

Groaning, he called for the stable boy.

"Unhitch him," he gestured to the horse, "and put him back in his stall." He was halfway across the cobbled yard when Jonathon stopped him.

"My lord, you've got baskets in here."

Picnic baskets for happy people doing pleasant things. He did not belong with them.

"Help yourself to anything in there." Then he thought better of it. "Hold on."

Jameson went back and snatched the wine bottle out of the spare basket. He didn't need a drunken servant getting injured and falling on a pitchfork or being trampled by a horse. Besides, he had a feeling he would need the wine himself.

Back indoors, he ran into Mr. Wynn in the hallway.

"Please send someone with a message to the Blackwood cottage at Norman's Corner. I won't be attending the young ladies on their outing to Smithson's orchard."

And if something happened to them, it would be on his head, he supposed.

THAT EVENING, MAISIE SAT outside with her aunt and cousin, each with a glass of sherry. The weather was fine, the day had been perfect, and despite Lord Turner's absence, Eleanor had sketched a few lovely drawings.

Maisie felt nothing but compassion for the man who'd been unable to enjoy a picnic. She'd wandered the old orchard, explored a building, and nearly fallen into a poorly covered well with rotten boards for a lid.

What would their cautious Lord Turner think about that?

After their picnic, they'd sat and read books before having an earnest discussion of the various dance partners from the prior Season. They tried to remember them all and consider with whom they might wish to dance again.

Maisie kept quiet about the one man who'd frightened her by maneuvering her away from the other dancers and, before she knew it, down a hallway, all the while whispering words of devotion. And then he'd attempted to reach down the front of her dress, pressed his lips upon hers while she struggled, grabbed the soft flesh of her rear end, and even tried to lift her skirts.

It had happened so quickly. But she hadn't stopped fighting, twisting her head from side to side so his kiss couldn't land properly when he had her pressed against the wall, the molding digging into her back.

When she'd continued to struggle, he'd eventually stepped back with an exasperated sigh.

"Can it be you don't want my advances?"

With enough room to straighten up, Maisie had slapped his chest ineffectually and brought her knee up between them before pushing past him to flee the room.

She'd never even spoken. *What would she say?*

The cock-sure viscount who'd assaulted her had given up and let her leave, as if she wasn't worth the trouble. Or, more likely, he'd initially believed she'd wanted his groping hands upon her and was flummoxed by her denying him.

She'd sat out every dance afterward that evening, trying to determine if she'd mistakenly encouraged his passion. Keeping her eyes upon him, he danced with others, and even seemed perfectly charming and gentlemanly. She didn't notice him herd any other young lady toward the hallway.

Had she invited his misbehavior?

She'd never told anyone about the frightening incident, not even Eleanor, and had never danced with the man again, although he'd tried to scrawl his name on her dance card.

"You're quiet, Maisie," her aunt said. "What did you think of the orchard?"

"There's a badly sealed well. Someone could get hurt."

"You sound like Lord Turner," Eleanor pointed out.

Maisie nodded. "Poor man! Imagine being so tormented he couldn't enjoy an outing on a lovely day."

"He used to drive in his open carriage with his wife," Lady Blackwood said. "She wasn't so fond of the country, but she went on rides with him because he liked it. They were such a lovely couple."

"They probably would have had children by now," Eleanor said. "Lord Turner used to play with Jenny's babies, and I remember he said more than once what a pretty child Lady Turner would have."

"*Hm*," her aunt said. "I'm not sure."

"What do you mean?" Maisie asked her.

"I mean no disrespect to the departed," Aunt Anne said, "but I do not think Lady Turner was interested in bearing children, at least not at the time she died. Lord Turner might have bounced Lionel on his knee, but Lady Turner never touched my grandchildren. She may have settled down to it eventually, or maybe she was fearful of the childbed. And who can blame her?"

They all contemplated the great risk necessary to bring a baby into the world.

"But no one can know for sure," Lady Blackwood added. "She might even have been carrying a child when she passed. That might explain his lordship's deep melancholy. Perhaps he lost two that day and has never mentioned it."

The notion sent chills down Maisie's spine.

In any case, she had decided not to give up on the man. She'd seen glimmers of his past good humor and was unwilling to let it lie dormant forever. Perhaps a frivolous outing with her and Eleanor had been too much to demand of him.

Tomorrow, she would try something more reserved and on her own, regardless of what her aunt thought proper. No one could ever think Lord Turner, deeply mourning his wife, would ever behave as the viscount had to her that evening in London.

The next day after breakfast, without mentioning her comings and goings to Eleanor, Maisie put on a bonnet and strolled toward Jonling Hall. She brought no gifts, no jam or meat pies, only herself and her determination.

The butler allowed her entrance, a good sign, and even said he would seek out his lordship. She had a feeling Jameson Turner wouldn't make her wait too long. They had moved past that petty posturing, designed to demonstrate his desire for solitude. At least, she hoped they'd moved past it.

In a couple minutes, she heard him on the stairs from where she stood in the center of the drawing room. He came in on heavy footsteps, looking bleary-eyed. His hair, far shorter than the day before, stood on end as if he'd run his hands through it a hundred times, and, clearly, he hadn't shaved. His clothing was beyond rumpled. Moreover, he smelled strongly of liquor.

"Have you slept?" she asked.

"No. Yes. I'm not sure." He collapsed onto the sofa, forcing her to sit quickly in case he became embarrassed by his own lack of manners.

"I was asleep at some point," he added. Then he laughed, despite neither of them having said anything humorous.

"You don't look well, I'm sorry to say."

He shrugged. Since he didn't take offense, she continued to pester him. "Have you eaten today?"

"No." He said this with certainty. "I only just got up when Mr. Wynn said you'd arrived."

He'd drunk himself into a stupor and passed out in his clothing. She glanced around for the bell pull, and gave it a yank.

He laughed again. "Women and bell pulls," he muttered.

When Mr. Wynn entered, Maisie took charge the same way she'd done in her own household after her mother passed.

"Please bring his lordship some porridge and bacon, and a pot of strong tea. The sooner the better, I'd warrant."

Mr. Wynn had the grace to glance at his master for permission. When Lord Turner did nothing more than shrug, the butler turned back to her.

"Yes, miss. Would you like anything?"

"I'll have some tea, too. I like milk and sugar."

"Yes, miss." And he disappeared. She hoped he would be quick.

"I'm sorry you couldn't come out yesterday."

"Well," he said, sounding cavalier and tossing his hands up before letting them fall on his lap.

"We had a lovely picnic, but you were correct. There was a little danger lurking in the form of some worn out boards over an abandoned well."

"What can you do?" he said, cocking his head and eyeing her a little sideways.

He was still in his cups. She would swear to it. *Had he been drinking all night?*

"I hope I didn't catch you at a bad time."

He stared at her, his eyes widening. "A bad time, Miss Maisie? Is there any other kind?"

Miss Maisie!

"You seemed in better spirits yesterday."

"Did I? I don't recall."

"May I ask what caused you to change your mind about accompanying us?"

"You may," he said emphatically, nodding his head.

She waited, but he remained silent.

Realizing he was waiting for her to ask, she did. "What caused you to change your mind?"

"None of your business," he said.

"I see." She took no offense. Besides, the answer was clear. He'd started ruminating on his dead wife and probably never made it past the front door.

"You probably do see. You seem like a stute . . . an astute young lady."

He had slurred his words; she was certain of it. *Where was that blasted tea?*

A maid entered carrying a tray with a large bowl of porridge and a plate of bacon, which she placed on the low table in front of Lord Turner. Just behind her, Mr. Wynn carried the tea tray. In a minute, his lordship was enthusiastically eating and drinking.

Maisie stirred her tea, wondering he hadn't a terrible headache, although perhaps that was still to come. She let him eat in silence, and the hollow, smudged look to his eyes cleared a little.

Finally, setting his bowl down, he burped and sat back with his teacup in hand. He'd already devoured five rashers of bacon.

"Do you feel better?"

"Did I say I didn't feel well?" He took a healthy gulp of tea and sighed, perhaps relishing the taste.

"No, but you didn't look particularly well." Maisie wasn't going to beat about the bush. "Frankly, you looked peaked."

"No one has ever called me that before."

"Hopefully, you don't end up in such a state very often."

She hoped, in fact, he continued to improve, to feel better, to come out of his melancholy if possible. If he couldn't do it himself, she was happy to help lift him as much as he would allow her.

"I don't know to what state you're referring, Miss Darrow, but I was a little hungry, to be sure."

He'd said her name correctly, which she took as a good sign.

"Would you care to take a turn about your back garden?"

He stared at her as if she'd grown a pig snout.

"No one has ever said that to me, either."

She smiled. "You and your wife never walked around your lovely garden? Or do you mean she never asked you."

Blast! Simply mentioning Lady Turner caused him to withdraw behind a somber mask. Leaning forward, he set the saucer down. Maisie prepared for him to become angry, toss her out, or to leave the room.

Instead, he steepled his fingers together, elbows resting on his knees.

"In fact, my wife didn't care for gardens much," he said, his voice toneless and tight. "Truly the opposite of Miss Blackwood, who seems to have an affinity for nature. You like it, too, it seems, what with rivers and orchards."

Maisie let out the breath she hadn't realized she was holding.

"My cousin is far more of a nature lover than I am. I don't climb trees or spend hours staring at a flower or a honeybee. But I love Sheffield. Every time I visit, I am never disappointed in its beauty."

He nodded. "I feel the same way about the area." Then he stood up. "Yes, I will show you around the garden." He ran a hand over his head, not improving the state of his hair, and then looked down at himself.

"Would you wait while I clean myself up?"

She feared he would not return once he went upstairs.

"You're fine for strolling on your own property, Lord Turner. I wouldn't change a hair."

His handsome face cracked into a shadow of a smile.

"Speaking of which, do you like the cut?"

She could be entirely honest, which it pleased her to be. "It suits you perfectly."

When combed, she was convinced it was very stylish, and uncombed, it gave him a rakish, devil-may-care appearance. Probably the last thing he wanted, but it did suit his face, nonetheless.

She let him lead her through the house to the back. He held the door for her, gesturing for her to proceed him through the French doors to a stone terrace lined with empty plant pots. There was a small table and a single chair, which looked as if they belonged in a more squalid dwelling than behind a lovely country house.

He ignored them and took her arm in his, making her jump.

"My apology," he said at once. "I should have asked and not presumed. Shall I release you? It's just that the stepping stones are uneven until we get to the grass."

Truthfully, touching him and being touched by him was pleasant. She felt no urge to pull away. The sensation of his body close beside her was distracting and exciting. She hoped it didn't make her grasping or depraved to enjoy the inadvertent attention of a disinterested man who was completely in love with his deceased wife.

She nodded when he pointed out a feature, such as a raised flower bed, an ancient willow, or a birdbath from Spain, although he choked on the mention of his wife's birthplace. He fell silent for a few moments, but then spoke again when they reached a white stone path through an overgrown rose garden, whose old plants were in riotous bloom.

Maisie stopped in the middle of it and faced him. "Eleanor would adore this. The fragrance is utterly intoxicating."

Closing her eyes, she breathed deeply, parting her lips slightly to inhale even more of the rich aromas of half a dozen or more varieties of roses. The flowers and their scents must come from Heaven.

Suddenly, and without warning, she felt Lord Turner's lips upon her own.

CHAPTER NINE

Maisie Darrow's lips were perfect. They were soft and full and pliable, and they were open under his own. And when he touched her arms, encircling each with his fingers to hold her in place, he relished her warmth and vibrance.

When Mr. Wynn had told him she was in the drawing room, he'd jumped up from where he lay sprawled on Esmera's bed. Knowing Miss Darrow wouldn't care about his grooming, he'd bounded downstairs, eager to see her, surprised to realize he still felt a little drunk, but with no headache. Perhaps it would come shortly.

He couldn't recall precisely why he'd changed his mind about going with her and Eleanor Blackwood the day before, but he was glad she'd returned. Then she'd made sure he ate before he even realized what the gnawing feeling in his belly was.

And when she stood in his rose garden and closed her eyes, she looked positively kissable.

Slowly, Jameson drew her close, and she didn't resist. He could feel her heart thumping wildly where her chest was pressed against his, and his own heart echoed the beat.

Kissing her was the softest, sweetest thing he'd done in a long, long time. And holding her when she was not soaking wet was a treat, her curves crushed against him delightfully.

In fact, everything about having his arms around Miss Darrow felt good. He wanted to groan with the sensations coursing through his body.

Finally, he lifted his head but, even as her eyes fluttered open, he didn't immediately release her.

Instead, he gazed down, seeing the surprise in her expression, but also the pleasure glowing there. And then, her face wavered out of focus, replaced by the burnished visage of his beautiful wife, and her dark, flashing eyes were accusatory.

He jumped back. *What on God's green earth was he doing holding another woman?*

"I'm sorry," he said at once, as much to Esmera as to Maisie Darrow. "That was unconscionable of me."

Miss Darrow didn't look the least bit affronted or concerned. *Shouldn't she?* A respectable woman wouldn't allow herself to be manhandled and kissed by someone whom she barely knew and who had absolutely no interest in forming a long-term relationship with her.

He was a little disappointed in her, frankly.

"I appreciate your apology, but no harm was done," she said.

While she spoke, his gaze was fixed on her lips.

He was fascinated with her petal-pink lips. Esmera's were wider, more generous, a dusky tan color when not made up, but usually crimson with the alkanet salve she wore. When made up, she looked like a goddess—alluring, desirable, sexy, all of which she was well-aware.

Miss Darrow's lips were plain, and he should forget them at once.

"I cannot believe how very muddled my head is from too much liquor last night. It's unlike me to drink that way. Even more unlike me to kiss strangers in my garden."

She took a step back, her cheeks becoming pinker. "Are we still strangers even after you saved my life?"

He shook his head, not knowing how to answer.

Esmera was his wife. That was the only truth he knew. And he wanted to pretend as though he had never kissed Miss Darrow.

"Would you like to take some flowers back to Lady Blackwood?" He didn't know why he asked such a question, but he had to bring them back from the realm of intoxicating kisses to the mundane world of gardening.

Without waiting for an answer, he jogged back to the house. "I'll get some shears," he called over his shoulder.

When he returned, Miss Darrow had ventured farther into the four-quadrant rose garden, looking like a perfect English rose, herself, with her flaxen hair shining in the sun, and her blushing cheeks mimicking the blooms all around her.

Esmera had always looked out of place in an English garden while perfectly natural in a glittering ballroom. *Strange.*

"Did you pick out some?"

Miss Darrow shrugged. "A difficult choice. Also, they are blooming so gloriously together, like sisters. It seems cruel to cut one away right next to another. How could I choose which to condemn like a judge or executioner?"

Good lord! Death and execution. It was simply a rose garden. *Could she truly be so soft-hearted?*

"Turn your back on the *sisters*, and I'll cut you a bouquet to take with you."

She smiled at him, nodded, and turned her back. Slender, shorter than Esmera, but equally graceful, Miss Darrow had a nice way about her. And there he went again, comparing them.

He would stop it at once. He must!

Approaching the first clump of rose bushes, pale pink, he haphazardly cut a few, placing them on the ground. He should have brought a basket or a cloth when he went for the shears, but he had been thinking only of breaking the mood of desire that had swirled about them.

"'*Of all the flowers, me thinks a rose is best,*' Shakespeare said, but I cannot recall in which play."

"How lax of you, Miss Darrow." He continued to cut the flowers, glad to know she wasn't perfect, for she made him painfully aware of his recent lapses in civility and his fallibilities as a whole.

"Actually, I know precisely who spoke it, Emilia, when—in Act II, scene two. But I don't want to seem a know-it-all. For I am not only about Shakespeare. He mentions flowers, particularly roses, quite a bit. Of course, we all know where the line *What's in a name? That which we call a rose by any other name would smell as sweet* comes from."

She paused, perhaps testing to make sure he wasn't entirely plebeian.

"From *Romeo and Juliet*," he supplied, nearly certain, as he'd seen it on an advertisement in a flower shop window, with the play mentioned along the bottom. *Thank God!*

"Yes, but some are harder to place. Such as this passage, *At Christmas I no more desire a rose than wish a snow in May's new-fangled mirth, but like of each thing that in season grows.*"

He considered. "You have stumped me, Miss Darrow."

"I was not testing you, my lord. But it is from *Love's Labor's Lost.*"

"May I ask why this fascination with Shakespeare?"

She hesitated, and he hoped he hadn't asked anything too personal. Turning, she examined the growing pile of roses, from the palest, nearly white to the deepest red and even a violet one he'd never even noticed before, until she picked it up and sniffed it.

"My mother loved the plays," she began. "And when I was old enough—actually, even before I understood the language at all—we read them together, speaking different roles."

"You mentioned your mother before, I believe." When he interrupted her about thistle jelly and called her cold and passionless.

Their brief kiss had proved she was neither.

"I had a chance to try the jelly. Thank you. It was unusual." *Like you.* "And delicious." *Also, like you.*

She nodded. "My mother died five years ago, nearly six. I read and reread all of her Shakespeare collection many times since then. I can almost hear her voice still in my head when I do."

He released the rose he was about to cut, sparing its life.

"I am sorry for your loss, Miss Darrow."

"And I, for yours, Lord Turner."

They stared at one another.

"I'm glad the Bard gives you comfort." Even though he now realized her memorizing lines indicated how many times she'd comforted herself by reading those plays. Immersing herself in Shakespeare was her version of how he lay upon Esmera's bed and went over every detail of their marriage.

"How shall I transport the roses?" she mused.

"I'll carry them back to the house, and we'll find you a basket. You've brought me a couple recently."

"True. Did you enjoy Cook's meat pasties?"

He didn't want to confess having given them away. On the other hand, it couldn't hurt to seem beneficent.

"My stable boy is always hungry. I let him have the delicacies from the Blackwoods' cook. I hope you don't mind."

"Not at all. I'm glad nothing went to waste." They were nearly at the back entrance to Jonling Hall. "Pity he read the love notes I'd penned for you."

Jameson actually stumbled and dropped some of the flowers. Hastening to pick them up, as he stooped, he heard her start to laugh.

"I'm sorry, my lord. I was merely making a jest."

"Quite humorous," he admitted as he stood. And it had been. He couldn't say he didn't admire her wit.

Indoors, Mr. Wynn retrieved the first basket she'd brought over, and Jameson carefully lay all the roses in it.

"There must be thirty blossoms," Miss Darrow declared. "Auntie will be thrilled. We'll put them all over the house."

"Before the bushes lose their bloom, you must return and get more," he said.

Instantly, he wished he could call the words back. They sounded like a friendly invitation. *Is that what he intended?*

No, he did not want to keep company with a lovely young woman who deserved a proposal at some point in the future. He could never do that again.

The risk, the pain—both were too great.

Moreover, his heart was buried with Esmera. All he had left was involuntary desire as displayed when he got too close to Maisie Darrow. That, and raw lust. Neither were love, neither were appropriate for an innocent miss who would want a husband someday soon.

"Did you come by horseback?"

"No, I walked."

"Good, it's safer," he said and stepped out the front door with her onto the paving stones. He ran a hand over his face and hair, having forgotten for a brief while his morning shadow and his uncombed disarray.

"I would accompany you and see you safely home, but I am unfit to be out in the world in my present state. Unfit to be seen by you, too, of course, but you are most tolerant. And forgiving."

"Nothing to forgive," she said.

And then he realized he really should have begged her forgiveness the moment he'd stopped kissing her. Instead, he'd offered her flowers, almost as payment.

He shouldn't have kissed her at all. Yet a part of him, the base, feral part wanted to do it again, and so much more. When she was near, he could easily imagine slaking his desire, satisfying the natural urges, pent-up for so long. How easy to take her farther away from his house, behind the gardens, and lay her down on the soft grass in the afternoon sun.

He had a clear image in his mind of what it would be like to peel her clothing away, release her soft round breasts for his palms to cup, run his hands along the curves of her hips, touch her soft petals hiding under her womanly curls, smell her particular scent, and run his tongue over her—

"Good day," she said. "Thank you again for the flowers, my lord, and . . . the hospitality."

Was she referring to his kiss? Or the tea?

"Good day," he returned, watching her until she reached the road in front of his house, which led in one direction toward Belton Manor, and in the other, back toward the village.

At some point, she turned and waved, and only then did he realize he was waiting for her to disappear from sight.

In fact, he was watching over her with fascinated dread, imagining a carriage coming too quickly along and knocking her into the ditch beside the road.

After she waved and turned, he hurried back inside and closed the door firmly, leaning his back on it and closed his eyes. When he did, he saw Miss Darrow's face, upturned to his, awaiting his next kiss.

Yes, he could enjoy a casual tryst with her, find his release between her thighs, for in all these months, she was the only one who'd brought those thoughts and desires back to the surface. However, sweet Maisie Darrow was not the type of woman one used in such a way.

She was the type of woman one left alone in pristine, virtuous condition for the man who would become her husband.

In fact, as far as he was concerned, he had better not ever lay eyes upon her again, or he would probably lay lips and hands on her, too.

"Mr. Wynn," he called. "Start packing the household. We are going to London."

MAISIE WAS GLAD FOR the walk home alone to examine her feelings. She'd been utterly surprised by his kiss, surprised and delighted. Her skin had become prickly all over. The longer he held her, and when he drew her close, the way his firm mouth moved over hers—she had enjoyed every second of the experience. She hadn't even minded the way his night's growth of facial hair slightly scratched her cheek.

Quite the contrary. That particular sensation had excited her and awakened something, causing her insides to tingle and her body to heat while her heart sped up. In fact, she'd imagined she could hear her own heartbeat. *Was that possible?*

And where her breasts pressed against his chest, she'd felt impossibly sensitive, and when his fingers curled into the soft flesh of her upper arms, she'd trembled.

Despite the brevity of the kiss, it had cemented all the good feelings she'd ever had about Jameson Turner. And then, he'd offered to cut flowers for her aunt.

Gazing down at the gorgeous variety of roses in the basket, she allowed her affection for Lord Turner to expand. There could be no harm in acknowledging she had a *tendre* for him. Moreover, she hoped in the days to come, if she continued to visit with him, he might develop feelings for her, as well.

Aunt Anne had been correct, however. It wasn't proper for a young lady to visit a single man alone, not even a widower in the country. For as soon as tea had been delivered along with his lordship's badly needed breakfast, all the servants had disappeared.

Anything could have happened in the drawing room or in the gardens. And, in fact, something had! Moreover, any of his servants might have seen the quick kiss only to discuss it with the others, and any of them might be friendly with servants at Belton Manor. Word could get to Jenny and then quickly reach her aunt's ears.

Maisie fervently hoped that didn't happen. Next thing she knew, she might be sent back to Scotland by the fastest coach.

Shuddering, she decided to ignore such a possibility. *There is nothing either good or bad but thinking makes it so.*

Frowning, Maisie thought about that. It wasn't quite the right quotation.

As she passed Norman's Corner and entered the tidy, whitewashed home, she set down the basket of fragrant roses before removing her hat and gloves.

Something about hope, she recalled, taking off her lightweight mantle and hanging it on the hallstand by the door.

Then it came to her. *Hope is a lover's staff; walk hence with that and manage it against despairing thoughts.*

Perfectly apt if a little premature. Certainly, she could imagine herself falling deeply in love with the man whose kiss thrilled her. Realistically, however, she knew he was far from returning such a sentiment.

If he continued to let her keep company with him— although Eleanor or Aunt Anne would have to chaperone—then Maisie was confident Lord Turner would eventually see her as a viable interest for his heart. Ultimately, he must come out of mourning and stop freezing at every mention of his former wife.

Why, she wouldn't even mind being the second Lady Turner, if he fell in love with her.

AT BREAKFAST, MAISIE SENSED an excitement in the house as she entered the small dining room. She was not the earliest riser. Eleanor had probably already had a walk, and Aunt Anne had undoubtedly read an entire newspaper and had at least two cups of tea. If she had missed something important, however, they would tell her.

"Hurry! Fill your plate and sit," her cousin said.

"What is it? Is there some interesting news?" Maisie's thoughts flew immediately to Jameson Turner, although she couldn't imagine what had occurred between yesterday and that morning.

"Yes," Eleanor said, pausing dramatically and looking at her mother, who nodded.

"Go on. Hurry," Maisie said.

"Jenny sent word early today. Maggie and her husband are coming to Sheffield for a visit."

Maisie tried not to feel deflated, but it had little to do with her. She liked her cousin Maggie, to be sure. And John Angsley, the Earl of Cambrey, Maggie's husband, was Jenny's husband's absolute best friend.

However, another couple didn't change the dynamics too much in Sheffield, the way, for instance, a bachelor such as Lord Turner did.

"When are they coming?" she asked.

"You don't sound thrilled," Eleanor protested.

From then on, being thrilled would always be reserved for Jameson Turner's kisses.

"Of course I am pleased. I'm sure we shall have more dinner parties at Belton Manor," Maisie said, hoping she was partnered again with Lord Turner. "And Maggie is always great fun."

"More than a dinner party," Anne Blackwood said. "Simon and Jenny will have a large fall gathering. They are planning to host a ball in their great room to celebrate Margaret's return. All the fine families from around the area, and probably within a two-hour ride, will come. You girls will have suitable dance partners, no doubt."

Maisie did feel a shiver of excitement at the notion of a large country dance. Having the Earl of Cambrey and his countess come all the way from their Bedfordshire estate north of London was a cause for excitement after all. While she couldn't imagine Lord Turner relishing a large affair presently, by then, she prayed he would be less reticent about embracing his social duty. And she also prayed he would comb his hair and bathe.

How she would love to dance with him!

She repeated her question, wondering how much time she had to work on Lord Turner's fragile mental state. He reminded her of a skittish animal, but she would give him plenty of time to adjust to being among his fellow humans again.

"They shall be here within the fortnight. Naturally, they'll stay at Belton," her aunt said.

Two weeks. Maisie didn't think that was enough time to help the inhabitant of Jonling Hall mend his melancholy enough to embrace attending a magnificent ball, but she would try.

Later in the early afternoon, she strolled with Eleanor to Belton and suggested they stop by the hall to tell Lord Turner the news.

The servants were bustling. Some in the courtyard were tying things to a large carriage, while others were coming out of the house with trunks and bags.

"What's going on?" Maisie asked Mr. Wynn who already had on his coat and hat. "What is this turmoil?"

"Lord Turner's household is returning to London," the butler told her.

All the air seemed to leave Maisie's lungs, so shocked, so instantly distressed by this information.

"Why? Has something occurred warranting his lordship's departure?" She had a strange notion if she could understand the why of it, she could change what was happening.

"I couldn't say, miss. Yesterday, his lordship said to pack, and, thus, we have been packing. In fact, we are nearly done."

Perhaps Lord Turner was upset by their kiss, yet he hadn't seemed overly perturbed at the time. Surely, she was putting too much importance on something that couldn't have been as earth-shattering or exciting for him as it had been for her. He was an experienced man who'd been a husband and shared the marriage bed, while she keenly felt every interaction with a man, no matter how small.

"May I see him? When is his lordship leaving?"

The butler's expression didn't change.

"Lord Turner has already gone, Miss Darrow."

CHAPTER TEN

"No," Maisie exclaimed in dismay, and Eleanor put a hand on her arm.

"Yes, miss," the butler continued. "He left yesterday, not long after your visit."

Mr. Wynn narrowed his eyes at her, and she wondered if he blamed her for this upheaval. In any case, he didn't sound pleased.

"Is there anything else I can help you ladies with, otherwise, I must be on my way and catch up with his lordship as soon as I am able."

Maisie couldn't believe he was gone.

When she didn't answer, Eleanor said, "Thank you. Have a good trip." Then she grabbed her arm and led her away.

"How could he have left without saying goodbye?"

"I'm not surprised at all," her cousin said. "He didn't even show up for the picnic. He has become unfeeling and discourteous."

Maisie shook her head. "I disagree. He is simply sad. The most grief-stricken individual one could imagine. "

"I know it was terrible for him to lose his wife," Eleanor said as they turned their footsteps toward Belton Manor.

"Only, think of the parents who lose children, or the children who lose parents. One can never get another father or mother," she pointed out.

"But everyone knows the life of a newborn is fragile. What mother doesn't steel herself to lose one or two babies? And we expect our parents to die before us at some time. But Lord Turner was only at the beginning of a life with his beloved."

"He can find another to love," her cousin said, somewhat callously.

"That's easy for you to say. But imagine Maggie without her Cam or Jenny without her Simon."

Eleanor fell silent. "I suppose you're right," she said at last. "And now we will need more bachelors for the upcoming ball. Let us please put thoughts of Lord Misery out of our heads and—"

"That is unkind."

Her cousin shrugged. "I'm not the first to call him such. Anyway, let's put Lord Turner aside and focus on my sister's imminent arrival and then a magnificent country ball."

Maisie was certainly going to try. After all, he hadn't even said goodbye.

FIVE MONTHS LATER, MAISIE arrived in London on a coach seated beside her brother Ned, and his good-natured wife, Caroline. With Christmas and the new year behind them, the Season was about to start. Again.

Of course, Eleanor and her mother would be staying in the Lindseys' townhouse on Portman Square, occasionally staying with her other sister, Maggie, on Cavendish Square. It had been ages since Maisie had seen any of them as she had left Sheffield for Dumfries a month after the great ball at Belton Manor.

It had been a lovely experience, and she'd danced with some nice young men and even agreed she would let a few call upon her family's modest townhouse, which her brother considered his own, when she was in London.

Her father, Baron Darrow, hadn't made the trip to London from Scotland, which was not surprising, as he had no love for Town and rarely left Dumfries. That left her in the capable, sometimes tyrannical hands of her older brother. Ned had softened a great deal since meeting and marrying Caroline in the spring the year before. A viscount's daughter who saw something in a baron's son. It must be love, Maisie and Eleanor had decided, because financial gain didn't seem to have played a part.

Maisie could only hope for the same. They had come late to London because her father suddenly had a bad case of gout, and she'd refused to leave him. Thus, the first ball was only two nights away. It was the dance heralding the Season as surely as Ascot did.

She had a few dresses already made, and even borrowed a few of Jenny's since she and her eldest cousin were the same height and build. Beautiful gowns that Maisie didn't care a fig had already been worn. If they were good enough for Lady Lindsey, they were perfect for her, and spared her family a great deal of money.

On the night of the ball, Ned allowed their carriage to stop at the Lindsey townhouse to pick up Eleanor on the way. Jenny and Simon had not yet come to London.

"I vow when I see you, it is as if we've never been apart," Maisie said to her cousin.

"I know exactly what you mean. Now, which wealthy lord were we talking about last?"

They dissolved into laughter while Ned crossed his arms over his chest. He was their protector for the night. His wife gave them a doting smile.

"I love the first ball of the Season," she said. "Getting rid of any nervous anxiety and surveying the field of battle."

Ned blinked slowly at her. "Field of battle?"

"Why, yes, dear," Caroline continued. "The competition, those with whom one wishes to joust and perhaps to conquer. At the first ball, one examines the other combatants to determine who will enter the *mêlée* in earnest, who will be heroic and chivalrous and who won't, who will be more of a spectator, who will be an ally, although other single ladies are not to be trusted."

"Unless they're cousins," Eleanor pointed out. "If Maisie were to find a man who interested her and I liked him as well, we would discuss it in a civilized manner, not stab one another in the back. Perhaps we could even draw for the long piece of straw to see who gets him."

The women laughed, but Ned looked sour. "As if it doesn't matter one man from another," he said tightly.

Caroline leaned against his shoulder. "The girls are only teasing, Neddy. You, for instance, are one of a kind."

This statement caused Maisie and Eleanor to burst out laughing once again.

"Just behave yourselves," Ned said after their cackling had died down. "I'll be watching."

True to his word, Maisie felt her brother's eyes upon her at every turn. Her dance card was requested and written upon by many young men, a lot of them familiar looking, even if she didn't recall their names. She hoped to feel a spark of something exciting with one of them.

And no matter what else happened, she would keep her thoughts off of a particular man she knew wouldn't be at this ball, or any, for that matter.

Except suddenly, there he was. *Could her eyes be playing tricks on her?*

Lord Turner impeccably dressed in charcoal gray and groomed to perfection, appeared in her line of vision, as he had just come down the short staircase to the gleaming wooden floor of the ballroom.

He surveyed the room, spotted her, and then headed directly toward where she and Eleanor stood.

"You just gasped," her cousin pointed out.

"Did I?" She not only gasped but felt her heartbeat speed up at the sight of him. Maisie wanted this man above all others. It was painfully clear to her. She'd simply been passing the days until seeing him again, and the instant she had, she'd come fully alive with anticipation.

"He does look a fine jousting specimen," Eleanor quipped.

"Not at all," Maisie said, her voice sounding choked. "I simply didn't expect to see him here."

"You mean seeing Lord Misery out and about."

"Stop calling him such. Did you know about this?"

"Perhaps," Eleanor said.

Then he was directly in front of her, greeting them each with a shallow bow, which they returned with a deeper curtsey.

"Good evening, ladies. You both look lovely, if I may say."

"You may," Eleanor said, finding her tongue first. "And may I say you look dashingly fit and handsome."

Maisie saw his cheeks color at the compliment, and then his glance flitted to hers.

"Are your dance cards full?" he asked, although it seemed he spoke to her.

Eleanor, determined to be an imp tonight, thrust hers in front of him. "I have a space."

Dutifully, Lord Turner glanced down and wrote in his name.

"And you, Miss Darrow?"

"I don't know," she said. Then she wanted to shake herself. She'd turned into a shy, tongue-tied ninny. *How could her first words to the man who'd kissed her and left without a word be so mundane and silly?*

She took hold of the card dangling from her wrist and looked at it.

"It appears there are two spaces," she said, letting him choose and noting he took the waltz over the quaint, antiquated quadrille. He would be holding her closely for many minutes. Her already pounding heart began to gallop.

"Good evening, Lord Turner." It was Ned behind her. He and Caroline were seated at a table to view the night's proceedings.

"Good evening, Mr. Darrow, Mrs. Darrow. I don't want to intrude upon your gathering. My cousin asked me to keep an eye on his sister-in-law."

"Lord Lindsey needn't have worried over Miss Blackwood. My wife and I are here."

"I'm sure he greatly appreciates that," Lord Turner said, "but one can never be too careful in London. The more eyes watching over these young ladies, the better."

"True enough," Caroline Darrow agreed. "It is good to see you out in company."

He merely nodded, perhaps not wanting to get into a conversation during which he would be offered condolences.

"I will see you all later. I'm keeping my eye on you," he added to Eleanor, and he spoke with no hint of a smile. Then he nodded to all of them, turned, and disappeared into the throng.

"Still Lord M," Eleanor muttered. "What was Simon thinking appointing him as my nanny? I shall write to him in the morning and tell him what I think of this arrangement. Mummy said whenever she wasn't attending, Lord Turner would, but I don't want such gloom and worry hanging over even one of my social events."

Maisie still felt shock and wonder at Jameson Turner being not only out in public but at a ball, a place of merriment and mingling. Moreover, he looked vastly different from the unkempt creature she'd encountered in Sheffield. He was stronger and healthier of body, to be sure. However, his expression was positively grim, and nothing but disinterest shone from his gray-blue eyes.

He may have found a new valet and even accepted a charge from Simon to get out into the world on Eleanor's behalf, but inside, he hadn't healed his heartache. That was apparent. She imagined him haunting his wife's grave on the outskirts of London, like in a scene from one of Eleanor's beloved Gothic romance novels.

Poor man!

But he had been under no obligation to put his name on her card, nor dance with her. *Why had he done so?* She could hardly wait to find out.

Before she could think any more about it, she was claimed by her first partner of the night, and went off to be part of the ball's Grand March, with Eleanor and her partner by her side.

And where was Lord Turner? She searched for him even as she went down the line of other dancers. Eventually, after a few moments, as she strolled down the women's side of the partnered line, she saw him in a corner of the room. Naturally, she expected to see him alone, but he was full of surprises.

Standing beside him, leaning close, was a beautiful woman. *Lady Elizabeth Pepperton*, Maisie realized with a shock.

The widow owned a magnificent home on Belgrave Square and, while not considered immoral exactly, was known for enjoying her share of lovers, only from among the titled ranks, and only one at a time. In fact, she was becoming rather infamous and more than a little envied by women who had no such freedom.

And she was talking with Jameson, her bosom pressed on his upper arm, so her cleavage nearly popped out of the top of her gown. Not that she needed to do such a thing and probably didn't even do it purposely. She was lovely, available, wealthy, willing, and had a slew of bedrooms at her disposal in the privacy of her own four-story townhouse.

Maisie wanted to gouge her eyes out.

Did she? Goodness, no! What a strange, vile, and vicious thought.

She would simply like a little more candlelight to flicker between their bodies, a little breathing space. Lord Turner, however, didn't seem to mind the widow's closeness at all. Maisie nearly missed her step and had to turn away or ruin the dance for her partner.

A SHOCK HAD SIZZLED through Jameson's body at his first glimpse of Maisie Darrow in half a year. For the life of him, he couldn't figure out why she had that effect on him. She wasn't the prettiest woman in the room, but she certainly commanded his attention.

His eyes had sought her out and found her almost at once, her pale hair set off perfectly by a rich blue and silver gown. Like a moth to the flame, he'd gone over to her directly, feeling fortunate Eleanor, his charge from Simon, had been by her side. Otherwise, he would have had no reason to approach Miss Darrow except the obvious one— that he was attracted to her.

Now, despite standing next to his paramour of the past two months, he couldn't stop watching her, gracefully dancing with some besotted idiot. The man might be the next prime minister for all Jameson knew, but he didn't like him.

"Who are you staring at?" Lady Pepperton asked.

She knew everyone, and he had no intention of informing her of his inclination toward Maisie. Not that he and Elizabeth had an affair of the heart. She had approached him because she wanted no emotional attachment, simply companionship and someone to ease the loneliness and stave off physical frustration. She had determined he might be perfect for such a proposition.

After a week of considering her offer—questioning deeply whether he was betraying his love for Esmera—he had shown up at her door on Belgrave Square and spent the night. It had been like scratching an itch he'd had for too long.

For the most part, they only saw each other in the privacy of her townhouse. About half a dozen other times, Elizabeth had wanted to go to a dance. Since this was the first splash of the Season, she chose tonight to go out. He didn't mind accompanying her. The *bon ton* was sophisticated enough to understand their arrangement and didn't condemn two widowed people from having one, as long as they weren't demonstrative in public.

This was, however, the first time he'd put his name on a dance card or danced with anyone except Elizabeth, who did not have one dangling from her wrist and wouldn't dance with anyone else while they were a couple.

He supposed he'd better tell her something so she wasn't surprised.

"I am dancing with Miss Blackwood, my cousin's sister-in-law, since he asked me to keep an eye on her at events unattended by her mother."

"Very well." She took a glass of champagne from a servant's tray as he passed.

"I'm also dancing with her cousin, Miss Darrow."

She looked at him over the rim of her glass, then sipped the bubbling beverage. "I see."

Did she? Maybe she could explain it to him then. He had intended to come tonight to dance with his paramour if she wished, do his duty toward Eleanor, and then go back to Belgrave Square and have solid, satisfying sexual relations with Elizabeth.

Maisie Darrow was an unexpected, ill-advised kiss in the country, and nothing more. *So why had he put his name on her card?*

"Which one is she?" Elizabeth asked. "I don't recall Miss Darrow."

He glanced around as if he didn't know precisely where Maisie was. After a few moments, he said, "There she is, in the blue dress with silver trim. Blonde hair."

"Yes, I see her." She studied her a moment, perhaps comparing her to herself. He hoped not. There was no need. He had no intention of pursuing Maisie or of breaking off his comfortable, effortless association with Elizabeth. She did not touch his heart in any way, and he had come to terms with needing the release of sexual activity.

"She is as fair as I am dark," she pointed out, putting a hand to her perfectly coiffed hair.

"True," he said. "Of what significance is that? It's merely a dance."

In truth, though, he had never been attracted to fair-haired women. His wife had blacker hair than Elizabeth, and he'd considered Esmera stupendously attractive, even mesmerizingly beautiful at first sight. Before her, there had been a few ladies who'd perked his interest, all of them brunettes, as he recalled.

As for his paramour, Lady Pepperton was rather like Margaret Blackwood Angsley, the Countess of Cambrey, a dazzlingly perfect beauty. Elizabeth had no reason to compare herself to anyone.

Then there was Maisie. Blonde tresses he'd already seen both done up and hanging down, both in ringlets and soaked with river water, in sunlight and in shade. It wasn't simply flaxen, her hair had colors of caramel and gold, candle-flame yellow, too. *Blonde* seemed inaccurate and too simple for the intricacy of her hair.

"You've gone quiet," Elizabeth pointed out. "Which proves what I was thinking."

"Which is?"

"That nothing is *merely a dance*."

He shrugged. She might be right, but his intentions were unclear even to his own mind, and he wouldn't understand them any better until he had Maisie in his arms again.

The next time Elizabeth asked to dance, it was for a redowa, and a little while after, a galop. Then, he went to the Darrows' table to claim Miss Blackwood. She was a passing fair dancer, despite being far more interested in discussing the impossibility of seeing any stars from London and how much she missed the clear skies of Sheffield.

"I couldn't agree more, Miss Blackwood."

Quick as a whip, she shot back, "Then why did you leave us in such a hurry?"

He grunted. He hadn't seen that one coming at all.

"I remember telling you before how some things in my personal life are not your business. Just because Simon is your brother-in-law and my cousin, doesn't mean you can ask any outrageous question you wish and expect me to answer."

She laughed at him.

"Outrageous, am I? Only if the answer is something dark and mysterious instead of merely because you missed the theatre and the food."

Dammit! He should have said either of those things. Miss Blackwood enjoyed herself at his expense for the remainder of their dance, and he'd been relieved to return to Elizabeth's side.

God save the man who ended up with the lively Eleanor Blackwood!

And then, after an impossibly long time, it was his turn to dance with the other country miss. *At last!*

Maisie Darrow had come off the dance floor moments earlier on the arm of a handsome fellow Jameson vaguely recognized. *Viscount Rooster?* No. *Ruthless?* No! *Roleston. Lord Peter Roleston, son of an earl.*

The name came to him as the man released Miss Darrow and watched her walk away with his fixed stare on her swaying hips. Jameson didn't like that one bit and hurried over to claim his dance.

"Are you ready?" he asked, taking her arm.

Miss Darrow jumped at his touch, tilting her head to look at him with her understanding, gold-flecked, brown eyes.

She simply nodded.

"Not too tired from so many dances?" he asked, realizing he sounded like an old fusspot.

"No, my lord," she replied, looking surprised. "The evening is still young, I believe. In any case, as Shakespeare said, *what masques, what dances shall we have to wear away this long age of three hours between our after-supper and bedtime?*"

They most certainly did not have three hours to go, probably a bit more than an hour before he could go home and relax in his own study with a glass of brandy.

No, that wasn't his plan. He had intended to go to stay the night with Elizabeth.

Two seconds with Miss Darrow, and he wasn't thinking clearly.

Except he had one persistent thought. He wanted to kiss her again. And truthfully, as he led her onto the crowded floor, he had another thought—London had suddenly become the most interesting place to be.

And the most interesting thing about London was Maisie Darrow!

God help him, he might have to pack for Sheffield.

CHAPTER ELEVEN

The moment Lord Turner took her in his arms, Maisie felt the rightness of it. She'd been partnered all night with perfectly acceptable men. She'd engaged in light banter, laughed, danced, and even sipped champagne with them.

Being with Jameson Turner was entirely different. It was the instant and intense stimulation of her entire body.

That was the only way she could describe the sensation of every part of her being aware of his proximity. Even the fine hairs on her arms and the back of her neck seemed to stand up. Her stomach fell and her chest tightened, yet not unpleasantly.

It was lovely having his arms around her, despite him being a little stiff, even reserved, and it was hard to speak while waltzing. She would rather they were standing in his rose garden.

And he'd spent the night stuck like tar to Lady Pepperton's side. He had moved on from his deceased wife at last.

"You look well," she told him. "Much healthier than you did last year."

He merely nodded.

"It seems you are eating better."

He gave a vague grunt.

"You are happy?" She hadn't meant to ask that as a question. She'd meant to state it as a fact, since he now filled out his suit in correct proportions and had let a beautiful woman into his life.

"I am content," he agreed.

"How long have you and Lady Pepperton been a couple?"

He faltered in his step for the first time, and then, as he whirled her around, he stared down at her, his eyes narrowing.

"You and Miss Blackwood are entirely too familiar with me, asking utterly inappropriate questions, which I don't have to answer. In fact, I have no intention of answering. As I've said before, that is none of your business."

She couldn't help shrugging. It seemed to her once a man kissed you, you had cause to be somewhat familiar with him. Apparently, he didn't see it that way.

"*The lady doth protest too much, methinks.* Or in this case, the gentleman."

What else could she say? She seemed to have hit a nerve, which made her wonder about his relationship even more. *Were they going to announce an engagement?*

Highly doubtful given the widow's history of lovers. More likely, it was an *arrangement of convenience*, the term she'd heard for physicality between a couple without love.

Why didn't that make her feel any better?

"Stop that, at once," he commanded.

"What?" She blinked at him.

"Quoting your Shakespeare at me. I am not protesting about anything except your insolence. What if I start asking you about Lord Roleston?"

It was her turn to falter in her step. Quickly, with Jameson's smooth guidance, Maisie recovered. *How strange for him to ask her such.* True, the viscount was the only man she'd danced with twice that night, which for a first ball of the Season was perhaps something to remark on, but it had only happened because the man whose name was penciled beside one of her dances hadn't appeared in time.

Lord Roleston had also, luckily, been at loose ends, standing close by.

"He rescued me from embarrassment and has behaved as a perfect gentleman," she said.

"I see."

And then their dance ended, and he led her from the floor toward her brother and his wife. Barely hesitating, Jameson bent his head over her gloved hand, not actually touching it with his lips, and then disappeared again.

"How is your evening going?" Caroline Darrow asked. "Are you enjoying yourself?"

"I am," she told her sister-in-law before sitting down.

Was Lord Turner going to be at each and every dance? She liked seeing him. It brought a tingly measure of excitement to the evening. But she also didn't like the unsettling feeling that came with watching him with Lady Pepperton. It seemed to hurt somewhere in the vicinity of her throat, like a lump of emotion was caught there.

And he hadn't been particularly nice to her, not like the man who cut flowers for her to give to her aunt. This Jameson Turner was gruff and reserved, as if they didn't know each other at all.

How could that be when he'd saved her life?

How could that be after he'd given her the only kiss of her life?

She had almost decided to sit out the next dance, despite being certain there was a name on her card. She had on new dancing slippers and, although it seemed an improbability, they were rubbing on her heels.

Then she saw Jameson escort Lady Pepperton onto the floor. This would be their third dance, if she'd counted correctly. At that moment, a young man approached, stuttering how it was his turn to dance with her, wearing an out-of-fashion suit and a poorly tied cravat.

Maisie stood up quickly. She would not be rude or cause him embarrassment, simply because she was feeling out of sorts. Thus, she found herself dancing with a slightly awkward partner in the same vicinity as Lord Turner and the impeccably polished Lady Pepperton.

The widow seemed to turn her gaze upon them at once, and Maisie had the unpleasant experience of being studied. She could either shrink or shine.

Choosing the latter, she put on a smile, engaged her partner with a joke, making him laugh uproariously as if she were the wittiest creature on earth, and they whirled past the reserved, quiet couple.

Luckily, her man with his queerly knotted cravat was a good dancer after all.

Maisie decided then and there she would not let her fascination with Lord Turner ruin her Season. If he wanted a ribald relationship with a free and loose widow, then he was not the man for her anyway. She could not compete on that field of battle Caroline had mentioned, not without losing her virtue and her reputation.

Thus, she would not compete at all.

JAMESON FOUND HIMSELF THINKING of Maisie Darrow each day now he knew she was in London. If Elizabeth wanted him to escort her to a ball or dinner party, he would likely encounter the enticing woman again.

Besides, due to his promise to Simon, he was at the beck and call of Lady Blackwood as a chaperone when necessary, which was whenever she sent word she would not be attending an event with her daughter.

Thus, if he was with Miss Blackwood, undoubtedly, Miss Darrow would be somewhere close by.

Usually, he and Elizabeth stayed indoors—separately, each at their own homes—except for times he went to her townhouse to spend the night.

Thus, when very soon after the first ball, she suggested they attend another one, he had to question her motives.

"Why? You are not on the marriage market, and these events seem to have that one sole purpose."

"Not at all. For couples, it is a place to dance and be seen."

If she'd said only for dancing, it would have made sense.

He frowned. "You've never cared about being seen before. Why now?"

"You have never been with me at the beginning of a Season, so you cannot know what I've *never cared about* before. All the latest crop of young ladies and single men are out and about, as well as those held over from previous years who didn't make a match and might be starting to get desperate. It's entertaining, I think."

"Why? Are you interested in finding someone to marry?"

"If I were," she quipped, "would you return my interest?"

He hesitated, while inside, he recoiled. *Absolutely not* were the words forming on his lips.

Why did he have such a strong reaction? Not because of her marriage or her past lovers. That would be hypocritical of him. She'd assured him of her faithfulness when married, and she made it a point to have long-term relationships with only one man at a time. No one could fault her principles.

However, while he enjoyed her company and her body, he'd experienced far more in the past with Esmera—the rapture of being entirely spellbound by one woman—and he was unwilling to settle for tepid affection even when combined with lusty desire. He wanted more. He wanted . . .

"Your lack of answer is telling," Elizabeth, her face looking pinched, interrupted his thoughts, which had circled around to Maisie.

Her reaction was new. They never had conversations about marriage or the future, and she never got upset with him.

"I'm not asking for you to marry me or even offer for me," she clarified. "I suppose I simply want to be someone's first choice for a change."

"You were, for your husband."

"True, but he's been dead a while," she pointed out.

"Don't you think if you continue to choose men who are plainly ill-equipped for committing to marriage, then you will continue to be disappointed? You can't be someone's first choice if he doesn't want anyone."

However, as much as his words sounded like truth, they were a lie. He did, in fact, want someone more than he wanted Elizabeth. He couldn't decide if he wanted Maisie Darrow simply because she was different than other women he'd been with—in both her appearance and her disposition of quirky kindness—or if he also desired her company because something about the way Maisie thought and communicated intrigued him.

Either way, he was incapable of pursuing anyone because his heart was in a coffin in Brompton Cemetery, which brought him back to the reason he had fallen into an easy relationship with Elizabeth in the first place. A straightforward, unemotional attachment was all he was good for at present.

"Are you wanting a change in our arrangement?" It was a tad awkward considering they were lying in bed, having just completed the sexual act rather satisfactorily.

Yet if he were honest, which he tried always to be with himself, he'd had a little trouble keeping Maisie from his mind during the heated moments of passion.

That bordered on him being a rogue, at the very least. He didn't like that one bit.

"All this introspection," Elizabeth complained. "I simply want to go to a few more dances and a few dinner parties."

"And find someone who will tell you you're his first choice and sweep you off your feet."

Elizabeth rolled toward him, her breasts pressing against his arm as she reached out to stroke his chest.

"I suppose I am getting a little bored."

"Thank you," he said wryly.

"No, I don't mean *with* you. I mean with being merely a widow. Unlike you, I don't opine for my deceased spouse. I am ready to move on to my next grand adventure before I am too old to be anything but a mistress."

"I never think of you as my mistress," Jameson told her. "But as a companion. A mistress sounds too one-sided in terms of the power in the arrangement. A mistress can be easily abandoned."

She sighed, "Thank you for that. However, in any relationship, one person can easily abandon the other. The power, I think, is always in the hands of the one who cares less for the other."

She was probably correct in that assessment. When he'd first started courting Esmera, a brief, almost obsessive time of stolen kisses and demands from him for more of her, he'd feared all the while someone else would take her from him before he could secure her as his wife.

Even after they'd married, the power had all been Esmera's. If she looked sad or became angry, he worried he'd caused irrevocable damage, and she would leave him.

The entire matter of letting one's heart become entangled was terrible and frightening. He was glad he'd given it away and would never need it again.

"I am not prepared to change our arrangement to anything deeper," he said.

"I understand. And I will never play you false. While there is no one else in my life, I am yours exclusively as long as you want. If someone else catches my interest, I will tell you at once."

"The right of first refusal," he joked.

"If I thought you would exercise that right, I might let my heart open to you, Jameson, but I am not such a dullard. I expect the same courtesy from you regarding where your interests might lie."

"Of course."

"Enough serious talk. We have decided. You shall escort me to the ball at Tilton House tomorrow night."

"Is that what we decided?" he asked, laughing until her fingertips swept lower, down past his bellybutton to capture his staff. Then he caught his breath, and . . . *dammit all if Maisie's image didn't flitter into his brain.*

He groaned, easily imagining her hand on him as her captivating brown eyes gazed into his. He became hard as an oak staff.

"Nice," Elizabeth murmured.

Jameson rolled over onto her, battling to clear his mind of Maisie and fill it with the woman beneath him. And failing.

He was behaving like a cad, but as he sunk into the exquisite, porcelain-skinned Lady Pepperton, he could only take comfort in knowing theirs was a practical relationship of equal measure.

For all he knew, Elizabeth might be imagining some other man thrusting between her legs. As he helped her find her release before enjoying his own, all the while, he pictured blonde hair spread out on the pillow beneath him, and a peaches-and-cream complexion, with sweetly blushing cheeks.

And despite trying to reason it away, he felt guilty— toward Esmera *and* Elizabeth.

MAISIE'S JOY AT BEING with her family in London was tempered with the unsettling notion Jameson Turner had found happiness in the arms of Lady Elizabeth Pepperton.

She didn't want to begrudge him a moment of relief from his melancholy, but she couldn't deny she felt slighted, not to mention inferior. After all, compared to the widow, she lacked allure and sparkling polish. Certainly, Lady Pepperton was far more similar to Esmera Turner than Maisie could ever hope to be.

In fact, six months earlier, the viscount had kissed her, apparently found her lacking, and left Sheffield. It was one thing to think of a man too mired in his misery to consider taking up with another woman. It was quite another to see he simply needed someone else to help him out of his mire.

In short, Maisie's esteem had taken quite a blow. Tonight, however, for a ball at the Duke of Wellington's Apsley House, she was wearing one of Jenny's dresses, and dressing like a countess gave her a goodly dose of confidence.

Entering Wellington's home at Hyde Park's southeastern corner, with Eleanor by her side, she was instantly awestruck. Simply being in the home of the famous soldier and statesman, even though the eighty-three-year-old Lord Wellesley was not in residence, gave her the chills. She could only imagine the wonderful play Shakespeare would have written as a tribute to his grace, the duke, if he'd known him.

Maybe Lady Pepperton was the equivalent of Wellington to Maisie's Bonaparte, and this entire Season, forced to watch Jameson with the beautiful widow would seem like Maisie's Waterloo—in other words, *absolute defeat*.

Endowed with his renowned art collection, much of it Spanish paintings rescued from a baggage train at the Battle of Vitoria in 1813, Apsley House was a showcase. Everywhere Maisie looked, there were treasures, including Dutch paintings from a French auction, gifts from numerous heads of Europe, as well as gilded wood, rich tapestries, and thick floor runners.

"I feel like a princess," she whispered to her cousin as, with Ned and Caroline ahead of them, they followed the stream of other guests to the rooms set aside for the ball on the second story of the three-story mansion.

"Pity, his grace isn't here," her brother said as if the Duke of Wellington was a personal friend who would have bent Ned's ear for half an hour if he happened to see him.

"A pity," Maisie agreed, squeezing Eleanor's hand. "But we shall have a grand time nonetheless."

"Since my mother didn't come, my duly appointed shadow will undoubtedly show up."

A tremor of anticipation shot through Maisie at seeing Lord Turner again, followed quickly by the disturbing cloak of jealousy that draped itself about her at the idea of seeing him spending the evening with Lady Pepperton.

"Why are you sighing?" Eleanor asked. "I know this doesn't compare to Simon and Jenny's country ball, but we can suffer through it."

"Somehow, we shall bear it," she agreed in jest.

"What on earth are you girls saying? You cannot compare Apsley House and all its glory to Belton Manor."

Which proved Ned was listening to everything they said. They laughed. He hadn't attended the Sheffield ball, in any case, and still had a burr under his saddle over anything to do with the Lindseys since, at one time, he'd hoped to secure Jenny for himself and had been soundly rejected.

"The girls are only joking," Caroline told him and, after a backward glance over her shoulder, she dragged her husband into the fray of the Waterloo Gallery.

"I appreciate that woman," Eleanor said.

"As do I. She is sweet and smart *and* can put up with my brother."

"And she keeps him from tying you in leading strings," her cousin pointed out. "Although he tries."

They surveyed the room, and Maisie felt her eyes growing wide.

"It *is* as beautiful as they say."

"Who are *they*?" Eleanor whispered, tugging her arm toward the far side of the room where a bank of windows overlooked the park, lit at that hour by many gas lamps.

"Everyone," Maisie said, wondering what refreshments might be in store that evening.

She'd had a busy day with Caroline, who was redecorating the parlor in the Darrow townhouse and demanding her sister-in-law go with her to every furniture maker and fabric store in London.

Consequently, she hadn't eaten a real meal all day. Her stomach grumbled as a passing servant handed her and Eleanor dance cards, and she slipped the ribbon upon her wrist.

"Well, everyone is right," Eleanor said.

Maisie had lost track of their conversation. "Would it be terribly uncivil to seek out the refreshments directly, and see if anything has been put out yet?"

Eleanor hesitated. "We might miss out on our cards being filled. I would hate to end up a wallflower at the Duke of Wellington's ball."

Knowing her cousin would appreciate her thoughts from earlier, Maisie said, "Then this truly would be your *Waterloo*."

They snickered, then they laughed heartily. It must have been nervous energy, but Maisie couldn't seem to stop herself, and each time she believed she'd got her humor in hand, she had only to look at Eleanor's wide grin to start laughing again.

People began giving them a wide berth. They were making a spectacle. Their dance cards would remain painfully empty if she didn't do something.

To rein herself in, Maisie swiveled away from Eleanor and thought of her mother, wishing she could be there that night and experience the beauty of his grace's residence and enjoy a night of dancing and merriment.

Sobering instantly, she felt tears prick her eyes. She took a deep breath, turned, and faced Lord Jameson Turner, who had come up behind her.

❧ ⬦ ❧

CHAPTER TWELVE

Are you all right, Miss Darrow?" Jameson Turner's voice was awash with concern, and it was nearly her undoing. She wanted to slump onto the parquet floor and shed pitiful tears.

For above all, she did so wish she could share one more day with her mother, one small moment of the present instead of going over the precious memories of the past.

How unfair! Suddenly, she wanted to wail. *What on earth was wrong with her?*

"I think I need some air," she said, looking around, wondering where she could find a little space in the crowded room.

Eleanor frowned. "Perhaps you could escort her, my lord. I don't know where her brother is."

Lord Turner looked doubtful. He was probably considering it an inappropriate request. It wasn't as if they were in Sheffield where they could spend a little time alone without spying eyes immediately declaring him a rake and her, a ruined woman.

The room tilted.

"I think I'm going to faint," Maisie said when a strange buzzing in her ears accompanied a sensation of her head being too light to remain attached to her body.

"Or perhaps my head is about to float away."

Or she might throw up all over Lord Turner's beautifully polished boots. She clamped a gloved hand over her mouth, feeling at once clammy and hot.

"She's very pale," she heard Eleanor's voice, seemingly far away.

Apparently deciding to save her the embarrassment of either passing out or being sick on the Duke of Wellington's perfectly polished floor, he grabbed her arm and, moving quickly, skirted the thickest groups of guests to find a doorway at the far end of the long room.

In moments, they were in a wide, quiet hallway where he settled her onto a tufted ottoman next to a large, marble bust of a man with a Greek laurel wreath on his head. She had no notion as to his identity.

Above the ottoman, which was red as much of the duke's decor, there was a large gilded shield.

"Do not move," Lord Turner ordered and disappeared.

She had no intention of moving, except to rest her elbows on her knees and her head on her hands. Maisie didn't care how she looked, the lower she put her head, the better she felt, except for the hollow place in her stomach.

The ottoman was really more of a divan, she decided, and next thing she knew, she had leaned over to the side, letting her ringlets get squashed under her head, which she rested on the velvet.

One side of her coiffure might suffer, but her mother would never see it anyway.

Tears leaked from the corners of her eyes, running onto the soft fabric. She sniffled. If her nose started running, too, she would have to return home or hope they had a well-equipped ladies' retiring room to repair the damage she was doing to her lightly powdered face.

"What on earth?" Jameson Turner exclaimed, and she opened her eyes to see him standing over her. "Are you injured?"

"Yes," she moaned irrationally. "I mean, no. But I hurt. All of me hurts."

And then it hit her. *What a ninny!*

"Today is my mother's birthday, and I miss her."

Lord Turner crouched beside the ottoman, and she saw he had a glass of water in one hand and a napkin containing something else in the other.

"I am terribly sorry," Lord Turner said, and sounded as though he understood her pain. "Will you sit up and have a sip of water?"

She did as he asked, and in their present positions, her head was above his. She wanted to throw her arms around him and sob. Reaching out, she took the glass he offered and gulped some water.

"So much better from a country well," she said. "I think I can taste the Thames."

He smiled at her. "They said they boil it. I asked the servant."

For safety's sake, he had asked. How kind.

"Thank you. What else do you have?" Her stomach still seemed to want to heave, but she knew it was from emptiness, not from illness.

"A piece of savory bread. It has cheese baked into—"

She snatched the napkin and devoured the contents.

"Thank you," she said again, mumbling around the deliciousness in her mouth.

He moved to sit beside her, and waited until she finished. And then, shocking her, he brushed bits of bread off her skirt.

"We don't want any grease stains on your lovely gown."

"Thank you," she said again, using the napkin to wipe the corners of her mouth.

"Feeling better?" he asked, looking as if he truly wanted to know.

Did she?

"I feel as if my body knew it was a special day before my mind remembered it."

He nodded in a vague manner, neither calling her insane nor agreeing.

"Now I feel disrespectful for coming out tonight to dance on my mother's birthday. I should be home."

He considered for a moment. "Doing what? How would you honor her at home?"

She shrugged, watching him as he drew out a handkerchief from his pocket and wiped at her face. Hopefully, she hadn't missed any crumbs, and he was simply trying to clean any tear streaks from her cheeks.

A stupidly warm and cherished feeling welled up inside her

"I would probably sit and think of her, I suppose."

"You can think of her here, as you obviously are," he pointed out.

"But I shouldn't be making merry."

"Of course you should, especially on her birthday. I think your mother would want her beloved daughter to be happy. I'm sure she was no more pleased at leaving you than you were at losing her. So why not show her how well you're doing."

"*Show* her?"

He shrugged. "I tend to think the dead are watching. My belief can be good and, sometimes, not so good."

"I understand," Maisie said. "I always hoped somehow for some connection to my mother, if only she could contact me, or if I could tell her one more time how I love her. And sometimes, in a quiet moment—far away from the bustle—I believe she's with me."

She hoped she hadn't upset him with talk of the dead, but he continued to look interested, so she went on. "When I was younger, when she first passed away, I used to pretend she had done nothing more than slip into the next room, and I would stand on one side of a door and talk to her, as if she were simply on the other side."

She sniffed. He tucked a stray strand of hair behind her ear, and she shivered at his touch.

"Silly, I suppose."

"Not so," he said. "No more than my sleeping in my wife's room, hoping she'll visit me in the darkness, for even a disembodied wife seemed better than her being gone completely."

Maisie nodded and set the glass down on the floor, tucking the empty napkin inside of it.

"Do you still do that?" she asked.

He shook his head.

"I don't talk to my mother through doors anymore either."

After another moment, he asked, "Do you feel better for eating a little?"

"Yes." Also, for feeling his body next to hers, touching her from shoulder to thigh.

"Would you like more?" he asked.

Maisie thought he meant something other than food entirely. Then realized his intent.

"I could eat a whole roast," she declared.

He smiled. "They are not serving roast chicken, pork, or beef, but they do have pastry wrapped around something. I think it's duck. And there are trays of cheese, too. Anyway, it's better than the stale bread you would get at Almack's."

She smiled.

"There it is," he said.

"What?"

"Your smile. It's good to see it back again. Let's try to make it bigger, shall we?" He tapped a finger on the side of his head. "What is the difference between a light in a cave and a dance in an inn?"

"I'm sure I don't know. What is the difference?"

"One is a taper in a cavern and the other a caper in a tavern."

She laughed, and he joined in, which she appreciated. He had a wonderful laugh and very good-looking teeth.

Then, Lord Turner stood and reached for her hand, which she gave him. When he drew her to stand, she was close enough to see the steel gray threaded through the deep blue of his eyes. So lovely, if one was allowed to say that about any part of a man.

Briefly, she wondered where Lady Pepperton was and whether the widow would be jealous of his time away from her.

For a few minutes, neither of them said anything, and then Lord Turner raised her hand to his lips, her still-empty dance card dangling from her wrist as a reminder of what she was supposed to be doing there that night.

And then, it seemed all hell broke loose.

"WHAT IS GOING ON here?" came a man's voice, loud enough to wake the very dead they'd been discussing earlier.

Jameson turned to see Ned Darrow approaching, his wife beside him wearing an expression of dismay.

"Can I believe my eyes? Are you compromising my sister?"

Was Maisie's brother hard of hearing? Jameson wondered. *Why else would the idiot be shouting so everyone would know his sister had been caught alone with a man?*

"I insist you salvage her reputation by marrying her," Darrow declared.

Jameson's stomach sank. Not hard of hearing at all, her brother was clearly cunning and duplicitous and knew precisely what he was about.

Hearing her gasp, he dropped his hold on Miss Darrow's hand. Belatedly taking a step back, he studied her face. *Had she been in on this ploy, feigning distress so he would take her somewhere private to recover?*

Her gaze locked with his, and he knew the truth, for she appeared as vexed as he felt.

Turning her attention to her brother, she took a step toward him.

"Please lower your voice, Ned. Nothing happened except I felt faint, and Lord Turner gave me some bread and a glass of water."

"Bread and water," Ned repeated as if it sounded too improbable for his ears to comprehend.

"Not regular bread," she insisted, "cheesy bread. I hadn't eaten properly all day."

Ned's red face indicated he wasn't prepared to let this drop so easily. Except since no one else had come upon them, it was blatantly clear who was forcing this issue.

"Sir, are you threatening the ruin of your own sister with innuendo in order to force a marriage?"

"What?" Ned Darrow shot back. "That's absurd. You were caught in a compromising position."

"Yet your sister and I are telling you we were not doing anything untoward. Thus, you are the only one compromising her, casting a shadow upon her reputation. Miss Darrow doesn't want to marry me, nor should she be made to do so simply because you have seen an opportunity."

Ned Darrow's eyes became narrow slits of scrutiny. "How do you know she doesn't want to marry you? Have you asked her? Were you pushing your suit while she was fending you off? Or worse, *not* fending you off?"

Maisie Darrow sighed. "Caroline, talk sense into my brother. Lord Turner is in mourning for his wife and doesn't want a new one, certainly not me."

But it was her brother who answered. "He is unquestionably *not* in mourning anymore. If he were, he wouldn't be the beau of Lady Pepperton while also lurking in hallways with my sister!"

Jameson wanted to pop the man in the snout with his fist. One good bash!

Ned Darrow knew nothing of Jameson's inner thoughts and feelings. Nor should he be referring to Elizabeth in any manner at all.

"Take care, sir. I do not like the way you are casting about with your disparaging remarks. I am neither anyone's beau, nor do I have any intention of being forced into marriage."

He took care not to add "least of all to your sister" to push his point home, as that would only injure the lady in question, but it was true. The last thing he wanted was to feel something for someone so easily lovable as she was, and then potentially lose everything again.

Even tonight, she could as easily have been stricken with deadly influenza or cholera and die next week. He was lucky it had only been hunger pains and an overly great burden of sentiment for her dead mother causing Miss Darrow to feel unwell.

He most definitely did not want a closer connection with her.

"Brother, please, let us go back to the ball. I feel better, and I have yet to get a single name upon my dance card."

Ned Darrow looked, if possible, even more sour.

"An empty dance card, at least fifteen minutes since arriving." He looked at Jameson. "Because you have detained her, she will now sit out most of the dances. People will wonder why. She will be disgraced and, worse, whispered about."

Jameson considered, then he smiled. "Miss Darrow, do you have a pencil handy?" He was fairly confident all the ladies carried them tucked away in a hidden pocket or in their reticule. After a pause, she nodded and produced one.

Grabbing hold of her forearm, he snatched at the dance card and then scrawled "J. Turner" across every other line.

"There," he said, releasing her and looking around at the shocked faces of her brother and his wife. "Now she will dance at least half the dances. Surely, she can scrounge up a few more partners if she hurries back to the ballroom."

He turned to her to see a smile playing about her pretty lips, glad to see she wasn't offended by anything that had occurred.

"I shall see you for our first dance in a few minutes, Miss Darrow. I am glad you are feeling better. And wish your mother a happy birthday from me."

She nodded and offered him a ghost-of-a-smile.

Ignoring Mr. Darrow, he bowed to Mrs. Darrow before striding down the hall, looking forward to getting away from her over-protective brother. In truth, Jameson couldn't blame the man one whit.

For Jameson, who had announced in no uncertain terms he had no intention of marrying anyone, was very much looking forward to holding Maisie in his arms for much of the evening.

Only then did he remember Elizabeth.

MAISIE COULDN'T WAIT TO find Eleanor. So much drama and the ball had hardly begun. Like a proper attendee, her cousin was chatting with a man and another two young ladies. She broke away from them as Maisie approached.

"Are you all right? You looked positively white or maybe green. Either way, not good, but you look much better now. Your normal pinkish, creamy hue. We need to make the rounds quickly and fill up your card."

Maisie held up her wrist so Eleanor could see.

"What in blue blazes?" her cousin exclaimed, seeing all the writing. Then she read it. "Oh, dear. I'm not sure you should honor that. The entire place will be talking."

Maisie grinned. "I would like to fill in with some other partners if possible, and maybe I should cross off a few of Lord Turner's dances."

"Has he declared for you? Is he in love with you?" Eleanor asked, still staring at the most unusual card.

"What?" Maisie snatched her wrist away. "Of course not! Quite the opposite. Ned came upon us and practically demanded Lord Turner marry me."

Eleanor's hand went to her mouth as she gasped. "Gracious!"

"And then Lord Turner said he wasn't going to marry anyone."

Eleanor gasped again. "So why are you smiling?"

"Because then he filled out my dance card, and I'm going to spend much of the evening in his arms."

Eleanor's eyes widened. "I knew it!"

"Knew what?"

"You have a *tendre* for Jameson Turner," she whispered.

"I appreciate your quiet voice. My brother was shouting at the top of his lungs."

Then she saw Lord Roleston, who saw her at the same time, smiled, and approached.

"Two lovely ladies who outshine even this perfect venue," he said, bowing to them each in turn.

Maisie and Eleanor both curtsied.

"May I have a dance with each of you?" he asked.

"My card is full," Eleanor responded, "but I believe my cousin has a few spaces."

"How can such good fortune befall me?" Lord Roleston asked, lifting Maisie's card from her wrist before she had time to offer it. He already had a pencil in hand as he perused it.

After a moment, he glanced at her.

"I've never seen the like," he said. "Is it a new custom?"

"No," she said, "more of a little joke. I was late getting my card, and—"

"It's no matter," Lord Roleston insisted. "If it is done in good fun, then I shall follow suit. As Shakespeare said, *With mirth and laughter, let old wrinkles come.*"

Maisie stared at him.

"It's from *The Merchant of Venice*," he said as he hurriedly penciled his name into all the free dances.

"Gratiano speaks it, Act I, Scene one."

He looked up sharply, and she saw a spark of camaraderie in his hazel eyes.

"Remarkable," he said.

"What do you mean, my lord?"

"Beautiful *and* intelligent, too."

She saw Eleanor's eyebrows lift and her mouth quirk into a half-smile. Maisie shrugged slightly.

The musicians who had been warming up, signaled the first dance, a traditional grand march before a quaint quadrille. Since her partner stood right beside her, Maisie and Lord Roleston made it immediately to the dance floor and were right behind their hosts, the duke's oldest son and his wife.

Thus, instead of being disgraced as had nearly happened minutes earlier, Maisie enjoyed the first dance in the same foursome as Lord Arthur Wellesley, heir to the dukedom, and on the arm of a handsome viscount. Moreover, he quoted Shakespeare.

Everything was nearly perfect.

Except as they made their second promenade through the lines of dancers, Maisie noticed Lord Turner partnered with Lady Pepperton, who looked as if she might be vying for the most beautifully dressed woman in London. And she had succeeded!

Lifting her chin, Maisie summoned her mother. Marion Darrow would not have given a fig for Lady Elizabeth Pepperton, and so neither would Maisie. Her sweet mother had loved her greatly, always showering her only daughter with kisses and kind words.

What could be better than to dance in her honor?

"Happy birthday, Mam," she said aloud and felt her heart soar.

CHAPTER THIRTEEN

Maisie barely got off the dance floor when Lord Turner appeared at her side to claim her for the polka that followed.

She couldn't help looking past him and around him. *Where was Lady Pepperton?*

"What on earth are you doing?" he asked as he tried to herd her into some semblance of rhythm.

"Nothing at all. Just admiring the other dancers."

"You will be admiring them while lying on your back if you don't focus a little," he warned her.

She did as he asked and concentrated on the lively dance. Mostly, her mind focused upon exactly where his hands touched her and how he pulled her in as they turned and then let her draw back on the straight.

"Are you really going to dance all those dances with me?"

"I wouldn't break my word, and my name on your card is as good as my word."

"People will talk," she pointed out, as if he didn't know that already. He was stirring up a hornet's nest of gossip.

"Once you've had a great tragedy occur, such silliness as the *ton's* notorious rumor mill fade into insignificance."

Maisie thought about it. "I understand, but I don't think it gives one leave to flaunt all the rules of society, nor to use one's personal misfortune as an excuse."

"An excuse?" he asked, his tone low, and she sensed he didn't like their discussion.

"To be outrageous, for instance, as I'm sure you and I and even Lord Roleston will all be labeled such after today."

"What the devil does Roleston have to do with it?"

"He saw what you had done and did the same, filling up the rest of my card."

She felt his body tense.

"That will appear unseemly."

She laughed. "Undoubtedly. However, I suppose no one will be able to say you and I are in a relationship of any kind if I do the same number of dances with him as I do with you. It is brilliant in a way, as it will cancel you out."

"Brilliant?" he said harshly, then she heard him mutter, "cancel me out" before he whirled her around again.

They finished the dance in silence. As he led her from the floor, there was Viscount Roleston.

"My turn," he said, a charming smile on his face.

Maisie nodded and took his hand.

"Do you intend to go through with this?" Lord Turner asked him before he could lead her away.

"Why, yes. I think it's a superb idea." Lord Roleston looked down at Maisie. "There's no one I would rather dance with anyway, so why go to the pretense of having my name on a bunch of other cards?"

"Normally," she pointed out, "it is considered the duty of a single gentleman to dance with as many single ladies as he can in a night."

"For one purpose," Lord Roleston reminded her. Then he looked sharply at Lord Turner. "It seems as if you are distorting the purpose."

Lord Turner cocked his head. "What do you mean?"

"You already have an arrangement with a lady, do you not? Why would your name be on anyone else's dance cards at all while you are otherwise committed?"

Oh, dear. Maisie watched Jameson's jaw grind.

"Miss Darrow and I are friends," he said at last, then he offered a shallow, curt bow to her and turned on his heel, striding off toward the other side of the room.

"I hope I didn't offend him," Lord Roleston said, not sounding bothered if he had.

They approached the dance floor. "If he truly is your friend, then I suppose you should dance as often as you like together. I didn't think his other *friend*, Lady Pepperton, looked particularly amused, though. Her face was puckered like a child eating a lemon."

"I'm sure he will explain to her the circumstances," she said before taking her place in line and dropping low in a curtsey, waiting for the music to begin. The formal dance seemed very eighteenth-century to her, but was a break from being whirled and twirled.

Slower, the intricate steps performed with the other ladies and gentlemen, steps she'd performed so many times her feet did them without thought, gave her a chance to recover from the previous exerting dance, and to consider Jameson Turner. She had enjoyed every moment with him, and every moment without him seemed inferior.

Was that how he felt about the world he was inhabiting since Lady Turner died—a pale, watery existence in comparison to the vibrant one he'd had before?

Then it was no wonder he seemed so morose, feeling only half alive while those around him carried on and expected him to do the same.

When the long dance ended, she saw Lord Turner waiting at the edge of the floor. As soon as Lord Roleston released her, Jameson took her hand, and Maisie felt a little as if she were in the middle of a tug-of-war game.

After only a minute's respite, they began to waltz.

"How are you feeling?" he asked. "Are you ready for a respite after this?"

Being held by him again, she was instantly revitalized, her body tingling in unexpected places.

"I'm quite well, and I'm positive our hosts have built in an interlude for refreshments."

"Will it come soon enough to keep you from fainting?" Lord Turner wondered. "You could get a head injury if you slid out of my arms and cracked your lovely noggin on the duke's floor."

"Don't be silly." *How could he be so attentive when he was there with another?* "How is Lady Pepperton?"

"Well, as usual. Why do you ask?"

Maisie couldn't tell him of Lord Roleston's observation about her having an expression like a citrus.

"She is not dancing."

He shrugged, which was difficult to do while waltzing. "I will invite her to dance again afterward, if she wishes."

"But there are plenty of available partners," Maisie pointed out. She had an inkling Lady Pepperton would only dance with Lord Turner.

He looked directly at her. "That's not her way."

"I don't understand."

"You don't have to, Miss Darrow."

She sighed. *"Confusion now hath made his masterpiece."*

For some reason, this made him grin, which only increased his attractiveness, and considering they were talking about his paramour, only increased Maisie's annoyance.

"That was from *Macbeth*. Lord Roleston quoted Shakespeare earlier," she blurted. "Can you believe it?"

"Easily," he quipped after a moment.

What did he mean by that? she wondered. She believed he might not like the viscount.

Sighing, she remembered when dancing had been simply observing your dance partner, sometimes silently and with the merest of smiles or nods, and deciding rather swiftly if one wanted ever to dance with him again.

Now it seemed as if each dance was a complicated conversation.

When they left the floor and she saw Lord Roleston waiting, she blew the stray curl off her forehead and wondered how Eleanor was faring. *Where was her cousin?*

Spying her having a glass of something with a young man, Maisie said, "Would you gentlemen mind if I sit out the next dance and have a drink?"

Realizing she had addressed them both, she turned to Lord Roleston. "I should have asked you as I believe you have the next dance."

"Certainly. Although I shall miss your nimble soles upon the dance floor, I will settle for your sweet mouth sipping champagne. If you take a seat, I shall return as soon as possible."

Lord Turner, just behind Lord Roleston, rolled his eyes exaggeratedly. However, he didn't immediately leave. As soon as her other partner departed for the refreshment table, Lord Turner escorted her to the closest empty seats and sat beside her.

"Roleston is a tad insufferable, isn't he?"

"He's charming," she defended the man who had stepped in to help her make the best of the evening.

Jameson Turner crossed his arms over his chest. "*Settle for your sweet mouth?* Is that what passes for charm?"

What did he have against Lord Roleston? She was about to ask him outright when Eleanor arrived, escorted by Lord Foley, whom they'd known since their first Season.

Harmless, he was not the type of man she could see sweeping her cousin off her feet.

Lord Turner stood at once and offered Eleanor his chair before nodding in greeting to her companion.

"The musicians are wonderful, are they not?" Eleanor remarked.

"Yes," Maisie agreed, just as Lord Roleston reappeared with champagne for her and one for himself.

"Would you like this glass, Miss Blackwood?" he offered her.

"Oh, no, thank you," Eleanor replied. "I am fine. The only thing I think would make this evening more perfect would be meeting the great Duke of Wellington. It was nice to meet his son, but I understand his father makes an unforgettable impression."

"I believe he is in his favorite residence in Walmer Castle, overlooking the sea," Lord Turner reported.

"Who can blame him?" Eleanor asked. "I've been to Kent, and the seaside is stunning."

"A long way to travel," Maisie said, "at his age."

"Not so far on the train," Eleanor pointed out.

"The Duke of Wellington takes a coach," Lord Roleston informed them.

"Why on earth would he triple his traveling time?" Eleanor asked.

"It may seem strange for one of England's greatest soldiers to be timid about train travel, but he witnessed the death of parliamentarian William Huskisson, smashed by a train, years ago."

Maisie gasped as she was sipping her champagne, causing it to go down all wrong and coming back as a cough while she tried to breathe. Eleanor patted her back. Although her eyes watered profusely, she couldn't take her gaze from Jameson Turner. He had gone quite still and pale. She wished she could stop Lord Roleston from continuing.

"It soured Lord Wellesley to the British rail system except when absolutely necessary. Actually, Huskisson was incredibly clumsy, and the list of his various accidents was already legend, two fractured arms, a sprained ankle from leaping unsuccessfully across a moat, falling from his horse, having his horse fall on him—"

"Gracious!" Eleanor exclaimed, now rubbing circles on Maisie's back while the coughing fit abated.

"Indeed," Lord Roleston agreed. "He had some sort of internal infection at the time of the train trip and everyone told Huskisson to stay home, even our queen, then Princess Victoria. Not only did he go, but he took his wife, who witnessed the terrible accident. He got out of the train he was on at a break during its maiden journey, only to be hit by the famous Rocket train while he dithered on the tracks. Squashed like a bug, with his legs cut, he bled to death . . . oh! Did I say something wrong?" he asked as Lord Turner pivoted and walked hurriedly away.

"His wife," Maisie said, standing. "Lady Turner died in a train accident. I thought everyone knew about that."

"I didn't," Lord Roleston said. "Poor chap. Shall I go after him and make amends?"

"If you will excuse me, my lord, as he told you, we are friends. I will return shortly." Thrusting her unfinished drink into Lord Roleston's hands, she went searching for Jameson.

HE COULD BARELY BREATHE. Just like that, Jameson was transported to the terrible day when he was informed of Esmera's untimely death. Only now, because of that idiot's description, he had a new image in his head of her lying on the tracks, her beautiful body crushed and cut, yet that wasn't what had happened.

Standing at the end of the same hallway where he'd brought Miss Darrow earlier, he looked out over the back of Apsley House to a lawn and trees. He saw only Esmera. Her neck had snapped, and she had died instantly, looking as perfect as possible given the conditions.

When he first saw her, she'd appeared to be simply sleeping, except for the coloring of her skin, an unnatural chalky hue and the bruising on her slender neck. He knew she wouldn't have been pleased if she'd become bloodied or had cuts on her arms or legs or . . .

He heard a loud moan and realized he was making the sound.

"No," he ordered himself, as he often did, to bring his thoughts away from that terrible day. At the same time, he knew someone was behind him.

Esmera's ghost was his first hope when he whirled around to face . . . Maisie.

"I am so sorry, my lord. Lord Roleston didn't know about Lady Turner."

He nodded. It was hard to believe anyone in London didn't know, but no one would be so thoughtless on purpose. Or so cruel.

Seeing her in a pretty gown, her cheeks pink and healthy, her gold-flecked, brown eyes gazing at him, he felt uplifted. The squeezing around his heart eased.

Unthinkingly, he opened his arms, and she ran into them without hesitation. Clamping them tightly around her, feeling her soft flesh against him, her chest rising and falling with each breath, he wanted to weep.

Instead, he looked down at her concerned face and claimed her beautiful lips.

Warm and alive, vibrant, rose-complected Maisie Darrow—the epitome of a man's fantasy.

He touched his tongue to the seam of her lips and, miraculously, she opened them for him. He felt her gasp even as he slid his tongue inside her moist mouth, tasting her recent sip of champagne, recalling Roleston's ridiculous talk of *settling* for her sweet mouth.

Miss Darrow's mouth was not to be settled for, but worshiped . . . and ravished.

His body prickled with wanting, and by her soft moan, she wanted him, too. Fairly certain this was her first deep kiss involving tongues, Jameson took it slowly, his hands drawing her closer, letting her feel his heated arousal.

Relishing the way her body melted against his, he tilted his head and nibbled her full lower lip the way he'd wanted to do months ago in his rose garden.

They said nothing, simply kissing mindlessly and, for him, desperately, as each moment spent exploring her mouth chased farther away the awful encompassing feelings of loss and death which had come upon him so overwhelmingly fast.

When at last they drew back, each to take a few deep breaths, he stared at her. Despite Elizabeth's experience and eagerness, this kiss was the first since his wife had died that left him shaken—at least, the first since the last kiss with Maisie.

What was he doing? Playing false with this woman who deserved more than a man who couldn't give her his heart.

He stepped back. He needed to find Elizabeth. He'd been rude to her due to his obsession with Miss Darrow, and she deserved better, too.

"I don't know what to say," he began. He wanted to thank her for bringing him out of the spiral of melancholy, but one couldn't thank a woman for letting herself be kissed, basically for letting him use her to feel as if he belonged with the living again.

"You shouldn't be here, alone with me." That was obvious. "Your brother might show up again, and I'm not sure we can talk our way out of every indiscretion."

"I'm not sure I want to," she spoke her first words, and his heart sunk. She was pinning some sort of hope upon him.

"Don't let any of your future dreams include me, Miss Darrow. For I can guarantee they shall not come true. I must find Lady Pepperton at once, as I am being a poor companion. And I think it best if we return to the ball separately. I'll let you go first if you intend to go immediately. Otherwise, I shall take my leave of you here."

Her eyes had grown wider during his tirade. Finally, she nodded.

"I am glad to see you are feeling better, Lord Turner." Then she lifted her hand, reminding him of his commitment to dance with her.

"Miss Darrow," he began, but she shook her head and drew her pencil from her reticule.

"Please consider yourself released from the rest of our dances this evening." He watched her ruthlessly start crossing out his name. "You were beyond chivalrous tonight, helping me tremendously. I bid you good evening."

Inside, he was in turmoil, emotions he couldn't even begin to fathom swirling inside him.

Before she could scratch out every one, he grabbed hold of her wrist.

"Leave me one more," he said.

Miss Darrow said nothing, only pulling her hand slowly free from his. He watched her turn and walk away, looking regal as she did, head up, bustle swishing.

What he wouldn't give to be a man free of the painful clamp upon his heart and the numbing sadness, free to offer for Maisie Darrow, and spend the rest of his life keeping her safe and making her happy.

That frightening and unexpected thought, of trying to protect another life, propelled him in the same direction she'd taken. In moments, he was back in the Waterloo Gallery, searching through the throng for his uncomplicated paramour.

He had been foolish to consider letting Elizabeth go or even risk what they had by getting entangled with Miss Darrow. Elizabeth was safe. He would never love her, which was a blessing. Naturally, he still felt concern that something might befall her.

Luckily, Elizabeth didn't care to travel as she'd already done so much in her younger years, living abroad. When she went out and about in London, she had a large, safe enclosed carriage and rode with the windows up so she couldn't be thrown out of it. She always rode her horse slowly through Hyde Park, at least when she rode with him.

Moreover, she considered trains crowded and noisy and stayed off of them, like the Duke of Wellington apparently.

And he knew she didn't go on small rowboats alone, and if she did, he was confident she wouldn't lose her oar and then fall in.

Lady Pepperton was perfect for him. He'd questioned her on the use of unattended candles and made sure she had her fireplace flues cleaned to prevent chimney fires.

What more could he do to keep her safe?

He ought to be by her side when they were out in the world, just as he should have been next to Esmera when she was traveling to Bath.

Determined not to let his thoughts go into the darkness again while he was at Apsley House, he finally found her, looking entirely at ease, chatting with Lord Michael Alder. It ought to bother him since their heads were close, and Alder's reputation as a rogue was infamous and well-deserved.

Swerving away from them before Elizabeth saw him and waved him over—or worse, ignored him, since earlier she had let her displeasure be known—Jameson went toward Ned and Caroline Darrow's table. He could at least discover if Maisie had left him one dance after all.

"She left, my lord," Mrs. Darrow informed him when he inquired as to her whereabouts. "A sudden and piercing headache overcame her."

Frowning, he glanced around as if he might still see her.

"You let her go alone?" He couldn't keep the disapproval from his tone.

Ned, who quite discourteously remained seated, replied, "Hardly alone. My sister went in our family carriage with our driver, not in a public cab. She is capable of reaching our home by herself."

Her brother was probably correct. Yet his heart started pounding in earnest.

"Where do you live?" he asked, feeling as if every second mattered.

"Why do you ask? Surely, you don't—"

Stepping closer, he glared down at Ned Darrow. "What is the address?" Jameson practically hissed.

The man blinked and swallowed, looking like a carp.

It was his wife who answered. "We are on the south end of Cambridge Street, number one-sixty-three."

"Pimlico," he said with a trace of dismay. *Not terrible, but not Mayfair, either.*

"It isn't quite St. George's Drive," Ned said, referring to the best street in their area near the Thames, before puffing out his chest, "but a nice place, all the same."

If something happened to her on the way to the Darrows' townhouse, it would be Jameson's fault. As assuredly as she had left because of his appalling behavior, he had singlehandedly driven her from the security of the well-lit ball and her family, out into the darkness of London's fog, thieves, and rutted roads which ate carriage wheels daily, leaving people stranded.

With that terrifying notion, he fled the Duke of Wellington's ball in pursuit of Maisie.

CHAPTER FOURTEEN

Jameson had not discovered her carriage along the route
between Hyde Park and Pimlico's Cambridge Street,
neither overturned nor with a wheel broken.

When he found number one-sixty-three, he dismounted
from his carriage and ran up the three shallow front steps
of brick to the arched doorway. The entire design was a
cheap imitation of Elizabeth's home in Belgravia, but there
weren't prostitutes or thugs lurking on the street in front, so
he should be relieved.

Knocking sharply on the door, he felt impatient to see
her, to make sure she was safe. Not that he expected her to
open the door herself, as Mr. Darrow must have some
semblance of manservant, if not a true butler.

Thus, he was beyond surprised when the door swung
inward to reveal Maisie herself standing there.

If Jameson thought he felt startled, she looked positively
stunned, blinking at him as if she believed he might be an
apparition.

Raising a hand to her chest, she stepped back, which he
took as an invitation and entered.

"What are you doing here?" Maisie asked, moving
around him to close the door.

"Why are you answering your own door?" he demanded. "I could have been a murderer!"

Her impish smile overcame her shocked expression, and his knees weakened when he saw her dimples for the first time. *How had he not noticed before she had the most charming dimples?*

"Do murderers tend to knock politely?" she asked. "I assumed they dragged one into an alley and slit one's throat, or climbed into one's bedroom sometime after midnight."

"Do not say such things, even in jest," he said, still enjoying the relief at seeing her safe in her own home.

And he was alone, in the foyer with her. No servants had shown up yet.

"You didn't explain why you answered the door, and where are all the servants?"

"We have a manservant, but as we were all supposed to be out until the wee hours, he is off duty."

She glanced around the modest front hall. "The same for our housekeeper. After supper, she and our cook went off duty, as well. I was about to go to bed," she added, gesturing up the staircase. "I don't normally use a maid for undressing, although with this dress, I could use some help removing it."

She left that particularly vivid and enticing phrase dangling between them, and his mouth went dry.

"What of your companion for the evening?" she asked, when he said nothing more. "Is she waiting outside in your carriage?"

Still distracted by the notion of helping to undress her, he couldn't think whom she meant. Instead, he stared at her adorable face, framed by golden ringlets which had lost some of their coils by this hour. Moreover, he couldn't help looking at her kissable mouth. And as they were standing still rather than dancing and turning this way and that, he could also admire the length of her neck, her slender shoulders, and her impressive décolletage.

The valley between her firm, high breasts was deep and mysterious, one he longed to explore.

He frowned. She might catch cold in such a frock, showing so much smooth skin. But she also looked absolutely fetching.

"Lord Turner, are you listening to me?"

In truth, he hadn't been. "My companion?" he repeated, not completely confident those were her last words.

"Lady Pepperton," she clarified, annunciating each syllable.

He hadn't even told Elizabeth he was leaving. A part of him was mortified, another part wanted to laugh at his own asinine behavior.

"I will return to Apsley House and reclaim her."

"Reclaim her?"

He smiled at the outrage Maisie put into those two words.

"As if she were your property, like a horse that wandered from your stable?"

He shook his head at her imagination. "I only meant, at last glance, I believe she was being wooed by another, and I might have to . . . ," he trailed off. "At least, I must offer her a ride home."

She cocked her head. "Since I am already home and, obviously not in need of your assistance, I must ask again, why are you here?"

"You left so quickly and by yourself, thus I was concerned."

"Strange, after the way we parted, not half an hour later, here you are. Recall you said you would not be in my future."

"This isn't the future, Miss Darrow. This is the present."

She tossed up her hands, looking exasperated, which he also found charming.

"Which is all we have, Lord Turner. No one can predict what comes next, but you can be mulishly short-sighted about it."

"I fail to see—"

"Precisely," she said. "To be honest, I do not have a headache. I left the ball because of you. You were truly unpleasant earlier. Except for the kiss," she amended.

"The kiss was very pleasant," he agreed, his gaze dipping to her mouth. More than anything, he wanted to repeat it. However, being alone with her in her home was even more dangerous, certainly more of an infraction than their earlier flaunting of the rules, and he ought to depart at once.

In fact, she shouldn't have made reference to their earlier indiscretion. They ought to pretend as if it never happened. That was how these things were handled.

"We need to laugh again," she said unexpectedly. "The way we did earlier tonight with your cavern and tavern joke."

"I don't feel like laughing." Jameson didn't, not one bit. He was confused by Maisie Darrow. More precisely, his feelings for her confused him. Above all, he didn't want to feel anything for her whatsoever.

Speaking of having no feelings, what was he to do about Elizabeth? He'd always treated women with respect, but tonight he had fallen far short of the mark where she was concerned.

He was behaving like the bastard he was, not the gentleman he aspired to be.

"Please," she asked, tilting her head and looking up at him from under her brown lashes, proving all women knew how to get what they wanted from a man. "Tell me another good joke."

He vaguely recalled a young blonde lady asking him the same thing at a country party in Sheffield, and realized it must be a memory of Maisie from a few years back.

He shook his head. *What a strange woman she was!*

He began the first tired joke that came into his head. "When is a lover like a tailor?"

"Oh, pish, my lord" Maisie said. "Everyone knows the answer: When he presses his suit."

He couldn't make her laugh anymore tonight. He didn't have it in him.

"I had best be leaving."

She nodded, seeming to agree. "Most people would prefer to die like Joan of Arc rather than Mary Stuart," she said conversationally.

"I beg your pardon?" *What on earth was she on about?*

She repeated her bizarre sentence, which was good of her, since he'd been distracted staring at her luscious lips.

"Most people would prefer to die like Joan of Arc rather than Mary, Queen of Scots." She paused, then finished, "As they like a hot steak better than a cold chop."

Jameson's mouth dropped open at her irreverence. They stared at one another. Then, when she made a little gesture with her hand and muttered "chop," he started to snicker.

She joined in with a delightful snort, and then he laughed from his belly, and she did the same with huge guffaws, not delicate, glove-over-mouth feminine laughter.

Hers was the most attractive laugh he'd ever heard, making him want to pull her close again and ravish her.

In fact, almost without realizing, his arms had floated up and away from his sides, reaching for her. She didn't gainsay him as he took hold of her upper arms before realizing his own intent. Then he drew her toward him. Her pretty eyes crinkled in the corners, as she still had the look of laughter on her face.

Odd how he had never considered laughter or joking particularly alluring. Esmera hated the notion anyone might be laughing at her or laughing at something she didn't understand, so she was a rather serious person.

In a startling moment, Jameson realized he couldn't recall exactly what his dead wife's laughter sounded like, which sobered him instantly.

But he was glad Maisie looked happy.

He cared about her happiness.

Dammit!

Releasing her abruptly, he stepped around her to reach the safety of the door and the street beyond. He needed to prevent himself from the kiss which would surely happen if he held her again.

"Good night, Miss Darrow."

"Good night, Lord Turner. I'm glad we have become friends after all."

With a nod, he left her, slipping out into the smoky London night air.

Then he turned. "Don't answer the door to anyone else, promise me."

"I promise."

MAISIE LEANED AGAINST THE door a moment, thinking Jameson Turner might test her by knocking again. After a minute, she went upstairs to bed. It was early, but she would read Shakespeare aloud to her mother on her birthday. Something happy with a good, tidy ending, for that was all any of them could hope for.

She settled upon *The Taming of the Shrew*, one of her favorites for the relationship that developed between Petruchio and Katherine.

When she awakened in the morning, the play was still clutched in her hand, a small, red-leather tome, which she set upon the shelf next to the rest in the set. Her brother had long since given up requesting she leave her collection in Dumfries. It went where she went.

Last night, she'd been thoroughly kissed by a man who did not intend to offer for her. And today, as well as the entire Season, her calendar was undoubtedly full of events designed to find a man who would do precisely that.

When Maisie headed down to the morning room for some breakfast, she fully intended to arrange a visit with Eleanor as soon as possible. She desperately needed to speak to her cousin and closest confidante, whom she'd hardly said goodbye to at Apsley House.

Before she could pen a brief missive to send to the Lindsey townhouse, however, Maisie was intercepted by Caroline, who entered the morning room with a determined look upon her face.

"You have a choice, Maisie," she declared.

Two unaware hostesses had scheduled their outings on the same day. Thus, Maisie had her pick of Kensington Gardens or Kew Gardens with a walk around the Palm House. Either way, there would be a picnic involved.

"Do you know where Eleanor is going, if to either?" Maisie asked.

"I'm sorry, I don't, but you can't always rely on her company. Besides, I will be there."

Maisie appreciated Caroline being her chaperone in lieu of a mother, although it was nicer to do these events with a friend. Even if her brother's wife was only a few years older, a married woman was not the same as a single friend. But Maisie still counted herself lucky.

"I am grateful and glad you don't mind going with me. Are we going out tonight, as well?" she asked, still considering whether she preferred the closer proximity of the gardens just west of Hyde Park or whether to go all the way along the river to Kew.

"We are, indeed. Tonight, there is a soirée at Holland House."

"Then we shall be going back and forth all day." Maisie hoped she didn't sound as if she were whining, but she would be just as pleased to go find Eleanor and have a game of croquet.

"Why don't we skip the morning events altogether and go for a ride on Rotten Row. Then I'll visit with my cousin before dinner."

"I wish I could say yes, but you must choose one of the planned excursions, or Ned will have a fit. He and your father have determined this is your last Season, and all they can afford. I do so want you to find someone, elsewise you may end up in Dumfries tending your father's house."

While she didn't mind the house she grew up in, filled with mostly happy memories, Maisie shuddered at a life spent without a husband and children.

"Kew Gardens, then. If we are going, let us go far and make it worthwhile stepping out."

"There's a good girl. You had only to change your attitude. It will be a wonderful day. No hint of rain, either."

As it turned out, Caroline was wrong in that regard, and by the time they crossed the Thames and entered the botanical gardens through Elizabeth Gate, clouds had gathered. Maisie didn't really mind. The rain usually came and went, giving everything a just-washed patina.

Soon, with a group of other single ladies and gentleman, they were on a brisk stroll around the grounds. They managed to tour the Pagoda, two temples, and the so-called Ruined Arch before the heavens opened with a downpour. Luckily, they were just going into the Palm House when it began.

Maisie's group met up with another group taking shelter there.

"We were going to take refreshments overlooking the rose garden," declared one of their hostesses, "but if the rain doesn't let up soon, we shall try to serve in here."

"So, we are saved from the rain by being in a tropical rainforest," Maisie quipped, knowing Lord Turner would see the humor.

"All the ladies' hair will be a frizzy mess in about five minutes," she whispered to Caroline, for the Palm House was a wrought-iron framed glasshouse, the largest anywhere, and the air felt nearly as damp inside as outside.

Sure enough, wherever Caroline's brown hair had escaped her bun, it puffed almost instantly. Maisie doubtless looked the same, her blonde hair turning into curly sheep's wool anyplace short tendrils were loose.

"It's a good thing we will have plenty of time to get ready for Holland House," her sister-in-law said. "A cool sponge bath may be in order to get rid of the sticky feeling."

In the stuffiness of the greenhouse, no one felt like hot tea or biscuits, so the refreshments were ignored in favor of wandering the three-hundred-and-sixty-three-foot-long structure.

Maisie leaned close to see the name on a label of a large palm.

"That plant is rumored to have been brought to Kew in 1775," came a male voice at her elbow.

Turning, Maisie had a nasty surprise. Lord Granger! It was the unchivalrous brute who had taken all the joy out of the final weeks of her previous Season, making her feel frightened and unsure of her own good judgment.

How had she not seen him earlier? He must have been a member of the other tour. She supposed she was fortunate not to have encountered him prior to this unfortunate moment.

Turning on her heels, she decided not to speak to him at all, but simply to avoid him. Then she felt his hand on her arm. She shivered from head to toe with alarm, but she could see Caroline a mere few feet away and others milling about. She had nothing to fear from this particular viscount while in public.

Thus, she turned on him. "Unhand me at once," she hissed.

Slowly, with a smirk, he lowered his hand from her arm.

"It's good to see you," he said, his glance taking in her appearance before lingering on her bosom.

"I may not have been clear last Season," she said, "but I wish to have absolutely nothing to do with you. I don't want to dance with you, or speak to you, or even be near you. Is that clear enough?"

His eyes widened, but he continued to smirk. Hopefully, that was all it would take.

Before he could speak, Caroline arrived at her elbow.

"Would you like to introduce us?" her sister-in-law asked.

"Positively not," Maisie declared. "He is of no importance and not worth knowing." Then she threaded her arm through Caroline's and urged her back the way they had come.

Luckily, Ned's wife had a good head on her shoulders and didn't fight Maisie, or ask questions until they were out of Lord Granger's hearing. They climbed the circular staircase to the second level, putting them thirty feet above the floor for a better view of the palms and other plants.

Since it was hotter, there were less people on the walkway that wound the perimeter of the central dome. And when they were alone, Caroline stopped her.

"You must tell me at once what that was about. Who was he?"

"I would rather not."

Caroline sighed. "Then I will have to tell Ned, so he can look into it."

Maisie didn't want anything looked into, as her sister-in-law so aptly phrased it. Nor did she want Ned to become involved. He would make a hash of it for certain, and probably publicly demand Granger marry her.

"Very well. I will say this, Granger is a gnat on the dung heap of London's society. That's who he is."

"Is he?" Her sister-in-law looked over the railing, and Maisie joined her to see the viscount wandering around, talking to others. "He must have been quite disrespectful for you to say such."

"He was." She wouldn't reveal when exactly, as that would lead to more questions.

Caroline glanced at her sharply. "Did he hurt you, Maisie?"

"Only my pride. And I do not want Ned to know. Please, can we stop talking about him?"

"Yes. But if I see that man approach you, I shall intervene."

Her words actually gave Maisie a little comfort. She didn't have to face the debaucher alone.

"If he does bother you again, though, we should tell Ned."

Maisie nodded. She knew wives and husbands didn't like to keep secrets.

"Very well."

Turning, she looked out through the glass. "We are like birds up so high. The view is probably spectacular on a clear day."

THE WEATHER HAD CLEARED for the soirée at Holland House, once the site of the Dowager Lady Holland's coveted political and social salons earlier in the century, which the likes of Byron enjoyed. She had been forced to set up her rival 'court' west of London proper since as a divorcée, she was shunned by the upper stratum of society and the royals alike.

Now, events were held and hosted by Henry Edward, the fourth Lord Holland, and his wife. They charged for tickets and had sold off much of the surrounding land to maintain the house. Thus, Maisie and her family passed the newly constructed middle-class homes of tradesmen, artisans, and estate workers before their driver took them along the elm-lined avenue to the massive Jacobean residence.

Driving through the famed Inigo Jones' gateway, their carriage stopped at the main entrance. Even in the dusky evening light, she could see the enormous building's character of turrets and high chimneys, with gables and mullioned windows.

"Pity it's too dark to see the brickwork," Ned said, but Maisie was more interested in what was inside.

Eleanor had sent word she would be there, and since Simon and Jenny weren't in London, that might mean Lord Turner was attending as well, acting as chaperone.

Her hopes died when she saw her aunt with Eleanor in the vaulted front hall. Marbled busts stood guard all around them. And with Lady Blackwood watching over her youngest daughter, there was no need for Lord Turner.

The cousins met, kissed cheeks, and dashed off through the inner hall to the grand main staircase, large enough for an army of horses to mount, ascending to the reception rooms above. Artwork and antiquities were everywhere, many garnered by the Dowager Lady Elizabeth Holland while on her Grand Tour of Europe, as a young woman, causing guests to call Holland House "the house of all Europe."

At another time, Maisie knew she would enjoy examining the pieces, but at that moment, she wanted only to talk to her cousin.

As soon as they were away from their family, proceeding through the startlingly ornate Gilt Room to the adjoining Crimson Drawing Room, Eleanor squeezed Maisie's hand.

"Tell me what drove you away last night."

In five minutes, she'd told her cousin everything, including Lord Turner's strange appearance at her home after the ball.

"I doubt I'll see him again for ages, not until Lady Pepperton decides she wants him to escort her to another ball."

"I can safely say you will see him very soon," Eleanor said, and turned her to face the entrance to the great room.

There he was, fastidiously clad in his customary charcoal gray evening attire, entering with other guests, and speaking quietly to the current Lady Holland.

CHAPTER FIFTEEN

M Maisie waited for the immediate rush of excitement upon seeing him to subside before she spoke.

"Do you think he has brought Lady Pepperton?"

Eleanor didn't simply lift a delicate shoulder when she was unsure. She gave a proper shrug.

"I have no idea."

Maisie couldn't take her eyes off of him, except when other guests blocked her view.

"When I saw Aunt Anne here, I didn't think he would come."

"He's not here for my benefit," Eleanor declared. "That's for certain. And if Lady Pepperton didn't come with him, then he's not here for *hers* either." She let her words hang meaningfully between them and blinked her knowing eyes at Maisie.

"Perhaps . . . his melancholia has lifted somewhat," Maisie proposed, although it seemed unlikely Lord Turner would show up at a ticketed event with the intent of making merry with strangers.

"We should get back to my mother and your brother before they start to search," Eleanor said, and so before she even had a chance to make eye contact with him, Maisie returned to the Gilt Room.

"Can you imagine living in one of these houses?" Eleanor asked, sounding repelled.

Maisie laughed. That was her naturalist cousin, preferring to sit on a tree branch rather than residing in a magnificent mansion.

She surveyed the room they were in. Every wall panel had embossing or engraving, carvings, mirrors, and paintings. And of course, gilded decorations. It was enough to make one's head spin and want to close one's eyes.

What Holland House lacked, at least in the parts Maisie had seen, was warmth. The scale alone made it set up perfectly for large gatherings. She could only wonder what it would feel like for a husband and wife, even with children, to try to make it a home. Surely, there was a private, cozier apartment hidden behind all this glamour.

She preferred the scale of Jonling Hall.

Not that her living there was any more of a reality than living at the Duke of Wellington's Apsley House or here.

"I'm sure the dowager loved her time as mistress of this estate. She truly made this place what it is."

"She was admired," Eleanor agreed, "but not often liked. I think the most pleasant word I've ever heard about her is 'formidable.' And most recall her as sharp-tongued and imperious to a fault."

"Her husband doted on her, don't forget," Maisie said. "I don't think she gave a fig for what anyone else thought."

If Jameson Turner held her above all others in his regard, she wouldn't mind if the rest of society turned their back on her.

Her aunt hailed them toward the edge of the great room, and Maisie didn't get a chance to look behind her to see if Lord Turner had come from the Crimson Drawing Room behind them.

There were no dance cards tonight, and the dance floor was not huge. Rather, this evening was a gathering, a place to mingle, to dance if one felt the inclination, and to eat a sumptuous buffet. When they all retired for the night, probably around one o'clock in the morning, their purses would be lighter from the cost of entrance, but hopefully, their heads would be full with fond memories.

Maisie simply hoped to see Lord Turner again in the vast rooms and even to speak with him. Unfortunately, as if her earlier interaction at the Palm House had heralded a turn of bad luck, she also spied the odious Lord Granger in the crowd, making her stomach twinge with nervousness. He didn't need to behave wickedly. Not bad looking, he was rumored to have a sizable inheritance coming his way, but still, he trifled with young ladies such as herself. Just for his amusement, apparently.

"You've gone quiet," Eleanor said.

"Where were you this morning?"

"Sketching—or trying to—in Hyde Park, next to the Serpentine."

"I wish you'd come on the outing." Maisie hadn't told Eleanor, or anyone until she'd spoken with Caroline earlier that day, about her previous frightening encounter at the end of the prior Season. If Eleanor had been with her at Kew, she probably wouldn't have been alone even for a second. Having him touch her arm again and speak with her so casually had caused all manner of unsettling fears she couldn't tamp down.

"I'll go to Kew with you anytime, as long as I can bring my sketchbook." Then Eleanor smiled. "I must admit, I'm glad we are not forced to dance and socialize tonight."

Maisie nodded. "I know you find the Season somewhat taxing on your quiet sensibilities. But how will you find a husband if you don't embrace the social aspects of it?"

Eleanor shook her head. "I am sure I don't know. However, I have no intention of worrying about it. There are men elsewhere than in London's great houses and ballrooms."

"True." Maisie had enjoyed seeing Jameson Turner as much on the riverbank of the Don as here. The recollection made her crane her neck to look for him again.

"If you like, we can stroll around a little more and try to cross paths with Lord Turner," Eleanor offered.

"Am I that obvious?"

"Only to me, dear cousin. I fear your heart is well and truly entangled with that man."

"Why fear?" *Didn't Eleanor like him?*

"Don't look at me that way, Maisie. I think he is a nice man when he is in his right mind, but also, I believe he is still off-kilter. He is not the same man we first met at Jonling Hall years ago. Do you agree?"

She nodded, but she had certainly seen glimpses of that earlier man when they laughed together, and his eyes sparkled with momentary mirth. All too soon, he would become somber again.

"Still, if you'll indulge me," Maisie entreated, "and help me at least to get in his vicinity tonight."

"Of course," Eleanor agreed, and then shrieked in her wonderful childish way that was better done at home than in the exquisitely refined Gilt Room of Holland House.

"Maggie! My sister is here. I had no idea she was coming."

Just like that, Eleanor dashed away. Maisie noted the crowd had parted slightly to make way for the spectacularly beautiful Lady Margaret Cambrey and her dashing husband, whom Simon called simply Cam. Two earls, best friends, marrying two sisters.

Pity, Maisie thought, *there wasn't a third best friend, also an earl, for Eleanor.* A gentle, kind man with a nice country house where her cousin could spend her days lying on the grass sketching flowers and bugs. Eleanor would be exceedingly happy, which would make Maisie happy, too.

At the moment, she would let Eleanor reunite with her sister and continue exploring the house. If she encountered Jameson, so much the better.

To that end, Maisie found the gorgeous library, reputedly one of the finest private collections in Britain. Despite being unable to spend any amount of time searching the titles when there was so much more to see, she took a cursory glance for any Shakespeare collections before moving on.

Meanwhile, musicians were practicing in one of the reception rooms as Maisie made her way to the smaller, so-called Yellow Drawing Room, instantly struck by the Flemish and Italian old masters. *To have such art in one's own home!*

She thought fondly of the landscape painting she'd memorized while waiting for Jameson that day in Sheffield. And then she heard footsteps enter the otherwise deserted room. He'd found her!

Turning, she gasped.

Lord Granger stood in the doorway, and her breath caught painfully in her throat. She could scream and people would come running. Knowing that kept her silent. She wouldn't give him the satisfaction of seeing her fear.

"Good evening, Miss Darrow. Twice in one day, I get to see your loveliness. It must be fate."

"I attribute it to incredibly bad fortune."

As with every one of the rooms, there were multiple doorways. She skirted a library table and headed toward the door at the far end.

"I wonder you never told anyone about our pleasurable tryst."

She froze. *Did he think she'd enjoyed herself when he'd pressed her against the wall in an arched alcove at Lord Wallingford's townhouse?* Granger's mouth had covered hers, stealing her ability to breathe deeply or to scream for help. His hands had suddenly roamed her body, one sliding down to squeeze her bottom, the other cupping her breast before she'd managed to raise her knee high enough to push him away.

As soon as he'd taken a step back, she'd fled.

"No one from your family ever said anything to me, neither an inquiry nor a request for a marriage proposal."

"I would never marry you," she ground out over a dry tongue.

He laughed. "And I would never propose to you. You're a full Scot, aren't you? Wild, barbaric people, known to drink the blood of the slain. As if I'd want any of your brutish ancestry in my offspring."

Maisie's temper boiled. *What hogwash was this idiot spouting?*

"You weren't worried about my brutish ancestry when you assaulted me."

"Assaulted you? Please! I assure you, I hadn't planned on spilling my seed inside you. Or at least not in your reproductive orifice."

Since Maisie was unsure what he was saying, only knowing she was being insulted further, she took another step toward the door, which she opened. Knowing she could step into the hall at any moment, she turned.

"*Would thou wert clean enough to spit upon!*" she hurled the words at him from *Timon of Athens*.

She saw him take a deep breath, nostrils flaring.

"What did you say to me?"

"I should have known an uncivilized brute such as yourself wouldn't know Shakespeare," she said.

He took a few steps toward her, but she didn't feel frightened of him anymore. She could hear people walking by, women laughing.

"*You starveling, you elf-skin, you dried neat's tongue, you bull's pizzle, you stock-fish!*"

"How dare you!"

She delighted in Granger's stunned expression.

"*Thou elvish-marked, abortive, rooting hog!*"

"Stop it," he commanded. "Stop saying such vile things."

Maisie laughed. "Your face is becoming quite red. *Truly, thou are damned, like an ill-roasted egg, all on one side.*"

He had crept closer, but she had one foot over the threshold.

"How dare you speak to me like that!" he sputtered. "You low-lander!"

She mustn't double over with laughter as she wanted to do, for that would give him the advantage.

"Is that the best you can do? *Thou loathed issue of thy father's loins!*"

"Don't you say another word to me," Granger yelled, charging toward her, looking apoplectic.

"*You are not worth another word, else I'd call you knave.*"

Maisie practically yelled the last word before she fled, colliding with a solid mass that stopped her going anywhere. Indeed, it pushed her back into the Yellow Drawing Room.

A moment's heart-stopping panic gave way to relief when she realized whom she'd slammed into.

"Good, you've caught her," Granger crowed. "I shall teach the guttersnipe some manners. I should have finished what I started last year." He stepped closer to Maisie, who whirled to face him. "Then you wouldn't be so insolent. There's obviously only one good use for your insulting mouth."

Everything occurred so swiftly, she barely realized what was happening. First, she felt Lord Turner's arm reach out across her midriff, sending her back toward the doorway behind him. She squealed as he did so.

Then, as she regained her balance, she saw him swing at Granger, hitting him squarely in the face. Blood spurted everywhere, and she realized she'd seen her first broken nose.

It looked painful. By the way, Lord Granger yelled and held his face, it must be as bad as it looked.

"You bastard!" he screamed, yet his words sounded muffled with his hands still clutching his nose and over his mouth.

"Be that as it may, I have better manners than you," Jameson said. "Don't drip blood on the Hollands's rug. It's probably worth more than your entire year's allowance."

He turned and offered her his arm, which she took.

Over her shoulder, seeing Granger's defeat, Maisie said one of her favorite lines from *As You Like It.* "*I desire that we be better strangers.*"

IT HAD FELT DAMNED good to clobber that idiot. Admittedly, before he became a viscount, Jameson had spent more than a couple hours at a pugilists' club, but he'd nearly forgotten the surge of vivacity one well-thrown, properly landed punch could give a man.

Not sure where he was going exactly, he led Maisie along with him, down the stairs, past late-coming guests, and out into the gardens closest to the back of the house. He knew the way; he'd been there many times.

"I heard someone spouting the very best of Shakespeare," he said to the silent woman beside him, "and, by the tone of your voice and the quotations you were choosing, I had a feeling you needed assistance."

Still, Miss Darrow said nothing, and her hand remained gripping his arm.

"I was wrong, though, wasn't I? You had already handled Granger beautifully, dazzling him with your words."

"Not *my* words," she spoke at last.

"Still, your sharp memory brought the right ones forward at the perfect time."

"I did feel as if they were coming from my brain," she admitted. "But I am terribly sorry to have provoked you to violence."

"Are you sorry I broke his nose?"

She didn't hesitate. "Of course not. He deserved it."

"Will you tell me to what he was referring?" He had a feeling she'd escaped something unpleasant in her previous Season.

He felt her lift a shoulder in a delicate gesture.

"I was caught unawares. I thought we were . . . ," she trailed off.

Jameson had reached the garden he knew well and, with a start, realized he'd only ever been there with Esmera. But it was beautiful and quiet, and there was a fountain which calmed one's disposition and soothed most troubles.

Someone had kindly put a stone bench where there hadn't been one before. He pulled her to sit beside him.

"You thought you were what?"

"Moving toward a relationship. He'd asked me to dance often, and by the end of the Season, started monopolizing my time. I had become comfortable in his presence, which was a mistake. I believed I understood his intentions. I let him kiss me once or twice, quickly, without his hands even touching me," she added.

It infuriated him knowing she'd been deceived, and calculatingly, too. Deeper than that, the new image in his brain of Granger kissing her mouth, especially when the cad had just disparaged it, made his blood boil with . . . *jealousy?*

"I suppose I should have known he wasn't seriously courting me when he let the weeks slip away until there were only a couple events left. Then he scared me," she admitted, and his hands tightened into fists again.

If he could go back in time to last year and encounter the rogue then—

"Nothing happened really, just a different type of kiss, one I didn't want, and then his hands were upon me. I don't think I wish to speak of it ever again except to say I managed to get away from him by myself then, too."

"How?"

She leaned her head against his shoulder, completely trusting him, making him feel unworthy. *Hadn't he'd taken liberties with her, too? Also, with no intention of offering for her hand?*

"I thought of something my mother had told me once. I was young, probably eight or nine, and asking about the differences between men and women." Unexpectedly, Maisie laughed softly. "I remember now—my questions were brought on by mention of a codpiece in one of the plays." She nodded to herself. "My mam gave me a general notion of what you . . ." She stopped and looked up at him, their gazes locking.

"I mean, of how men differ, and Mam said it hurt them to be hit there as they had parts that hang outside of the body. So, I brought my knee up and made hard contact with Granger's dangly bits. He doubled over and stepped back, and I ran away."

Jameson couldn't help laughing, and she joined in.

"Excellent work, Miss Darrow."

"You, too, Lord Turner."

"I really feel like plain Mr. Turner most of the time. And to you, I am Jameson, if you will allow it."

"I am happy to think of you as Jameson, and you may think of me as Maisie, but we dare not say the names aloud in company."

She raised her head then and looked around. It was dark except for the multitude of torches, as well as the lights shining out of nearly every window in the house. However, nestled in the garden, with walls of shrubs, he didn't think party guests could see them.

"How did you find this place?" she asked him.

He hesitated.

"You've been here before," Maisie surmised.

"I don't think I've ever lied to you. Yes, I used to come here with my wife. It reminded her of Spain. The flowers all around us are dahlias. The seeds for all these were given to the Dowager Lady Holland when she was in Madrid about fifty years ago. It was her husband's librarian who successfully grew the first ones. Naturally, there are more in England now, as Lady Holland created what they called 'dahlia mania,' at the time."

He recaleld how delighted Esmera had been when they'd first discovered this little paradise.

"We would come here sometimes simply to sit, although there was no bench. This is new." He gestured to the stone seat under them. "I liked the quiet, and she liked the flowers, but I had to stop her from picking them."

He chuckled at the forgotten memory.

"Have you come here since . . . since she passed?" Masie asked tentatively.

She probably believed he was like gunpowder, ready to explode with anger or grief at any moment.

"No, I didn't want to intrude on Lord and Lady Holland. Then when I realized the house was open tonight, I thought . . ."

"You thought you would punch a man in the nose and then share these gorgeous dahlias with your annoying friend."

"Something like that," he said, and couldn't help smiling at Maisie's ability to bring lightness to him where before everything had felt heavy.

In truth, he'd wondered if he could ever come back there alone. The notion of stepping into that garden without his own Spanish flower by his side had terrified him. He probably would have dissolved into abject sadness. Maisie made it bearable.

"I am glad you are here with me," he said, meaning it with all his heart.

"And I am glad you brought me. And honored. I wouldn't mind coming back here in the daylight and seeing the colors better."

"I will bring you. They are every color, just like roses—pink, red, and orange. Also, white and lilac. Yes, you must see them in the daylight. There is even a poem, which I think I can recall."

"Tell me," she ordered.

He looked up at the night sky and thought. *Yes, he remembered it.*

"The dahlia you brought to our isle
Your praises forever shall speak;
Mid gardens as sweet as your smile,
And in color as bright as your cheek."

Maisie clapped.

"Lord Holland wrote it for his wife," Jameson told her. And once before, he had recited it for his. Esmera had smiled and kissed him.

Now, he'd told it to Maisie, which suddenly seemed wrong. He couldn't recreate what he had with Esmera, and if he felt the need to tell Maisie a poem, it ought not to be about his dead wife's favorite flower.

Suddenly, he wished he had memorized some of Shakespeare's sonnets. Maisie probably knew them all. But they were all about love, weren't they? That wouldn't be appropriate, either.

"Shall we go back inside?" he asked, when all he really wanted to do was take her in his arms, feel her warmth and her heart beating soundly against his chest, and kiss her again.

He hadn't stood yet when she turned to face him. They were so close, her sweet face upturned to his.

Placing his hands on her slender shoulders, he paused, staring into her tawny eyes.

If he kissed her now, would he be any different from that cad Granger?

Jameson had no right to do so, simply because he wanted to, simply because she was exquisitely kissable.

Suddenly, noise bursting into the serenity of the dahlia garden had them both rising to their feet.

"Unhand my sister!"

CHAPTER SIXTEEN

Internally, Jameson took himself to task for letting his guard down, while, at the same time, he wanted to roll his eyes at the absurdity of the situation. This was a serious matter. He knew that, but it was also the second time Ned Darrow had found them and would, undoubtedly, try once again to force him into marriage with Maisie.

And for the second time, it was not going to work.

He had willingly and ecstatically rushed headlong into marriage with Esmera, knowing nothing could stop him from claiming his beloved. He would be damned if he was going to be coerced and manipulated into his next nuptials.

As long as it was merely Ned and his wife, Maisie would make them understand they were simply sitting in the garden admiring flowers. They wouldn't even mention the odious Granger and what brought them outside in the first place, in case it embarrassed her.

Casually, he and Maisie turned their heads toward the interlopers. At the same time, he released his hold on her upper arms. If only he hadn't been touching her, it wouldn't have looked so damning. Still, it was only his hands upon her. His lips hadn't been touching her. Yet.

Maisie gasped first as they saw the extent to which they'd been found out. Not only Mr. Darrow and his wife. Also, a group of other guests, as if they'd begun a search party. Loud tapping on the mullioned windows above drew his attention to the house, where, with the interior lighting, he could easily see people looking down at them from the second story, like a gallery of observers.

What on earth?

"Are you all right, dear?" Mrs. Darrow stepped forward.

"Yes!" Maisie said at once. "Why are you all here?"

"We've been looking everywhere for you," Eleanor explained, coming out from behind Ned. "There was blood on the floor in one of the drawing rooms," she added, "just like in a Gothic novel!"

"That was Lord Granger's blood," Maisie said, and a collective gasp rose from the crowd.

"He had a handkerchief clasped over his face," came a voice from the group, confirming her words.

"Lord Granger told someone who then told me that you had been abducted by violent force," Ned Darrow said, his hard glance landing on Jameson. "It appears he was correct."

"He lied," Maisie protested.

"Did Lord Turner strike him and then bring you outside alone?"

"Yes, but—"

"Then Lord Granger did not lie," Ned declared.

"He threatened your sister," Jameson said. "The man is dangerous."

"Yet *he* is the one with the bloody face," Ned pointed out. "Maisie, did Lord Granger touch you?"

Jameson knew she had been put in a bad position. She wouldn't want to bring up what had occurred the Season before, as most would condemn her for being alone with a man, especially when she'd been found alone with another tonight.

"Maisie told me Lord Granger had been rude to her earlier today, at the Palm House." These words came from Ned's wife.

"What?" Ned said with visible outrage, turning on his wife. "And you didn't tell me?"

Jameson felt the same way. *Why hadn't Maisie told him she'd encountered the rogue earlier that day?*

"Thus, perhaps Lord Turner was simply defending her honor," Mrs. Darrow said reasonably.

The throng of onlookers were hanging on every word and even murmuring comments with each bit of news they heard.

"I think we should go inside to continue this discussion and speak privately," Jameson said. "Or perhaps you wish to take Miss Darrow directly home."

"The best way to handle this, Lord Turner, is publicly," Maisie's brother insisted. "Nothing good ever came from secrets. Or from a man being alone with a woman."

Jameson glanced at Ned's wife, for it was a strange statement for a husband to make, to be sure. In his opinion, a lot of good happened when the right man and woman were alone.

"Taking my sister home so you can disappear like a snake in the grass," Mr. Darrow continued, "will accomplish nothing. Moreover, I fail to see how a man can defend a woman's honor by bringing her to a secluded place and laying hands on her."

The crowd murmured appreciatively, and Jameson feared someone would bring out chairs next and offer refreshments.

"Ned, I would very much like to go back inside," Maisie intervened. "It is early yet, and we've paid for the tickets," she reminded him.

Jameson nearly laughed at her appeal to her brother's bank account.

"We will go back inside and spend a celebratory evening," Ned agreed, "as soon as Lord Turner declares his intention to marry you if he has not already done so. For I cannot imagine why else he would bring you alone to a secluded place."

The man raised his tone as he spoke the last two words, and Jameson thought Ned Darrow had missed his calling—he should be an actor upon the stage.

"Ned!" Maisie implored, but the crowd was growing louder.

Jameson looked around him. The entire situation of his unintentionally compromising Maisie had exploded, becoming out of hand, and escaping his control. His inevitable, obligatory path was becoming clear. If he walked away from her now, news of her ruin would spread all over London by morning—for, without doubt, the uninteresting story of two people caught standing in a garden would be transformed into a scandalous tale of lovers being caught naked rolling in the dahlias.

He would be considered a despicable cad who, in front of everyone, destroyed her reputation so no man would ever offer for her unless that man wanted to be laughed at and considered a dupe.

And Maisie . . . her life as she knew it would end. Any existing invitations would be abruptly canceled, and no future ones would be forthcoming. All tickets to events of the Season would be revoked. She would be a pariah, whispered about and shunned.

Jameson obviously had no choice. Even if he didn't consider her a friend, which he did, even if he hadn't already saved her life, he couldn't leave her to the terrible fate the *ton* would gleefully dish out.

"Of course, I wish to marry Miss Darrow," Jameson said loudly. "She is femininity perfected. I admit, Lord Granger was also going to offer for her, at least, that was what I understood. My emotions overcame me, and I had to fight him for her. As the knights of old would say, I won the day *and* the lady!"

The onlookers cheered. Instead of ruin, Maisie had two suitors vying for her hand, which all but proved her innocence. There would be no stain attached to her name ever.

"I only regret I couldn't wait to determine if her affections lay with me. I know I should have spoken with you first before I asked her for her hand," he addressed Ned, who nodded as if he were wise King Solomon himself.

"And since I already declared my intention to her mere minutes ago, I would have shown up at your door to do the very same, first thing tomorrow morning."

Lying through his teeth was easier than he'd ever imagined, when it was for a good deed like saving Miss Darrow.

"Now we shall go inside and find some of Lord Holland's champagne," Ned Darrow said, appearing to warm to the patriarchal role, his only by default in the absence of their father.

Maisie's brother went so far as to clap Jameson on the shoulder, even though no mention had yet been made of sending a request to Maisie's father. Perhaps her brother really did have the final say. It would undoubtedly expedite matters of engagement.

Jameson swallowed. In absence of the elder Darrow, either approving or disapproving, it seemed he was now engaged to Miss Darrow. He glanced at Maisie, who had gone quiet. Her face had paled, too. Before he and his new, good chum Ned could take a step toward the path leading back to the house, she halted them with her words.

"Isn't anyone going to ask *me* if I wish to marry Lord Turner?"

MAISIE COULDN'T BELIEVE THE evening's events, neither the speed with which they had occurred, nor the serious turn they had taken. One minute, she and Jameson were discussing the colors of flowers, and now, they were all but engaged.

No, they were engaged.

Except no one had truly asked her.

And she knew Jameson Turner most assuredly did not want to marry her, or anyone. If she let this continue, it would not go well.

"What can you mean?" Ned asked, looking askance at those who still listened in on their family drama. "You would not have come outside and sat alone with Lord Turner if you didn't want to accept his proposal of marriage, which he has stated he made."

Dear Ned. Despite often being a thorn in her side, he was trying hard to protect her, or, at least, to protect the family name.

She couldn't thwart him by refuting Jameson's bold lie that he'd proposed, nor could she refuse him in front of witnesses. That would bring disgrace not only on herself, but also on her brother and even Caroline, who stood with Eleanor, seemingly fascinated.

She was not normally a hand-wringer, but she found herself doing precisely that. *Was there no escape?* Perhaps Jameson was relying on her to get them out of it as she had the previous instance when they'd been discovered alone.

"*Many a good hanging prevents a bad marriage.*" The words popped out of her mouth.

Looking startled, both Ned and Jameson stared at her. Eleanor's eyes widened, and Maisie could see her cousin was holding back laugher. But then she stepped forward to hold Maisie's hand for support.

"No one is going to be hanged," Eleanor said, "whether you marry or not."

Was she telling her this wasn't as serious as it felt?

"I mean," Maisie tried again, "some prefer death to marriage if the couple isn't really right for each other."

Her brother's mouth formed a harsh line of disapproval. Apparently, he thought this engagement was all done and dusted.

"Do you prefer death to marrying me?" Jameson asked, his tone neutral, while she could see apprehension in his eyes.

She gasped. "No, of course not. I was speaking *for* you."

"Unnecessary," he said with a shake of his head.

Most of the guests had wandered back indoors to the music and dancing, so Maisie tried again.

"For what is wedlock forced but a hell, an age of discord and continual strife?"

Even as Eleanor squeezed her hand encouragingly, Jameson sighed with exasperation.

"Miss Darrow, I have been to the gates of hell, and I am certain marriage to you will not be anything like it. As for discord and strife, I believe we can comport ourselves without either."

Stepping away from her brother, Jameson offered her his arm.

"Would you come inside now, so we can end this spectacle and have some champagne? I assure you Holland House will serve a decent glass of it."

Maisie felt trapped yet not the way Jameson must truly feel. He was putting on a good face, but she knew this was not what he wanted.

In front of Ned and Caroline, what could she do?

Releasing Eleanor's hand, she took Jameson's arm.

"You may do that," Ned said, indicating their touching, "but nothing more. And do not forget, you must not be alone together, either, until after the wedding."

Maisie wanted to dispute him, and she felt Jameson bristle at her side, but they both remained silent. There was no point in arguing with her brother. Better to simply arrange to go around his wishes, or even to ignore them outright.

Because one thing Maisie knew, she was going to speak to Jameson Turner alone and talk him out of this chivalrous nonsense. Her refrain about everything seeming better with jelly was blatantly not applicable. Not even thistle blossom jelly could fix this.

Already, she was thinking of a plan. After a little time had passed, no one would recall tonight's unfortunate farce. Then they could break off their engagement, and her reputation would be none the worse. As long as they weren't caught alone again. For then, she would be known as soiled goods, and finding a decent husband would be next to impossible.

In any case, with her mind and heart entirely taken by Jameson, she didn't want to search for another husband, decent or otherwise.

On the other hand, she would find it simply unbearable to be partnered for life with a man who was in love with his dead wife.

At that moment, his caring, amiable presence beside her reminded her of the love she wanted, not to mention children! She didn't even know if the marriage would be real.

Would he even take her to the marriage bed?

If he did, would it be awkward?

Back inside Holland House's Gilt Room, Maisie found herself the center of attention, which was particularly strange given that the beautiful Lady Margaret Cambrey was there as well. Eleanor's sister usually commanded any room she entered. However, not only did Maggie stay out of the limelight, she looked perfectly content to linger by her husband's side and raise a glass to toast the newly engaged.

Lord Cambrey had one arm around his wife's waist, his fingers caressing her through the layers of her gown and petticoats. Every once in a while, Maggie looked up at him at the same time as he looked down at her, and their love—as well as their blatant desire—took Maisie's breath away.

She wanted that!

Looking over at Jameson, who was listening to Ned drone on, probably about the intrinsic value of a woman with a small dowry and a penchant for spouting couplets, Maisie doubted she would see such a look from him.

She sipped the champagne someone had thrust into her hand and tried not to cry.

MAISIE AWAKENED WITH THE feeling something wasn't quite right, and then the memory of the previous night, which had lasted well into the early hours of the morning, overtook her.

She popped out of bed, only to stand in the middle of her moderately sized bedroom and dither. If she weren't now an engaged woman, she would be thinking about what gown to wear midday for a lunch Caroline had mentioned previously.

However, she was unsure of her status or her social commitments.

Was she released from the rest of the Season's events? Or was she supposed to go bask in the admiration and envy of those still hoping to make a match?

Maisie doubted Jameson wanted to escort her to a multitude of frivolous balls, soirees, and dinner parties. He was still in mourning and only went when . . . Lady Pepperton wanted him to.

Lady Pepperton!

Maisie groaned. She needed to speak alone to Eleanor and to Jameson, although probably she should speak to Jameson first. Unfortunately, she couldn't think how to do so without causing further damage. She needed her mother!

Since she couldn't have her, and since Caroline was more loyal to Ned than she could possibly be to Maisie, she decided to kill two birds with one stone by seeking out Eleanor and hoping to speak with Lady Anne Blackwood.

Her aunt had raised three daughters and seen two successfully married. Surely, kind Aunt Anne could give her some advice on how to proceed.

To that end, Maisie dressed in a demure day gown and, after snagging Rachel, the maid, as a companion, she headed over to the Lindsey townhouse where Jenny's mother and sister always stayed when in London.

Eleanor greeted her despite the lack of invitation. Soon, in the drawing room, with the maid seated at a distance with a cup of tea and some biscuits to bribe her into turning a deaf ear, Maisie had disclosed the truth about the awful events in the Yellow Drawing Room, and then the lack of proposal in the garden.

"He was manipulated into asking for my hand. Lord Turner does not want to marry me."

"But he has already kissed you upon occasion, and he took you into that secluded garden."

"We were discussing his wife!" Maisie pointed out. "Anyway, he had the opportunity to kiss me again and didn't take it. Thank goodness!"

She recalled being discovered by so many. "I would have been mortified if my brother saw me kissing anyone."

"Do you think Ned ever kisses Caroline? It's hard to imagine them in a truly passionate embrace."

Maisie stared hard at Eleanor until her friend blushed and smiled sheepishly.

"Sorry, I suppose imagining your brother in that capacity isn't something you wish to do."

"Definitely not." Maisie rolled her eyes. "I need to speak with Lord Turner alone, but how will I manage it?"

"Maybe I can help," came a voice from the doorway.

CHAPTER SEVENTEEN

Both Maisie and Eleanor turned their heads at the familiar voice.

"Maggie!" Eleanor greeted her. "I didn't know you were stopping by."

Lady Margaret Cambrey swept in, all sapphire-blue silk and pearls, breathtakingly lovely from head to toe.

Maisie smiled. "How do you do it, cousin?"

"How do I do what?" Maggie asked and took a seat next to her.

"Glow, shine—look positively radiant all the time."

Maggie laughed. "That's ridiculous. I look like everyone else when I wake up in the morning, before I begin my toilette."

"No," Eleanor said, "she doesn't. She wakes up with fairy dust sparkling in her eyes and her hair perfectly untangled."

Maggie sent them both a smile. Like everything else about her, it was dazzling.

"I didn't come here to talk about me. In truth, I hoped Eleanor was going to see you today, and I intended to come along. But here you are, which is lovely, because Jenny's cook makes the best buttery breakfast pastries." She turned to her youngest sister.

"Eleanor, order some of those and coffee, too, and we'll have a proper chin-wag."

In a short while, they were happily seated in the morning room having an impromptu snack.

"I wish Jenny were here, too," Eleanor said.

Maggie nodded. "She's either just had a baby, heavy with one, or about to deliver." She stirred her coffee, then tasted the hot brew. "Of course, Simon is nearly as handsome as my Cam, so I can see why they are in a constant state of reproduction."

Eleanor shook her head at her sister's irreverence, but Maisie considered the countess to be correct. Both Jenny and Maggie had married attractive men, although neither could hold a candle to Jameson, in her opinion.

"Anyway, let's get to the important topic, shall we?" Maggie stated, setting down her cup. "Our Miss Maisie is engaged to Lord Jameson Turner. The big question is, are you happy about it?"

Maisie hadn't thought about that. Certainly, no one else had asked her.

When she considered becoming Jameson's wife, she wanted to yell with amazement, and her primary emotion was, indeed, happiness. They had a way of making each other laugh, which she cherished. Moreover, she delighted in being near him, and his touch made her tingle.

More than anything, though, she wanted him to want her, too.

A marriage he didn't want could, in fact, be hellish.

"*Hm*," Maggie said. "A myriad of emotions crossed your face, dear coz. I'm sure the first was happiness, followed rather quickly by doubt. Now, you appear worried. Cam and I stayed indoors during your garden discovery and public engagement, and I tried to get others to come away from the windows, but to no avail. Tell me what's going on."

"The public spectacle of our engagement was nothing compared to yours," Maisie reminded her cousin. Lord Cambrey had gone down on bent knee in front of Queen Victoria, the Duchess of Sutherland, and most of the *ton* at a ball at Lancaster House two and a half years earlier to ask Maggie to become his countess.

"Even saying the word *engagement* makes me feel like a fraud," she continued. "Lord Turner is in mourning."

"It's been over a year," Eleanor pointed out.

"Time has nothing really do to with grief," Maisie reminded her. "Merely someone's artificial measure of how long a woman should wear black, that's all."

"I wonder who came up with it," Maggie mused. "Never mind, if he was in mourning, he wouldn't have taken you to a garden alone, would he?"

"His *wife* used to go there because of the dahlias," Maisie said, feeling morose. "Her favorite flower."

Her cousins remained quiet a moment, digesting this bit of information. Then Eleanor reminded her, "He has kissed you before."

"What?" Maggie said. "Do tell."

And so, Maisie went over her and Jameson's brief history, even the rescue from the River Don.

"It sounds to me as though he's interested in you. If you ask me, your first kiss caused him to leave Sheffield because he felt too much for you and wasn't ready. Now, he probably is."

"What of Lady Pepperton?" Maisie asked, her thoughts having flitted over the woman numerous times since the night before.

"What of her?" Maggie asked with a lift of her shoulder. "Everyone knows her type and what their relationship is, or rather, was. She was utilitarian at most. Healthy men—and women—have urges. We women have no recourse out of wedlock but to assist ourselves to physical release when frustrated, but men have ample opportunity to gain relief with the opposite sex. She could as easily have been an east-end tramp servicing him."

Maisie looked at Eleanor, who wore an expression undoubtedly mirroring her own shocked one. That Maggie would speak openly of self-stimulation and of prostitution awed her.

"I don't know what to say to any of that," Maisie declared, feeling out of her realm of knowledge.

Maggie chewed on a piece of pastry infused with strawberry jam. "You don't have to say anything," she mumbled, then swallowed. "I simply wouldn't worry about the widow if I were you. Undoubtedly, word has already reached her and, thus, she knows it is over. Or Lord Turner, being the decent sort he appears to be, has visited her to apprise her of the end of their arrangement."

"Even though I know he does not wish to marry—"

"You think you know," Maggie interrupted.

Maisie nodded. "While I believe he has no interest in being married, you think I should go through with it. Why?"

"If he makes you happy, and you say he does, then everything else will follow," Maggie assured her. "You are pretty and smart and kind. If he doesn't love you already, he will in time. There's no reason to think otherwise. And he has a good heart, first trying to help his father who, according to Jenny, never treated him well, then buying Jonling Hall, hoping to return it to his half brother. The way he stood up to Granger and then saved you from a badly tarnished reputation proves it further."

Maggie sipped her coffee again before adding, "Why, he's practically a saint. Along with all that, he has a thick head of hair, good height, and a rather fine physique, if I may say so."

"He has interesting eyes, too," Eleanor tossed in.

"I agree with all of that," Maisie said, "but his heart remains with his wife. What if he is never able to give it to me? Maggie, imagine if you'd married Lord Cambrey and loved him as you do, but he didn't return your affection, except with friendship. Wouldn't that be torture?"

Maggie sighed. "Yes, but there's no reason to believe Jameson Turner won't fall head over heels for you. A dead and buried wife is no match for a vibrantly alive one, no matter how strong their love was or how vivid his memories of her. You must make your own impression upon him and create new memories."

"And once you start bearing his children," Eleanor pointed out, "then you will become first in his regard."

"My dear sister," Maggie said, "I know you speak with sincerity and the best intentions, but you don't know of what you speak. My advice to Maisie is to secure Lord Turner's regard, in his heart and in his bed, *before* she gets in the family way. Many a man has sired a child upon a wife without loving her, and then gone off to seek his pleasure elsewhere. If he's not deeply in love with Maisie before she produces his heir, he may not be able to then separate the passionate woman you are from the mother figure."

Shaking her head, Maggie's glossy locks fell perfectly across her shoulder. "You must make him love you and desire you first, then when your children come, he won't be tempted to stray to a mistress."

Maisie's heart sank. "I feel as if I have a lot of work to do where regularly engaged people simply get to enjoy their wedding day and their honeymoon."

"You shall do both," Maggie promised, "and you'll find it worth it once you gain his utter adoration."

"You didn't have to work a minute with any man to be adored," Eleanor said to her sister.

"True, but John and I had our own tribulations to overcome. Everyone does. Again, I tell you, it's worth it."

"I would very much like to speak to Lord Turner alone, despite Ned saying I cannot."

"You must come to my townhouse tomorrow at two o'clock. That gives me time to get word to Lord Turner to come as well. I will not mention your name in anything written," Maggie said.

Turning to Eleanor, she asked, "Can you bring Maisie to afternoon tea without Mummy?"

"I shall certainly try, although I don't think Mummy would mind if she knew."

"Probably not, but she wouldn't want to be put in the position of lying to Ned and Caroline if asked."

They all nodded solemnly.

Then Maisie added, *"The day shall not be up so soon as I, to try the fair adventure of tomorrow."*

"That's the spirit," Eleanor agreed.

JAMESON WAITED UNTIL A civilized hour of the morning, one when it was considered beyond acceptable to go visiting, and then another hour longer. He wasn't looking forward to the unpleasant business of meeting with Elizabeth. In some regards, they had a loose arrangement. Notwithstanding, as it had been going on for two months of exclusivity, she should have been told of its ending by him, not by reading the morning papers—if it had even taken that long for the news to reach her.

At the very least, he should have spoken to her ahead of getting engaged. He would have, of course, if he'd known it was going to happen.

He was engaged.

Every time he thought of it, he waited for a wave of dread to crash over him. Instead, except for annoyance at being coerced by Ned Darrow, Jameson couldn't really dredge up any outrage or even true opposition to it.

If it had been anyone else, he might be in a blind fury at the sudden loss to his freedom and the public's new, incorrect perception he was over Esmera. He would no longer be considered a mourning widower but a happily engaged man looking forward to life with a new woman.

That seemed disrespectful and patently false.

Was he happily engaged? Because his fiancée was Maisie, he could imagine a future of easy conversations and laughter with her. So, he was not unhappily engaged.

But loving her the way he had Esmera? He didn't think it was possible to do that. He was already fond of Maisie, and kissing her had been a revelation of what desire could feel like again, his body reacting with surprising intensity, familiar but also new.

He hadn't felt anything like that with Elizabeth, nothing beyond feeling satisfied in a physical sense.

Sometimes, however, he'd felt lonelier afterward and sadder, longing to be back on Esmera's bed in Sheffield, alone with his memories.

And recently, the memory of first kissing Miss Darrow in the midst of the blossoming roses plagued the forefront of his brain. The last time he and Elizabeth enjoyed each other's bodies, he couldn't keep his mind off Maisie.

He should have ended it with his paramour then.

"I was expecting you," Elizabeth said as soon as she entered her drawing room after letting him wait for ten minutes, standing in contemplation. She took a seat and gestured for him to do the same—on the other sofa.

"I haven't been taken off guard in quite a while," she said. "You succeeded. You and your Miss Darrow."

He nearly said she's not *my* Miss Darrow when he realized she now was precisely that, and soon to be *his* Lady Turner.

"It's not that I didn't think it might happen," Elizabeth continued. "I'm not blind. I simply didn't think it would happen so quickly. You move fast when you find your first choice in a woman." She made sure to remind him of the words they'd used previously.

"I had no choice," he protested.

"Everyone always has a choice, Jameson."

He waved her words aside, knowing he would do the same again rather than leave Maisie to the wolves. Gossipmongers would have torn her apart, and she didn't deserve that.

"Your thoughts are already drifting," Elizabeth said. "You cannot keep your mind off her. What happened to right of first refusal or, at least, being courteous so I wasn't humiliated. You could have given me the chance to publicly break it off with you before you became engaged. You showed everyone I was simply your easily abandoned mistress after all."

Apparently, she had a very good memory.

"I am here to offer my sincere apologies. Miss Darrow and I were discovered in a compromising position."

The look on Elizabeth's face made him quickly amend his statement. "I mean, we were in a compromising *situation*, as in we were unchaperoned alone in a garden. Before I knew it, I was forced either to let Miss Darrow face ruin or become engaged to her."

He looked Elizabeth squarely in the eyes. "If there had been a way to keep it quiet until you had the opportunity to end our relationship first, I would have. It wasn't possible when all the guests at Holland House were witness to our indiscretion."

She stayed silent a moment.

"It is hard to blame you when you are being so chivalrous. Unfortunately, your chivalry is all for another woman, therefore I can at least be a little angry." She tilted her head. "And also, a bit sad knowing we have kissed for the last time."

"I don't want you to be sad. I don't want anyone to be sad, for that matter, especially not over me."

She stood, and he rose to his feet, as well.

"Don't worry," she assured him. "I won't go into a steady decline of melancholy. In fact, I am going to the theatre tonight with Lord Alder, so you must excuse me if I throw you out, but I have to find the perfect gown."

He smiled, relieved down to his toes. Except . . .

"Are you sure about Lord Alder? You know he's been called Lord Vile for good reason."

She cocked her head.

"Jealous?"

At that moment, he would lie to her. He owed her that. "Somewhat."

She smiled and looked radiant.

"I predict he and I will have an arrangement similar to ours, and it will last no more than half a year. That would be long enough with any man."

"What happened to you being bored as simply a widow?"

"I've changed my mind. The excitement over a new companion has reminded me how nice it is to be free to do what I want. The idea of having the same man in my life and in my bed for the rest of my years is frighteningly confining. During our attachment, I forgot how thrilling it is at the beginning of a relationship, and I intend to keep my liberty to have this same thrill whenever I want."

Actually, her words did sting a little—that she was so looking forward to starting up with a new man.

He took Elizabeth's hand, bent his head over it to kiss her fingers, and then he bid her goodbye. He hoped Alder would treat her well, but that was a gamble she was willing to take, and which no longer concerned him.

Next, Jameson stopped in at Crocky's, his old gambling haven, to while away a few hours and relax. He deserved it. Many of the men offered him their congratulations.

He waved these off at first because, while real, his engagement was also a sham. After a few more claps on the back or raised glasses, though, he started to accept them with a smile or a nod while lifting his glass in return. For deep down, he felt a sense of contentment marrying Miss Darrow.

Even if they weren't madly in love, even if he wasn't desperate to claim Maisie as his own—and remove her from the grasp of any other potential suitors the way he'd felt with Esmera—he was pleased to be saving her from ruin.

After all, he already knew he could be a considerate husband. But this time, he must do two things which he'd failed to do before—he must not give her his heart and soul, for doing so would open him to the terror of loss once again; and secondly, he must keep her safe.

That would be his main responsibility.

When he returned to his townhouse, there was a missive from the countess, Lady Margaret Cambrey, inviting him to her home on Cavendish Square.

"When did this arrive?" he asked Mr. Wynn.

"Just after you left for Lady Pemberton's home, my lord."

Still, it seemed short notice. He could think of no reason not to go the next day, and he was curious as to why Maisie's cousin wanted to speak with him.

Probably not simply to offer him her congratulations, he'd wager.

While he was particularly close to Simon and, thus, also friendly with Jenny and Eleanor who lived nearby, Maisie's other cousin, Lady Cambrey, rarely went to Sheffield, nor did Jameson travel in the Earl of Cambrey's circles in Town. That was reserved for inherited titles.

"Send a message round to accept, unless it's too late, in which case, it can wait until morning." He still wasn't certain how these things were done.

Mr. Wynn nodded. "I shall take care of it, my lord."

"You needn't call me that," he muttered.

Sighing, he had his butler pour him some brandy and then went into his study to write letters—to Simon, who would probably hear about his engagement by way of the Blackwoods anyway, and to his father, who would not give a damn.

Then, for want of anything else to do and unable to settle his thoughts, he searched his bookshelf for any Shakespeare, finally drawing out a thin tome of sonnets.

He felt more like reading one of those tragic plays in which everyone was slaughtered by the end, with bodies piling up like leaves in the autumn. They were so outrageous, they transported one completely, and without the complicated deceptions of women pretending to be men, everyone at cross-purposes, and the main characters falling in love with the wrong people as had happened in the one comedy he'd seen.

He took another look. No other work of Shakespeare was on his shelf.

Never mind, Jameson decided, he might even try memorizing a sonnet or two so he could impress Maisie next time.

After all, if Lord Roleston could make her eyes light with a quotation, he could, too.

Not that he wanted to light Maisie Darrow's lovely brown eyes.

Wasn't it enough he would make her his wife?"

CHAPTER EIGHTEEN

Maisie had never felt nervous about seeing Jameson Turner before. Since the previous year, her feelings for him had developed from wanting to help the man to simply wanting him.

And now, she felt a twinge of nerves at the thought of meeting with him, making her skip anything heavy for lunch. Besides, Maggie would undoubtedly set out tea and, at the least, sandwiches. It would be her first meal with him since the dinner party at Belton Manor the previous year. Then, like now, he didn't know she would be there.

While choosing the ideal gown, wanting to look fetching but also as if she were casual about looking her best, she rehearsed what she would say. Naturally, she would start with an apt quote. Perhaps *"hasty marriage seldom proveth well"* would illustrate her trepidation, particularly when the haste was entirely created by external forces and not by his overwhelming desire for her.

She decided on a dusky mauve, soft cotton gown with deeper-hued lace trim and gray cloth-covered buttons. She felt stylish in it, neither demure as a debutante, nor too flashy, either. Attractive, it was form-fitting over her curves but not revealing.

Maisie spun in front of her looking glass. Perfect for boosting one's confidence as long as she didn't spill anything down herself.

Hours later and unable to think of anything except seeing Jameson, she sat in the parlor, staring at nothing, her gloves and hat already on.

Unfortunately, Ned found her in her contemplative state.

"What are you doing?" he asked bluntly.

What was she doing? Trying to decide whether to graciously accept Jameson's marriage offer or talk him out of what was plainly a bad idea.

"I'm waiting for Eleanor. We're going to visit Maggie and have tea."

He hesitated. "Is Caroline going?"

"No." Maisie's stomach started to churn. *Was he going to make this most simple outing difficult?*

She could make insinuations that Caroline might be off who-knew-where doing who-knew-what to send Ned off on a wild goose chase, but she couldn't make her brother worry over his own wife.

"She has gone visiting with friends, I believe, but I'm not certain."

"Shall I accompany you to Lady Cambrey's?"

He insisted on calling their cousin by her title, which irked everyone. She'd always been plain Maggie before becoming a countess. Maybe Maisie could use it to her advantage.

"I don't believe it is wise to go uninvited to the Earl and Countess of Cambrey's home. It could be seen as vulgar."

"Vulgar!" Ned repeated, flaring his nostrils. "Very well, although I can't imagine why I would not be welcome amongst my cousins."

"I'm sure another time you will be." She heard a carriage draw up outside their modest home and stood up.

"That must be Eleanor."

Snatching up her lightweight mantle and reticule, she was at the door in a flash. Their manservant, always a few steps behind, missed opening it before she yanked it inward and strode outside. To her dismay, Ned followed her.

One of the Lindsey footman had lowered the folding step and held the carriage door open. Ned came all the way to the barouche to peer under the leather roof. Eleanor smiled at him.

"Good day, Uncle Ned." She had always called him such due to the difference in their ages.

"Good day, Eleanor. Where are you off to today?"

Maisie rolled her eyes at his attempt to catch her in a lie.

"To my sister's," Eleanor said at once. "I thought Maisie would have told you."

He simply nodded. "No chaperone?"

"Dear brother," Maisie stepped in, "I know you think we women are a frail and fragile lot, but even you cannot believe we need someone to watch over us at Maggie's home. And we have a driver and a footman, both wearing the Lindsey livery, to get us there safely."

"Very well," he said, stepping back and letting the footman assist her into her seat.

"Aren't you going to wish us a merry time, uncle?"

"No, just behave yourselves," he said and retreated behind the front door.

"My brother is a strange man," Maisie said. "For a moment, I believed he was going to try to go with us, and then we would have had to call it off entirely."

"Maggie would have taken care of him," Eleanor said.

Maisie loved how her cousins helped each other and, in turn, treated her as the fourth sister. She would be lost without them.

"Now, let's just hope your fiancé comes."

Maisie swallowed. The word seemed unreal, as did her situation.

When they passed the recently relocated Marble Arch, and took a right onto Bond Street, Maisie knew they were only minutes away.

"Strange to see the arch standing there, isn't it?" Eleanor remarked, as it had always stood before the *cour d'honneur* of Buckingham Palace.

"It makes for a grand entrance to the park," Maisie agreed, "and I'm glad they scrubbed the marble clean."

"That won't last long," Eleanor said. Then a moment later, she added, "They say policeman use it as an outpost?" She even craned her neck to look back at it. "Imagine, there are policeman hiding inside there right now. With no windows!"

But Maisie had stopped listening, her stomach doing flips of nervousness as Cavendish Square came into view a few minutes later.

"Don't worry," Eleanor said, sensing her withdrawal. "It's only Simon's cousin. Think of him like that."

Only Simon's cousin, she repeated silently. *Her fiancé.*

Maisie was still trying to quell her nerves as they entered Maggie's blue and white drawing room. They were earlier than the appointed time for Jameson to show up, giving the Lindsey carriage a chance to go around back to the mews.

While they were getting settled, Lord Cambrey, having come home midday from Parliament, entered and gave them each a friendly wave and nod, shooting them his famously charming, crooked grin.

"Don't try your charms on my sister and cousin," Maggie said, before he swept her into an embrace.

"I wouldn't think of it." He looked down at her and she, up at him, and Maisie thought they were going to kiss.

Instead, with eyes only for his wife, he said, "I have to go out again. There's an important bill coming up through the house. I sent word to Simon. I am sure he'll be in Town soon."

"Meanwhile, you will keep everything held together in the House of Lords," she said, giving him her dazzling smile.

He groaned. "I love you."

"I love you, too."

And then positive she and Eleanor had been forgotten, Maisie watched the earl lower his head and kiss her cousin, who seemed to melt into his embrace.

Maisie's skin became a little prickly, watching this intimacy, but she was too fascinated at seeing such a display to consider looking away.

"Oh, for goodness sake," Eleanor said after a few moments, and tossed a small, satin pillow at the couple. It bounced off Lord Cambrey's head, and they at last broke apart.

"I'll forgive you for that," he said to his sister-in-law, "only because I truly must leave now."

Maggie touched a hand to his cheek, and they shared another glance before he released her, nodded at his guests, and left the room.

That was when Maisie heard him greet Jameson Turner.

Her fiancé had arrived.

"Go right on in," they all heard Cam say. "The ladies await you."

Maggie exchanged glances with both of them as they stood, and Maisie cringed, especially when she heard him repeat, "The ladies?"

Then Jameson was at the door, eyebrows lifted.

"I have been waylaid before," he declared, "but never by three such beautiful ambushers."

He greeted Maggie first, taking her hand and bowing over it. "Thank you for inviting me, Countess."

"The pleasure is mine," she insisted.

Then he turned to Maisie and Eleanor, greeting each in turn without taking their hands. Maisie breathed a sigh of relief, glad it hadn't become odd and formal between them.

"May I ask what's going on?"

"Our dear cousin needed to speak with you alone, Lord Turner," Maggie told him. "Eleanor and I were happy to facilitate such a meeting."

Jameson turned to Maisie. "I suppose your brother wouldn't be happy if he knew."

"You suppose correctly. And if my sister-in-law knew, she would probably feel it her duty to tell him."

He nodded. "Rightly so." Then looking questioningly from Maisie to Eleanor to Maggie and back again, he asked, "How do we begin?"

"I think you two may stay in here, and my sister and I shall take a few turns around the square in front." Maggie went to the door and Eleanor followed. "We have much to catch up on, and then, if everyone is amenable, given the hour, I have a light luncheon prepared."

Just like that, the door clicked closed behind her cousins, and by Maggie's command, Maisie was finally alone with Jameson.

"Do you think your brother and his wife wish to make the formal announcements, the banns and all that, or shall I go ahead?" Jameson asked. "And what of a date? I don't think we need an overly long engagement, nor should we seem in too much of a hurry. Perhaps four months. But I would have called on you soon and spoken with your brother about all this. I assume your father will be in agreement to whatever Mr. Darrow arranges, or is there a trip to Dumfries in my future?"

Maisie found herself speechless. His words were buzzing in her brain like incomprehensible bluebottle flies.

"Are you all right?" he asked, gesturing for her to sit. When she sank back onto the sofa, he sat beside her.

"I am amenable to any arrangements your family wishes," he continued.

She took a long breath. "Will you please stop?"

His mouth snapped closed on whatever his next words were going to be, probably already deciding upon food for their wedding meal.

"The last thing we said in private," Maisie pointed out, "was how we would go back to the gardens at Holland House to see the colors of the flowers. Hardly a precursor to marriage. And yet, you're behaving as if we were already on the path to matrimony, and it simply got sped up a bit by our being discovered."

He crossed his arms over his broad chest but said nothing more.

"Well?" she persisted.

"I don't know what you want me to say. There's no use crying over spilt milk, as they say."

"Unless it is Macbeth's *milk of human kindness,* which apparently you are overflowing with. However, I cannot let you marry me. You are being incredibly congenial, but the sacrifice is too large."

He sighed. "I don't see it that way at all. In fact, to be honest, while I wouldn't have done so if not cornered, I do not mind marrying you."

She put her head back on the sofa and closed her eyes. *He didn't mind marrying her.* The way one didn't mind choosing raspberry sponge over strawberry sponge or buying a new pair of shoes.

This was not the relationship she wanted with a husband, nor had it ever been her aim when first pestering him. *Did he know that?*

"When I visited Jonling Hall, I went only to cheer you up, or try to, anyway. It was not with Shakespeare's famous words in mind—*Thou art sad; get thee a wife, get thee a wife!*"

"Famous?" he questioned, sounding confounded. "What play is that from?"

Maisie didn't open her eyes. "*Much Ado About Nothing.* That's not important. What matters to me is Ned is taking advantage of your good nature, and I find it unconscionable."

"I think we are in too deep to worry about that now." Jameson did not sound as bothered as she felt.

"But you understand I did not set out to trap you, don't you? I didn't think to myself, there's a grieving widower. I think I shall snag him for my husband."

When he remained silent, she opened her eyes to see him apparently fighting back laughter.

"How is this amusing?" she asked, giving him her most serious and earnest expression.

"It's not," he agreed. "I never considered you were attempting to trap me."

That was a relief. "As long as we're clear about that," she said. "But you are being trapped nonetheless. And what about Lady Pepperton?"

Oh, dear. She hadn't meant to bring up his paramour. It had slipped out. His expression now mirrored the severity of her own.

"I've spoken with her, and I will never see her again, except in public. And I don't wish to talk about her anymore."

Maisie considered this a moment. He sounded utterly dispassionate when he mentioned her. *How could that be?*

"So, you broke it off with her, and she was perfectly fine with our engagement? No tears or recriminations?"

Jameson sighed. "Your questions make it difficult *not* to talk about her anymore as I just stated."

Yet, she wanted to ask more, particularly how he could break off with someone so easily. *Could Maggie have been correct, and Elizabeth was no more to him than an east-end tramp?*

"Then your arrangement with Lady Pepperton was strictly utilitarian?"

He leaned forward, as close to her as he had got since he'd entered the room.

"If I answer this one question, will you stop asking about her? Because I promise you, she has no bearing on our future."

"All right." Her voice didn't sound like her own, but rather an emotion-clogged croak.

"Yes," he said. "As ugly as that sounds, our arrangement was utilitarian. Having said that, I found her companionship pleasant."

"Thus, you *did* like her as a person?"

He threw his hands up in the air. "One question was all I had to answer," he muttered as if speaking to the wall opposite.

Then he turned to her again, and his blue-gray gaze locked with hers. "It is similar to how you don't mind speaking to someone at a party because otherwise you would be standing there alone."

"But you were doing much more than speaking," she couldn't help mentioning.

Maisie thought she heard him growl deep in his throat.

"All right," she gave in. "I don't want to hear any more about her anyway, as long as I can be assured she isn't going to come after me in a jealous rage."

"I can assure you she is not. Besides," he added, "she will be out at the theatre tonight with her new beau."

"Gracious!" *That was fast!* But she didn't say such a thing in case his feelings actually were hurt.

"Indeed," he agreed with her unspoken words. "Isn't there a line from Shakespeare about the speed with which someone moves on after the end of a relationship?"

Maisie mused on this. "Juliet said it well. '*O, swear not by the moon, the inconstant moon, that monthly changes in her circle orb, lest that thy love prove likewise variable.*'"

He grimaced. "Not exactly accurate, as Lady Pepperton was *not* my Juliet, and I was certainly *not* her Romeo."

Maisie felt a blade of relief slice through her. She might have to deal with the ever-present specter of Esmera Turner, but not the living Elizabeth Pepperton.

"I didn't want to speak to you about her anyway today," she confessed.

"No? Yet we have spent precious minutes doing precisely that."

She ignored his rejoinder. "I wanted to tell you, I have a plan to get us out of this farce."

His eyes widened briefly, then he sat back and crossed his arms again. "You have a plan?"

"Yes, I do. We shall remain engaged for a good while, and when no one remembers why you were forced to propose to me, then we shall break it off."

"Impossible," he said at once.

"Why?"

"If I break it off, then I'm behaving like the bastard I was born as, and which I'm sure many still call me behind my back. Leading you on and then breaking a marriage contract will make me a pariah. I might as well show up at Buckingham Palace with leprosy for the welcome I'll receive anywhere in London."

"I can't believe you care that much."

He shrugged. "Even if I didn't, there's Simon and Jenny. I do care what they think of me, and if they believe I've hurt you, then my own cousin will cut me out of his life. Unlike you, I've got very little family."

"We could always tell them the truth," she reminded him.

Jameson shook his head. "If one person knows, everyone will know. Any card player understands that."

"Then I shall be the one to break it off with you. I am positive you won't mind being the sympathetic figure."

He cocked his head at her, which she deemed quite charming.

"Possibly. But you will need to have a good reason. Another man, perhaps. You cannot simply change your mind, or you will not find another man in all of Britain who offers for you again. But we can keep your plan in mind, if you like. It has merit."

Abruptly, he took her hand, which distracted her and caused her pulse to race.

"Why don't you tell me why you are so desperate to save me from this terrible entrapment?"

His thumb brushed over the bare skin at her wrist, where her glove ended.

She could think of nothing except being Jameson's wife and having him stroke her wrist forever.

"Very well," she said after a few moments. *"Hasty marriage seldom proveth well."*

She couldn't tell him her real worry—that a second marriage, particularly a forced one, would never result in love. Shakespeare said, *"The instances that second marriage move are base respects of thrift, but none of love."*

Not that she thought Jameson was marrying her for anything to do with money, but she knew he wasn't doing it for love.

She supposed as long as she could break it off when she was ready, she could let the sham of an engagement continue for a few months.

"Then we shall draw out the engagement to five months," he agreed. "That's really the entire Season. Do you want to stay in London?"

Frankly, she would rather be in Sheffield, or Dumfries for that matter, where things were not so complicated, and her brother didn't watch her every move. However, Esmera had vanquished the *ton* and been the darling of every host and hostess. Not only had it reflected well on Jameson, he'd loved and admired the Spanish beauty for her social graces.

Maisie would at least try to be a fiancée he could be proud of.

"Yes, of course," she said. "After all, it is the greatest city on earth. Why would we ever want to leave?"

Jameson abruptly stopped caressing her skin, and she keenly felt the loss of his touch.

And then he stood up.

CHAPTER NINETEEN

Her words sent a shiver of disappointment running through Jameson. Naturally, Maisie Darrow had fit perfectly well into every venue at which he'd encountered her. She had always appeared as a golden flame of beauty, all blonde and bright, a capable dancer and good conversationalist.

However, she hadn't seemed to him as though she truly gave a fig about the Season. He had imagined coming to London, while enjoyable for her, was merely a means to an end—to secure a husband so she could stop the madness of continuous social events.

He'd guessed she felt similarly to Eleanor Blackwood, who'd said she preferred the air outside of London and, certainly, the night sky.

Sadly, he had guessed incorrectly.

"In fact," Maisie continued as he started to pace the exquisitely decorated Cambrey parlor, "it will be the best Season ever because I won't have to worry about impressing my peers or dancing with strangers. I'll have you."

He nodded, although it brought back a painful memory of Esmera saying something similar. Once they were engaged, she'd said he was her ticket to freedom, no more dance cards or demure pastel-colored gowns. As if a fiancé were merely a useful accessory.

A feeling of unease about marrying Maisie settled over him for the first time. That, in itself, should surprise him. While he'd lain awake in the morning hours after Holland House and begged Esmera to forgive him his betrayal, he'd felt a sense of peace and accepted the fact he was on the right path, feeling satisfied he could offer Maisie his protection.

She seemed like someone who especially needed it.

Facing her, he studied her pensive face. It was a face he wouldn't mind looking at the rest of his life, if he could remove the worry lines currently etching her forehead.

"Is something wrong?" she asked before he could do the same.

"How does a caterpillar improve in morals?"

"I beg your pardon?" She looked confused for a moment, and then she smiled, her frown fading. "A joke, yes?"

"Yes. Do you know?"

She considered, and he assumed she might know the answer but kindly wanted to let him say it. She shook her head.

"He turns over a new leaf."

She laughed, but barely.

"You did know it," he accused.

"Perhaps."

He tried again. "The cabbie has the only business in which you can drive your customers away and keep them, too."

This time, her spontaneous laugh came out as a snort. It was enchanting. He came back to her and offered her his hand. She stood beside him.

"If we ever get too serious, I'll tell you a joke," he promised.

"All right. I would like that."

"I will send a formal announcement to the newspapers."

She nodded her agreement, blinking those lovely eyes.

"My dog," he blurted when a notion came to him.

"What?" she asked, obviously startled. "Another joke?"

He put his hand on her chin and raised her face to his so he could look more closely.

"I only just realized who your eyes remind me of."

She attempted to bat his hand away. "A dog? I remind you of a dog?"

He smiled, and her gaze went to his mouth, disconcerting him.

"Not just any dog, and only your eyes. Your gorgeous, rich, gold-brown eyes. They remind me of my childhood collie, my constant companion when I was growing up."

"What was its name?" she asked, her gaze returning to his.

"You're going to like it."

"Am I?" Those very eyes they were discussing sparkled up at him with merriment.

"Will," he told her.

"Will! For William Shakespeare?" She clapped her hands.

He laughed. "No, for *will* you stop barking?' and *will* you stop chewing my shoes?' He was trouble, my mother said from the time he was a puppy, but I adored him."

At that moment, he could easily imagine adoring Maisie, too.

Leaning close, he claimed her mouth under his. The sensation didn't disappoint him. Her lips were as soft and warm as he'd remembered. When she parted them for him, he released her chin and swept both his arms around her to hold her close.

He felt her hands creep up his chest and lace behind his neck. There was something sweet and trusting about the way she did so. Yes, it was enticing, and his body reacted instantly to the taste and scent and feel of her.

However, kissing and holding her was also deeply comforting. His spirits soared as he explored her mouth, and their breathing became as one.

She was like a balm to every miserable musing that liked to flit through his mind unbidden. In fact, when he was with her, she staved off the descent into misery which often occurred in his quiet moments. That was when he replayed his last words to Esmera, or imagined her final terrifying moments.

Perhaps Maisie would be the one saving *him* from ruin and not the other way around.

There was a tap at the drawing room door, and he stepped back quickly, causing her arms to drop away from him. When it opened after a polite moment's delay to reveal a maid, they were three feet apart, looking composed, although he could see a distinct difference in the color of Maisie's mouth from before he kissed it. Her sweet lips had reddened and looked plumper.

How could that be?

"My lady requests you in the dining room," the girl said before retreating.

Just when things were getting interesting, too. He should have taken hold of her and kissed her the moment they were alone.

"We have run out of private time, it seems."

Maisie nodded, still staring at him.

"Is something amiss?" he asked her.

"When you kiss me, my worries seem to disappear."

He took her hand and tucked it under his arm. "I feel the same way, Miss Darrow. Do you know the way to the dining room?"

"Yes."

"Then direct me, and we shall see what your cousins have in store for us next."

"*Lay on, Macduff,*" she said, "*and damned be him that first cries, 'Hold, enough!'*"

"It won't be me to cry hold," he told her. He was determined to see this through all the way to marriage.

"Nor I, Lord Turner."

Saucy minx.

MAGGIE AND ELEANOR WERE discussing something to do with the River Great Ouse that ran through the earl and countess's country home in Bedfordshire. Something about fishing, but Maisie's mind had wandered while watching Jameson. The same had happened through the leek soup course and the ham sandwiches on thinly sliced bread served with cheddar and piccalilli. Nothing too fancy but everything quite delicious.

She hadn't managed to talk him out of marrying her, yet he hadn't entirely discounted her plan to call off the engagement after a few months if it could be done without recriminations. He seemed to think she would need to fancy another man for that to appear realistic. She would never desire another man.

When they touched, and when he kissed her, it was perfect. Yet she knew he could do such things with a woman and not have his heart engaged. To him, she might be as utilitarian—a word she was growing to detest—as Lady Pepperton.

Even in the marital bed, he might perform the sexual act with her and feel no more than he had with his paramour. Maisie would never know the difference. Except she knew he had desperately loved Esmera. Their marriage had been entirely real.

"You sighed loudly, Maisie."

Maggie's voice interrupted her thoughts. When she blinked and came out of her reverie, she realized she'd been caught staring at Jameson while he sipped tea and polished off a piece of vanilla sponge drizzled with lemon icing. Three pairs of eyes were upon her.

She felt her cheeks start to heat up.

"Would you like a piece of cake?" Maggie offered.

"It's delicious," Jameson said. "I was about to ask for another. I think mine was on the small side."

Eleanor smiled. "I think you had the largest slice, my lord."

They all laughed, and Maisie was pleased at how easily he conversed with her cousins. Ned was awkward in most social situations, forcing Caroline to verbally tidy up after him.

In truth, Jameson would be the ideal husband, except he'd already been that for someone else. For her, he would be simply a *pretend* husband.

To keep from ruminating on that depressing notion, Maisie helped herself to a piece of cake and devoured it in silence.

"Will you be escorting Maisie to the Parkland ball in two nights?" Maggie asked, filling in the silence.

Instead of answering, Jameson looked at her, one eyebrow raised, questioning.

Their first appearance as an engaged couple. All eyes would be upon them. People would easily detect if theirs was a union of affection, or something else entirely. They'd all seen the arranged marriages in which both parties had walked into a business arrangement willingly for title or money. No one frowned upon such a thing, but some—women, mostly—considered it a pity.

Rather a waste of two hearts which might be happier elsewhere.

Far worse was an arrangement when only one of those involved was a willing participant. The other—again women, mostly—had been forced into it by parents or guardians.

Maisie shuddered. This could be so much worse. She might have been caught in the Yellow Drawing Room with

Granger. Her brother would have tried to get her to marry such a man, and then Granger would have loudly told everyone about his bias against the Scots.

She was lucky indeed.

"I hope you will be my escort for the Parkland ball," she said to Jameson. "Nothing would please me more. I shall have to go with Ned and Caroline, of course, but once I arrive, I will reserve all my dances for you."

"I would pick you up at your home if it were allowed," he told her.

"I suppose at some point we will be allowed in the same carriage if Ned is with us, or maybe even Caroline, but I don't think my brother will consider Eleanor to be an adequate chaperone."

If she got to spend any time alone with Jameson except on the dance floor, Maisie would consider herself fortunate indeed.

"A FALL WEDDING," CAROLINE said over breakfast two mornings later. "That's a grand idea."

"Depends on where it is held," Ned retorted, despite Maisie's sister-in-law having been speaking to her and not to him upon seeing the announcement in the paper.

"It looks very fine in print," Caroline continued, "Lord Jameson Carlyle Turner to marry Miss Maisie Marion Darrow."

"He's barely a viscount," Ned sniffed, "but I'm satisfied I've done the best I can for you." He fixed her with a stare. "Let's not mess it up, sister. If he doesn't like Shakespeare, don't chase him away. I sent word directly to Father a few days ago. We shall try to get him to your wedding when the time comes. I was surprised at the length of the engagement, frankly. Gives Turner too much time to back out of it."

"He wouldn't do that," Maisie said. "It's more likely I will be the one to—" she closed her mouth abruptly.

What on earth was she thinking?

"One to what?" Ned asked sharply.

"To become skittish." That sounded realistic. Better than disclosing she would be the one to break the contract if the falsity of their relationship became too burdensome and torturous for her.

"You? Skittish?" Caroline said. "I don't think you will be, dear."

"She had better not," Ned said. "We're selling that crumbling old place in Dumfries. Then where will you live when you're not with our cousins or with me?"

This was the first Maisie had heard of it. "Where is Dad going to live?"

"Hopefully, with you," Ned said.

"What? Why didn't anyone tell me? Are you saying Dad will come live with me and Jameson as newlyweds? He hates London."

"Not in London, silly girl," Ned scoffed. "He'll want to move into Jonling Hall with you."

"Why wouldn't he live with you and Caroline?" Her brother and his wife had a tidy house south of Dumfries on the River Nith, barely twenty minutes for their family home.

Ned pushed his chair away and stood up. "You have no say in it." And he left the room.

"I don't understand," she said to Caroline.

"I'm sorry, but your father doesn't want to live with Ned and me. I think they are too peas in a pod, but you can't have two men like that under one roof. Hopefully, your husband will be amenable."

"And if not?"

Maisie loved her father, but he had never been overly demonstrative in his love for either one of his children. He had let their mother do all the nurturing. And after her death, he had become an even more prickly individual, spending all his time in his brewing hut, leaving Maisie to Ned's watchful eye and leaving Ned up to his own devices.

She could no more imagine her father wanting to up and move to Sheffield and sit across from her each evening as a guest in her home than she could envision inviting the Prince Consort to tea. Nor could she expect her father to be happy living in England.

"Is Dad pleased to sell his house and to move?"

Caroline shook her head. "I do not believe Ned has asked your father's opinion on any of it. Yet."

Oh, dear! Ned was overstepping, like the time he bought a herd of sheep, and her father had ordered him to sell them back, humiliating her brother. Or when he tried to plant hops in their lower acreage, wanting to please their brewer-of-a-father. Instead, Fintan Darrow had laughed at his only son, calling him a farmer.

"The Darrows aren't farmers, boy," he'd said to Ned, although her brother was well into early manhood by then.

Maisie wasn't sure what the Darrows were, and only knew her surname meant something about an oak tree. Before her father stopped doing anything much except brewing, fishing, and drinking, he'd been a sergeant in the British Army and fought in the east in the Emirate of Afghanistan. He refused to speak of it even when, as a young girl, she'd discovered some of his weapons and asked him.

What Ned was to make of such a legacy, she couldn't imagine, but her brother had made his way in the world as best he could. In truth, she wasn't too sure what he did all day.

"I will certainly ask Lord Turner his opinion of the matter," Maisie promised, despite thinking she wasn't in a position to push her father upon a man who, likely as not, would be far happier if he'd never taken her into his precious dahlia garden.

Many hours later, dressed not in one of Jenny's gowns but in her own best new gown as a newly engaged woman, all thoughts of her father fled when Maisie entered the Parkland ballroom. Not as grand as either Apsley or Holland House, still it was an admired venue and would be well-attended. Most importantly, she would be with her fiancé.

Going through the receiving line, her neck craning to catch a glimpse of Jameson, she curtsied low when she reached the gracious duke whose wife had passed away only the year before, and who now put on the event with his sister by his side. They were both in their eighties, and she could only wonder at their stamina for still entertaining during a Season at such an advanced age.

Ned and Caroline were behind her, and she hoped many years from then, she and her brother would still be close.

Since the Earl and Countess of Cambrey were already there, and Maggie was inadvertently holding court, it was easy to find Eleanor, who preferred to stay close to her middle sister rather than wander off to speak with strangers. As soon as Eleanor saw her, they grabbed hands.

"Is he here yet? Have you seen him?" Maisie asked.

"I haven't seen hide nor hair, I am sorry to say."

"Never mind. I didn't take a card. Look." And she held up her arm with only a sheer organza glove but no dangling ribbon and dance card.

Eleanor sighed and held up her own hand. "I did. And two gentlemen so far have written their names. It was convenient having Maggie here, so they could introduce themselves to her and John, and then be properly introduced to me."

"Do you fancy either one?"

Her cousin shrugged. "Too soon to tell. They weren't repulsive. That's all I can say."

Just then, a tap on her shoulder had her spinning around to see . . . Lord Roleston.

"Oh," she said, surprised at the depth of her disappointment.

"Good evening, Miss Darrow. Miss Blackwood."

Maisie had recovered her manners, and both she and Eleanor curtsied.

"May I have a dance?" he asked Maisie. "I promise I won't do anything outrageous like take half of them."

"You won't take any of them." Jameson was suddenly at her side.

Lord Roleston frowned. "What the deuce, Turner? Can't a man have his turn?"

Jameson took her hand and rested it on his arm. "Not with my fiancée, he can't. Or hadn't you heard?"

"Heard? I've been out of the country since we met at Apsley House. Not so long ago as all that. Are you saying you and Miss Darrow are engaged?"

"I am." Jameson sounded rather pleased with himself, which imbued Maisie with contentment.

"Is he teasing me?" Lord Roleston addressed her directly.

"He is not, my lord. And if my fiancé does not wish me to dance with anyone else during our engagement, I am happy to honor his wishes."

"I have some space," Eleanor chimed in, perhaps to save the viscount from embarrassment.

"Of course," Lord Roleston said. "I was about to ask you next."

After he hastily scrawled his name on her card, he congratulated Maisie and Jameson before bowing and disappearing into the crowd.

"I was only five minutes late and already having to fend off my rivals."

He looked dashingly handsome in his black suit, starched white shirt, and lavender ascot with matching gloves.

"There aren't too many, my lord. I don't think it will be a full-time chore."

"I am positive, Miss Darrow, you have many more admirers than you've even noticed. The color of your hair alone makes you stand out like a glowing beacon. No offense, Miss Blackwood."

"None taken," Eleanor said. "It is simply a fact of nature that while we have a goodly number of blondes and lighter brunettes in England, people with Maisie's flaxen pigment—or is it the lack of pigment—are rare."

"There you are, Turner," boomed the Duke of Parkland, overly loudly due to being notoriously hard of hearing. He had cut a swath through his guests to reach Jameson, but now that he'd reached him, he looked past him.

"Where is she? I've been looking forward to seeing your lovely wife."

Maisie could feel Jameson's arm turn to stone under her hand, even as those close enough to hear quietly gasped.

CHAPTER TWENTY

It was not an auspicious beginning to their first social appearance as a couple. Maisie knew it was not done maliciously, but it was the worst possible time for the old duke to blunder.

Jameson drew away from her to give the duke his full attention. Everyone fell silent around them. Even Maggie and her husband were watching, as those around them turned to view the spectacle.

Maisie wished there was something she could do. At that moment, she wished she could become Esmera simply to ease Jameson's pain. However, she could only stand uselessly by his side, not the woman their host wanted to see and certainly not the woman Jameson wanted.

"My wife died last year," Jameson said succinctly, and the Duke of Parkland's face crumpled in shock.

"No!" he protested. "Last year? Did I know this? I'm so sorry, my boy. Such an extraordinary lady. I will never forget dancing with her."

"She enjoyed dancing with you, as well, Your Grace."

"We talked long that night. Do you remember? I spent a good deal of my younger years in Spain. Beautiful country.

Beautiful woman, your wife." His gaze wandered over Maisie, plainly found her appearance lacking in anything remarkable, and then went back to Jameson.

Maisie only hoped the duke didn't ask how she had died, for it was rather gruesome, more so than slipping away from influenza or cholera.

"I recently lost my wife, too," the older man continued. "We had sixty years, but it wasn't enough. You understand?"

"Yes," Jameson sounded choked. "I do."

Maisie felt helpless.

Jameson said nothing more, and the duke stared at him, obviously still digesting the information of Esmera's untimely demise.

"I made sure to have Spanish wine on hand for her tonight."

Jameson groaned, and Maisie could stay silent no longer.

"Your Grace, it is wonderful you recall the late Lady Turner, as we all recall the generous nature of your Lady Parkland. Perhaps we can take comfort in the following thought: *Death makes no conquest of either woman. For now they live in fame, though not in life.*"

Both men looked at her. Jameson's pallor was a little gray. The duke seemed thoughtful, however, and then he nodded.

"This young lady speaks the truth," he said loudly.

"Oh, it's not really me, Your Grace," she protested. "It's Shakespeare."

"Either way, good words, well said."

His sister approached him and whispered something in his ear.

"I take my leave of you both," he said.

Maisie dropped into a low curtsey, and Jameson bowed.

The duke nodded to each of them before taking his sister's arm. As they walked between the gathered guests, his rumbling voice came back to them, "Turner's wife is dead, too. Can you believe it?"

"Would you like to get some air?" Maisie asked immediately.

Jameson nodded and walked stiffly toward the room's doorway. He hadn't taken her arm or even invited her along, and Ned would insist on the propriety of a chaperone if she went with him.

Looking at his retreating figure, her heart ached. *Was there anything she could do to help?*

To Eleanor, she said, "If Ned comes looking for me . . ." Then she stopped and shook her head. "Never mind. The devil take propriety. I am going after him, and Ned can lump it!"

With that, she hurried in the direction Jameson had gone before she lost him altogether.

JAMESON KNEW HE HAD handled it badly. He ought to have introduced Maisie as his fiancée. She was probably furious with him. But Esmera was suddenly right there before him. He could see her flaming orange silk gown the night she'd mesmerized the Duke of Parkland. The old man had been enchanted and, along with the duchess, they had sat in a quiet corner between dances, and he'd listened to his wife and the duke speak about Spain.

Now, they were both without their wives.

What he wouldn't give to turn the corner and see Esmera in the same gown, eyes sparkling, red lips parted in a smile. She was at her happiest in this type of setting, especially when adored by someone as important as his grace. And Jameson had adored watching her happiness.

No one was outside yet as the ball had only just begun. Alone, he walked to the edge of the terrace and then descended the steps to disappear into the lush garden. In the center of it, or what he supposed was near the center, there was a large marble statue gazing upward. Hands fisted, he let out a loud yell.

He hadn't done such a thing in a while, and never outside the privacy of his own home or carriage.

He listened in the silence that followed. Other guests didn't come running, so he assumed he would not be escorted to Bedlam that night. But then, a few moments later, he heard footsteps. In truth, he barely heard them on the gravel path and wouldn't have heard them at all if he hadn't been carefully listening.

Those were dancing slippers, not men's shoes. He imagined he could hear the swish of her gown. She had answered his call.

As the steps came closer, he closed his eyes and made a wish.

"Esmera," he whispered, and then he turned, just as Maisie came into the moonlight—all golden-haired and pale blue shimmering satin, looking like an angel.

She hesitated, and in that hesitation, he knew she'd heard him and that he had caused her pain.

"No," she said. "I am sorry. It's only me. I wanted to check on you. I'll leave you alone."

When she turned to go, something inside him shifted. These were very high stakes, he realized—their future, a marriage, and possibly offspring. Yet, he was still hoping for cards that could never be in his hand again. And in doing so, he risked losing her.

What was wrong with him, living in the hazy falsehood of memories?

"Wait," he said, and she did. That, in itself, was a blessing, for she could have kept on going and left him to his misery. Rightly so, too.

He reached out his hand, and she took it, letting him draw her close. He needed to feel her warmth.

For long minutes, he simply held her, and she let him. Her presence made him stronger, driving out the wispy vestiges of unwanted remembrances.

"I am sorry," he murmured against the top of her head.

"There is nothing for you to be sorry about."

He shrugged. "I should have introduced you properly to Lord Parkland."

"You were taken by surprise."

She was making it easy on him. He sensed living with her would always be easy. Free of drama.

Again, he wanted to compare, for he'd had his share of dramatic encounters with Esmera, but this time, he stopped himself.

"Your quotation was well-timed, and I appreciate it." He leaned back and looked down at her. "You know your brother is probably about to storm out here."

"What can he do? Force us to marry?"

They both began to laugh, and all the tension drained out of him. *How did she do that?*

Gone was the desire to howl with sadness or even to shake his fist bitterly at the mercurial twist of fate. Life did go on, and he could stand there and laugh and feel affection for another woman.

"I would very much like to dance with you tonight."

"I would like that, too," she agreed. "First, tell me another joke."

Since he was getting ready to kiss her, the request caught him off-guard.

"Very well." He'd heard something at the club recently. "Mrs. So-and-So said to Mrs. What-Not, 'What black eyes that baby has!' And Mrs. What-Not said to Mrs. So-and-So, 'Yes, his father is a pugilist.'"

Her lovely face broke into a broad smile. "That's a good one."

"*You* are a good one," he said, the words spilling out of him with the grateful emotions he felt.

And then he couldn't wait another second to kiss her. It was expected, in any case, that engaged couples would sneak away to get to know one another better. That was how some knew to break off an engagement or others decided to speed it up.

Her lips under his were perfect, and as he touched his tongue along their seam, she parted them. The sensual feeling of slipping his tongue between her plump, soft lips made the blood rush heavily through his body. His hands drifted down to her backside and, without wondering if she would mind, he reached under her bustle and squeezed her.

She gasped, and her grip on his shirt tightened. When he tilted her hips to cradle them against his own, she moaned and, instantly, his shaft, nestled against her heat, hardened. For the first time, he considered how a long engagement could be torture.

That didn't give him the right to shred her reputation before the marriage. As he pulled back, he nibbled her lower lip, tugging it before he released it.

"I liked that," she confessed.

"I'm awfully glad, for I hope we can do it often." He took her hand again, lifted it high, and made her twirl in a circle for his viewing pleasure.

"I didn't yet take the time to tell you how lovely you look in that gown. You are stunning. The blue suits you beyond anything."

She dipped her head, which surprised him. *Was she blushing?*

"The only flaw I can see," he began, which brought her head snapping up, "is the neckline seems a bit high. Have a word with your seamstress about showing your décolletage to your fiancé, would you?"

And the smile reappeared on her face.

Jameson settled her hand on his arm, tucked her close, and headed back inside to dance with his spectacular fiancée. Truthfully, he would like to see a little more of Maisie's beautifully shaped breasts and couldn't wait for the wedding night, when he would finally see all of her shapely form.

He would do his best to make her happy.

Reentering the Parkland mansion, Maisie wished she knew whether she should say something glib about how much she liked Spanish wine. She wanted to reassure him she wasn't the least sorry the duke had it on hand. Perhaps she should offer to toast Esmera with it. However, she didn't think Jameson was ready for any of that.

Anyway, she preferred French wine. Claret was her favorite.

Miraculously, their absence seemed to have escaped notice, or perhaps Eleanor and Maggie had handled it and distracted Ned. In any case, as the beginning notes to a waltz sounded, Jameson led her immediately onto the dance floor. Being in his arms had become her most favorite thing, along with being kissed by him.

Recalling the exciting manner in which he'd handled her bottom, she could almost imagine how thrilling the wedding night would be. Almost! He would undress her and himself! She would see Jameson Turner entirely bare. *Gracious!*

"Are you all right?" he asked.

"Yes, why?" her voice came out all breathy, imagining him naked.

"You missed a step."

"Did I?"

"Actually, you nearly tripped me. I would have sprawled across the parquet and possibly cracked my skull."

He was teasing her.

"I barely hesitated," she protested.

His broad shoulders would be available for her to run her fingers over. And then his bare chest and his stomach. She glanced at his face. The most handsome man she could imagine would be hers. And then she would be able to touch his . . . all of him. She swallowed.

"Why are you staring at me like that?"

"Like what?" she croaked, licking her suddenly dry lips. His gaze went to her mouth, and her insides flipped.

How would she ever break off their engagement when all she wanted was for the time to speed by until he was her husband?

"Like I'm the last piece of roast beef on the platter."

She could hardly laugh for the heavy, tingling feeling between her hips. At the same time, she would swear her nipples had hardened.

Did that happen? In fact, her entire treacherous body was committing a mutiny of sensations designed to make her go through with the ill-conceived notion of marrying a man who loved a ghost.

She might not inspire such love in him, but after each kiss, she became more certain she had garnered his desire.

MAISIE DESCENDED THE STAIRCASE the next morning dressed in her favorite blue riding habit. Since Jameson had complimented her in blue the prior evening, perhaps she would only wear this color when keeping company with him.

"That's ridiculous," she muttered to herself, imagining an entire wardrobe of one color. People would laugh at such an affectation.

"What's ridiculous?" Ned asked. "And where are you going?"

"Riding with Lord Turner."

"No," he said.

"Yes," she said. "Ned, you are not my father, and I am not a child. I greatly appreciate your looking out for me," she added, when he flushed. "However, I will not be ruled by you any longer. I am an engaged woman. The announcements have been made. Lord Turner will not renege on the agreement. And I will not act like a simpering debutante for the next five months. I will conduct myself with all due decorum, I promise you, and I will always have a third person with me when I am with him." *At least in public.*

Ned's mouth opened and closed. Then he gave a long put-upon sigh and asked, "Who is accompanying you today?"

"Eleanor *and* Maggie. They should be here momentarily."

"Both of them?"

"Caroline was busy, and the Countess of Cambrey offered to join our little group." She tossed in Maggie's title to impress him.

More to the point, if Eleanor had come alone, they would have had to stick close like pages of a book since Maisie would no more let Eleanor ride by herself than she would do so herself. With her two cousins riding together, she and Jameson were more likely to have an opportunity to spend time alone.

"If you plan ahead next time," Ned said, "I'm sure Caroline will make herself available. Or even I might have time."

"I will," she promised.

They both heard the sound of arrivals outside, and, beating their man to the door, Maisie opened it to see her cousins. Sticking her head farther out, she looked up the street and spied the tall figure of Jameson on horseback, leading another horse.

"It seems everyone is on time," Ned said beside her.

Maisie snagged her crop from the hall stand and was nearly down the front steps when she remembered to ask her brother a question.

"Have you written Father about my engagement?" She could only assume he'd had sense enough to couch such a letter in respectful terms asking their sire's permission. If her brother had made it sound as if their father had no say in the matter, she feared he was as likely to forbid the marriage as not.

"Yes. I sent word directly."

"When you receive a response from Father, I would appreciate knowing what he says."

Ned gave her a curt nod and shut the door.

Her cousins looked beautiful on their horses, while Maisie had to wait for Jameson to bring her a promised mount from his own stable. Ned and Caroline kept only one carriage horse in London, and Caroline was out in the carriage. Maisie was relieved as their horse was long in the tooth and not the caliber of what the Cambreys, Lindseys, or Jameson Turner would ride.

"Beautiful weather," Maggie called down to her. "Are we coming in to visit with Neddy for a few minutes?"

"No," Maisie said, looking behind her at the closed door.

"Wonderful," Maggie added, wickedly. "You look gorgeous in blue, by the way."

Maisie knew the color was also her cousin's favorite, and she was fortunate Maggie was in pale gray today.

Eleanor was in a becoming fawn-colored habit, and slid off her horse to hug her.

"Good day, Lady Cambrey, Miss Blackwood, Miss Darrow," Jameson greeted them and dismounted. "Perfect day for a ride."

"It is," Maggie said. "Where are we going today?"

"Since you have all made your way down this far," Maisie said, her arm around Eleanor, "I think we should go to Battersea. There's a tea garden and, of course, the fields."

Jameson frowned at her.

"Why are you making that face?" she asked him bluntly before she could think better of it.

"Am I? It's only that Battersea Bridge seems barely to be standing, and certainly not straightly upright. I can imagine all of us plunging into the Thames."

"Really?" Maisie had read nothing in the newspapers about warnings. "I've been over it a number of times recently."

"Maybe you should stop doing so," Jameson said.

She laughed, then realized he was serious. "I'm sure the bridge can handle another day with the four of us," she said. "And if we're up for a long ride, we can come back via Vauxhall Bridge. Do you deem that one safe, my lord?"

"Are you mocking me?" he asked, leading her horse to her.

"Only a little. We shall put it to the other ladies. Do either of you have objections to crossing the Battersea Bridge?"

"We can all swim," Maggie said, as if that put the matter to rest.

"And we have Lord Turner to save us if we get into difficulty," Maisie reminded him.

Even though it had been a frightening day on the bank of the River Don, she remembered it fondly. From the way Jameson looked at her, perhaps he did, as well.

Without further response, he cupped his gloved hands for her, and she stepped up and onto the saddle, hooking her leg over the pommel.

"Good?" he asked.

"All set," she agreed.

When he winked, she thought it one of the most intimate gestures she'd ever received.

Then he held his hands together for Eleanor to regain her saddle. When he had mounted, they were on their way, falling into an easy procession with her cousins in front, and she and Jameson following behind.

"Keep close and alert," he called out. "I will let you know if a carriage approaches from the rear."

Eleanor twisted in her saddle to send Maisie a querying glance. All she could do was shake her head. Jameson seemed to be taking all their safety very seriously, but she hoped he would relax and enjoy himself after they had crossed the Thames.

It was actually a wonder to be suspended over the wide, rushing river and felt vastly different on horseback than it did from the inside of a carriage. The wooden structure swayed a little in the light breeze.

Eleanor called out, "Isn't this wonderful?"

Maggie didn't seem as thrilled, and moved steadily forward, keeping her face averted from the river. Maisie didn't think her cousin minded heights, but she was not a tree-climbing daredevil like Eleanor.

"Keep moving," Jameson advised. "Let's get off this infernal thing."

Maisie had been on the bridge enough times it didn't worry her one bit, but she wasn't trying to alarm anyone, so she did as he said. It wouldn't be wise to tell him she sometimes stopped in the middle and watched boats pass underneath.

When on the other side of the Thames, they took a left to go down river, toward the fields. Birds were circling and diving near the marshy grasses, and the blue sky was brilliant.

Maisie hoped everyone was as happy as she was. The horses fanned out, and Jameson rode closest to the river, while Eleanor and Maggie rode the field. All at once, something slithered across Maisie's path, and her horse reared.

Within seconds, she'd gone from a pleasant ride to shrieking with surprise and clinging to her mount's neck, in danger of sliding off.

◇◇◇

CHAPTER TWENTY-ONE

If her foot caught in the stirrup and this horse, unfamiliar to her, took off, Maisie could be gravely injured. Thus, she clung even as the beast windmilled its front hooves and seemed to approach a nearly vertical angle. And then, it was over.

As the horse went back on all fours, with Jameson at its head holding the bridle, Maisie settled back into the saddle and tugged down her smartly fitted jacket. While she caught her breath, her cousins drew around her.

"Well done," Eleanor said. "You held on like one of Philip Astley's trick riders."

"Are you hurt?" Maggie asked.

"No, I'm fine. Just a little winded."

Jameson had said nothing, but as the others rode on, he didn't release her horse's bridle.

"We should return home at once," he said through tight lips.

"Whyever for?" she looked past him to where her cousins were trotting along toward the tea garden at the far end of Battersea.

"Because you were nearly killed, and it would be folly to continue as if it hadn't happened only to have it happen again with tragic results."

She gave him all her attention. "I was not *nearly killed*. Yes, I was a little frightened, but no more so than the horse."

"You might have slipped off the saddle."

"True, but I didn't. And if I had, I might have broken a bone at the most or had a bruised back." She decided not to mention her musing upon the stirrup and possibly being dragged to her death.

"Maisie!" he exclaimed, and it was the first time he'd said her given name. Pity he wasn't saying it with soft, amorous tones. Rather, he sounded exasperated, and even angry.

"Please release the bridle, and let's continue," she said. "I am fine, and we shouldn't let them get so far ahead."

"My heart is still racing," he told her, but he let go of her horse.

"As is mine," she admitted. "But it doesn't mean I wish to stop riding. I am not afraid. *Cowards die many times before their deaths. The valiant never taste of death but once.*"

With that, she urged her horse forward, and they caught up with the others.

Jameson remained quiet for the remainder of the ride, and also watchful. In fact, two hours later, when they were crossing Vauxhall Bridge for home, Maisie finally turned to him.

"Stop it, please. I feel like a zoological creature."

That made him smile for the first time since the incident.

"*Female beautifulis Britannicus* on display," he said.

"*Beautifulis* is not a word," she pointed out, but felt happiness flow through her like warm treacle.

He shrugged. "The meaning is clear."

"Flattery," she scoffed, tugging down her jacket again despite knowing it was perfectly in place, as were her blonde curls, artfully clasped to one side and draped over her shoulder. Their maid had done a grand job of making her presentable.

"No," he protested. "Flattery rings of something false. I truly think you're a beautiful woman. And there is nothing wrong in my telling you so. After all, you are my fiancée."

"I am still trying to get used to that notion."

"As am I," he agreed. "But it sits well with me."

He seemed in a good mood, and Maisie decided to broach what might be a turbulent topic.

"How would you feel if my father came to live with us?"

His expression registered surprise.

"Since you've barely mentioned the man, I had no idea you were considering it."

"I wasn't, but Ned said our Dumfries house is to be sold. Apparently, Father is to live with me."

After a pause, Jameson said, "If I had to choose between living with Ned or you, the choice would be clear, so I can't blame your father. Is he easy-going?"

"I wouldn't call him that." She wished she could think of something positive to say. "He stays out of the way a lot, and keeps to himself."

"So, we can put him in a closet, and he'll be perfectly satisfied."

She couldn't help the snort of laughter his words produced. Then covered her face with her gloved hand. *Dear God!* She sounded like a wild boar.

But he ignored it, except for a brief, wry smile. Then he added, "Better we have your father with us, than mine. In any case, we'll deal with what comes when it comes."

"Thank you."

He cocked his head. "For being reasonable?"

"Yes." Such a pleasant man. She was extraordinarily lucky of all the men Ned had to force upon her, it had been Jameson.

"Do you realize by asking about the future means you no longer plan on breaking our engagement after a few months and running off with another man?"

He was right. Every moment she spent with him made that plan seem impossible.

"That one might read the book of fate, and see the revolution of the times."

"Who knows what the future holds?" he echoed her quotation.

"Exactly."

JAMESON WAS LOOKING FORWARD to picking Maisie up at her home and taking her to the play. He could think of no better way to enjoy Shakespeare than with a woman who was passionate about the Bard. He had not grown up going to the theatre, not in the countryside of South Wingfield, which had nothing of interest but a fifteenth-century manor house. There was an even older church where his mother, Callie Turner, was buried after lingering her whole life near Jameson's profligate father's home.

He wasn't sure whether his mother had hoped Lord James Devere would raise her from an impoverished chambermaid to lady of the manor, or she simply could see no earthly reason to move away. In any case, there they remained, until one day, rather matter-of-factly, when he was sixteen, his mother told him who his father was.

Strangely, Devere, the younger son of a prominent family, didn't deny it, probably because, even then, his father thought Jameson could be useful to him.

After moving to London to take up the life of a gambler, Jameson saw no point in going to the theatre. Later, as a married man with a wife who preferred opera, he was happy to do whatever she wanted, even to watch her singing along to words he couldn't understand from their seats in the balcony. And while Esmera also enjoyed ballet, she didn't care for plays, particularly not plays spoken in Elizabethan English.

He hoped Maisie didn't think him too uncultured for barely knowing the few plots of Shakespeare he had encountered. She'd been especially excited about this play, *Richard II*, because of the famed actors who were in it, Charles Kean as King Richard and John Ryder as Bolingbroke.

Jameson didn't know if there was a play about any other King Richards, nor did he know anything about the second one, but he intended to do his best to follow along. It couldn't be worse than opera, and he had the pleasure of Maisie's uplifting company.

Unfortunately, Ned and Caroline would be seated with them as the four tickets had already been acquired, and Eleanor had agreed to give up hers so the newly engaged couple could go together.

The outside of the Royal Princess's Theatre on Oxford Street was rather plain, with double doors under an awning, but inside, it was elegant and large, with the building stretching all the way back to Castle Street. More importantly, its management had been taken over a couple years earlier by the esteemed Charles Kean, whom Maisie was so excited to see perform, and it had become the home to his authentically historical Shakespeare productions, often co-starring the actor's wife.

Despite three tiers of boxes, the Darrows didn't have one of their own, and Ned hadn't thought to ask—or perhaps hadn't wanted to ask—the Lindseys or the Cambreys, if either kept a box. So, the four of them found their seats in the "pit," as Maisie called it, about ten rows back from the stage.

She was fizzing with excitement, her head on a swivel from the moment they entered the auditorium, and Jameson found it contagious, growing more excited by the moment.

"The royal box is empty," Maisie said, but it didn't dim her enthusiasm one bit.

Ned took the aisle seat with Caroline next to him, then Maisie, and then Jameson. They read their programs and examined the advertisements in case there were any wondrous new types of tooth powders or hair creams.

As the commodious theatre filled up, it became noisier, but in minutes, the gas lights running down the aisles and the lamps in the walls flickered, creating a hush as well as causing him a moment's alarm in case it was a gas issue. And then, with everything properly lit again, the curtains drew back.

Drummond limelight, a flaming blend of oxygen and hydrogen directed onto quicklime, lit areas of the stage, and into these the actors strode to great applause.

As soon as they began to recite their lines in rapid-fire speech, Jameson was entirely lost.

Maisie clapped and gasped, occasionally making *oohing* noises along with others in the audience. Leaning forward, Jameson noticed Caroline seemed to be following along, although occasionally, she, too, looked as confused as he felt. And Ned dozed off after about ten minutes and didn't awaken until intermission.

Jameson sat back puzzled. At least with the opera, no one expected him to understand what in blue blazes was going on.

During the intermission, they went into the lobby for drinks.

"Perhaps if I'd seen *Richard I*, this play would make more sense to me."

Maisie laughed good naturedly, then at his undoubtedly blank expression—for he felt completely confounded when he considered the acts he'd just seen—she stopped and looked at him quizzically.

"Are you in jest or serious?" Ned asked. "For I cannot tell."

"Lord Turner has a wonderful sense of humor," Maisie told her relations.

Jameson didn't know what he'd said that was so amusing, but he wasn't looking forward to returning to the auditorium.

"I would watch the play like Mr. Darrow, through my eyelids, but I thought I should keep vigilant in case there is any mischief."

Caroline laughed this time and elbowed her husband.

Ned looked sour. "I close my eyes to better listen to the cadence of the language."

Hm, maybe that would help. Jameson might try it. That or going off to sleep as Ned had blatantly done and awakening when it was over. Maisie could always tell him the plot later.

"But are you enjoying the story, and the intrigue and drama of it?" she asked.

"I like the scenery and the costumes," Jameson said truthfully, unwilling to lie about the story of which he hadn't a clue. "The main fellow, he's very good. I can tell," he added.

Maisie gave him an endearing smile. "That's Charles Kean, himself. He's brilliant."

"And the lighting is good, too." He was thankful there were no more wax candles dripping from chandeliers. He'd had a painful experience years earlier.

Her smile broadened if possible, and she looked as if she wanted to lean into him and let him kiss her. Or maybe that was merely his own dream, for she was ravishingly beautiful that night, in pink instead of blue. She looked fresh and kissable.

All too soon, they'd finished their drinks and returned to their seats.

"Will there be another intermission?" he asked.

Maisie shook her head and then, when he tried to ask her how many acts were left, to his amazement, she shushed him. She certainly took her Shakespeare seriously.

He opened his program to check on their progress, and even though he could plainly hear others murmuring around him, she elbowed him when the paper rustled loudly.

Thus, he sat back to "enjoy" the performance. He hadn't been lying about being impressed by the costumes and scenery, easily envisioning himself transported to another time—if only he knew in what period Richard was king.

Some medieval century, he mused vaguely.

A few minutes later, he spied the mischief of which he feared and sat up straight, then leaned forward, peering intently at the stage to make sure he wasn't imagining it.

A reddish orange flame flickered at the front of the stage, but he couldn't be positive it wasn't intentional. The limelight was on nearly all the time but occasionally, it went out for great effect when a character left or entered. But it was always bright white with the merest green tint. This was definitely flickering a fiery orange.

"Maisie," he began.

"*Sh*. I will explain it to you after."

He leaned closer, his lips near her ear. "I think there is a fire. Do you see it?"

"What?" This time, she turned her head, their faces colliding.

"Fire," he said. "Do you see it?" He pointed to the right side of the stage. "Is it part of the play?"

She peered in the direction he pointed. "Sometimes, they use crimson glass over the limelight to make it look like red flame."

"Do you think that is crimson glass?" he asked calmly, sure he could smell smoke.

"No, I don't think so." She wasn't whispering anymore. "I think we'd better mention it to—"

"Fire!" a man a few rows closer yelled. Then a woman screamed.

Immediately, Jameson jumped up and took Maisie's hand.

"Get up," he yelled to Ned, who was dozing. "There's a fire under the stage."

Caroline and Ned, looking bewildered, got to their feet.

Already, panic was ensuing as those closest to the stage filled the aisles and those behind them rushed to clog the exits.

"If we get separated, and we shall," Jameson said, "I will bring Maisie back to Pimlico. Climb over the seats and go toward the stage."

"Are you mad?" Ned asked.

"No, he's right," Maisie said. "I've toured the entire theatre in the daylight. Either to the right or the left, there are passages leading to Carlisle Street."

In a booming voice, Charles Kean called out from the stage, "Good people, the fire shall be contained momentarily. No need to panic. We have many exits. Use them. Don't blockade them."

The other actors had fled and, while the general air of hysteria seemed to be slightly placated with Kean's reassuring words, people still surged to get outside. Stories appeared in the papers of fires in London, and all over Europe, especially in theatres or any venues where crowds gathered. Many died from the smoke, trapped and unable to exit.

Why, the very land they were on had once held the Royal Bazaar, which was destroyed by fire twenty years earlier! Jameson was not about to be listed in the column of the dead in the *London Times* morning edition. Nor was Maisie Darrow.

Then the lights all went out abruptly, and Maisie screamed at his side, clutching his arm.

"It's a good thing," he said. "They've turned off the gas so there won't be an explosion."

However, they could still see the wicked flames flickering under the stage, darting into the small, empty orchestra pit.

Practically hauling her from seat to seat, Jameson made it over the ten rows toward the stage, then with her hand clasped firmly in his, he darted past the red glow into the darkness on the right.

They had to slow down to find the side hallway, which was in pitch blackness. He kept his hand on the wall of the narrow passage and the other on Maisie.

"We should be nearly there," she said, sounding breathless but not afraid. "I hope Ned comes this way, too."

Jameson, too, hoped his future brother and sister-in-law made it out safely. Shakespeare was the balm for Maisie's mother's death, and it would be a terrible loss for her if the Bard became associated with any harm befalling the Darrow family. Still, he refused to offer unkeepable promises that they would be all right, not until he saw them with his own eyes.

And then they could see a little light from streetlamps filtering in under the door at the end of the passageway.

"I hope it's not locked."

He would break it down with his shoulders if it were. Luckily, because he was fond of his undamaged shoulders, the door opened to his touch, and they were outside on Carlisle Street.

Jameson pulled out his pocket watch. "Nearly 10:40. We could find a cabbie on Oxford Street, except that's where everyone else will be. Do you mind walking a little to get out of the mayhem?"

"We should go that way," Maisie pointed past him to the west. "I believe Cavendish Square isn't too far."

"You're correct. Do you think the Cambreys will mind?"

"Not at all. We're family."

Thus, Jameson found himself alone with his fiancée on foot in the sooty air of London. It was a good thing they were engaged, or her reputation would surely be blighted by this. He could take her in his arms on the guise of comforting her, and no one could say a word. After all, they just escaped a theatre fire.

He drew her closer. "I have to confess, I didn't love that thespian experience."

She giggled. "Usually, all the excitement happens on stage."

"Again, I must disclose I hadn't a clue what that play was about or who was who. I didn't find much exciting happening until the fire. And there is no Richard I play, is there?"

"No, but there is a Richard III and there is a Henry IV Part One, but no Henry I either."

He shook his head. "I should have read about King Richard II before the play. Just the same way I would take the time to learn all the rules of a card game before I would go to a club to gamble."

She thought for a moment. "We can read the play together." Then she hesitated before adding, "If you wish. Some time. But only if it suits you."

She offered him her time so sweetly, and then became tentative, as if she feared he might refuse.

"If you would share your knowledge with me, Miss Darrow, I would be most grateful."

He felt her relax and drew her more tightly against him. Only a few blocks to go, but anything could happen. This was the time for thieves and murderers to roam the streets, not people dressed for the theatre.

A notion struck him since he had on a wool suit, and she was wearing something made out of butterfly wings for all he knew.

"Are you cold?" he asked as they turned onto Regent Street. The very next left would put them onto Margaret Street, and then they would be able to see the square on which the Cambreys lived.

"No, not at all. I was far too stimulated by our evening's activity to feel the night air, but the pavement is rather hard on the sole of my foot."

He yanked her to a stop. "What are you saying?"

"I lost my shoe when we were climbing over the seats. I'm lucky I didn't lose my reticule, too."

"Good grief, Miss Darrow! What is it with you and your shoes? Moreover, why didn't you say so?"

"To what end, my lord? Do you carry spare ladies' footwear on your person?"

She had a point, but she could step on something sharp and get a nasty infection.

"Turn yourself a little," he ordered her, but she didn't move, not understanding in the darkness what he was about. In another moment, he swept his hands under her knees and lifted her into his arms.

"Oh!" Maisie exclaimed. "Lord Turner!" Then she said nothing more, and he had the distinct notion she liked their new arrangement.

"Put your arms around my neck," he told her. "Hold on." And then he began to walk again, glad she was a petite female, since, while he considered himself fit, he didn't have the muscles of a longshoreman.

"You are very strong," she said after a few moments of him striding along.

"It's quite a bit easier than when you were soaking wet with river water."

Still, he wished he wasn't breathing so hard. After another block, able now to see the first street that made up Cavendish Square, he stopped to adjust her in his arms, giving her a quick toss upward, which settled her higher in his arms.

"Oh!" she said again.

He smiled. This speechless Maisie was new, and he had a feeling it wouldn't last once they reached her cousin's home. Fortunately, the Earl of Cambrey's townhouse was on the closest side of the square, and he had only to turn the corner and go halfway down the block to reach the elegant, four-story home.

"Lights are on," Maisie said as he set her on her feet.

He rapped on the door before he noticed the bell and rang it. It took a few moments before the door swung inward.

"Mr. Cyril," she declared. "It's me, Miss Darrow. My apology for showing up so late and uninvited. Is my cousin here?"

"No, miss. The countess and his lordship are out."

"Are they expected back soon?" she persisted.

"I do not know precisely when, miss. I will tell her ladyship you came by."

The butler stepped back as if he might turn them away. Indeed, almost before Jameson knew what was happening, the door was being closed in their faces.

He thought not!

❈

CHAPTER TWENTY-TWO

Jameson put his hand on the door, holding it open. "There was a fire at the Royal Princess's Theatre. We came here as the closest place to seek assistance. Miss Darrow has lost her shoe."

He glanced down, and Maisie dutifully lifted her skirt to show her torn stocking and bare toes to Mr. Cyril.

The butler's eyes widened, and he hastily looked away.

"I cannot think Lord and Lady Cambrey would appreciate our being turned away," Jameson insisted. The idea of carrying Maisie back along the street in search of a cabriolet-for-hire didn't enthrall him as much as resting on a comfortable sofa.

"Will you let us wait in the drawing room for them?"

The butler looked a long moment at Jameson, then back at Maisie.

"Yes, my lord, Miss Darrow. Come this way."

In two minutes, they found themselves alone with Mr. Cyril having left them after promising hot tea and biscuits.

Maisie sat on the sofa, a little bedraggled from the evening's adventure. Jameson couldn't imagine her looking more enchanting. Seeing no one was going to tell him otherwise, Jameson sat close beside her. Then, deciding he'd be a fool to waste the opportunity, he took her in his arms and kissed her.

The familiar sizzle of heat welcomed him along with her warm, soft lips.

When he drew back, he looked around. They were still alone, and the earth hadn't crumbled at his indiscretion.

"It seems fate has kindly provided for us," he said. "*Carpe diem,* Miss Darrow?"

"Positively," she agreed, so he kissed her again, pushing her back against the arm of the sofa until he could stretch out over her. When he'd ravished her willing mouth, he trailed kisses down her neck as she arched it back on the armrest.

He raised his head. "Have I told you how good you smell?"

Without opening her eyes, she answered, "No, I don' t believe you have."

"How remiss of me. You do, in fact, smell heavenly. A floral scent but not cloying, and with a hint of citrus."

"You have a good nose, my lord. Will you please kiss my neck again? I liked that."

"I intended to, anyway." He resumed nibbling on the smooth skin at her throat. Her fingers clasped in his hair, and he realized for the first time he'd lost his top hat somewhere along the way, or perhaps it was still under the seat at the theatre.

The feel of her fingers against his scalp, then tugging his hair, set his loins to throbbing. He wanted her bare and underneath him, with her fingers doing exactly that as he thrust into her.

He continued his mouth's exploration, kissing her collarbone, then amazingly, his mouth was on the upper swell of her bosom. He reached between them to cup her breasts, feeling her gasp at his touch. Then, through the thin fabric of her evening gown, he had the delightful experience of her nipples pearling under his caressing thumbs.

If he tugged a little, he might be able to free the straining bud for his lips to taste.

He had just managed to splay his fingers beneath her neckline to determine if there was any give to the fabric of her gown, when she said, "The water has probably boiled by now."

She was right. They probably had only moments. With another quick kiss placed on the valley between her breasts, Jameson drew back, yanked her to a sitting position, and let her smooth her skirts and hair.

There was a quick rap, and the door opened. The Cambrey butler found them seated a few feet apart, undoubtedly looking guilty, overheated, and incredibly happy.

"Your tea, my lord, Miss Darrow." And he placed the tray on the low table in front of them. "Will there be anything else?"

He had a way of asking which discouraged any further requests.

"Thank you, no," Jameson answered for them both, realizing lords hardly ever thanked their servants, but this wasn't his butler, in any case.

"We appreciate your hospitality," Maisie added, as if Mr. Cyril had graciously invited them in.

"Yes, miss," Mr. Cyril said stonily and departed.

"At least he closed the door again," Jameson said. "Do you really want tea?"

She shook her head. "We should probably pour it in a minute so it doesn't seem wasted or as if we . . ."

"As if we were otherwise occupied."

She blushed prettily. He grabbed the small milk jug, poured too much in the bottom of both their cups, and then nearly overflowed each with tea before he set the pot down.

JAMESON POUNCED. IT WAS the only way she could describe how he suddenly covered her body with his once more.

Maisie laughed with delight. Yet, when he held the sides of her face with his palms and looked into her eyes, her laughter died.

Was he searching for something? She wanted to provide whatever he needed. And she longed for the moment he could ease the wanting he'd stirred deep inside her.

Her body felt tingly in places, and her nipples hardened each time he kissed or touched her. And all the while, a steady tension was building, demanding release. If they weren't in danger of discovery—if they could lock the two doors to the room—she'd be willing to go further than a kiss.

His hands left her cheeks to splay across her breasts again. She looked down, watching with fascination as he slipped fingers into the neckline of her gown, and stroked her breasts. It was not enough. She squirmed.

Obviously, he felt the same, for he began to hike up her gown, drawing the diaphanous fabric over her knees and thighs until it pooled on her lap.

She had on split drawers of the softest cotton and, without hesitation, he touched her core, the very place that felt damp and hot and throbbed for him.

Silently, she watched him do all this, and then she put her head back and closed her eyes.

Unerringly, he stroked her, and her body bucked under his capable ministrations. His mouth suddenly was upon her neck again, this time working his way upward to her lips, claiming them, sliding his tongue inside before—*gracious!*— he mimicked with his tongue what his fingers were doing down below. It was heavenly!

She moaned. The tension that had curled inside her coiled tighter.

"Jameson," she breathed against his mouth. "Help me."

"Yes," he promised. "Let me. You are so ready. You'll go off like lightning."

Not even thinking about his words, she grasped his shoulders as she felt him caress the little bud between her legs. It was as though he were performing magic upon her. Barely had he stroked her a few times when the muscles low in her stomach tensed even more tightly and blissfully released.

She found herself gritting her teeth with the intensity while her body soared and opened, softened, and finally relaxed. Utterly spent.

"You are so beautiful," came his words, breaking the spell, reminding her where she was. Her eyes popped open, and she panicked. While her body wanted to curl into a comfortable position and relax, she knew she was in danger of being entirely compromised.

Slamming her legs together, she heard him mutter, "Ow! You've trapped my hand," and hastily unclamped her thighs until he removed his hand and sat up.

"Hurry," she said. "I think I hear them. Do you hear them?" Her brain was racing as was her pulse.

"Stand," he ordered, and she did. Then he proceeded to smooth her dress, making sure the scant two layers were properly hanging and aligned.

"No, I don't hear them," he said, and her heartbeat calmed. "Turn, please."

She did, and he made sure no lace was torn and all her buttons were fastened.

"Now sit, and have tea."

However, she was trembling from the intensity of the experience, so she paced instead. It was strange to feel the soft oriental carpet under one foot, her toes relishing the sensation while her body savored the rest of what had happened.

"I cannot believe what you did. What I let you do."

She should be embarrassed at how and where he'd touched her, but she wasn't. She felt closer to him than anyone in her life.

"I apologize if you felt—"

"No," she interrupted. "Do not apologize. It was wonderful. Beyond that, it was extraordinary. And exhausting. If I weren't so stimulated, I could fall asleep right now."

"It's a feeling unlike any other. I am looking forward to it again, myself."

She stopped pacing and stared at him. Then it dawned on her.

"You need release, too."

After looking over her shoulder at the firmly closed door, she sat beside him again. "Is there time? What shall I do?"

"Nothing." Picking up a saucer, he put it in her hands. "Just drink tea and be happy." Then he offered her a smirking grin. "I'm glad you enjoyed it."

"But you—"

"I am fine." He shifted on the couch. "Or I will be when my body calms a little more."

Just as he reached for his own saucer, they heard the front door open, and an exchange of voices. Then the drawing room door burst open.

"Maisie, Lord Turner!" Maggie greeted them, looking concerned. "Cyril said you were here, escaping a fire! Are you harmed?"

Jameson and Maisie stood, and he spoke first. "There was a small conflagration at the Princess's Theatre. We left through the back and came here."

"I hope we didn't overstep," Maisie added as Maggie came forward to hug her.

The earl was right behind her. "Not at all," he said, shaking Jameson's hand. "You did the right thing. We were in the opposite direction, but we could see more traffic than usual, snarled to a halt on Oxford Street."

Jameson nodded. "You didn't see flames or smoke, though?"

"No," Lord Cambrey said. "What happened?"

"It looked like flames coming from the front of the stage," Jameson described it, "from directly underneath."

"Oh, dear God!" Maggie exclaimed. "It's always something. I'm very glad you came. Where is your carriage, or did you go by cab?"

"Lord Turner picked us up in a cab," Maisie told her cousin. "We went with Ned and Caroline and got separated. Do you think we might take your carriage back to Pimlico? They will be worried sick until we show up."

"Of course," the earl said. "Let me see if we can stop our driver unhitching the horse." He left the room quickly.

"As long as you two are all right," Maggie said, spying the tea. "Sit, finish your tea, and tell me about the play."

"And the loss of footwear," Maisie confessed, showing her.

Maggie laughed. "I think I can help you. We don't want you going home like Perrault's Cinderella, do we? You've already caught your prince."

Maisie rolled her eyes but noticed Jameson reddened, perhaps slightly abashed. Then her cousin rang for the maid, before glancing at the mantle clock.

"I'm not certain if anyone will answer that bell right now."

In fact, it was Lord Cambrey who returned before a servant. "We will have a mutiny on our hands. First, tea and biscuits, and now you're ringing for the parlor maid. Cyril is having fits and said the girl has already retired."

"I'm so sorry," Maisie said.

"No matter," Maggie promised, and she slipped off the shoes she was wearing. "Take these."

They were stunning, pink satin ankle boots with bows on the front instead of buttons and little heels. *Perfection,* Maisie thought, *just like her cousin.*

"No, I couldn't possibly."

"Absolutely, you can. They even match your outfit," Maggie said.

Maisie slipped them on, and they fit. "I really do feel like Cinderella."

Since the earl was yawning, Jameson stepped forward and shook his hand again. "We won't keep you a moment longer from retiring."

Maggie's handsome husband gave them a rueful smile. "I'm sure our Rosie has plans for us before we retire. It is uncanny how that child knows the minute we go upstairs. The nanny says our little girl can be deeply asleep and then her eyes flutter open. I swear she's feral and can smell us."

"An exhausted parent renamed his first infant 'Macbeth,'" Maisie announced.

"Why?" Jameson asked, without a pause, knowing by her expression what she was up to.

"Because he murdered sleep," Maisie finished.

A moment of silence greeted this declaration. Jameson laughed first, and the others joined in as they realized her little jest.

Then Maisie and Jameson took their leave, climbing into the Cambreys' luxurious brougham. Sitting close by Jameson's side, Maisie felt as if the evening had been a turning point. At least, for her. After the liberties she'd allowed, she could never break off their engagement and set him free, not unless he asked her to.

In her mind, she was now his, and equally, he was hers.

"You're unusually quiet, Miss Darrow," he said, tracing a finger along her arm, causing goosebumps.

"It has been a night of hurly-burly, but Shakespeare was right to say, *'Fortune brings in some boats that are not steered.'*"

"Meaning?" He turned on the seat to face her.

"Only that without our planning it, and even though we began our evening under Ned's watchful eye, we spent a great deal of time alone."

Jameson took her hand in his. "True, yet we had to escape a theatre fire, lose a shoe, and greatly annoy a butler in order to do so."

She laughed, her heart full. "I love . . . I love the way you spin a story, my lord." Then she stuck her feet out from under her gown to admire Maggie's pretty shoes.

She had nearly slipped and said something she was positive he did not want to hear. At least, not yet.

"And I love the way you make me feel," he responded immediately.

Considering what he had done to her on Maggie's sofa and how he'd made her feel, Maisie believed herself firmly in his debt.

"I do hope we find Ned and Caroline safely at home." It would be terrible if she'd mistaken the seriousness of the fire, and something had happened to them while she was sipping tea and doing other things.

He squeezed her hand. He didn't offer any silly reassurances, which she appreciated. They would know when they got back to Cambridge Street.

Then, they sat back in silence. With the traffic of other theatre-goers and those out at balls, it took nearly half an hour to reach her house.

Just before they turned onto Cambridge Street, Jameson suddenly spoke again, "Promise me you won't go to the theatre without me."

She considered his strange request. *Was he worried she would go with another man?*

"I believe Eleanor, having given up her ticket tonight, asked me to go with her to another play. I would like to."

"May I accompany you?"

She saw no reason why not. "Of course. My cousin won't mind having you escort us."

He relaxed back onto the leather seat.

A few moments later. "Will you also promise not to go riding without me?"

Maisie squeezed his hand. "I will not accept a riding invitation with any other man. Does that satisfy you?"

She had not expected this type of possessiveness from him, considering his heart was not engaged.

"No," he said, surprising her further. "I am serious about this. I do not want you out riding. And certainly not across that blasted Battersea Bridge or in those snake-ridden fields."

Oh, so that was what was on his mind.

"If I ride, I shall go to St. James or Hyde Park."

"Why are you fighting me on this?" he asked. "As your fiancé, I merely ask you ride only with me, so I can keep you safe."

Keep her safe? "I am not fighting you, my lord, but I am a capable rider. That was a chance encounter with a snake and may never happen again."

"If it did—" he started.

"If it did, and you were beside me, how could you prevent it? May I remind you, you were beside me, and still, it happened."

He fell silent, and she scolded herself. She hadn't meant to hurt his feelings.

"You did help calm the horse afterward."

He sighed. "You shouldn't have been on an unfamiliar mount, I suppose."

"Then we shall ride more often so your horse gets to know me." She would have to ask Eleanor again to accompany them for Caroline was not keen on riding sidesaddle, preferring carriages.

"And promise you won't go riding without me," Jameson persisted. "Something could happen."

Apparently, he was not going to rest until he got the answer he sought.

"Very well."

"Thank you." Then he frowned. "Please . . . are you listening, for this is important?"

"Yes." *Was he going to declare his love for her?* That would make this moment perfect.

"Do not stand too close to the fireplace or the cookstove or any lamp for that matter. I have read of ladies becoming terribly burned. Your dresses are so poofy, you have no idea when you are putting it directly into the flame."

Maisie wished he'd said he loved her, but, obviously, he cared. "The skirts are actually narrower this Season," she soothed him.

The carriage had stopped, and the driver opened the door. Lamps were lit inside their modest townhouse, and the curtain twitched. Maisie felt confident all was well with her brother and sister-in-law.

"I think I have been in a fantastical world, not the one I first went out in earlier this evening."

"I understand what you mean," he agreed. "And when we step out of this carriage, all will be as it was before."

"I'm sure Ned is already scowling at us through the window. The sooner you escape from here to your own home, the better."

"I know there is some pertinent line from a play you're dying to say."

"The driver is waiting," she pointed out, "and my front door just swung open."

"Say it," Jameson ordered, stepping down so he could offer her his hand.

"You must know it, from the end of *A Midsummer Night's Dream*, when Puck tells the audience they were all sleeping."

When he smiled and shrugged, she quoted, "*If we shadows have offended, think but this, and all is mended, that you have but slumbered here while these visions did appear. And this weak and idle theme, no more yielding but a dream.*"

"The evening *was* like a dream," he said, and she let him walk her to the open door.

"Tell me there is a chaperone inside that carriage," Ned said.

"Of course, there is," Jameson said as he bent over her hand and kissed it. Then he dashed back to the curb before her brother could ask more or go look inside the brougham.

"His name is Puck," he called back.

Maisie laughed as she went inside.

"Puck? Puck!" her brother exclaimed and followed her into the drawing room where Caroline was seated, drinking sherry with her feet on an ottoman.

"You both look well." Maisie was relieved.

"We got out quickly, but it took ages to hail a cabbie," her sister-in-law said, patting the seat beside her. "Sherry?"

"Yes, please."

"Ned, pour your sister some sherry."

Her brother did so but continued to stare at her. "Maisie arrived in a strange carriage with Lord Turner and some fellow named Puck."

He handed her a small glass, and she yawned, realizing she was exhausted by the last few hours.

"It was Maggie and Cam's carriage. We ended up at Cavendish Square." She upended the thimble-sized amount of liquor and stood.

"If you'll excuse me, I am ready to sleep. I can hardly keep my eyes open."

Without waiting for a response, Maisie leaned over and kissed Caroline's cheek. "I'm very glad you are well."

Then she patted her brother's arm as she passed him.

On the stairs, her limbs felt leaden, and she knew she would scarcely have time to recollect all the wonderful moments of the evening before slumber overtook her.

UNFORTUNATELY, THE VERY NEXT day, Maisie received an invitation to go riding, one which she simply could not turn down, nor could she invite Jameson along.

When the missive came with unfamiliar handwriting, she barely skimmed the short body of it before reading the signature—*Sr. Inigo Maradona*

At first, she was puzzled, and then it dawned on her exactly who this was. The late Esmera Turner's brother.

Why did he want to go riding with her?

CHAPTER TWENTY-THREE

Maisie appreciated that the invitation stated there would be a professional chaperone, but Ned would never let her go riding with a stranger without meeting both Mr. Maradona and his hired chaperone. And for once, Maisie entirely agreed with him.

Dressed in her blue riding habit, her hair in a tidy low bun, she felt the sense of confidence resulting from being well-dressed and groomed.

When the stranger arrived at their home, thankfully, their man servant made it to the door, saving Maisie or her brother having to answer it. And still, even in her favorite blue, she felt almost coarse next to the impeccably clad man who entered wearing a European-tailored sack coat in a stylish plaid linen.

With his olive-complected, chiseled features and thick, soot-black hair, Mr. Maradona was as strikingly handsome as Esmera had been gloriously exotic.

He bowed low to Ned, then took first Caroline's hand and then Maisie's, bending over each and brushing his lips across their knuckles.

Only then did Maisie notice he was followed into the room by a heavy-set, older woman with gray-streaked hair, wearing a full skirt for riding. She must be the professional chaperone.

Mr. Maradona turned to her and spoke in Spanish, and then she stepped forward and curtsied to each of them.

"I am Señora Huerta," she said in heavily accented English. "The duenna." Then she stepped back, her sad glance cast to the floor.

"When Esmera was first going out, you understand, she had to have a duenna, a chaperone," her brother explained. "Like a nanny, only for an older girl."

Ned brushed all that aside and got right to the point. "What do you wish with my sister? Even with Mrs. Huerta, this is unusual."

"I understand your position, Mr. Darrow. I have a fine horse at your sister's disposal, and my intentions are to ride with her and speak privately."

"That tells me nothing," Ned protested.

Señor Maradona had apparently had enough of Maisie's brother. He turned to her.

"Will you go riding with me, Miss Darrow? It appears you are dressed for such an outing."

Maisie shot Ned a quelling glance. Hopefully, he remembered her diatribe of a few days earlier. He was *not* her father.

"Yes," she agreed, "as long as Señora Huerta stays close." She offered the dour woman a smile, hoping to win her over should protection be necessary. The woman's gaze remained somber.

"Of course," Señor Maradona said. "And we will return whenever you tire."

"Very well. Then let us be off." Maisie was dying of curiosity, knowing only one thing—this was to do with Jameson's first wife.

In a few minutes, without a backward glance to Ned, who was undoubtedly looking out the window, Maisie rode down Cambridge Street with Jameson's dead wife's brother and her duenna. They rode in silence for a few minutes, which suited Maisie. She didn't want to prompt him by saying the wrong thing, nor offend him by presuming she knew what this was about.

When they went north, rather than toward the river, she didn't have to break that promise to Jameson about crossing Battersea Bridge.

Relieved, she finally asked, "Shall we go to Hyde Park or St. James's?"

"Hyde Park, if you don't mind. I enjoy a good trot along Rotten Row."

She nodded. He said nothing more for a while. Curiously, when she would have gone along Elizabeth Street to Sloane Street, he went easterly to Belgrave Place, then followed this until it put them directly on Belgrave Square, home to Lady Pepperton.

Could it be coincidence?

She was freed of any such notion when Señor Maradona took the first right, taking them off the most direct route to Hyde Park, and slowed directly in front of the block of townhouses containing Lady Pepperton's home.

"Do you know who lives there?" he asked.

Maisie drew herself up straight and stared him directly in the eye. "I do."

"What do you think of your fiancé's relationship with that woman?"

"I fail to see how that is any of your business. And, since it is not a current relationship, it has no bearing whatsoever on me, either."

He nodded, but he didn't urge his horse forward. "When my aunt passed away, my uncle wore black the rest of his days."

Maisie waited. She turned to make certain the duenna was still close by. The lady sat hunched on her horse, looking neither particularly happy to be out riding, nor unhappy, for that matter.

When Esmera's brother said nothing more, Maisie said, "He sounds like a devoted man."

"A devoted husband," Señor Maradona corrected, "and widower."

"I assure you, because I know this to be absolutely true, Lord Turner was a devoted husband, too." That she should have to be defending the fidelity of her fiancé regarding his previous wife, seemed strange indeed.

The man shrugged, and his horse took a few steps, but he reined it in. "My sister's husband was careless with her, giving her too much freedom, and look what happened."

Maisie started to protest, but he cut her off, "He may have loved her, but he didn't deserve her. Nor does he deserve you, Miss Darrow."

She gasped at the dramatic tenor of his voice and the way he now stared at her with his nearly black eyes.

"I don't think that is for you to judge, nor was it with your sister. They chose each other, and a terrible accident took her from Lord Turner. He wishes it were otherwise. Believe me."

If he could have Esmera back and brush Maisie from his life, she was of no illusion Jameson would do it in a heartbeat. Nor could she blame him. He loved Esmera, and his heart knew the same longing as Maisie felt for him.

"Then why did he quickly take up with this loose Pepperton woman, and now you?"

At least he hadn't included her in his low estimation of Jameson's paramour. If he could have seen her on Maggie's sofa, though, Señor Maradona might change his opinion and say she deserved whatever she got.

Maisie urged her horse forward. She didn't want to be seen loitering in front of Lady Pepperton's home. However, when she'd only moved a few feet, unsure if Esmera's brother was following, the front door opened. Lord Michael Alder stepped out wearing a formal tailcoat, obviously from some event they'd attended the previous evening.

Lord Vile, as he was called, for quite valid reasons, froze at seeing three people on horseback, at least two of whom were staring at his lover's townhouse. Maisie averted her gaze, fairly certain he did not know her and, thus, couldn't possibly report back to Lady Pepperton that Lord Turner's betrothed had been outside her door.

Moreover, while she saw him tip his hat out of the corner of her eye, Maisie kept her horse moving along.

In a few minutes, they were at Hyde Park Corner, near the Duke of Wellington's Apsley House. She swallowed the lump in her throat and wished Jameson were there. Going off with strangers had been folly.

Since Señor Maradona still seemed inclined to ride, they directed their horses along the tan and gravel surface of the *Route du Roi*. Maisie turned again to make sure Señora Huerta was still there, plodding behind. Satisfied, she faced forward again. Enough of this tiptoeing around.

"Did you invite me to ride in order to warn me away from Lord Turner because you believe he made for a bad husband and an even worse widower?"

"Yes," he said. "My family has suffered much because of him. My parents lost their only daughter."

She was not going to argue the ridiculousness of blaming Jameson.

"Luckily, they have a son to carry on the family name and give them grandchildren."

"I cannot do so while they mourn my sister still. There can be no festivities for us. Only Turner seems ready to forget her existence and move on. My anger at him has grown instead of dissipating, as I see him live his life as if Esmera never existed. She would be heartbroken to see how he has forgotten her."

Maisie considered all the time Jameson spent mourning, and how he still became visibly upset when he thought of Esmera.

"Perhaps your family should direct their anger toward the British railway, señor. It was a senseless accident over poorly laid track. There was no need for a lovely young woman enjoying life, heading to a splendid city like Bath, to end up with a broken neck."

He cringed, and she felt sorry for her vivid description, but the man was being unfair.

"You hope to honor her by disparaging her husband, but I think you are dishonoring the man she loved. And if you try to hurt him by dissuading me from marrying him, it will not work. Those of us who know Lord Turner understand the depths of his grief."

She would not ride with this twisted, bitter man another moment. To that end, she drew her horse to the side and stopped. Señor Maradona reined in his horse, too.

"I can only advise you to get on with your life. Your sister lived life fully, by all accounts, and I think you should do the same. As Shakespeare said, *'the miserable have no other medicine but only hope.'* You should give your parents some hope for the future with grandchildren. As for your anger, it will give you nothing but dyspepsia. You should try to let it go."

And then, as she lifted her leg over the pommel to slide down the side of the horse, she heard her name.

"Miss Darrow!"

"Drats!" she exclaimed aloud at Jameson's voice. Her luck had run out.

JAMESON COULDN'T BELIEVE HIS eyes. Maisie—*his* Maisie, as he thought of her—was swinging her leg over the saddle of a horse and next to her, not even trying to assist her descent, was his former brother-in-law, the ever-serious Inigo Maradona.

What the hell!

Which is precisely what he asked as her riding boots hit the gravel surface.

"What is going on here?"

Maisie was now sandwiched between her horse and Inigo's.

Before anyone could answer, Jameson added tersely, "Move your mount so the lady can exit. You're crowding her, and she could get trod upon."

Esmera's brother didn't acknowledge him, but simply moved forward a few steps. That was when he noticed the other member of their little riding party. Señora Something-or-other, a woman who had cried at his wife's funeral nearly as much as Esmera's mother.

"Miss Darrow was in no danger," Inigo insisted. "Yet you seem to be overly concerned for her safety, unlike my sister's."

The verbal slap was nothing new. Esmera's brother had been lashing out at him since her death, and for the sake of the man's grief, Jameson allowed the misplaced anger. However, he would not allow the man to put Maisie in the middle of it.

And yet here she was, directly centered amongst the horses and the insulting words flying at him. He could hardly sweep her onto his horse in the middle of Rotten Row, nor would he berate her for breaking her promise. Not in public. That would come later.

Dismounting quickly, Jameson offered her his hand, grateful she didn't make a scene but simply took it and let him draw her to his side.

"What is the meaning of this?" he asked again, hoping she would speak now because he didn't want to hear any more nonsense from Inigo.

"Señor Maradona invited me riding, and I accepted since he provided a chaperone."

Jameson tried not to purse his lips in disapproval and disappointment but failed. After he ground his molars a few moments, he nodded.

"It appeared your ride has finished. Will you leave with me?" He still wasn't sure if she would be compliant.

"Yes, we had concluded our conversation, and I had decided to walk out of the park and hail a cabriolet to get home."

She looked up at Señor Maradona, shading her eyes from the sun since at that angle, it shone under her jaunty little hat.

"Good day, señor. I wish you peace and a happy future. For your parents, as well."

Jameson could see the man's jaw tighten, but he nodded slightly.

"I wish you a happy future as well, Miss Darrow. As I said, you deserve better than this man."

The devil! If Maisie wasn't there to witness, Jameson would drag Inigo off his horse and beat the tar out of him.

His former brother-in-law merely leaned over and grabbed for the reins of Maisie's gentle horse, then he turned back the way they had come.

The duenna followed without a word, despite managing to glare fiercely at Jameson before looking away. He could practically feel her gaze slicing into his heart.

Silently, Jameson and Maisie watched for a few minutes before he turned to her. She wore what he could only describe as a defiant set to her mouth, knowing she'd broken her promise not to ride without him. However, she wasn't going to cower because of it.

He was annoyed but felt grudging admiration, although he would never tell her. If this was the pattern for how she would behave after they married, he was in for a smattering of trouble.

"Are you going to walk me back to the corner?" she asked. "There will be many cabbies there."

"On the contrary, since everyone rides carriages or horses to Hyde Park, I doubt there will be many at all."

Maisie hesitated, then lifted a delicate shoulder. "You may be right. I hadn't thought considered that."

They began to walk back toward the triumphal arch marking the eastern end of Rotten Row, with Jameson leading his horse.

"Where were you coming from and going to?" she asked.

He hesitated. *Should he tell her?*

"Occasionally"—*some might say too often*—"I go to Brompton Cemetery, just to visit with her. On the way home, I like to cut through the park."

"A strange coincidence," she said, "that I was with her brother."

He would not tell her today's visit had been a special one. He told Esmera about Maisie, unsure what she would have thought of her. He couldn't recall his wife and Maisie interacting, but he knew they'd been at the same parties at Belton Manor, and probably at a few London balls.

When he told Esmera he was marrying again, lightning hadn't struck him dead on the spot. He'd considered that a good omen.

And while he was visiting her grave, Esmera's brother was trying to come between him and Maisie. *Could his dead wife have sent her brother?*

"How did this come about?" he asked.

Looking sideways at him, Maisie said, "Señor Maradona sent an invitation to my home."

"So, you simply went riding off with the man out of sheer curiosity. Frankly, I'm shocked Mr. Darrow let you go."

"In truth, Ned was not thrilled," she confessed. "But there was a chaperone."

"A woman who, by her expression, would as soon stick a knife in me as not." Jameson recalled the duenna's hawk-like attention when he'd been courting Esmera. Señora Huerta had been as fierce and effective as Cerberus guarding the underworld. Never would he have been allowed alone with his future wife in the Holland's garden, for instance, nor anywhere else.

In fact, Jameson couldn't recall a single moment's intimate encounter with Esmera *before* their wedding night, except holding her on the dance floor.

"She held no animosity toward me," Maisie interrupted his musings, "so I felt perfectly safe with Señor Maradona. I believe his main purpose was to warn me away from you."

Jameson thought about this. "I doubt it was because he gave a fig for you, in truth, but only to do me harm. Do you understand that?"

"Yes," she sighed. "I do now. The poor man."

"The poor man!"

She glanced at him. "He is quite trapped in a bog of anger and sadness, perhaps even worse than you."

That felt as if she'd slapped him. *Is that how she saw him? Trapped in a bog.*

"I think my grief has been quite normal."

"Of course," she agreed at once. "Besides, who is to say what is normal? Yet, it can be overwhelming and stifling, too. Señor Maradona carries his parents' grief as well as his own. Were they a very close family?"

"Yes, very. They were kind to me after we were engaged, but I do not think they considered anyone good enough for Esmera. They were right. She should have been the wife of a king."

How many times had he marveled at how incredibly lucky he was she'd given her heart to him?

Perhaps he shouldn't be praising his former wife to his next wife. However, Maisie looked pensive, yet not perturbed. What's more, she did not appear as if she were about to fly into a jealous rage. He'd experienced that before, and hoped never to again.

"At her funeral," he added, "I confess I had no more tears left. Her mother and father and even Inigo cried so hard, it was almost frightening. I half believed we would stand at her grave all day and night. I simply wanted to go home and be alone."

He felt her touch his arm gently. "I understand."

"From that day on, they became cold to me. I represented the loss of her."

"I told him to give his parents hope, perhaps grandchildren," Maisie informed him.

He laughed. "You told the supercilious Inigo Maradona what to do."

"He wasn't too pleased, I admit."

"I don't doubt it. I suppose it is as hard to bend him to one's will as it is you."

He felt her startle beside him. "Whatever do you mean?"

"You broke your promise."

"I am terribly sorry. I didn't want to make the promise," she pointed out. "And I shouldn't have made it because I cannot imagine how I will keep it. Eleanor and Maggie will want to ride again, and you cannot always be there."

Helplessness—that unpleasant suffocating feeling washed over him again. He wanted to tuck Maisie away in a box and only take her out of it when he could protect her.

He didn't know what to say. His feelings were real, and as she'd said, sometimes overwhelming.

"You were right. There is a cabbie." He hailed it for her, dropping the reins of his horse to help her in. Then he gave the driver the Pimlico address.

"Are you angry with me?" she asked before he could shut the door.

Angry and sad, wasn't that what she accused Inigo of being?

"No. I will follow the carriage and make sure you get home safely."

"That's unnecessary."

She didn't understand. It was as necessary to him as breathing. If he turned away, went home, and found out her carriage was in an accident, if she so much as scraped her elbow, he would be devastated.

Leaning in, he kissed her quickly. Before she could react, he closed the door.

If he were going to marry and not be driven out of his mind with worry, he should have married a woman he didn't care about. But then, he hadn't intended to marry anyone ever again.

Following closely behind, he contemplated the cab before him, containing his bride-to-be. He didn't think of dark-haired Esmera, only of sunny, blonde Maisie, and knew the familiar feeling deep in his bones. He was falling in love with her, had known in his rose garden it was possible, and thus, had fled her presence.

Now, he would have to be vigilant, on pins and needles of worry the rest of his life.

Her precious head popped out the window at that moment. She looked back at him, waved, and smiled.

He released a long sigh. No matter what it cost him in sanity, Maisie Darrow was worth it.

CHAPTER TWENTY-FOUR

Maisie waved goodbye as Jameson rode away. He had followed the cab all the way to her home, but left her without coming inside, only with a promise to escort her to a dinner party and dance at week's end.

She couldn't help feeling she'd let him down.

At least they could get back to their previous footing at the party. She would be as social and dazzling as she could, as similar to Esmera Turner as it was possible for her ordinary self to be, and make him happy and proud to be her betrothed.

During the week, she thought herself lucky to be able to choose *not* to participate in social events. However, she went to a cricket match with Eleanor and the Cambreys, and agreed to play croquet when Lady Turbity wrote to her the very morning of the event saying she was short one female.

"If it's not too much trouble, and if your fiancé doesn't object, of course."

After lunch, upon Lady Turbity's beautifully flat lawn, they all gathered into their teams. Maisie was relieved to see her foursome contained another young woman she knew at least by sight, Lady Adelia Smythe, the daughter of an earl, painfully shy and quiet, as well as Lord Roleston and Lord Whitely.

Maisie tried to engage Lady Smythe in conversation immediately, but she barely responded. When Lord Whitely made the next attempt at conversation with the young lady, Maisie turned to Lord Roleston.

"How are you enjoying your engagement?" the viscount asked while they awaited their turn.

She considered the highs and lows, particularly the disheartening incident of hearing Jameson say how extraordinary Esmera ought to have married a king.

"It is satisfactory, Lord Roleston. Rather the same as not being engaged, quite frankly."

"True enough, I suppose, for here you are without your fiancé."

"This was rather a last-minute decision," Maisie clarified. "In any case, I don't believe Lord Turner is one for croquet."

"Oh, to the contrary. I watched him and his wife win as a team against Lord and Lady Rutherford. Since it was at the Rutherford's country estate, I can tell you it was bad form to defeat the hosts. Even so, Lady Turner was fairly crowing about her victory, and everyone was fascinated by her, thus, she got away with it."

Maisie digested this information as she left Lady Turbity's croquet match behind. Jameson had been aware of the week's schedule and had not offered to partner with her. Perhaps he believed she couldn't possibly be as good as Esmera. And he was probably correct.

She was not in competition with a dead woman.

Nevertheless, as she fussed and fretted over what to wear at week's end, she did not want a recurrence of the Parkland ball with the host looking past her, hoping for Esmera Turner.

When she arrived on Jameson's arm on Friday evening, she wanted to look stunning. When she considered how to best accomplish this, one thought came to mind . . . *Maggie!*

Thus, two days before the ball, she went with Maggie to a dressmaker's, a modiste of the highest caliber, obviously not to have a new dress made but to get one of three choices altered.

"The former Lady Turner wore a lot of reds and oranges, and they looked stunning with her black hair. She could even wear saffron yellow," Maggie pointed out with admiration. Maisie stood upon a low dais in front of a mirror, dressed in her favorite blue gown.

Madame Courvage agreed with a nod. "She could. You," she said, turning to Maisie, "have unusually pale hair for one with brown eyes, yes?"

"I suppose I do." She turned to Maggie. "I am washed out, sickly and wan."

Her cousin shook her head. "Don't be ridiculous. You must stick to what you can wear. You would, for instance, look stunning in black satin, but seeing how Lord Turner is a widower, that will only remind people of his previous mourning. You can wear pale pink so well, but it is too immature for your status as an engaged woman. You've worn too much blue to be able to make an impression."

"He likes me in blue," Maisie defended the fact she wore a blue day gown.

"Nevertheless, I am thinking you can make his eyes pop from his head if you wear another jewel tone like amethyst or emerald. Madame Courvage, what do you think?"

"None of these dresses Miss Darrow has brought me are amethyst or emerald," she pointed out. "So, I think, countess, you already have a plan."

"I do. Miss Darrow and I are of a similar size, we can even wear the same shoes, as we recently discovered."

Maisie covered her mouth as she gasped. "I forgot to return them to you."

Maggie waved her hand, dismissing the boots. "That's no matter. Keep them if you love them. As I was saying, though we are similar, she is *exactly* the size of my older sister, Lady Lindsey. I had my sister send more gowns after

Miss Darrow's engagement, as my sister most likely won't need them for a while. She is in the family way."

Looking over her shoulder, Maggie smiled her winning smile that made women and men adore her. This time, she directed it toward her footman who stood by the door.

"Jack, the box, please."

In a moment, he had dashed outside to the carriage, returning quickly with a box, which he brought forth and placed on the floor before returning to his station.

"Jenny wore it only once, and since it was at *my* engagement at Lancaster House, I don't think anyone noticed except her husband."

Maisie hid her smile. Maggie was not speaking vainly, only truthfully. For the Countess of Cambrey, then still Margaret Blackwood, wore a stunning blue gown that night and commanded all of London high society's attention. That particular gown could never be worn again by another lady, as everyone would remember it.

Maggie began to untie the string around the cream-colored box. Inside was a layer of tissue, which she pushed aside to reveal a verdant and vivid green.

She lifted it out for Maisie to see. "Not to speak ill of the departed, but Lady Turner was not subtle in her fashion. She was all drama and tight satin. Stunning, to be sure, but there is something to be said for fresh and crisply sparkling. This shade of green, some call it 'shamrock,' will remind everyone of the best of the English countryside, especially with a new panel in the front of the bodice and the skirt of pink roses on a gold background. You have such a fabric, do you not, madame?"

"You chose it yourself," the seamstress admitted and went to get it.

Maisie admired the gown. "I like it just as it is, with the paler green panel underneath."

"Just wait, cousin, until you see the fabric I selected. The gold will reflect in your hair, and the pink will remind everyone of your lips and cheeks. But let's get you into the dressing room first."

ON FRIDAY NIGHT, WHEN Maisie stepped out her front door, she was cloaked in a floor-length, blush-colored evening mantle, also borrowed from Maggie, with only her pink lambskin shoes visible when she walked. Her gown was hidden, and she wouldn't even need to change into dancing slippers as these shoes were butter soft.

Jameson came to collect her, along with Ned and Caroline, in a hired hackney. Ned immediately sat next to him, so Maisie and Caroline would sit together facing the gentleman.

"Lord and Lady Westing will have an excellent meal laid out and superb musicians," Ned informed them, as if they needed his guidance. He was no more friends with the Westings than Maisie, nor had he been to a party at their house before.

It was only because the Duchess of Westing wanted to have a gathering to showcase her daughter Amanda that there was a party in the first place. They'd had a terrible gas explosion and fire the year before, effectively blinding the marquess, heir to the dukedom, and this was the first dinner dance in their newly renovated townhouse on Grosvenor Square.

"Will the marquess and his fiancée be there, too?" Maisie wondered, knowing of Christopher Westing's long recovery and happy engagement to Lady Jane Chatley, since the engaged couple were both Maggie's friends. In fact, that was why any of them were even invited.

"You can depend upon it," Ned continued. "My sources say yes."

Beside him, Jameson rolled his eyes, and Maisie smiled at him.

"What? Is there something amusing?" Ned asked.

Jameson spoke up. "Not yet. How about this? When is it no misfortune for a young lady to lose her good name?"

"I beg your pardon," Ned exclaimed. "It is never a good thing. What can you mean by such a question?"

"It is joke, husband," Caroline explained. "Go on, Lord Turner. Tell us when."

"When a young man gives her a better one," Jameson finished.

Maisie thought it would have been better if Ned hadn't interrupted the quip.

Ned frowned. "I do not understand it at all."

That made Maisie want to laugh out loud at her dear brother's perplexity.

"How about this then?" Jameson persisted. "The intention of fencers is each to touch their opponent, but in this, they are often foiled."

Maisie and Caroline laughed, and then all eyes turned to Ned who was frowning. Then his brow cleared.

"Foiled! *Ha, ha*," and that was the extent of his laughter, but Maisie could tell her brother appreciated it.

"Well done," she said to Jameson, who tipped his hat.

They entered the Westings' foyer amongst a small group of other arriving guests, single men for Amanda's perusal with an equal number of single ladies to round out the dinner and, naturally, some established couples to provide a stellar example.

And then, it was time for the unveiling of her new gown. Two servants awaited to take ladies wraps and, less likely, men's overcoats, were any foolish enough to have worn one on this balmy summer evening.

Maisie unhooked the neck fastener of her wrap and let it slide off her before handing it to the servant. Jameson was speaking with someone on his other side, but as she rejoined him, he glanced at her to take her arm. And he froze.

The look on his face, particularly when he stepped back to better view her, was one she would never forget. She felt instantly beautiful. The man she loved had an expression of wonder on his handsome face, along with primal desire.

"You look stunning." He leaned close and whispered, "Kissable and edible."

She didn't even know exactly what he meant, but felt the heat creep up her face with pleasure at his approval.

He grinned at her, setting her insides to fluttering. "And now you've brought the rose to your cheeks. Even more lovely."

As they approached the Westings, he whispered, "I was going to try to behave myself tonight, too. But it will be impossible."

Then they were curtseying and bowing to the blind marquess, Lord Christopher Westing, and his fiancée, Lady Chatley, her telling him who stood before them. They were a charming couple.

Next, Maisie and Jameson met Lady Amanda, who was like every other debutante at her coming out, looking self-conscious and wide-eyed, and finally, Lady Helen Westing, the renowned artist, and her husband, patriarch Lord Spencer Westing. He was known to be a bit eccentric but an excellent statesman.

Maisie hoped Ned, directly behind her, wouldn't say anything embarrassing.

When she and Jameson had cleared the receiving line, they were directed into a large drawing room for drinks. It was like many other events of the Season except they'd gone through the line together and were clearly a couple. No one mentioned Esmera, and her specter didn't seem to hang over the party. There wasn't even any Spanish wine being served.

As Maisie drank champagne and watched the young men try to capture Amanda Westing's notice, she relaxed and knew herself to be the happiest woman in London.

"I need to get you alone at once," Jameson murmured in her ear.

For a moment, she felt a frisson of alarm, but when she saw the wicked gleam in his eyes, she knew what he was about.

"I don't think that will be happening, my lord. Only think of the example we are here to set for the likes of young Lady Westing."

"Only think of how much I want to admire your dress . . . and what's underneath it."

That did it! At his words alone, her body tingled.

"Behave," she scolded. "They don't even have a large garden for us to explore. We would have to go to their private park in the middle of the square."

He lifted his gaze upward.

"I refuse to disappear upstairs with you and have the Duke of Westing suss us out."

Jameson made a frustrated face, and she couldn't help but laugh. She was, however, extremely ready for dinner to be served and finished, so he could take her in his arms on the dance floor. She was under no obligation to dance with any other partner, and she couldn't wait to feel his hands upon her, his firm body close to hers.

"I think that is the prettiest dress I have ever seen," he said later when they took to the parquet in the Westings' great room and the dancing began. "Perhaps you should wear it on our wedding day. Then I will get the added pleasure of removing it."

He was incorrigible, but, in truth, she hadn't considered a wedding dress. She knew women often wore a favorite gown or their best gown, and those who were wealthy enough wore a new gown made for the occasion.

"We'll see," she said, again knowing in her heart it would be impossible to break it off with him.

Plainly, he wanted her, but if she suddenly came to a halt midst the other dancers in the Westings' lovely ballroom and asked him to declare before these people and God if he loved her, she knew he would hesitate, break her heart into pieces, and then declare a fondness for her. Probably respect, too, and admiration, and, of course, desire.

Could she live on those sentiments the rest of her life, while showering him with love?

She was coming to the conclusion the answer was a resounding yes! She could share him with his perfect memories of his dead wife, who would always remain youthful and gorgeous while Maisie grew ungainly with children and then soft with age and eventually wrinkled. Maybe hairless!

"Are you all right?" he asked. "You've grown exceedingly pale. Shall we stop?"

If they stopped, his hands would have to fall away from her, and even that small connection would be lost.

"No, I am fine. I would like some water after this dance."

The fact Jameson was so concerned and attentive brought a lump to her throat, and Maisie reminded herself, he, too, would be paunchy, wrinkled, and perhaps hairless. If they were lucky, they would grow old together, making each other laugh.

It would have to be enough, for she could not see herself with any other man.

She wished she could look up into his eyes and tell him she loved him, but she wouldn't embarrass him for anything, certainly not to unburden herself.

Instead, she made a silent vow. In the privacy of their own bedroom, on their wedding night, before ever she let him consummate the marriage, she would tell him she loved him. For she couldn't have him thinking she was the kind of woman who could give her body to a man without loving him.

She was not Elizabeth Pepperton.

CONSIDERING HER MISGIVINGS DURING the evening, Maisie thought the Westings' soirée was the best night of her life. Jameson never left her side, and they danced until one in the morning. And, thanks to Maggie's perfectly designed gown, he never took his eyes off her.

Afterward, when they arrived in their neighborhood of Pimlico, Jameson surprised her even more by asking Ned's permission to spend a few moments alone with her.

"That would not be proper," her brother began, and she glared at him. She hated to create a scene in front of Jameson, reminding Ned yet again he was not her father, nor was there any danger of his lordship reneging.

"We will keep the door to the parlor open," Jameson offered.

"As long as you do not remain directly on the other side," Maisie added.

Still, Ned hesitated. Maisie was about to inform him she would go back outside and get in the hackney with Jameson if that's what it took to get privacy, when Caroline intervened.

"We shall leave the door open and retire, just like my parents did for us," she reminded her husband, who stared at her open mouthed.

"There is still a maid on duty if you need anything," she added. "And as you're aware, voices and . . . other sounds carry up the stairwell, so simply call us if you need us."

That was fair warning they might be overheard. Maisie nodded her thanks.

Taking hold of Ned's arm, Caroline half-dragged him from the room not looking the least bothered by her husband's shocked expression, undoubtedly mirroring the way Maisie felt.

"That was a surprising turn," Jameson said.

"Indeed. I like my sister-in-law more every day." She was beginning to think there was more to Caroline than she knew.

However, as Jameson took hold of both her hands, she could focus only on him.

"I simply wanted you to know I was teasing you at the Westings'."

"You were?" *What did he mean?*

"I don't need to be touching you every moment and stealing a kiss." But as he spoke, one of his hands cupped her cheek, and he bent low to kiss her.

She sighed afterward, as he drew away. "So, you didn't need to do that?"

"Correct." And then both his hands cradled her head as he kissed her again.

When it ended, he remained with his forehead against hers.

"I am exceedingly glad you were persistent at Jonling Hall," he murmured. "It was you who caused me to begin to live again, spurring me out of my lethargy. The bog, as you called it."

She wished she hadn't spurred him directly into Lady Pepperton's arms, but he was with her now.

"I longed to see you as the man I recalled."

"And am I?"

She looked into his gray-blue eyes and couldn't lie. "You have a somberness lurking, always ready to overtake your mood, but I suppose every one of us must experience such at some point in our lives. That you are going about your life despite it is a tribute to your strength."

He shook his head. "Only you would see a weakness in me and make it positive."

"Grief is not a weakness," she assured him. "In this world, when so many children die before reaching even the tender age of five and loved ones are taken swiftly through disease or accidents, it is only the unconquerable human spirit that keeps us from constant despair. Knowing life is short and living it anyway—isn't that an amazing feat?"

"Shakespeare?"

"No, merely my thoughts."

He nodded. "They are good ones."

"I am so happy tonight," Maisie added. "I don't mean to carry on about the certainty of uncertainty."

"And I don't mean to be a bore."

They heard coughing from the upstairs landing and grinned at each other.

"I believe I have overstayed," Jameson said. "That is a cue if ever I heard one."

She nodded. Her brother had been more than tolerant.

"I greatly admire you, Miss Darrow," Jameson added, and, as Maisie assumed they would, his words of admiration rather than love stung a little. But they also gave her hope.

THE NEXT MORNING, MAISIE awakened with an outlook she could only describe as sanguine. Her marriage was going to work. Her life was going to be happy.

She entered their dining room and saw mail on the table next to the newspaper and the teacups. It was addressed to Ned, but it was from their father, so naturally, after the briefest hesitation, she opened it.

As she read, her heart started to pound. In a few lines, her father, Fintan Darrow, had destroyed her happiness.

CHAPTER TWENTY-FIVE

Maisie's father got right to the point in the first line.

I do not give my permission for your sister to marry this Turner fellow. To be clear, I forbid it. I don't know him or his character. Send Maisie home at once, and I will discuss her future with her myself.
F. Darrow

Normally, she would have wondered why her own parent couldn't sign his note with love, but at that moment, all she could do was panic. He had forbidden her marriage to Jameson, and he wanted her to go home to Scotland in the middle of the Season.

Why had her normally disinterested father chosen this moment to suddenly become involved in her life?

Ned's letter to him regarding her engagement must have riled him. Her brother had obviously not been respectful enough.

Tossing the letter onto the lace tablecloth, Maisie fisted her hands in frustration. She ought to have been the one to write to her father, for she could only imagine Ned saying how *he* had found the perfect husband and how *he* had given his permission as if it were his to give.

Dear God!

Well, there was nothing for it but to make the long trek home and get it sorted out. She was not giving up the love of her life while Ned and Fintan Darrow battled over domination of their little family.

When Ned came downstairs, she went over their father's letter with him. He had the grace to look abashed at the turn of events now out of his control.

Within an hour, with Caroline along for guidance, Maisie went to Euston Station to map out her journey. In the past, she had travelled mostly by long and tedious carriage ride betwixt London and Dumfries, but for expediency's sake, she would take the trains. The rail went nearly all the way with a few gaps in the line where there would be coaches handy for traversing.

However, at home, with tickets in hand for the following day, and Ned and Caroline's willingness to give up one maid as chaperone, Maisie still needed one thing—to tell Jameson.

They had made no plan to see each other that day, or even the next, when she would depart early in the morning on the London and Birmingham Railway. She knew he wasn't going to like the content of her father's letter, which she would not disclose, or her traveling by train. But there was no choice.

While Rachel, who would travel with her, packed her trunk and their cook packed food that wouldn't spoil over the next two days of travel, Maisie settled down to pen letters.

She didn't bother writing to her father, as he would see her at the same time as her letter arrived. Instead, she wrote to Eleanor, explaining the situation and vowing to return triumphant.

And then, she tried to write to Jameson. Tried twice and failed. With the third sheet of paper, she decided to be direct.

Dearest Lord Turner,

I am forced to take an unexpected but necessary journey. I hope to be back at the end of next week, although I have no idea truly what my schedule will be. I am sorry to leave so abruptly and will greatly miss your company.

I understand your nature and know you will fret. But this is not my choice and, as Shakespeare said, we are "the slaves of chance, and flies of every wind that blows."

Yours with sincere affection,

Maisie Darrow

She reread it and decided it would suffice. In her heart, she knew if she made an attempt to meet with him before she left, Jameson would make every effort to stand in her way and perhaps even ask her to promise not to go. In short, he would forbid her traveling the same way her father was forbidding her from marrying him. Then she would be utterly stymied.

Feeling a heaviness of spirit, she sealed her envelope and gave it to their man servant to deliver mid-morning the following day.

JAMESON BELIEVED HIS HEAD would explode, if not his heart. As he read Maisie's brief note, his hand began to tremble. He wasn't sure if it was rage or fear causing the strong and violent reaction. Pushing his chair away from his desk, he decided to go immediately to her home and stop her.

Saddling his horse himself, he had never crossed London so quickly. Spurred on by fear gnawing at his gut, he hammered on the Darrows' front door. It seemed to take a lifetime for their manservant to open the door.

"I must speak with Miss Darrow."

The man's next words made the blood chill in his veins. "Miss Darrow has gone away, my lord."

He couldn't breathe, and his ears seemed to be ringing. *Too late!* Yet, perhaps not. If he knew where she was going, he could ride faster on his horse than she could travel by coach.

Caroline appeared in the foyer. "Lord Turner, come in. Darryl, why did you leave his lordship standing outside?"

However, Jameson remained on the step. He intended to ride as soon as he knew her destination. Seeing Maisie's sister-in-law only alarmed him further.

"You are not with Miss Darrow on her trip?"

"No, we were not invited, nor would it have been prudent for all three of us to take such a costly trip. In any case, my husband would only throw oil on the fire where his father is concerned."

"You have lost me, Mrs. Darrow. Are you saying Maisie went alone?"

"Of course not. She has our maid as companion." Caroline frowned. "I know she sent you word of her departure. Didn't she explain the circumstances?"

"No," he said curtly, keenly aware of wasting time. Every minute he stood there she was getting farther away from him. He wished he could keep the frustration out of his tone, but he could not. "Where is she going?"

"On her way to Dumfries, my lord, summoned by her father. Ned and he ... how shall I say it? They have discordance between them, so it seemed best for Maisie to do as her father said, given the delicate nature of their discussion."

"Delicate nature?" he prompted, shifting from foot to foot. At least, the situation didn't seem so dire now he knew Maisie was in her family's carriage with a maid heading home. Hopefully, Ned knew which inn was safe to direct the driver to take the women. They probably were going by way of Sheffield, stopping off to see Jenny and Simon, but would likely need to spend the evening in Leicester first.

"Is she stopping in Sheffield?" He could race like the devil and meet up with her there, perhaps convince her to have dinner with him at Jonling Hall.

"No, my lord, the train does not go that way, nor is there a close enough station."

At Mrs. Darrow's words about a train and a station, his brain emptied of thoughts, only to fill again a moment later with the image of Esmera at the morgue.

He clutched the door frame and felt the bile rise in his throat. Not just one railway, a hodgepodge of them. One rickety train to the next, and his Maisie willingly endangering herself by boarding each and every one of them.

The devil! She could have told him sooner, and he would have taken her himself, with a hundred chaperones if need be. She knew what this would do to him when he discovered how she was traveling.

What callous betrayal! For her to take a willy-nilly family journey, leaving him to suffer with worry, it seemed so unlike the woman he'd imagined he knew.

Just like Esmera going off to play in the ballrooms of Bath without him. She could have waited a few days. A few short days, and she would have been alive.

Ned was lucky it was Caroline who'd come to the door, for if Maisie's brother were there, Jameson would have blistered him for allowing his sister to go.

"Thank you for telling me." He turned away, and despite it being early in the day, he went straight to Crocky's for the best food and the prettiest serving women and the highest stakes. He intended to stay there all day and maybe all night and put the selfish Miss Darrow out of his head.

All women were thoughtless, selfish creatures, he mused to himself, except Elizabeth. He'd been a fool to destroy that pleasant relationship for another one like he'd had with his wife, full of uncertainty and heartache.

An hour later, battling every minute with himself, he finally let go the notion of going after the train. It was pointless. The fast iron beast could beat his horse any day. He would be trailing her until she stopped.

Then what? She would look at him with her lovely eyes all surprised, wondering why he had intruded where he hadn't been invited.

Maybe she would even scoff at him for worrying like an old woman.

She'd broken her promise about riding, and now she'd withheld the truth and put her life in danger needlessly.

He could not possibly live with such a wife.

IT WAS THE LONGEST, most uneventful journey of her life, and Maisie felt as if she'd aged a century overnight.

They'd been fortunate to find a "Woman's Only" carriage on the first train for a long stretch of their journey. Her maid had slept most of the time except when Maisie tried to engage her in conversation. Mostly, Rachel looked wide-eyed and uncomprehending, and thus, Maisie let her sleep as much as she liked. The poor girl probably needed it, since Ned had not hired enough staff to run even their modest home, and the two maids, the man servant, and the cook all kept very long hours.

Caroline was going to suffer the loss of one maid over the next week.

In the course of the first day of travel, when Maisie had the luxury of losing herself in a novel, she had decided to teach Rachel to read when they returned home. Some said it was a worthless endeavor, and could even be detrimental to a servant's happiness, but she didn't look at it that way. Rachel might get restless if she had new skills she couldn't use and even leave the Darrow home for a better position.

But that would be a transition to be celebrated, like a budding flower.

Ned wouldn't see it that way.

Maisie didn't know for sure what Jameson would think of the idea of bettering the servants, but she had a feeling he would agree with it. After all, he had gone from being a bastard to a viscount. Not many did that.

On the second day, a thought struck her. She had never seen inside his home. The realization came to her as she stared out the window, momentarily seeing her reflection before her eyes focused on the landscape beyond. What she knew of his life in London was only that he'd lived elsewhere before, somewhere above Hyde Park, until he'd married Esmera. Then, they had needed a better address and had purchased a place on Princes Street.

Maisie understood the necessity of location, especially for a viscount. Pimlico was clean and safe, but decidedly middle class, and, thus, they could never entertain there. Mayfair was out of reach for the Darrows, but the Turners had managed a residence on the outskirts of the wealthy, close enough not to be embarrassed by their street address, and even within walking distance of many venues.

With a start, she realized they hadn't been too far from his townhouse the night of the theatre fire. He could as easily have taken her there as to Maggie's.

Why hadn't he?

She mentally scolded herself. For one, it would have shredded her reputation should anyone discover such an egregious infraction of decency. But he hadn't even mentioned it, or suggested walking by and letting her look at his home from the outside.

Wasn't it to be her future home, too?

Maybe it wasn't. Maybe it was already too much Esmera's home to ever have another woman take up residence. Everyone knew Lady Turner had loved London. She probably had loved her townhouse, too.

Maisie swallowed. Every night, Jameson might go back to a place filled with Esmera's little touches of Spanish artwork and decorations, furniture she'd chosen, and wall colors. Maybe he felt happy surrounded by her things, ensconced in the memories of their life. It might even seem like a shrine.

Staring out at the countryside, knowing they were within a couple hours of her home, Maisie contemplated the changes that had occurred after her mother's death. Not many. Certainly, no one had ever suggested getting rid of her favorite vase. Or even moving it for that matter. For all Maisie knew, Marion Darrow's clothes were still hanging in her wardrobe.

She had been too young and grief-stricken to consider her father. Now, however, he would have her full attention.

They had ended up on the Lancaster and Preston Railway, having to disembark at Carlisle due to track issues and take a coach over the border into Scotland and west toward Dumfries. Their coach stopped at Gretna Green, letting off a couple, and Maisie had to wonder at their story.

If her own father refused to give his permission, would Jameson want to marry her in such a sneaky manner? The excitement of the girl, probably too young to marry in England, was palpable. Yet her parents might even now be close behind, frantic with worry.

It was far more likely Jameson would use her father's refusal as the ideal way to break off their engagement, while saving face and with no shadow on either of their reputations.

Perhaps he wouldn't be happy knowing she was up here in Scotland trying to persuade him otherwise.

Oh dear!

Maisie tried to keep her spirits up, but as they approached the Dumfries coach station, near the road that led to her home, butterflies took flight in her stomach. She never thought she would miss her annoying brother, but facing their father without Ned left her anxious.

As soon as they disembarked at the coach house, Maisie bolstered her courage by taking charge in the familiar surroundings.

"Come along, Rachel. The wagons for hire are over there. Let's get a man to move our trunks."

Like most Scottish market towns, Dumfries had a long main street where its weekly markets were held. The largest landmark was the Mid Steeple, built at the beginning of the previous century, and which could be seen from a fair distance. Her mother had called the ancient border town small but beautiful, and Maisie had hoped to show it to Jameson someday.

Despite having small industries of hat- and shoe-making, as well as brewing and tanning, it was their weekly Wednesday market that brought the largest insurgence of people from many miles away, making it a premiere place for Anglo-Scottish trade. While Maisie sometimes found the boisterousness of the market overwhelming, particularly the cattle sellers, she loved their tidy port and watching the ships dock and unload on the banks of the River Nith. It was practically an ocean compared to the River Don from which Jameson had saved her, and whenever Eleanor had visited, that was where they went, down to the riverbank so her cousin could sketch.

The Darrow house was on Great King Street, with a large plot of land farther back from the river for keeping their horses. Within minutes, she and Rachel had traversed the town's center on a wagon seat, and were dropped off at Maisie's own white-stone house with its pale gray front door and trim. Three stories high with two dormers at the top, Maisie looked up at it and felt the same way she always did—that her mother might be inside waiting.

By the time she'd put her hand to the door handle and entered, she had waved away such foolish notions.

Knowing her maid must be already leery of being dragged so far from London, she hoped the girl would settle in with the family's servants and make friends for the short time they were there.

Andrew, who sometimes worked for them and sometimes didn't—depending on his whiskey intake—was polishing the dark wooden banister.

Tall and in the middle years of life, blunt to a fault, he exclaimed, "Good lord, if you don't look like the spit and image of your dear mother, God bless her!"

And just like that, Maisie was welcomed home.

"Where is Father?" she asked. "Is he here or . . . ?" She left her question hanging because she half hoped he was out, and she could avoid a confrontation at least until morning. It was already an hour until supper time, and her travels had exhausted her.

"Aye, he's here," Andrew said. "Brewing in the back."

Her father enjoyed brewing ale, nearly as much as other men enjoyed drinking it.

"Will you show Rachel where she can put her things and sleep tonight? And introduce her to Gail and Jordie."

"Yes, miss. Come along, girlie." Rachel followed Andrew, with a backward glance at Maisie, partly apprehensive but also a little excited.

Undoubtedly, this traveling and meeting others was good for her. She would be fed and given some of Fintan Darrow's brew which all the staff drank. Maisie sighed. At least the maid would sleep well that night.

Feeling assured either Andrew or Jordie would take her trunks upstairs, Maisie decided not to put off the inevitable any longer. Even if she had dust and grime from her travels, and although her stomach was beginning to grumble, she went along the passageway to the back of the house, and stepped into the tiny garden where there was definitely not a dahlia. Without knocking, she entered her father's brewery.

It was a small room with curtainless windows, but little light entered due to the way he had piled things up on all sides. Sacks of hops and barley on one side, jugs empty and full everywhere, and in the middle, his fermenter.

"There you are," her father said, hardly glancing at her and looking no more surprised than if he'd seen her recently.

She let go of any hint of English accent. "Yes, Dad, I'm here. As requested."

"You took your time about it, Maiz," he said.

"I came immediately as your letter reached our home in London."

"Home? In London? *This* is your home."

She sighed. "You know me. I'm rather easy-going. Dumfries or London or even Sheffield with my cousins. I can adapt."

He looked at her sharply. "This man your brother *announced* you were marrying, like *he* has the say of it, his home is in Sheffield?"

"True. He's a cousin of Jenny's husband."

"*Hm.*"

What did he mean by that?

"You might like him, Dad. He's smart, and not a dandy. And your grandchildren would be bonnie indeed."

He folded his arms. "I shouldn't have let you go to Sheffield apparently. Did he take advantage of you?"

"Of course not," she spluttered, surprised her father was thinking such a thing.

"Then why are you thinking of children. It's not proper."

Her father was being difficult. *But why?* "Just letting you know I think him handsome, that's all."

He grunted.

Maisie idly picked up a cup and looked inside, then she sniffed it and wrinkled her nose at the pungent aroma.

"Set it down, girl," he said sharply. Then, in a kinder voice, he said, "Taste this." And he poured her a little cup of golden brew from a jug.

Smooth, not at all bitter, it had a taste that reminded her of fruit, like pears perhaps.

"I like it very much."

He grunted again, but she could tell he was pleased. He had a license, and the Beerhouse Act was his favorite law ever created, as he could sell from his own little brewing hut.

"Why did you sound set against Lord Turner in your letter when you've never met the man?"

Her father shook his head.

"It doesn't matter if it's Turner or the King of Persia, you're not marrying him."

He turned his back and opened another sack, digging into it with his fingers and sniffing whatever it contained.

"You're already promised to another."

CHAPTER TWENTY-SIX

Maisie thought she must have heard him incorrectly. "What are you saying, Dad? That's impossible. No one has ever said a word of this. I don't believe you."

"If you'd close your piehole, I'll tell you." Then he shook his grizzled head. "No, I'm ready for my supper. Let's go in and talk over a meal."

She'd entirely lost her appetite, but seeing how he was stoppering jugs and tying closed his sacks, she knew she would get nothing more out of him until they were seated at the dark oak table in the dining room. Her mother loved it and said a solid table was good for the family.

Unexpectedly, tears pricked her eyes, and she left her father to his tidying, heading back into their house to wash her hands and face.

Her room was the same, and with her trunk at the bottom of her bed, it looked as if she'd never left. The counterpane with roses fastidiously sewn around the hem by her mother reminded her of the dress she'd worn recently. *The perfect dress on her happiest night.*

Her mother would have liked that dress, Maisie was certain.

She didn't change for dinner, since removing her outer layer of mantle, hat, and gloves, and changing into softer shoes removed the worst of the traveling dust. Their long-time housekeeper, Gail, had put fresh water in the jug, and Maisie poured it into her washing bowl, before sniffing the cake of soap that smelled like home. She lathered up her hands and then patted her face with a damp washcloth.

In five minutes, she was back downstairs and found her father already in the dining room. Fintan didn't stand when she entered, merely nodded in greeting, and she realized with a jolt how used to such customs she now was that his behavior seemed rude. How her father would hoot with laughter if he knew her thoughts.

Maisie didn't immediately jump on the question burning in her brain. He knew she wanted to know the identity of her mysterious mate, and he was not a cruel man, so she wouldn't ask again.

As soon as she poured herself a glass of beer and settled her napkin on her lap, she looked at him expectantly. He reached for a slice of bread and quickly slathered it with creamy butter from the pot.

"It's nice to have you home," he said, then took a large bite of the bread, washing it down with his own glass of ale. "I know you're curious, so I'll say it quickly. Your mam had a best friend. Do you remember? Lorna Dugan."

"Yes! I do, but I haven't thought of her in ages." The face of the woman swam into Maisie's memories, brown hair and round cheeks. Lorna used to be with her mother while they did chores or had tea.

"Mrs. Dugan's son is a year older than you. Do you remember him?"

Dear God!

"Now, Maiz, don't look like that. Roddy's a nice lad."

A stranger, for whom she had no feeling whatsoever. She vaguely recalled him, but she hadn't spent any time with him, nor any boys, and he was much younger than Ned, so he hadn't been one of her brother's childhood friends, either.

"I'm sure he's nice, but—"

"He's your betrothed. I promised your mam on her deathbed."

She scrunched her napkin into a ball in her lap.

Why would her mother do such a thing? And why hadn't he told her before?

"Then why did you let me have a Season? Two of them? Why did you even bother to send me to London?"

Her father shrugged. "Your mother always wanted you to experience it. Said it was the most exciting thing for a girl, especially if you were going to come back home and spend your life in Dumfries. As you are," he added decidedly, and finished the rest of his bread before starting in on the sausages and mash.

"But she must have known I might find a husband." Her father frowned, and she decided to press her case. "I have agreed to marry Lord Turner. I've given him my word."

Fintan Darrow shook his head. "Your word means nothing."

She bristled, but he held his hand up. "Don't go getting all feisty on me. I don't mean it like that. I know you are a good girl and don't lie. What I mean is, no one can hold a woman to a contract or a promise, for that matter. Your word isn't the same as a man's word, and that's the truth."

She might not be able to sign a legal contract. In that, her father was correct. However, Jameson had already taken her to task for breaking her promise about riding without him. And that was inconsequential compared to this.

On the other hand, she could not be certain he wouldn't be relieved at not having to marry her.

Except, they'd had such a heartfelt talk in her drawing room . . .

And now there was Roddy Dugan.

"Why would Roddy Dugan wish to marry me? He doesn't even know me."

Her father shrugged. "For one thing, you're the most beautiful girl in Dumfries." He said it matter-of-factly, but it amazed her to hear. Her father had never commented on her looks before.

Strange how much pleasure a parent's approval could still give her even though she was all grown up. Especially when he added, "You look just like your mam."

Maisie nodded. Despite there being no likeness of her mother anywhere in their home, she could still recall her dear face and knew his words to be true.

"*Thou art thy mother's glass, and she in thee calls back the lovely April of her prime,*" she said quietly.

"What play?" her father asked.

"Not a play, a sonnet actually. Number three."

"You are a wonder, Maiz."

JAMESON'S HEAD ACHED, AND he sorely missed Maisie. He'd stayed late at Crocky's club for the past two nights. She'd only been gone three days, but he felt as if he hadn't looked into her doe-brown eyes for a lifetime.

Dammit! He wasn't supposed to feel this way again. He'd vowed when Esmera died never to let his heart become entwined with longing for another woman.

Hadn't he learned his lesson?

Apparently not, because he missed Maisie terribly. Not only was he worried she hadn't made it safely to Dumfries, he was terrified she wouldn't make it back, either. And when she did, he would worry every moment she was out of his sight for the rest of his life.

How could loving her—or anyone—be worth it?

Surely, he had been happier in the year of mourning when he had nothing and no one to care about.

Well, he thought wryly, *perhaps happier was the wrong word.*

He hadn't felt a spark of true joy until Maisie Darrow barged into his home in Sheffield. Keeping company with Elizabeth had done little more than stave off the insanity of being utterly alone for such extended periods of time. He couldn't say he felt joy with his paramour, only relief.

And then Maisie had reappeared in a London ballroom, looking, if possible, even more beautiful than he'd recalled.

Yet she had as much power to strip him of his happiness and plunge him into the depths of misery as she had to bring him joy.

He loved her!

That realization brought not a whit of surprise. Of course, he loved her.

Wandering into a pub two streets away from his townhouse, two streets in the wrong direction for the privileged and the titled, he sniffed the air, thick with pipe smoke and spilled beer. Here, a bodacious serving wench with sweat dripping off her was hurrying between the tables, and a fierce barman with a scar on his forehead ruled the roost. It wasn't his first time in the seedy establishment, nor doubtless his last.

Ordering whiskey, and having the wench leave the bottle at his table, Jameson considered how he would survive until he knew Maisie was back safely on Cambridge Street.

But then what? If she stubbed a toe, he would feel it. He knew, rationally, she was correct about the certainty of uncertainty. Yes, illness and death were all around them, especially in filthy London. *But what if he caused her death through something as careless as making love to her?*

He drank and set the glass down empty. He had looked forward to having children with Esmera when she was ready to leave off her form-fitting gowns and come away from the ballrooms. That might have happened in another year or so of her enjoying late evenings dining and dancing with society's highest echelon.

When he had offered for Maisie, deciding to wed her, he hadn't considered having a family at all. His thoughts were all on initiating her into the wonders of the sexual act, for they were obviously well-suited in that regard. If he was patient and gentle, he knew she would enjoy that aspect of being a wife. He had been all eagerness, like a green youth, wishing to speed up the days until he could slowly undress her and worship her body as she deserved.

Then, they'd had the morbid discussion of infants dying. She had been right. They all knew people who'd lost siblings or parents who'd lost children. And that had reminded him how nearly as many mothers died giving birth as babies died afterward.

What if Maisie died in childbirth? That would be entirely his fault, as plainly as if he'd shot her or slit her throat.

His mind was racing with fear until he could scarcely breathe. He refilled his glass. There were ways to prevent his seed implanting in her womb. Esmera had known them and used them successfully, but they weren't assured. Like everything in life, there was the possibility of things going wrong.

If his mind's contemplations continued circling this way, from Maisie to Esmera, from life to death, always with fear, he was going to be fit for nothing but Bedlam. He took another long drink. Maisie didn't make him happy anymore. In fact, he now felt the same overwhelming misery as he had when first she encountered him. He simply couldn't continue this way.

He would have to embody the worst rogue, a most heartless cad. He hoped he had it in him. For he needed to be free of this mantle of worry, and loving her as he did, the only way to set it aside was to set himself free of her. Free from her gold-flecked brown eyes and sweetly rounded cheeks, her bowed lips nearly always curved in a winsome smile.

He had to cut her out of his life or drown in misery.

When he saw her again, he would tell her it was finished between them.

Even so, he had to tamp down the fear he wouldn't get the chance to tell her. That something would snatch her from him, taking the last breath in her body before he could lay eyes upon her one last time.

He ordered whiskey and started to pray.

TIRED, CONFUSED, CONFLICTED, AND feeling betrayed by her own mother, Maisie had dropped the strained discussion on her first night at home. She had decided to take up the challenge again the next morning, hoping her father had considered her feelings during the night, perhaps softening a little.

They would have scones and thistle blossom jelly, which Gail made faithfully from Marion Darrow's recipe. After all, Maisie thought, as she went downstairs to breakfast, everything seemed better with jelly.

Nearly everything anyway.

While they sat outside having breakfast on the flagstone terrace with the view of her mother's now-overgrown garden, Maisie sipped tea to wash down the scones, and her father drank beer. She began again.

"Dad, tell me what Mam said exactly, will you?"

"She wrote it down so I wouldn't forget. As if I'd cock up anything to do with our only daughter," he scoffed.

Maisie set her teacup down. "Mam wrote it down, like instructions?"

"Aye, she did."

"May I see what she wrote? I have nothing of hers except her name in my Shakespeare books."

He left the terrace for a minute and returned with a wooden box she remembered seeing after her mother's death. Her father had made it himself, polishing it to a high sheen. She'd assumed it was a project merely to keep himself busy in the aftermath—and the terrible quiet in their home.

When he lifted the lid, she couldn't help leaning forward.

He gave a small sigh. "Just a few things I saved. All for you, of course."

He drew out a necklace she'd forgotten about, with a small amethyst pendant set on a simple gold chain.

"I gave her this." He brushed his thumb over the gemstone, then set it down. "And here's her hair." He had a skein of her mother's hair, braided, with a ribbon at either end to keep it tidy. "Lorna Dugan did this."

He held it up to Maisie's head. "Same as yours."

She held out her hand, and he set the braid on her palm. Feeling tears flood her eyes, she closed them, easily envisioning her mother smiling at her, with her hair gathered in a loose bun, brown eyes shining with love.

"You can read it for yourself," her father said, bringing her out of her reverie as he held out a piece of paper.

Putting the braid back in the box, she took what he offered her. As soon as she began to read it, she felt a wash of emotion. A note from her mother. *What a treasure!* She couldn't hold back the tears any longer.

"Are you crying, Maiz?"

She could only nod, her throat being too closed with emotion.

Unexpectedly, she felt her father's hand on her back, patting her gently.

"I know it was hard on you losing her, a soft girl ending up with just me and a lout-of-a-brother."

That made her chuckle.

"You did fine, Dad, and Ned has always tried his best."

"I'm not selling this house," he said unexpectedly. "I'm living here until I die. Is that understood?"

What Maisie understood was her brother and father needed to communicate better, but at that moment, she wanted only a little peace so she could enjoy her mother's note.

Wiping her eyes, she held the paper down so the full glare of the morning sunlight illuminated the page. There was Marion's gently curving script. It stole her breath, reminding her of the precious moments when her Mam taught her to read and write. Surely, those were the best gifts of all, better even than having her mother's beauty.

She read the page and felt new hope start to shimmer inside her. Rereading it, she wanted to laugh with relief.

"Seeing it in her handwriting makes it impossible to disobey, isn't that right?" her father asked.

"Yes, Dad. Impossible. She's given me permission to marry Lord Turner, and I am beyond grateful."

"What are you saying, Maiz? Right there, she says to tell you Roddy shall be your Paris, the husband chosen for you by your parents. *Remind her of how much happier Juliet's life would have been if she had fallen in love with Paris.*"

"Honestly, I agree with Mam. I think Juliet was a rash fool, for Paris was a better choice. I think she could have grown to love him, and he was plainly devoted to her."

"Then you agree with your mam."

"Yes, I do. Particularly when she says, 'If Maisie should meet her Romeo, then let it be *As You Like It* that rules her heart and her marriage."

"Yes," he agreed, "as I like it, meaning as the parent has dictated, and marriage to Roddy, just as your mam chose."

"No, Dad. It's not as *you* like it. It's *As You Like It*, the play, which of all the plays, ends in the most love marriages, all with the father's blessing. Don't you see, she didn't want me to have to die for love like in *Romeo and Juliet*, but to marry for it instead."

He stared at her. "Juliet's life would have been happier if she'd fallen in love with Paris."

Maisie smiled. "Thank you for reminding me. You've done exactly as she asked. But I have, indeed, found my Romeo. And I would rather not have to defy you and stab myself."

Her father looked aghast. "What are you saying?"

"It was a terrible ending for Juliet, but in the other play Mam mentioned, lovers wooed and married happily."

"Maybe you'll love Paris—I mean, Roddy."

"I already love Jameson Turner. And you're the first person I have told."

Fintan Darrow seemed to draw himself up in his seat, and his smile beamed from his face.

"Truly? You haven't told your brother?"

"No. I wouldn't dishonor you that way. I haven't even told Lord Turner."

Now, her father simply looked shocked.

"Then I suggest you do so if you plan to marry the man."

She smiled at him, seeing no reason to burden him with the complications of Jameson's profound grief and widowhood. Her father already understood all those things only too well.

"I suppose you'd best tell me about him, then. Shall we go for a walk, so I can show off my engaged daughter?"

Maisie enjoyed the rest of her visit in her hometown, deciding to stay five days. Even Rachel liked it, which was surprising for an east-end Londoner, although she said the air seemed too thin to be real. Maisie laughed at the maid's perception of clean air and couldn't wait to tell Jameson. It would surely make him laugh.

When not talking with her newly garrulous father, who let her try her hand at creating her own beer, she was trimming back the shrubs and rose bushes, and weeding her mother's garden. She'd found out the servants had been reluctant to touch it after Fintan yelled the very first time Jordie had trimmed a rose bush. That had been five years prior, though.

Under her loving care, her mother's garden began to take shape again, and by the third day of working on it, Maisie hoped the new plantings would take hold and be there the next time she returned home.

"Your mam would be very proud," her father declared.

"I may visit Lorna Dugan tomorrow," she told him, "as long as Roddy isn't around or harboring any expectations."

"Nah, Maiz, he's not even in Dumfries at present. He's making pig iron in the north. Mrs. Dugan will want to see you, I'm sure. You'll hear over and over how much you're like your mam."

"I don't mind that at all."

She hoped he didn't mind her bringing up a sensitive issue, but their relationship had changed now she was a woman, and she felt she could ask him.

"So, you never wanted to marry again after Mam died?" There, she'd finally asked what had been mulling in her mind since getting to know Jameson.

"Whatever for?" he asked, his expression surprised.

"For company, or if you fell in love again, I suppose."

He turned a distinct shade of red. "As for company, I don't need a wife for that," he said, blushing harder.

Maisie knew he was right in that regard, but didn't want to think exactly what her father meant or how he went about obtaining that "company." She guessed at his age, he didn't need a Lady Pepperton at his continuous beck and call, but someone more occasional.

"As for love, there is no one like your mother," he added.

That was undoubtedly how Jameson felt about Esmera.

"If I wanted another woman hanging around besides Gail and Cook, then I could have asked Mrs. Dugan when she was widowed. But it wouldn't have been right. I would have kept thinking it ought to be your mam, not Lorna in her place. I know it would have made me sadder."

Maisie nodded, more convinced than ever she shouldn't move into the townhouse Jameson had shared with Esmera. *Could she ask him to sell it and start over?*

Then she thought of Jonling Hall with regret. It was the perfect size for a family. It was also one of the prettiest homes she'd ever seen, and, best of all, her aunt and two of her cousins lived in Sheffield.

But what if all Jameson saw was Esmera in the drawing room and the dining room and on the stairs and, worst of all, in the bedroom!

On the journey back to London, she wondered how she could help Ned and her father make peace. After all, it had been the best visit she'd had with her father since her mother had passed, and Ned, too, should enjoy such a relationship. In all likelihood, Caroline would have to take charge. One thing was certain, her father wanted to keep his own home and wouldn't be living with her and Jameson.

Weary and dirty, she and Rachel took a hackney from Euston Station, expecting glad faces when they walked in the front door in Pimlico.

Instead, Caroline looked as if someone had died, and Ned was equally grim.

"You had best sit down for this," her sister-in-law said, and directed her to the wing-backed chair. Then Ned stood before her.

Blinking up at him, dread curling in her stomach, she said, "Tell me. Quickly."

"It's Lord Turner."

She gasped. She couldn't face it. Something terrible had happened to him. She loved him with all her heart.

"He has reneged on his offer to marry you. In short, he's called off your engagement."

CHAPTER TWENTY-SEVEN

Maisie heard the words with relief, for they were not news of Jameson's death. She breathed deeply, taking a moment to regain her composure. Then their true import sunk in.

There would be no marriage to the man she loved, no happily-ever-after, no *As You Like It* ending.

What had happened to change his mind?

"You spoke with him directly?"

"I did," Ned said. "He came to the door a few days ago, and we met right here."

Maisie looked at the sofa as if Jameson might appear.

"Were you here, too?" she asked Caroline, in case Ned had been demanding or off-putting. Her sister-in-law would have tempered any such meeting.

"I was," she said. "He didn't ask me to leave, so I didn't."

"Tell me what he said," Maisie said, surprised at how calm she sounded when inside she was starting to shatter.

Ned answered. "Turner apologized, as if that does us any good. He said he'd come to the conclusion you and he were not suited at all. Obviously, he did not go into detail. I assume he has an affliction. Or perhaps an unusual preference."

Maisie stared at her brother, knowing she was frowning, yet trying to comprehend what he was implying.

"For goodness sake," Caroline interrupted. "An affliction!" She rolled her eyes. "Lord Turner seemed terribly out of sorts. Tormented, I would call him. He said he was sorry how this would affect you and would make sure everyone knew it was on account of his own failing and nothing to do with you."

"That won't help Maisie's reputation," Ned grumbled.

Maisie didn't know what to say, stuck on the word *tormented*.

"I suppose I could go see him." Tomorrow, in the daylight, perhaps it wouldn't seem so final.

"You will not. Word has already got out. I heard it mentioned at White's that the engagement was off."

"It would look bad," Caroline agreed, "for you to be seen with him now that he has broken it off."

Maisie nodded, too exhausted from the trip and the emotional upheaval to want to fight. In the morning, she would at least write to him and ask for an explanation. Surely, he owed her that.

JAMESON RECEIVED THE LETTER from Maisie and let the relief of her safe return wash over him. That was all that mattered. If she was angry over his breaking their engagement, he could deal with such. She was alive and well, having survived the long train ride in both directions. He could relax and breathe properly for the first time since he'd learned of her departure.

He'd also managed to climb out of his self-destructive despondency, ceasing to drink everything in sight by the bottle instead of the glass. He'd kept that up for three days and nights before realizing the liquor only increased his anxiety over her absence.

However, that night, after ten days, finally, knowing she was home in London, he would sleep well again.

Dear Lord Turner,

I was surprised by the news you had ended our brief engagement and no longer wish to marry. From all my brother and my sister-in-law indicated, your mind is made up and cannot be altered. Thus, I won't attempt to do so. I only want to let you know I was happy during our engagement, maybe more than you could understand. I wish you had felt the same.

Also, as it leaves me unsettled, I would appreciate knowing why you came to the conclusion we do not suit one another. I was under the notion that we did. I will be unable to alter any grievous flaws in my character for future relationships if you don't tell me how I disappointed you.

Yours sincerely,
Maisie Darrow

Not a word of Shakespeare. *How strange!*

He nearly set pen to paper to respond to her but decided against it. Anything he said would be hurtful, and then she would write back, and then he would feel the need to respond again. Before he knew it, he would be inviting her to take a stroll so they could more easily converse. *And then, where would he be?*

As soon as he laid eyes upon her, he would want to hold her. And if he held her, he would be hard pressed not to kiss her. They would have to get engaged again if he did either.

Feeling like a cad, he folded her letter and slid it into his desk drawer. Jameson had no plans to attend any more of the Season's events, as he had absolutely no wish to make merry or to be the object of the *ton's* speculation. Thus, if Maisie reentered society, as she ought to, he would not run into her.

In fact, he might pack up and return to Sheffield. He had a few business dealings to secure, and then with nothing to hold him in London, he could retire to the country.

If only that didn't feel like a coward running away!

Meanwhile, knowing she was in London, he confined himself to his townhouse for the remainder of the day and the next as well, while he set up meetings with his banker, his accountant, and his stock exchange broker. Staying in all the time only exacerbated how unsettled he felt in his own home.

Esmera had furnished the drawing room with ornately carved sofa and chairs, their dark wood trim reminding her of Spain. He found them to be as uncomfortable as church pews. The dining room was also dark, with blood-red wallpaper and a chunky-legged table. She forbade modern lamps while eating and entertaining, and lit the room with the candelabra and wall sconces. He couldn't be bothered to light enough candles to chase the shadows away, and therefore, never used the room anymore.

His study was piled with old papers he needed to throw out. It held no appeal. So, he retreated to the main bedroom upstairs, throwing his jacket upon the bed. However, he could not shake the feeling she haunted the room, far more than in Sheffield since Esmera had made no impact on their country home. Here, however—this was her domain.

In this bedroom where Esmera loved trying on her clothing and where he'd enjoyed stretching out on the bed to watch her, he could still see her plainly. If he looked toward the wardrobe, she was choosing that evening's gown. In front of the full-length looking glass, she was twirling to catch a glimpse of her own backside. At the ottoman by the dresser, his wife brushed out her hair, then snapped at the maid to hurry with the styling so she wouldn't miss a moment of the ball or dinner party.

He hadn't changed any of their room, and now, he found it discomfiting. Too empty of her, yet also too full of her.

Indeed, his bedroom didn't give him any peace or joy. No wonder he'd never brought Elizabeth there.

Their small townhouse had a single spare bedroom, which Esmera had ignored. Dinner guests never saw it, and she didn't use it, so it was as the previous owners had left it. Jameson wandered into it and sat on the sagging mattress. He'd had little money when he'd first purchased this home. Yet, due to his hard work for Simon's estate, the stipend which came with the viscountcy, and his own smart investments on the stock exchange, he'd had enough to furnish his townhouse properly. Now, he had no heart to enjoy it.

No heart for anything anymore.

Lying back upon the dusty counterpane, he stared at the faded canopy overhead. Above that was a flaking ceiling. The dilapidated state of this one room in his London home must be indicative of his spirit, he decided. Utter negligence.

He had been negligent in his marriage, he assumed, or his wife would be alive. Images rushed into his brain, unbidden and unstoppable.

Esmera declaring her intent to go to Bath without him, eyes flashing defyingly.

Maisie's sunny expression as her train hurtled along the tracks.

Esmera on the marble slab at the morgue.

Maisie gazing up at him just before he kissed her.

He threw his arm over his eyes and moaned. Allowing himself to indulge in this foolishness for a minute or two, he then grew weary of being so close to derangement.

"Snap out of it, man!" he muttered aloud. "Time to sell this place."

That surprised him, but when he thought about it, it felt right. He would be happy if he never had to sleep another night under its roof.

No, he wouldn't be *happy*. He would be *less miserable*. The only happiness he'd felt in the past year was through Maisie and her silly Shakespeare quotations. And her eyes and her laugh and her lips.

Tomorrow, he would go to Chesterton's in Kensington and meet with the established old firm of estate agents. The sooner they found someone to take the place off his hands, the better.

MAISIE HOPED FOR A response from Jameson, waiting patiently the first day after she knew her letter had been delivered. The next day, still hopeful, she felt less patient, even while strolling with Eleanor and Maggie along the Serpentine. They were aghast to discover she'd gone to Dumfries to fight her father into letting her marry Jameson only to have him call it off while she was away.

The following day, she became downright annoyed, which turned into unleashed fury by the next morning.

How dare he ignore her? She stomped through her house. Then, just to spite him, she rode the family carriage over Battersea Bridge. Twice.

On the fifth day, Lord Roleston sent his condolences on the ending of her engagement, and said he hoped to see her at a Mayfair ball the next night.

"Yes!" she exclaimed.

"What is it?" Caroline asked, startled in her seat by the window doing needlepoint.

"A ball. Tomorrow night."

"You said you were finished with the Season!"

Maisie had. In a rash moment, two days earlier when Ned pointed out there were many weeks left and many events to attend, she'd declared herself entirely done with all of it.

"I've changed my mind. Lord Roleston expressly asked if I would be there. And he can quote Shakespeare," she added.

Caroline nodded, looking bemused. "Well, that's a good thing to have in common, isn't it?"

Maisie found herself feeling lighter for the first time in days. It *was* something in common. A handsome man who had never been married, who liked to dance and was plainly interested in her, and who didn't consider her ruined despite her brief interlude of engagement.

Moreover, he had not only read Shakespeare but taken the trouble to memorize some excellent lines.

What a prince! He would certainly not have been confused during *Richard II.* Regardless, she couldn't be positive Lord Roleston would have carried her through the streets of London, either, that glorious evening when she lost her shoe.

Shrugging, she hoped she never needed to find out.

Meanwhile, the memory of what had happened on Maggie's sofa would have to be buried and forgotten. *Like an unloved corpse*, she thought cruelly.

Resigned to not ever hearing from Jameson Turner again, the next night Maisie put on her favorite blue silk gown and looked forward to the ball. It was very near to the Lindseys' townhouse, so Eleanor would be there as well.

When Maisie swept into Lord and Lady Felton's spacious corner house and spied Eleanor, it felt as if the past few weeks had never happened. Unfortunately, they had, and as she went through the small receiving line, she was taken aback by condolences from the host and hostess and their offspring, twin girls for whom the ball was being thrown.

"So sorry to hear about your misfortune," said Lady Felton.

Maisie nodded, gasping inside, having believed in polite society no one would even mention it. She was wrong. As she crossed the foyer and climbed the stairs to the great room where the ball would take place, she heard whispers. No one had ever had cause to whisper about her before—at least, not until the dahlia garden incident.

With Ned and Caroline beside her, she held her head up, ignored the gossips, and searched for Eleanor.

Luckily, Lord Roleston was already there and was the first to approach her.

"They may be brutal tonight," he warned her. "Did you realize such could be the case?"

"No, I hadn't even considered the wagging tongues. *Opinion's but a fool, that makes us scan the outward habit by the inward man.* They shall see what they wish to see by my appearance here tonight. Probably, they'll deem me shallow and too flighty for already being out after so recently being thrown over."

"Did your trip away from London have something to do with your break from Lord Turner?"

At first, Maisie thought him too forward, then she sighed. *What did it matter now if she became friendly with another man?*

After all, the rest of her Season would be spent trying to eradicate the love she felt for Jameson. And, if she found another who would make an adequate husband, even Lord Roleston, then she would deem herself lucky. Otherwise, there was always Roddy Dugan and his pig iron.

"I went to Dumfries to prevent being treated like the *Merchant of Venice*'s Portia who said, '*I may neither choose who I would, nor refuse who I dislike; so is the will of a living daughter curbed by the will of a dead father.*' Or in my case, my dear mother. As it turned out, my father had mistaken my mother's intent. In any case, it was all for naught, as Lord Turner changed his mind while I was away."

Oh dear! She recalled she was supposed to say something to put herself in a favorable light, but couldn't think what.

"How could he do such a thing to you?" Lord Roleston looked aghast. "Does the viscount love another?"

"Yes," she answered, thinking of Esmera. "I believe he does."

Lord Roleston snatched at her dance card and held it still, while he searched his pocket for a pencil. Eventually, she drew a miniature one out of her reticule and handed it to him.

Taking it, he said, "I am sorry if you were played falsely, Miss Darrow."

She glanced past him. In her heart, she couldn't really accuse Jameson of such. She'd known from the beginning his first marriage was the perfect union. Nothing she offered him could match up to that.

Glancing back at Lord Roleston, she realized he was busy writing on her card.

"Not too many times, please, my lord, or new gossip water will be poured by tomorrow."

He grinned at her. "I am happy to be in the same pot of water as you, Miss Darrow. Still, to protect your sensibilities and your reputation, I have only marked my name down thrice, which is only once more than entirely proper."

She smiled at him. "Thank you. For if we were entirely proper, what would anyone have to talk about?"

Thus, as the evening progressed, Lord Roleston returned to her side more than once. He made Eleanor choke on her lemonade with a joke about Gothic romance, and, most importantly, he kept Maisie distracted. When they weren't dancing, he told her about his small estate in Yorkshire, his interest in cultivating sheep, and his two sisters and brother.

At the end of the evening, she was exceedingly grateful for his existence. Without Lord Roleston in attendance, she would have sorely missed Jameson and probably vowed never to attend another event of the Season. Instead, she found herself looking forward to going boating near Chelsea in a few days. She had agreed to be in the same party as Lord Roleston and his sister, Emma, and share a picnic blanket with them.

However, that night, as she undressed and climbed into bed, the heaviness of wanting Jameson's company settled upon her again like an iron blanket. She wondered if he missed her at all.

They didn't suit. That was his only explanation, and not even given to her but to her brother. She hadn't believed him cruel before, but now, she did. She also thought him a liar. Plainly, they did suit, and very well, too. But he didn't love her, and ultimately, he'd chosen the dead woman who had completely captured his heart.

JAMESON HEARD AT HIS club about Miss Darrow and Lord Roleston. Their names had become linked. The feeling upon learning this information was unpleasant at best and downright gut-wrenching at worst. *His* Maisie was being wooed by the son of an earl. Still a viscount, however, as anyone would be happy to tell her, a wealthier one who would end up with an earldom, even if it was a bloody sheep farm in the north.

He had chosen this path, Jameson reminded himself daily as he made himself scarce so the estate agent could measure the rooms of his home. He had wanted the worrisome care of Miss Darrow to be on someone else's shoulders. The annoying thing was how he still kept thinking of her and worrying over her just the same. When he found out she'd been boating, he knew he should have been there in case she fell in and needed saving.

What if Roleston wasn't careful with her precious life?

He strolled along to Dolly's Chop House, passing under the arch from Paternoster Row and into Queens' Court Passage. The delicious aromas were already wafting out from his favorite casual dining establishment. He would while away a couple hours, as he always met people he knew there, catching up in the smoking room with the latest news of Parliament, and, by the time he went home, the estate agent would be finished poking around.

Unfortunately, the first thing he saw was Lord Roleston dining with a man who looked similar enough he was obviously a relation. Instantly, it gave Jameson a sour stomach, but when the viscount's gaze rested upon him, he nodded to the sandy-haired fellow and moved past to find an empty table as far from him as possible.

Not for the first time, he shook his head at the twist of fate that snatched his half brother Tobias from the world precisely when Jameson was ready to defy his father and tell him of his existence. Their cousin Simon said he looked very like Tobias, and it would have been a gift to sit at Dolly's with family.

Roleston had sisters, too, Jameson recalled. Truly, he was a blessed man who now also had Maisie.

He could only hope the townhouse sold quickly, for he was more than ready to quit London for Sheffield. He ordered food from the waitress—the owner, Mr. Howell, always employed pretty ones to the delight of the customers—and sat holding a daily rag in one hand and a drink in the other.

"I say, Turner, you turned out to be a bit of a rogue."

He looked up from his glass of beer to find Roleston standing beside the table, a belligerent expression upon his face. Just behind him was the other man, plainly his brother.

"What are you on about?" Jameson asked.

"I could ask the same of you. What were you about, putting your name on her card all those times to bring notice to the two of you, even before you were formally engaged? And then waiting for her to leave town before breaking it off with her like a gutless coward?" The man sneered. "You give viscounts a bad name, frankly."

Jameson stared at him. He wanted to tell him to go to the devil or that it was none of his business. Yet, it was Roleston's business if he now cared for Maisie. And Jameson had to hand it to the man for coming over to him in public. In fact, Dolly's had grown quiet with the other patrons wondering whether this scene would turn nasty.

"Nothing to say?" Roleston added into the silence.

If he was hoping to cause a scene, perhaps even a fight, he would be disappointed. Jameson wasn't going to give him the satisfaction. He only wasted a punch on reprobates of the caliber of Granger. The man who stood before him, who was comforting Maisie, didn't deserve his wrath, only his gratitude.

"I thank you for stepping in and partnering with Miss Darrow." He wasn't sure exactly how he got the words over his now dry tongue, but that should satisfy Roleston.

However, the man didn't leave. He stood staring down at Jameson until there was nothing else he could do. Slowly, Jameson rose to his feet.

"Is there something more you wish to say?"

Roleston leaned closer. "Aren't you going to respond to my calling you a coward?"

Jameson sighed. "I understand your desire to defend the lady's honor."

A searing memory of Maisie writhing under him on Lady Cambrey's sofa chose that moment to flash in front of his eyes. Her honor did, in fact, need defending. He had behaved badly and deserved a thrashing.

Glancing around at the eager faces, he wondered if he owed it to Maisie to let Roleston pop him one in public.

"Everyone here has heard you call me a coward, and, thus, you have done your duty."

"Have I?" With that less-than-stirring comeback, Roleston hauled back his right arm.

Good grief! Jameson thought. *Don't damn well give me so much warning.*

CHAPTER TWENTY-EIGHT

It seemed the viscount was moving in slow motion. *How long would Jameson have to wait for his soul-cleansing punishment?* he wondered.

And then he recalled how Roleston was going to enjoy all Maisie's warmth and passion next, if he was lucky. In a flash, his blood boiled with jealousy.

As the man's fist finally came toward him, Jameson ducked and sent a quick jab in return. Not into the viscount's face. He didn't want to leave a visible mark or break his nose. He only wanted to end this.

His fist met solidly with Roleston's stomach, and the man doubled over like a pecking hen.

Jameson drew coins out of his pocket, which he deposited on the table, picked up his newspaper, and turned into the fist of the other Roleston brother, which sent him toppling to the floor.

Damn it all. He had been right. It would be good to have family!

MAISIE OPENED THE NOTE from Eleanor. "Come to Portman Square tomorrow at 1 p.m. Lunch and pleasant surprise awaits."

For a brief, heart-stopping moment, she imagined it might have something to do with Jameson. Then she realized how foolish an idea that was. Her cousin would undoubtedly have told her if, somehow, she was holding the man captive in the Lindsey drawing room.

Then, she went riding with Lord Roleston, his older sister, and his younger brother. They were very sweet people. Naturally, Ned approved of this new beau, as the viscount would be an earl one day. Ned was looking forward to parties at the man's Yorkshire country home and telling people his sister was a countess.

"Fie," she muttered the following day, as she adjusted her hat and got into the hired cabriolet, setting out for Lord and Lady Lindsey's townhouse. Despite her brother's happiness, she would rather have been a bastard's wife than Queen of England.

As soon as the door at Portman Square was opened by Mr. Binkley, she knew what the surprise was. If the Lindseys' beloved butler was in Town, then so were the Lindseys.

"Come in," Eleanor called from the drawing room doorway.

Maisie nodded her thanks to Mr. Binkley as she handed him her mantle, and headed over to her cousin, giving her cheek a kiss before peering past her. There was the eldest Blackwood sister.

Jenny opened her arms wide, and Maisie rushed over for a hug. She was the calm, capable sister who Maisie had often longed to have as her own.

"You are showing," she declared as she drew away from Jenny, still holding both her hands and looking down at her slightly swelling stomach, barely disguised by the fall of her gown. "How do you feel?"

"Very healthy," Jenny declared, her brown eyes being nearly the same shade as Maisie's own. In fact, she looked most like Jenny, if her cousin's hair were about ten shades blonder.

"Is everyone here?" she asked, meaning Simon and Jenny's eldest son, Lionel, and the twins, Daniela and Pamela. "It's so quiet."

Jenny laughed. "The nanny has taken them out for a stroll. And Simon went directly to Parliament."

"When did you arrive in Town?"

"Only yesterday," she said, taking a seat and gesturing for her sister and Maisie to do the same.

Maisie felt honored. "And you invited me so quickly?" She turned to Eleanor, hoping she wasn't intruding while the Lindseys were still settling in.

"Why, yes!" Jenny said. "You are family. Maggie should be here soon, too."

"Strange," Maisie said, "I didn't see Ned's invitation to this little gathering."

They all burst out laughing. Then Jenny shook her head. "Ned and Caroline will come to dinner very soon, and you, too, I hope." She cocked her head. "And, from what I hear, we should set an extra setting for Simon's cousin."

Maisie's stomach twisted. "If you do, then I shall not attend."

Although at first, she'd longed to run into him, now, too much time had passed. It would be mortifying to get together over dinner as if nothing had happened, with everyone knowing he'd broken it off.

"What! I don't understand." Jenny looked between Eleanor, whose head sunk, her palm on her forehead, and back to Maisie, who felt her cheeks redden.

"Oh, the blasted slow post," she exclaimed. "The last news I had was of an engagement. Eleanor! Why didn't you tell me?"

"You came in late last night and only just got up," the youngest sister protested. "I could hardly start with how was your trip and, by the way, Jameson Turner is a cad."

In five minutes, Maisie had explained the situation, leaving Jenny looking a little morose.

"Do not be sad on my account, coz," Maisie implored. "I have a new suitor. A very nice man, Lord Roleston. Do you know him?"

Jenny shrugged. "Heir to a sheep family, I believe," she said, summing him up succinctly and dismissing him with a frown. "But where is Jameson now?" she asked. "How is it you haven't spoken to him?"

Maisie could only shake her head. "He has no wish to see me or speak to me."

Jenny's expression changed to exasperation. "I confess, he has not been right since Lady Turner died, but I truly believed you'd brought him out of his melancholy, restoring not only his good humor but his manners, as well. That night at our home, before he went away, we had such a delightful dinner party. It was the first time I'd seen him smile or laugh in months."

What could Maisie say? "Can we relinquish the subject of Lord Turner?"

"But I just got here," Maggie's voice came from the doorway. "And I haven't had a chance to pile on the agony yet."

She sashayed gracefully across the thick carpet, looking stunning in a violet gown trimmed with silver.

"Oh, don't get up," she ordered as they all started to do exactly that. Sinking gracefully onto the sofa next to Jenny, Maggie kissed her sister's cheek.

"You look well," she told her.

"And you look gorgeous," Jenny said in return.

Maggie smiled, while lifting a perfectly sloped shoulder, as if to say, of course.

"So, what did I miss? Lord Turner is behaving like a frightened ass, and our Maisie is suffering the consequences."

"Frightened?" Jenny asked. "What do you mean, Mags?"

"It's obvious, isn't it? He is terrified at having fallen in love with our delightful cousin."

Eleanor took Maisie's hand and squeezed it. "It makes sense."

"No," Maisie said. "It does not. I know the reason why Lord Turner broke off our extraordinarily brief engagement, which he was forced into by Ned, by the way."

They all stared at her with questioning eyes.

"He's still in love with Lady Turner. And honestly, who can blame him. He had a perfect marriage, and she was perfect in every way."

"Pish," said Maggie.

"Certainly not perfect," remarked Jenny quietly.

Eleanor simply squeezed her hand again.

"No one is perfect," Maggie added, then she reached up and smoothed her already perfect hair, as if giving the lie to her own words.

"Marriages unquestionably are not," Jenny said emphatically.

They all looked at her.

"No, there is nothing wrong with mine," she said. "Simon and I are in love as ever." She patted her stomach and got a fond look upon her face.

"Were you going to say something else?" Maggie asked. "I think you drifted off into a baby daze."

"Baby daze?" Jenny repeated, then seemed to snap to the present. "Those are the exact right words. Anyway, I would never disparage the dead, but I spent more time with Lord and Lady Turner than any of you. Yes, they were in love. Their marriage barely had time to get out of the honeymoon stage, after all. But—" she broke off.

"But?" Maisie and Eleanor asked at once.

"As I said, I don't like to speak ill—"

"Yes," Maggie interrupted her sister, "we know. Go on."

Jenny sighed. "Lord Turner seemed to spend an inordinate amount of effort keeping his wife happy or, at least, content."

Into the silence, Maisie felt the need to defend him. "That was nice of him, don't you think?"

"I do. I think he is a good man, a self-made man, too. Meaning no disrespect to Maggie's husband or my own, but Jameson has done it all on his own despite having a difficult, cold, and unreasonable father in my husband's uncle." She seemed to be thinking of him when she shuddered.

"Anyway, their marriage was far from perfect. I cannot imagine working so hard for someone who . . . seemed . . . well . . . ," she trailed off.

"Say it," Maggie ordered.

"A tad ungrateful, full of herself, selfish, immature. Dear God, if another woman so much as spoke or took the limelight, as they say, for a moment, Lady Turner would speak louder or simply get up and leave. Petulant, self-centered, vain as a peacock."

Maisie was stunned. She had never heard Lady Turner spoken of in such a fashion, and she had never heard sweet, reliable Jenny say anything like that about anybody."

"I'm so glad, sister dear, you don't ever speak ill of the dead," Maggie said drolly.

Jenny realized what she'd done and clamped a hand to her mouth. Eleanor was laughing uproariously, which was terribly irreverent of her.

"Anyway," Maggie agreed with another shrug of her beautiful shoulders, "that was my experience with her, too."

Since Jenny had started, she seemed to think she had best be the one to finish.

"Esmera Turner had Jameson so twisted around her finger, he was completely wrung out by her death. Truly devastated, with a terrible lost look when Simon and I first came to London to help him home. I think he had given so much of himself to her, he didn't know how to live without her. Not that any of us can imagine what it is like to lose a spouse."

She paused, then added, "Truly, I don't want to imagine my life without Simon."

Again, she placed a protective hand on her stomach. "However, Lady Turner lived for London and the *bon ton*, whereas Jameson lived for Lady Turner."

Her words seemed to prove Maisie's supposition. Jameson was still deeply in love, perfect marriage or not. And Esmera was the only woman for him.

Suddenly, they heard male voices in the foyer.

"Simon is home," Jenny exclaimed, jumping up and looking as excited as if he'd been at sea for a year.

Their marriage had to be perfect, Maisie thought.

"And he's brought company. Someone from the House of Lords, I'll warrant."

"Maybe it's Cam," Maggie said, "although I think my dearest said he had errands to run for his mother before he came over."

Maisie already knew. She could tell. Her ear had caught the particular cadence of his voice. Her body could tell, perhaps sensing his particular breath and skin and smell. She felt the lurch in her stomach and began to ring her hands. She wanted to run to the adjoining room through the other doorway. Or hide under the sofa.

Anything rather than see him now, in front of her family, especially after they'd just been talking about him.

He crossed the threshold after Simon and any awkwardness she had felt disappeared when she saw him.

"Dear God," she exclaimed. "What happened to your face?"

JAMESON RAISED A HAND to his mouth, where the cut had bled quite a bit the day before but now was just a messy reminder of his own stupidity. His cheek had also developed a large and colorful bruise.

He opened his mouth, which hurt, then closed it. He was speechless.

Maisie looked breathtakingly beautiful. He wanted simply to gaze at her, drink in the happiness her appearance gave him, like clear, cool water to a parched man.

Maisie!

"Good day, Jameson," Simon's wife was the first to speak and remind him of his manners. "What a surprise!"

Quickly, he approached her as she stood to greet him. Taking her hand, he bowed over it, getting a good view of her blossoming stomach.

"You are looking very well, Jenny." He was glad they were on a given-name footing and considered her to be his family. He hoped she felt the same way.

"I wish I could say the same." She indicated his face.

After offering her a tight smile, he paid his respects next to Lady Cambrey, who uncomfortably reminded him of Esmera—something about her satisfied smile, beautiful as it was, and her knowing glance. She had a way of looking right inside a man, taking his measure, and knowing his flaws. Or maybe that was only Esmera who did such.

Next, he went to Eleanor, feeling as if he were heading closer to the gallows with each Blackwood sister, with everyone in the room awaiting the inevitable.

Eleanor let him take her hand while giving him a strange, examining look, as if she had only just been thinking about him.

In that instant, he was certain he'd been the topic of conversation right before he and Simon had arrived.

Why else had the ladies all stared at him with that same judging look?

Then, at last, he was directly in front of her, her gold and brown eyes, like shiny topaz gems, narrowing as she took in his appearance. Her lovely bowed lips slightly parted questioningly.

"Miss Darrow," he greeted, taking her hand.

What more should he say? The truth. "It is good to see you again."

She flinched, and he felt instantly remorseful for the way he had callously—cowardly—left her letter unanswered.

"In answer to your question, Miss Darrow, my face met with another man's fist. As I was not looking at him directly, I could not duck in time."

Simon, now standing beside his wife, her hand in his, laughed at this remark.

"I don't think Jameson being hurt is funny," Jenny said, elbowing her husband in the stomach.

"*Oof,*" he said, looking pained, then he grinned again. "But it is."

"Who did it?" Lady Cambrey asked, her intelligent eyes seeming to already know the answer.

He wanted to lie. He did not want to invoke the name of Maisie's new suitor in this place, causing all the ladies to begin silently speculating, nor did he wish to cause her any embarrassment. However, Simon already knew the truth. He'd run into his cousin near the Palace of Westminster as the House of Lords was concluding their day's business, and they'd caught up over ale at a nearby politician's pub.

Jameson was thrilled to have his cousin close again, despite the harsh conversation they'd had.

"Congratulations!" Simon had said as soon as they'd sat down in the pub.

"None needed."

Simon slapped the table. "It's not every day a man gets engaged."

"No, that's true," Jameson had told him, "but I am not."

"Not what?"

"Engaged. I broke it off."

Silence, then, "You idiot. Dullard. Witless dunce!"

Jameson had simply shrugged.

Simon had stared another moment. "I don't know whether I'm angrier at you or sadder for you. Maisie Darrow is a wonderful young lady."

Somehow, Jameson had defended himself, explaining as best he could. They'd moved on to other topics, with his cousin falling silent again every few minutes, then muttering "fool" under his breath.

Eventually, Simon had invited him home to visit Jenny and have lunch.

Now, he had no choice but to answer Lady Cambrey's question. However, before he could say anything, he felt a gentle tug and realized he was still holding Maisie's soft hand in his.

Instantly, with their gazes locked, he released it.

"I believe it was Roleston," Maggie added, tired of waiting apparently, and he watched Maisie's face pale.

"No!" she said.

"Actually, it was, but not *your*...I mean, not the Viscount Roleston. Not your friend." *Dammit*, he was babbling. *Spit it out, man*, he urged himself. "It was his brother."

"What!" Maisie asked. "Why on earth would he hit you?"

Jameson sighed. "I suppose because I had just punched his brother in the stomach."

Why Eleanor and Simon found this funny, Jameson would never know, but they both were laughing at his tale. Maisie, however, was not amused.

"And why would you punch Lord Roleston in the stomach?" she asked him, her voice sounding thin.

He considered this. "Because I didn't think it sporting of me to break his nose or leave a mark on his face."

Her gaze went to his own split lip.

He grinned slightly, although it hurt. "Apparently, his brother had no such compunction when it came to my face."

"Maybe he considered you were already as ugly as could be, so what did it matter," Simon quipped.

His cousin apparently considered himself witty, but Jameson still felt too raw, seeing Maisie, especially seeing her looking displeased with him. Knowing the next man she kissed would not be him didn't help his mood.

"I should go," he said.

"Ridiculous," Maisie said. "You only just arrived. Besides, I was about to leave."

"I thought you were staying for lunch," Eleanor said to her cousin.

"And I thought you had come to lunch," Simon reminded Jameson. "Remember, we discussed leg of lamb."

Jameson glared at his cousin.

"I don't wish to make Miss Darrow uncomfortable by my presence."

Maisie sniffed and looked at him. "I can assure you, my lord, your presence makes no difference to me one way or the other. If you wish to dine with your cousin, as I wish to dine with mine, then stay. As long as we are not having *beef and iron and steel* or we shall *eat like wolves and fight like devils.*"

"I beg your pardon?" Simon asked. "I'm sure it will be lamb."

Jameson was thrilled to hear her quote the Bard again.

Maisie shook her head. "Yes, I'm sure you're right, Lord Lindsey. We shall all dine together, cousins and more cousins. *If this were played upon a stage now, I could condemn it as an improbable fiction.*"

"*Twelfth Night,*" Jenny said.

"Oh, I do hope John gets here soon," Maggie said, sitting back down, a saucy look of enjoyment upon her face. "Is it too early for wine?"

HOURS LATER, JAMESON FELT as if he needed air. Great lungfuls of it, and he stepped into the Lindseys' attractive back garden with Simon, a cigar in each of their hands. The homes on Portman Square were fortunate to have a little greenery between them and the mews for their horses and carriages. His fervent desire to remain in Maisie's company had warred with his desperate need to fight the unbelievable attraction he felt for her.

Consequently, he had been on tenterhooks all through the meal, wondering how the encounter would eventually conclude, and how they would part. The lamb on his plate might have been iron and steel, as she'd quoted, for all he could taste of it.

Every time she looked at him with a hint of hurt in her glorious eyes, his food turned to sawdust. Every one of her disappointed looks where her beautiful, sunny smile used to be, cut him to the quick.

"What are you going to do, cousin?" Simon asked.

There was only one thing he could be talking about.

"I don't know."

Simon puffed at his cigar. "You aren't happy," he pointed out.

Jameson grimaced and shook his head. "I am never happy."

"That's not what I hear from our Miss Eleanor or from Maggie. They said you were a different man with Maisie." Simon stopped looking at the small garden and faced him. "I want you to be happy after all you've been through. It might not be the same intensity as it was with Esmera, but if you've found a measure of contentment with her, why are you fighting it?"

"You have it all wrong," Jameson told him. "It is precisely as intense with Maisie, but not the same, naturally. You can't compare people, but the feelings are all there, just as strong. My feelings are so far beyond contentment, it's frightening. That is the problem. I'm not up to going through it again."

"Going through *it?*"

"You were in a bad way after Toby died in Burma," Jameson reminded him. "What if you had to go through that again? What if you had to put yourself in the same position? Then, imagine instead of Toby, it were Jenny."

Simon nodded. "I understand what you mean, but there is no certainty for any of us."

"That's what Maisie says, too. I know that. I'm not an imbecile. But it seems more desirable to not experience anything like Esmera's death ever again if I can avoid it."

Simon nodded. "Of course, but then, I ask you, what's the point in being alive? You've already lost a parent and a brother and a wife. That's a lot, I know. You may lose a child or two or three, but you may also have a delightful family of ten kids."

"What!" Jameson exclaimed, and they both chuckled

"Not ten then, but even one is a blessing. You may enjoy a long life with Maisie or a short time. For me, I wouldn't trade a minute I've had with Jenny or my children, even if I knew it would end tomorrow. They are the reason for my being alive, if you see my point. I would be safe from pain without them, perhaps, but that sounds like death to me. I would rather live."

Jameson considered his cousin's words.

Then, against propriety, Maisie came out alone onto the back terrace. She looked like a woman with something on her mind.

Simon nodded to them both and, also against all rules of decorum, he went inside and left them alone.

CHAPTER TWENTY-NINE

"You know you shouldn't have come out here by yourself," Jameson admonished, yet he didn't look upset.

"Oh, *pish!*" she said, mimicking Maggie. "Besides, we've had some good experiences in a garden." *And in a drawing room.*

"You came to give me hell for treating you badly?" he asked. Then added, "And rightly so."

"It was bad of you not to respond to my letter." She felt the need to be nonchalant since he hadn't, in fact, apologized for his treatment of her. "I found ways to occupy myself without you."

"Roleston," he bit out quickly.

"Yes, Lord Roleston, among other diversions. Is that why you came to blows?"

Jameson hesitated. "He felt the need to defend your honor against my shabby treatment of you, and I fully intended to let him. Then he took too blasted long, and I reacted. I ducked and punched, and next thing I knew, his brother had taken care of upholding your honor for him."

He touched his chin. "If you intend to remain with Roleston, you better keep his brother near for protection because your man cannot hit for trying."

Jameson was purposefully making light of it all. It infuriated her.

"As long as you've given me your blessing, my lord, I do find Lord Roleston and I *suit* very well."

She noticed he winced slightly, his own words tossed back at him.

"Why did you leave without telling me?" he demanded suddenly. "And on a train? Just like that?"

Her mouth dropped open at his harsh tone. *Did she owe him an explanation after the way he had treated her?*

"Is that why you broke off our engagement? Truly?" she asked.

"You must have known how it would affect me. How can I forgive you putting me through that pain with utter disregard?"

Maisie had only meant to spare him the argument, knowing she had to go with or without his approval.

"So, you cannot forgive me for going on a train?"

He dashed her words away with his hand and then, when he saw the cigar between his fingers, he puffed on it, before blowing out a large cloud.

"I cannot forgive you for endangering your life and not caring what that would do to me. You said we were friends," he reminded her.

"We were more than that, weren't we? Yet my life is only valued for how it affects your well-being? I suppose I should remain a prisoner in a room with soft pillows." She could not keep the derision out of her voice.

"I was trying to keep you safe. Don't you see that?" he asked.

"You were trying to keep me safe for *you*, to somehow make amends and gain redemption for losing Esmera, even though you couldn't have done anything to prevent her death. The train accident was not your fault, but you are carrying the weight of it as if it were."

If he wanted an explanation as to why she'd left without talking to him, she would give it to him.

"You had forbidden me even to ride a horse. I knew you would forbid me to take a train journey north, but it was imperative I do so. Instead of arguing with you and breaking another promise I couldn't make, nor keep, I left. And then I came back. Safely."

He stared at her. After a moment, he asked, "What did your father want?"

"I thought you knew. You spoke with my brother and his wife."

"Mrs. Darrow said only that you were summoned. I did not pry further. The reason was not important, only that you had left me."

The way he said the words softened her to him. Yet, she didn't want to forgive him, at least not easily. He had cut her from his life as if her own feelings were unimportant.

"My father wanted to discuss the man I would marry."

"Me?" he asked, a charming tilt of his head, causing his hair to fall across his forehead.

She sighed. *Why did everything about him appeal to her?*

"No, not you, as it turned out. He wanted me to marry Roddy Dugan."

"Who?"

Maisie waved her hand, dismissively. "He isn't important. It was a misunderstanding. By the time I left, my father had given us permission . . ." It was humiliating.

"For us to marry," he finished.

She nodded. They stared at one another.

"I wish I . . . ," he broke off, then ran a hand through his hair, looking away from her, out over the pretty garden. Then he set his cigar down on a stone plant pot.

"I know," she said.

He made an exasperated sound. "What do you *know*, Miss Maisie Darrow?"

"I believe you wish you could love again the way you loved your wife, but it is impossible. She was the perfect woman for you, and no one else, certainly not I, can ever measure up to her perfection."

As she spoke, he began to shake his head, then he closed his eyes and groaned.

"Dear lady," he said, "you have got the wrong end of the walking stick this time."

"I don't understand."

"Apparently not." Jameson looked heavenward and then back at her. "I will be frank, and probably inappropriate, but that hasn't ever stopped me before with you, has it?"

"No," she murmured, feeling a little nervous about what he might say. She hoped it wasn't too painful.

"When I was with Elizabeth, our last week," he paused, "I closed my eyes when I was making love to her. Do you know whom I saw?"

She swallowed a lump of emotion. Of course she knew! She even wondered if he'd been thinking of Esmera when he was kissing and touching her in Maggie's drawing room.

"Your wife," she said flatly.

"No, God forgive me. I saw you."

She gasped. As she did, his glance landed upon her mouth. In another moment, he closed the distance between them and kissed her lips. His kiss wasn't soft and tender, not tentative or gentle. It was desperate and lustful. It was ardent and left her trembling with need for him.

"I have missed you tremendously," he said when he pulled away, before claiming her mouth again.

For many minutes, they kissed with his hands at her waist and then upon her back, his fingers stroking up and down her spine while she clung to him. Maisie didn't want it ever to end.

When it did, instead of gazing at her with love, however, he spun away with another groan.

"I should be horsewhipped," he said, not looking at her. "I cannot treat you in such a manner."

He could if he loved her. If he intended to make her his wife, she would allow him anything.

If he merely desired her, she could not settle for that, even if he offered her some sort of arrangement the way he had with Lady Pepperton. She could not dishonor herself or her mother in that fashion.

"What do you want?" she asked.

A long hesitation met her question. She started to regret asking.

Then, in a rush of words, Jameson said, "I don't want to worry about you. I don't want to feel responsible, and I don't want to be scared of losing you."

She frowned. Those were not the answers she'd expected.

Had she been the one to cause him to think her helpless and in need of his constant vigilance?

"I went to the river that day with only one oar on purpose so you could rescue me."

He cocked his head. "You what?"

"I only had one oar."

"That's madness," he declared. "You could have drowned."

"Oh, I never intended to fall in. That truly was an accident. But I thought if you simply helped me from the boat, being my savior would bring you out of your melancholia. It was helpful, wasn't it?"

His mouth was slightly open. "You are a rash female."

"No." She shook her head. "Truly, I'm not. I don't climb trees like Eleanor or race my horse beyond a reasonable cantor. Even so, my plan seemed to awaken something a little too protective in you. You are not responsible for me, nor can you shield me from anything and everything. You simply cannot."

"I am in agony over this," he said. "If I let you go, I have to worry that numskull Roleston will not be able to keep you safe."

She threw up her hands. "You are not listening. If that is the only reason you do not want to let me go, then I would not stay with you anyway. I asked what you wanted, Lord Turner, and yet you told me only what you didn't want."

"I want *you*," he ground out.

Maisie took a step back, propelled by the emphatic way he said it. Then she experienced a moment of sheer joy.

He wanted her. Whatever that meant, it sounded promising.

However, in the next instant, he shook his head. "I am sorry. Forgive my weakness." And he stepped around to go inside.

"Where are you going?" she asked.

"Home. Actually, soon I'll be leaving for Sheffield. I am selling my townhouse. Dreadful thing, I wish the next owner more joy of it than I had."

"Jameson, wait," she begged, not caring about the pathetic beseeching tone of her voice.

"When I have left London, it will be easier for you to finish your Season, and perhaps even make a satisfactory engagement for your future," he reasoned.

"With the numbskull," she said bitterly.

Nodding, he said simply, "Good evening, Miss Darrow."

Then he disappeared inside the house, and she knew he would not still be there when she followed.

NOT FOR THE FIRST time, Jameson wondered what it would be like to have a father with whom he could speak about important matters, but his own was self-centered and useless. He had already heard Simon's advice on the matter, and he agreed with his cousin up to a point.

Except for actually being able to let go of his fear.

He even agreed with Maisie, knowing he couldn't shield her each day of her life.

That was the problem, and it would grow monumentally worse if they had children and he had to protect them, as well.

Strange as it seemed, he even knew of Hobbes's famous view on the matter. He might not have read a lot of Shakespeare, but his half brother's library, now his, was filled with philosophers. As Hobbes said in his poem *Leviathan*, the life of man was "solitary, poor, nasty, brutish, and short." Or it could be.

But did it have to be? Jameson had never thought so until Esmera's train accident. He had assumed he could control his life, his destiny, and his happiness. Until his wife had been snatched from him. Then he realized he had no control at all. It was terrifying.

The estate agent from Chesterton's had already found an interested buyer, so Jameson could pack up and be assured of a tidy profit in his account by month's end.

He ought to make better use of his townhouse while he had it. To that end, he sat outside in the back with a glass of whiskey and contemplated what a cock-up he had been. By the second glass, he realized the sound he heard was not the pathetic whining in his head, but something real in his yard.

Still, it took him a moment of searching in the evening dusk before he located the source. Under a bush, mewling with distress, was a small black and white cat. Setting his glass on the ground, not caring too much if he were scratched, he reached under and took hold of soft fur and sharp claws.

What he drew toward him was not a cat at all but a kitten. He had never held one, never seen such a tiny animal up close.

Like a squirrel, almost, except for the distinct markings as if it wore a little black mask over its white face and had a black coat draped over its back.

Its blue eyes weren't even open very wide, and he knew instinctually it was very young. He was holding a baby cat in his arms.

Somewhere nearby was undoubtedly a worried mother.

He called for his servants. Mrs. Williams took the cat and said she'd give it some milk at once. That seemed the correct course of action. Mr. Wynn agreed to help search for the mother.

Unfortunately, after half an hour of fruitless looking in the garden and then around the front and side of the townhouse, and then in the mews, they finally found what Jameson didn't want to find. A dead mother cat. It appeared to have been hit by a carriage, the very evidence of the brutish, short life he'd been recently contemplating.

He supposed it was a common enough occurrence, but it saddened him all the same. And then, he heard the sound again. *Dear God, it was multiplied a hundredfold!*

"Mr. Wynn, am I losing my sanity, or do you hear it, too?"

"Yes, my lord, I hear it."

"Mewling in the mews," Jameson quipped.

Mr. Wynn only nodded.

Jameson knew Maisie would have at least smiled at his quip.

Buried in the hay, they found five more black and white kittens.

"Very well, Mr. Wynn, let's get them back to Mrs. Williams's capable care."

"My lord?" his butler asked, startled at such an undertaking.

"You didn't think I would leave them here to die, did you?"

"No, my lord," Mr. Wynn said with a sigh out of proportion to the simple task of carrying two kittens in his lanky hands. Jameson managed to carry three.

Mrs. Williams's eyes opened very wide at seeing her new charges. But she found a basket for them, realized it wasn't big enough, and found another.

"Gracious!" she exclaimed. "I had better double our milk order and skim the cream for them."

This warranted a rolling of the eyes from Mr. Wynn.

"Come now, Winnie," Jameson teased. "It will do us good to have something to care for. However, be a good fellow and take some kind of rag out there to scoop up that dead cat. Not something we want to leave lying out there, is it?"

"No, my lord."

"Where will they sleep?" Mrs. Williamson asked, still trying to get milk into them with a teaspoon.

He was tempted to put them in Mr. Wynn's room, but only in jest. "They can have my bedroom, and I'll sleep in the spare."

She looked agog, but later that night, when he checked, there the kittens were, wriggling around in two baskets. All blue-eyed when they bothered to open them. One kitten fell out as he watched. He went in and scooped it up, returning it to its litter mates.

He doubted they would all survive, but he could give them a fighting chance.

That was all he or anyone could hope for. That's what he would have given Esmera if he'd been by her side. That opportunity was robbed from him by her refusing to wait and travel with him.

She had made her choice. Not only the date of travel but the carriage and the seat, as well.

Chance and fate and choice.

Maisie would love these kittens; he simply knew it.

A POUNDING ON THE door heralded a visitor, and Maisie beat their manservant to the opening.

"Jameson!" she exclaimed, then realized she'd said his first name aloud. "My lord," she amended.

"I am here to present you with new life."

"I beg your pardon."

From the pocket of his jacket, he withdrew a black and white kitten, holding it out toward her. Adorably, it looked as if it were wearing a black mask and jacket.

Her heart melted at once, and she snatched it from him like a hungry child for a boiled sweet, cradling it to her bosom.

"Where did it come from? Whose is it?"

"It came from my garden. The only thing to grow there for years, as far as I know. And it is yours, if you'll take it. Along with this one." He drew another out of his other pocket. "I have four more just like them at home."

"No! Do you? Are you keeping them all?"

"I think they will like Sheffield very much. Far less likely to get hit by a carriage as their mother did."

She gasped. "I am terribly sorry." The kitten had settled down against her warmth and closed its eyes, but Jameson still held the other one.

"I think it likes your hands better than your pocket," she pointed out as it rubbed its face against his fingers. "Will you come in?"

"I had hoped to, although you have every right to slam the door in my face."

"Don't be absurd," she said. "I am not one for theatrics."

"True, that was more my wife's style."

Maisie looked at him sharply. It was the first slightly critical thing he'd ever said about Lady Turner. Plus, he had brought her up himself, matter-of-factly, and didn't look distraught.

He entered behind her, and when they went into the drawing room, she set the kitten down on the sofa. Luckily, it remained there instead of falling off.

"I have no idea how to take care of it," she confessed. "My mother had two cats when I was little, but they were quite wild and lived mostly in the area between my father's brew house and the back door to our kitchen."

"It's no matter, I can keep them with me if you like until we get to Sheffield. Mrs. Williams has turned out to be a crack hand at feeding them."

She blinked at him. Something was not making sense. More than one thing actually.

"Lord Lindsey mentioned you were selling your townhouse. I take it you have done so."

"Yes!" he said, looking pleased. "I shall be glad to close the door upon it."

Finally, their manservant stuck his head in the drawing room to see who had arrived.

"Do you need Rachel, miss?"

Both Ned and Caroline were out, but she truly didn't worry at this point.

"No, I'm fine. You can leave the door open." That should suffice to keep the servants from talking. Or not.

After he'd left, she gestured for Jameson to take a seat. "Do you intend to keep a place in London?"

"I don't know, to be honest. While I enjoy a good party as much as the next fellow, I am not overly fond of the noise and smoke."

Maisie was puzzled. "You spent so much time away from Jonling Hall."

"Only *after* I married. My wife was very fond of Town."

Again, he had brought up Esmera. And again, he seemed composed, even serene.

"What about you, Miss Darrow? What is your penchant for Town versus the country? You once told me London is the greatest city on earth."

She felt her cheeks heat up. "I might have overstated. I think perhaps it is, but I haven't been many places. I suppose I am happiest in the country. Not like Eleanor, of course, who wants to be right in the midst of nature most of the time. But I do like the clean air and open space, and the more relaxed manner."

"If you were to live away from all this, you would be satisfied?" He gestured around them as if the Darrow home represented the best of Town.

She nodded. "I confess, even though I like the gowns one sees in London, I do not always admire the women wearing them."

Then she realized how insulting to his wife her words might be. She bit her lip.

Luckily, he simply smiled.

"One of the most eloquent rebukes of the *ton* I have ever heard," he said.

She relaxed. "I, too, enjoy a dinner party, as you said, but during the Season, between the constant need for persiflage and the lack of substance, dinner engagements become a chore. Not to mention, hardly anyone knows which play is which."

He was laughing again, but she didn't feel insulted. After all, he was one of those who didn't know his *Hamlet* from his *Macbeth*, so if he was not upset, she certainly wasn't.

Moreover, he looked incredibly handsome when he laughed. He was a man who ought to do so far more often.

"It is good to see you happy," she confessed.

"Why is it so effortless with you?" he asked.

Shrugging, she hoped her cheeks were not growing any redder.

"Miss Darrow, will you marry me?"

CHAPTER THIRTY

Maisie wanted to say *pish* once again, pretend he was making one of his jokes, and send him on his way.

However, Jameson suddenly looked extremely serious.

"You are leaving for Sheffield." She said the first thing to come to her mind.

"I hoped we would be going together. How else can Mrs. Williams look after your kitten with the others?"

So, that was what he had meant.

"My lord," she began.

"I wish you wouldn't call me that. You said my name earlier. It sounded good. Will you say it again?"

"Jameson," she repeated, experiencing a little thrill up her spine at the intimacy of speaking it aloud to him.

"May I call you Maisie as I do in my thoughts?"

She nodded. *He thought of her?*

"When are you leaving?"

"When would *you* like to leave?"

She sighed. "This conversation seems vaguely improper. We are not formally or otherwise engaged, announcements have not been made—"

"None of that matters, does it?" He looked like he was going to say more, perhaps even refer to all the improper things they'd already experienced, but he waited, gazing into her eyes.

"No," she said. "I suppose it doesn't."

"Because what really matters," he insisted, "is whether you will accept me as deeply flawed as I am."

She took a quick breath. She loved him, and for the second time, he was offering her a chance to live her life with him.

"I could accept your flaws," she admitted.

Unfortunately, she remained conflicted. Reaching over, she stroked the small creature sleeping beside her.

"What worries you?" Jameson asked after a moment. "About saying yes to my proposal."

Maisie didn't know if she could be brave enough to expose her utmost vulnerability to him. *Should she tell him what worried her most was how she loved him?*

"Mostly, that you are asking me again as rashly as before." True, Ned was not forcing the issue this time. But Jameson was behaving as impetuously as she feared any gambler would—deciding to wager on a future with her and hoping for the best. "With little basis for wanting to marry me."

She'd nearly managed to ask him if he loved her, or imagined he might grow to love her. *Nearly.* How was it she could let him touch her in the most intimate fashion, but the discussion she most wanted to have was too difficult for her to begin?

"I am never rash," he said, sending her a charming smile.

Then he leaned forward, elbows on his knees, looking as if he were about to impart something serious.

"Clearly, the basis for our marriage would be happiness. I never laughed with Lady Pepperton," he confessed unexpectedly. "With my wife, I did laugh because I found her entertaining, even though I knew she wasn't trying to be. But you are the only woman who laughs with me. I lied about our suitability. It is perfect. You make me exceedingly happy, and I delight when I can give you even a glimmer of that same happiness."

Maisie nodded. They did seem to have a kindred sense of humor.

"When you ask me to tell you a joke, I feel it an honor to bring out your smile and your lovely laughter," he continued. "Let me try it now."

"I don't feel very much like laughing at present. This is too serious a discussion."

"Regardless," he said, "which is heavier, the half moon or the full moon?"

Not even considering, she said, "I am sure I have no idea the weight of the moon."

"The half-moon, of course, because the full one is *twice as light.*"

She mulled it over.

He made a grimacing face. "A good riddle but not a particularly funny one, I suppose. Why is the horse such a peculiar eater?"

She shook her head. Jameson was madness personified.

"Because he eats best *without a bit* in his mouth," he finished.

"Without a bit," she repeated, then giggled.

"That little laugh is good enough for now, but I would like to see you doubled over with mirth."

"I must remind you, my . . . Jameson, you gave me a cold and heartless set down, breaking our engagement as if you were stopping delivery of a newspaper. It is difficult to trust in your commitment once again."

"That's not fair," he said. "I would never stop delivery of the *London Times.*"

She opened her mouth but couldn't think what to say to this rejoinder. Then she realized he was joking again.

"Now, the *Manchester Guardian,*" he added, "I could easily give up, but you are definitely the caliber of the *Times.*"

"Perhaps this is not the time for quite so many jokes," she told him.

He nodded. "Fair enough. In all seriousness, while I may live in fear for your safety for the rest of my days, any moment I spend with you is preferable to time without you."

That was undoubtedly serious and wonderful.

"A lovely sentiment," she told him. "I feel the same way, except for the terror. I have no wish for you to feel afraid, certainly not daily. If we marry, will I ever travel by train?"

"As long as I am with you."

"As long as you are with me," she repeated, feeling her spirit sink a little. "And then, I may ride a horse and swim in a river and stand by a fire?"

"Yes, and juggle with sharp knives," he added with a wry grin.

At least he recognized the ridiculousness of his fear-inspired demands.

"I will not be treated like a child," she told him.

"I will treat you like a queen, with the greatest care," he promised.

Because she loved him, she could live with his restrictions and eventually would make him feel secure enough to relax them. However, after how easily Jameson had given up on their engagement the first time, Maisie was no longer of the mind to marry a man who didn't whole heartedly love her. It was as simple as that.

After the discussion with her father, she no longer wished to be a man's second best.

She had to ask him.

"And what of your heart?" she asked.

His expression instantly went blank, his emotions shuttered. He didn't want her to know the truth.

Maisie decided to press the issue. "I know I agreed to marry you once without either of us declaring our feelings, but I am no longer willing to do so."

She had thought to wait until the wedding night to tell him she loved him. *But wouldn't it be an awful moment of silence before they consummated?*

"I see," he said. "You are no longer willing."

At that moment, the kitten on his lap stretched and mewled, then went back to sleep.

"They were fed before I brought them," he told her. "They'll need to eat again soon."

She nodded but continued to stare at him, waiting. *Could he say anything to give her a modicum of hope for gaining his love in the future?*

"My heart," he began, then stopped. He seemed to be clenching his jaw. Then, abruptly, he lifted the black and white ball of fur from his lap, stood, and absently slipped it into the large pocket of his sack coat.

"I am unable to tell you what you want to hear. Only know I feel a great deal for you. I hope you will consider my offer. I must be off."

He literally ran from the room, leaving her with a kitten and a dreadful weight of disappointment.

She supposed it was entirely up to her whether she could marry this man, or anyone, under these circumstances.

JAMESON WAS ADMITTED TO Simon and Jenny's townhouse by their faithful butler, Mr. Binkley, and wasted no time asking, "Is Lord Lindsey receiving?"

"Yes, my lord."

"I wish you wouldn't call me that," Jameson muttered. "You recall knowing me *before* Lord Lindsey slapped the ridiculous title of viscount upon me."

"I do, my lord."

"I have not changed."

"No, my lord."

"Then why . . . never mind. Where is he?"

"In his second-floor study, my lord."

"Now, you're just doing it to annoy me, aren't you, Binkley?"

The man shrugged and gestured for Jameson to head up the stairs.

A few moments later, he was pounding on Simon's closed door.

"Come." He heard Simon's familiar voice and pushed the door open.

His cousin was seated at his desk, papers on one side, ledgers on the other, and newspapers strewn over both.

Jameson didn't care how busy he was. "I need help."

"As in you need a second for a duel, which I would have to think about because Jenny is opposed to my doing such stupid things, or as in you need money to pay off a debt, which I will gladly do."

"Neither." Jameson sunk into the chair opposite Simon's desk. "I need you to punch me in the face or throttle me senseless or perhaps—" He heard the kitten mewling and dragged it from the pocket of his coat, plonking it onto the papers on his cousin's desk.

Simon stared at it, fascinated.

"What on earth?"

"It's a baby cat," Jameson informed him as the creature wobbled to its feet and began to explore the desktop.

"I'm aware of that. Should I ask why you're keeping one in your pocket?"

"Dammit all! I meant to leave it with Miss Darrow." Jameson stuck his hand out and chucked the kitten under its chin. It closed its eyes and enjoyed the ministrations.

"Well, that explains everything," Simon said drolly. "If it pisses on my paperwork, I shall not thank you. So, you went to Maisie's and took her a gift of a kitten and then took it away with you, and now you want me to beat you. Is that right?"

"No, I did leave her a kitten. I simply meant to leave her two, but I got distracted and left in a hurry. I didn't even realize I'd put it back in my pocket."

His cousin sighed and rubbed his forehead. "Why did you go see her and why did you leave in a hurry?"

"I went because I cannot live without her, so I asked her to marry me. Again."

"And she said no, I take it, causing you to run away."

Jameson shook his head.

Simon grinned. "She said yes, after the shabby way you've treated her. You are a very lucky man, indeed. Jenny feared Maisie might never speak to you again. Especially as she's being wooed by Roleston. And perhaps his younger brother. And she was even spotted riding with your former brother-in-law. A little odd, come to think of it. But Inigo Maradona is considered dashing to a fault, so maybe not so odd after all."

"Is there any whiskey in here?" Jameson thought that might be the answer to his problems.

"Brandy will have to do." Simon pulled out a bottle from his bottom desk drawer, as well as two glasses. He poured and handed a glass to him over the kitten's head.

"I take it we're not toasting your romantic success?"

Jameson shrugged. "Miss Darrow wanted to know if I love her. To put it plainly, she asked about my heart, and I fled."

He stared at his cousin, daring him to laugh. Luckily, he didn't.

"She has a right to be loved, don't you think?" Simon asked. "Especially by the man who wants to be her husband."

"I haven't admitted even to myself how much I love Maisie." It was too frightening to feel such love again. And too disloyal. "Or rather, I have, but I can't really acknowledge it."

"Then it's unlikely she knows," Simon pointed out. "And if she doesn't think you truly love her, then she will always feel second to Esmera. Worse, she will doubt your loyalty and constancy. You broke the engagement once already. Undoubtedly, she thinks you can do so again on a whim."

"I told her she was the *Times*, not the *Guardian*, dammit! I will not break faith with her again."

Simon shook his head in dismay.

Jameson sipped the expensive French brandy. "I gave my heart to Esmera. If she were still alive, I wouldn't be thinking of Maisie at all. That's the truth."

Nodding, his cousin said, "I understand that. But she is *not* alive, and your heart is no good to Esmera anymore."

"I know. And Maisie is all I can think about. Except I promised to love Esmera forever. What kind of man casts that love aside? I don't even know how to do it." He smacked his hand on the desk, and the kitten jumped before returning to swatting at a pencil.

"If I no longer love Esmera, then it will be as though she didn't exist, as if we were never married. Yet I am her husband."

"You are not," Simon said in a gentle tone that made it all the more serious. "I've let you say it before without correcting you, but you cannot be her husband. You ceased being her husband the minute she died. You are *not* wedded to a ghost."

Jameson took a large gulp. "I feel guilty just considering telling Maisie how I feel. Yes, she has my heart, but to say it aloud to her, to make it openly known . . . it makes me a cad to stop loving my dead wife."

There was a knock on the door. Simon looked at Jameson for permission to interrupt their private and personal conversation.

Jameson sighed and nodded, before Simon repeated, "Come."

"Sorry to bother you," Jenny said, entering.

Both men stood at once. Simon's wife was the picture of glowing health with a pretty blush to her full cheeks.

"Oh, Jameson" she said, "I didn't know you were here. How are you? Good to see you again. Are you staying for supper?"

Before he could answer, she looked past him to her husband and noticed the kitten.

The expression crossing her face was the exact echo of Maisie's.

"Oh," was all she said as she leaned over and scooped the black and white bundle off the desk and squeezed it to her ample bosom. "Such a darling."

It mewled.

"Perhaps it cannot breathe," Simon quipped. "Don't squeeze it to death, love."

Jenny plopped down in the seat next to the one Jameson had vacated, and when he looked at her, she had tears in her eyes.

"Are you well?" he asked, feeling instantly on alert.

"Dear me," Jenny said, "yes. Please sit down."

"She is in the weepy stage," Simon explained. "It will continue for a while. She was sobbing over some pinkish-hued clouds the other day."

"I was," Jenny admitted, and then she laughed at herself. "I am a sentimental mess at present. Forgive me. Why did I come in?"

"She is also in the forgetful stage," Simon added, and husband and wife both laughed.

Jameson's stomach clenched. He wanted this. Desperately wanted it and realized in a traitorous moment, he had never had this easy camaraderie with Esmera. They'd had so much else, though, and he had no regrets.

But this was very nice, too.

"Let me think." Jenny looked at the door and stroked the kitten before setting it upon what was left of her disappearing lap.

"Oh, yes, I recall. Simon, love, I was examining the vineyard ledger, and I think we have a problem. I believe someone is selling off casks on the side. I know it sounds terrible to think one of our people would do such a thing, but perhaps that very someone is in desperate need of more money, I don't know."

She rested her hands on her blossoming stomach while the kitten stretched up and rubbed her fingers. She added, "All I can say is the inventory and the sales are not matching, and I think we should take a trip there as soon as possible."

Simon relied on his smart wife for the bookkeeping. Their partnership was truly a wondrous thing.

Instantly, a frisson of dread rushed through Jameson at the devastation his cousin would experience should anything happen to Jenny. Yet, there she was bearing his children, coming to London, traveling to their holdings.

He sighed.

"I'm sorry, Jameson." Jenny focused on his face. "I thoughtlessly interrupted."

"No, I was just leaving."

"Not on my account. Please, the vineyard can wait. Is there anything I can help with, or is this man's business?"

"It is man-and-woman business," Simon informed her. "Maybe Jenny can help better than I," he offered, raising a dark eyebrow.

Jameson supposed it wouldn't hurt to tell her.

When he awkwardly explained his dilemma—his loyalty to Esmera, having given her his undying love, his guilt over his feelings for Maisie—Jenny's forehead, which had been frowning as he spoke, cleared at once.

"Dear man," she reached over and touched his hand, startling him. Like a mother's touch. Their gazes locked, and he fell into the wise depths of her eyes. Whatever she was going to tell him, he would believe and know it for the truth.

As long as it wasn't some convoluted confusing Shakespearean quote.

"I confess," she began. "I had nearly the same problem."

"What?" Simon demanded.

"Just listen," she said to her husband. "When Lionel came along, the love I felt for him upon his birth was huge, overwhelming, so fulfilling. Do you remember?" she asked. "We talked about it every day. How could we be so fortunate? How could we love our son so much? It was frightening and beautiful."

"I remember," Simon agreed, his tone thickly emotional.

Jameson almost felt as if he were intruding on their moment, and he failed to see what this had to do with him.

Yet, she turned to him once more. "Then, I became in the family way again. I was happy, of course, but toward the time when I was ready to deliver, I began to worry, even to feel sad. How could I love this new baby the way I already loved Lionel? How could I love them equally? Was I betraying my son? He was the absolute center of our world. How could there be another center? So many questions and absolutely no answers."

Jameson having had no children, and growing up as an only child, he had never considered these questions before.

"Then a magical thing happened, which I never expected," Jenny said, shaking her head.

"You had twins," Jameson said.

"True, but that wasn't the only magical thing. As soon as the new babies arrived—I say that as if they simply flew down from the heavens instead of . . . well, anyway, the moment I saw them, my love tripled."

She picked up the kitten and kissed its soft head before returning it to her lap.

Jameson nodded and waited. Her eyes widened with emphasis, pretty brown eyes, nearly as lovely as Maisie's.

When Jenny said nothing more, he smiled and looked to Simon for assistance.

His cousin laughed. "I felt exactly the same way, so I know she is right."

Jameson shrugged. "I am happy for you both."

Simon laughed. "He doesn't understand, my love. You're wonderful with numbers. Explain it better so he understands."

"Don't you see?" Jenny demanded. "Our love didn't get cut in half so we had less to give Lionel. It didn't diminish at all! It multiplied." She looked at the whiskey bottle and frowned for a moment, perhaps realizing they were drinking early in the day.

"See this liquor. It wasn't like taking the bottle and trying to pour it perfectly evenly into three glasses, or worse, creating three unequal portions." She beamed at him. "Instead, suddenly, we had three full bottles of whiskey."

Simon was howling with laughter now at her analogy. She ignored him.

"Jameson, it is the most amazing feeling. Instead of our hearts being full once, they were full of love thrice over. Let Maisie have your whole heart. It won't diminish your love for Esmera one little bit. You will simply have even more love. I promise."

Jameson tried to believe she was speaking the truth, and he felt the clamp of fear around his heart loosen a little.

"I am not worried this time." She patted her stomach under the kitten. "I eagerly await the next addition to our family and the multiplication of our love."

"Even if we have triplets," Simon suggested.

She gave him a hard look, then smiled sweetly at Jameson.

"I swear, my heart's capacity is getting bigger each time."

She made sense. He had simply never thought of it in such a practical, mathematical—and magical—fashion.

"I can love Maisie as much as I want," he said to them, "and keep Esmera fully in my heart, as well."

Jenny nodded, and he nodded back to her, feeling light and happy.

"Thank you," he said. "Have I ever told you two how much I love being part of this family?"

Jumping up, Jameson rushed from the room.

CHAPTER THIRTY-ONE

Maisie was astride their carriage horse, not the best beast for riding sidesaddle, but it was all she had. She had asked Caroline to watch their new feline charge, told Ned she was going riding—alone—and left. She had hours before dark and knew she had best sort out her thoughts.

To put a fine point on it, she must decide what compromise she could live with. Feeling as she did about Jameson, and as happy as she felt with him, she knew she could compromise a great deal.

Stopping her horse in the middle of Battersea Bridge, watching the boats going under, she considered his offer. A life in Sheffield with a man who said he wanted to spend whatever time he could with her. It truly was practically, almost, nearly a declaration of love.

And she was warring with herself whether it was enough.

As if conjuring him with her ruminations, she heard Jameson's voice.

"Maisie," he called out her first name, despite how others were passing by.

Impropriety and ruin at every turn. She grinned.

"Ned told you where I was," she guessed as he approached on his handsome mount.

"Even if he hadn't, I would have guessed you were here, drawn to the most rickety bridge over the Thames, just to aggravate me."

"Not so. I come here for the view. But I wasn't too keen on crossing because of the snakes. See how cautious I have become."

He shook his head.

"Did you bring me another kitten?"

"No, in fact, I left one behind with the Lindseys. I'll have to get it back. For all I know, it might be the best mouser of the bunch. And it might miss its siblings."

She liked that sentimentality about him.

"Anyway, will you come off this infernal bridge?" he demanded.

Not if he had something important to say to her. It was as good a place as any, and perhaps more fitting than most.

Earlier, the wee cat had tickled something in her brain, another pertinent nugget from Shakespeare, and she was glad he'd reminded her. She believed it the perfect beginning to a discussion.

"Why are you here?" she asked. "*Art thou afeard to be the same in thine own act and valor as thou art in desire? Wouldst thou have that which thou esteemest the ornament of life, and live a coward in thine own esteem, letting 'I dare not' wait upon 'I would,' like the poor cat in the adage?*"

Jameson stared blankly at her a moment. Then he muttered, "Dammit!" And finally, more loudly, he said, "I understand you're saying something about a cat. Is this about the kitten I gave you, or do I need Roleston to come translate?"

She sighed. "Sorry. It's Lady Macbeth urging her husband to do what he said he would do and to act boldly. She refers to the famous adage about a cat. Do you know it?"

"Something about not getting wet. I don't want to either, which is why it would be prudent to get off this decrepit bridge before we fall into the Thames on our horses."

Maisie held up her hand. "The proverbial cat wants to eat fish but is afraid of getting its feet wet. Do you see?"

"Yes," he said. "They don't have poles like Miss Eleanor."

She stared at him, and he stared back, and the rest of the world fell away.

"I have to tell you something. It is a new thought about my heart and Esmera," he began.

She wanted to cry, recalling his diatribe in Jonling Hall, when he railed against her and his fate, when he first told her he was a man who had the perfect wife.

"I know you loved Esmera. And you loved her with all your heart. Jameson, I love you enough to be glad you had that. But I also envy her. How ridiculous for me to be envious of a dead woman! But I have been, more than once. For she enjoyed your unfettered heart, receiving all of it, and I never will."

He brought his horse beside hers, facing in the opposite direction so he could look directly at her.

"You love me," he repeated matter-of-factly. "Do you?"

"Yes," the word was torn from her. "But I have come to understand, and accept, you can never—"

"I love you, Maisie Darrow, with all my heart." He paused and appeared to be waiting for something. Then his eyes widened, and he clasped his hands to his own chest.

"Are you all right?" she asked him, for he wore a beatific expression tempered by shock.

"I am fine," he answered. "My heart doubled in size, and I needed a moment to get used to it."

Was he making a jest? And had she heard him correctly?

"Did you say you love me?" she asked.

"I did."

Tears sprung to her eyes and immediately trickled down her cheeks.

"Are you happy?" he asked, fishing a handkerchief out of his pocket.

"Extremely," she confessed, shaking the cat fur off of it before dabbing at her eyes. *"For which of my bad parts didst thou first fall in love with me?"*

He cocked his head. "I can think of none, not even this annoying habit of quoting Shakespeare. In fact, I love you more for it. What play is that from?"

"Much Ado About Nothing."

"I hope someday to identify them all if you're patient with me and read them with me."

Her heart swelled. How she would love to do so! She could already imagine sitting in their drawing room in Sheffield, under the landscape painting, acting out the parts.

"I have a surprise for you," he said.

"Is it another cat?"

"No." He took a deep breath. *"Yet in these thoughts myself almost despising, happily I think on thee, and then my state . . . my state,"* he hesitated, looking worried, then his brow cleared as he recalled, *"like to the lark at break of day arising from sullen earth—sings hymns at heaven's gate."* He nodded to himself.

She nodded, too, encouragingly.

He took a breath and finished, *"For thy sweet love remembered such wealth brings, that then I scorn to change my state with kings."*

He had entirely stolen her words, leaving her speechless. Moreover, she knew her face was nearly splitting with the size of her smile.

Clapping her hands, rather recklessly, for her horse was getting restless, Maisie leaned forward to kiss him.

He leaned the rest of the way, so she didn't have to fall out of her saddle, and he took her mouth with his.

Stepping back, her horse separated them rather frustratingly.

"I know it's only half a sonnet, but I wanted you to know how happy you make me," Jameson told her. "May we get off this infernal bridge now?"

Three months later . . .

SINCE NEITHER ONE OF them gave a fig about the approval of the upper level of British society, nor had they a need or desire to impress anyone or placate gossips, they remained engaged for a mere two months. They married in Dumfries, at the Greyfriars Church.

Her father boasted, albeit without delight, how he'd practically paid for the new church himself since the building was funded through an imposed tax on all beer brewed in the town.

"Dad, it was built in 1727," Maisie pointed out, deliriously happy on her wedding day, "and you have no such tax now!"

"All the same," he said, grumbling on behalf of his fellow brewers from over a century earlier.

At the wedding luncheon following the ceremony, Fintan Darrow provided all the guests with free beer, a new brew called "Maisie ale." Ned wondered aloud why his father had never brewed a beer with his name.

"Because none of my customers will drink such bitter brew."

Ned's cheeks flamed with color, and Maisie hoped her father and brother would work on their relationship *after* her celebratory feast.

Jameson's father and his second wife were there, looking as if they had already drunk a case of bitter Nedly. Such sour expressions Maisie had rarely witnessed. Moreover, even as Simon, with Jenny's help, attempted to placate his uncle, the man looked all the more dour.

At least he had come and courteously met his son's bride. However, Maisie wouldn't mind if she didn't meet him again for a while.

"There's no helping Lord James Devere," Jameson said of his father. "And I, for one, won't waste another moment worrying over him. He won't get one of our kittens, either."

Maisie and Jameson had left London a couple weeks after the second announcement of their engagement. Maisie went to Dumfries, and Jameson to Sheffield to prepare his home for his new bride, taking all six cats.

For Maisie, on the banks of the Nith, surprisingly, the weeks had flown by with letters and a visit from Jameson to meet the man who would be his father-in-law.

Jameson and Fintan got on well, for which Maisie was exceedingly glad. Her father even said he would visit Sheffield, at last, once she was settled.

"You can give your advice to the Lindsey brewers," Jameson offered, and Maisie saw her father's pleased expression.

Eleanor had declared she'd known how this would work out all along.

"Just like one of my Gothic romance novels. From death and despair to a happy country wedding."

Maisie thought it more like one of the happier Shakespeare plays but didn't gainsay her cousin.

Even Lord Roleston had sent his best regards of the day, along with his suggestion of an ardent recitation of Sonnet one-hundred-and-sixteen on the unfaltering steadfastness of time.

"*Love alters not with his brief hours and weeks, but bears it out even to the edge of doom,* will positively make all your guests weep," he wrote to her. "My loss is Lord Turner's gain. I am content you have your heart's desire, and I shall continue to seek out a similar attachment for myself."

On her wedding day, everything was perfect except for her mother not being there. Maisie brought her close as best she could by wearing her mam's amethyst pendant, which went perfectly with the dress Maggie helped her choose for the special day. The palest lavender lawn with the happiest looking lace.

"How can lace be happy?" Jameson had asked Maisie in a letter when she'd tried to describe it to her fiancé.

"I don't know, but it is. You'll see."

At the church, after their vows and in front of all their friends and family, he'd taken her in his arms and kissed her. As he drew back, he said, "You were right, as usual. That's the happiest lace I've ever seen."

When the lunch was over, Maisie and Jameson departed on their wedding trip. They had decided on a tour of Europe, concentrating on Italy, since so many of Shakespeare's plays took place there, and she wanted to tour all the cities. Particularly Venice.

To that end, they boarded a train and started the long trek south. Mutually, with unspoken agreement, they didn't have a discussion about railway travel or say anything significant about it. They simply planned their trip and boarded the train with the Lindseys, the Cambreys, the Blackwoods, the Darrows, and their friends seeing them off.

"Tell me a joke," Maisie demanded at least once an hour.

"I shall run out soon," Jameson protested, but dutifully obeyed. "Pity me, sir, I have a wife and six children,' said the beggar to the wealthy man. The gentleman replied, 'Dear fellow! Accept my heartfelt sympathy. So, have I!'"

She frowned at him. "That's your worst joke ever and not the least bit funny."

He laughed uproariously at her expression. Then he took her hand. "Mrs. Turner, I hope we have at least ten."

"Well," she said, feeling the heat rise in her cheeks. "Perhaps we shall start trying tonight."

And they did. On the same railway in which she'd ridden with Rachel, Maisie now traveled south with her new husband, heading for London where they would change rails for the Brighton Railway, ending up on the coast by midmorning the following day. From there, they would take a ferry to Dieppe, France.

Naturally, as a newly married couple, the Viscount and Viscountess Turner of Sheffield, they had one of the few bed-carriages on the London and Birmingham Railway. After traveling all day, the night porter came in to turn down their narrow but adequate bed, while Maisie hid in the tiny bathroom. Jameson had already helped her with the frustrating number of buttons and fasteners on her gown, and she'd removed the rest of her thin and soft layers while in the water closet.

When she exited, she had taken her hair down and had donned a silk robe and nothing else. Jameson, standing in the small space left available to him, wore a smile and his cotton drawers.

"Oh," she said, and her heart started racing at the sight of so much bare skin.

His manly body was hers to study with his muscled arms, capable of delivering a good punch, and a broad chest, which she'd already had the pleasure of resting her head upon, although not before without his shirt.

Now, she could see the smattering of curly hair between his nipples and lifted her hand toward him involuntarily.

"Given the confines of the carriage, I concluded it best to undress while there was room to do so."

"Very considerate," she praised him, utterly distracted by his solidly built legs, with well-defined thighs and calves. She nearly said, "Turn around," but thought better of it. She wasn't appraising horse flesh, after all.

Still, he was her husband to enjoy and to love. She knew she had a soppy, foolish smile on her face.

"Maisie?"

"Yes."

"May I remove your robe?"

She swallowed, her mouth suddenly dry.

"Yes." She was his wife to do with as he saw fit. "Please. Do. I would like that, I mean."

Then, nervously, without waiting, she began to untie the belt at her waist.

He stepped closer and finished what her trembling hands had started.

"Remember on Maggie's sofa?" he murmured against her temple.

"*Mm.*"

"It will be like that, only better," he promised.

She relaxed. That had been rather spectacular, and she was looking forward to whatever could be better.

Her robe slid to the floor, but he didn't embarrass her by standing and staring at her nakedness. Rather, he took her hands and pulled her down onto the bed with him.

"I have longed for this moment," he confessed, as somehow her breast knocked against his arm.

She giggled.

"You are all curves and softness, and the creamiest skin I have ever seen." His fingertips skimmed across her shoulders, and she shivered.

"Cold?"

"No."

He trailed his fingers along her breasts, speaking words of love and praise. His capable mouth, his tongue, and even his teeth soon joined the work of his hands, until all of her was aflush with desire.

"Jameson," she whispered, while he drew one of her nipples between his lips and sucked it. "I am throbbing everywhere. But especially between my legs where you touched me before. It is almost painful, but delightful."

Immediately, his hands caressed the skin at her waist before fluttering down over her belly button to her downy curls. He slipped a finger between her soft folds, and she gasped.

"You are very wet," he told her.

"Yes," she said, already wanting to moan at his practiced touch. "All day, every time I imagined tonight."

He claimed her mouth again, tugging on her lower lip as his fingers slipped between her legs.

"It's passion," he said, stroking her slippery moisture.

Maisie tried to have a rational thought but came up with only two words.

"It's love," she sighed against his mouth.

"Yes," he agreed while he teased her body until, low between her hips, she tightened like a spring. And then, as his touch flickered faster over the core of her desire, and his tongue mimicked his fingers, she found her release.

After a few moments, when she recalled where she was, on a train, speeding south, she sighed. It was already better than it had been the first time.

"Will you touch me?" Jameson asked, his voice strained.

She recalled what she'd been told by her older cousins and what she'd read on her own, and knew her husband needed to find his own release and would do so, if all went well, inside her. They might even create a new life that night.

Wanting more than anything to please him, she pushed him onto his back and echoed his approach. Exploring him as she'd longed to do, she stroked her palms lightly across his skin. The hair on his torso was far softer than she'd imagined. Then she followed the contours of his ribs and noted how his body narrowed but didn't flare out at his hips the way her own did.

And then, she drew off his drawers and let his staff spring free.

"You're magnificent," she murmured, glancing at his face, but his arm was over his eyes, his head tilted back slightly.

A bead of liquid was at the head of his manhood. His own liquid passion, a drop of love. *Amazing.* She might be afraid if she wasn't still so elated from what he'd just given her.

Without hesitation, Maisie grasped his stiff shaft, and he groaned. She nearly released it before recognizing it as a sound of pleasure.

With Jameson letting her explore him freely, she played with his body, touching him, stroking him, even squeezing the small sacks between his—

Suddenly, she found herself flipped upon her back, and her new husband hovering over her. He nudged her legs apart and nestled between them.

"Are you ready, Mrs. Turner?" he asked.

"Yes." Her voice sounded like a squeak, but she gave an emphatic nod of her head.

Resting on one of his forearms, he used his other hand to fit his manhood to her opening and then . . . he entered her.

It felt strange and unnerving. Moreover, his movements brought her out of the haze she'd been in since she'd spent.

"Relax," he murmured.

She tried, but her body was still opening for him, and then, a twinge of pain, more of a burning feeling, that made her gasp and then stole her breath.

"That's the worst of it," he said, halting.

"All right." She believed him, feeling a little less enthusiastic though, until he continued.

Dropping his mouth to hers again, he kissed her as his body continued to glide into hers. Slowly, in then out.

It was far more difficult for her body to reach the point of the coiling spring she'd felt twice already at his touch, but then—wondrously—even while kissing her and penetrating her, he slipped his hand between them and touched her nubbin.

Maisie knew it wouldn't take much more than that. With her body relishing the myriad sensations, she was entirely enthralled by their lovemaking until her release caught her suddenly and unexpectedly, whirling her in the same ecstasy she'd felt earlier.

This time, however, she wasn't alone. Mere seconds after her muscles had tightened and released, she felt Jameson thrust faster, harder, and then he, too, went taut before spending his seed deeply inside her.

IN THE DAWN LIGHT, their train chugged along, and Jameson had given up determining exactly where they were en route. He knew only he held in his arms the woman with whom he was madly in love.

They were beginning a new life together, something that had seemed an impossibility for him a mere few months ago, mired as he was in misery. Maisie brought him happiness, and making her happy was even better.

She stirred, and he kissed her immediately, knowing he would never waste a minute of time. That was something Esmera's death had taught him, and he'd almost missed the lesson. He'd almost missed out on Maisie.

"Where am I?" she asked, sounding wool-headed.

"With your husband. God knows where exactly."

She giggled. "Tell me a joke."

"No," he scolded. "It's too early. Go back to sleep."

"Kiss me," she demanded, sounding completely awake. "Or is it too early for that, as well?"

He grinned. Turning her in his arms and wriggling onto his side, they faced one another. Then slowly, thoroughly, he kissed her.

"*Mm*," Maisie sighed as his hand swept down her arm and over her hip before coming back to cup her breast. When he rolled her nipple between his finger and thumb her sigh became a moan, and his loins responded, willing and ready.

He slid his tongue over the seam of her lips. She parted them for him, and he plundered her sweet mouth until she arched her body against him. Finally, she drew back

"*You have witchcraft in your lips*," she murmured.

He halted. "What play?"

"*Henry V*," she responded, and grabbed his face between her palms, drawing his head down to kiss her again.

He decided he was going to like this life with both his Maisie and her Shakespeare in it. Very much.

❦

EPILOGUE

1852, Jonling Hall
Sheffield, England

Maisie laughed so hard, she feared she would disgrace herself and have to change her drawers. In any case, she sneezed tea out through her nose and had a choking fit. Hamlet had suddenly appeared over the arm of the sofa and ambushed Macbeth, who fell off the edge directly onto Portia, walking underneath. The latter two kittens fluffed up to nearly twice their size before taking off at a gallop.

Macbeth climbed the nearest curtain, making it to the top where he clung there, wild eyed. Portia ran in a circle before disappearing under the sofa.

"Naughty, Hamlet," Maisie scolded the young cat who now sat innocently in the sunny spot on the cushion, washing his paws.

Crossing to the windows, she reached up to rescue Macbeth, a nervous cat, unhooking his claws and lifting him off the drapery. She stroked him a moment, then set him down.

"Go play," she ordered.

Romeo, Juliet, and Puck were elsewhere, most likely under Mr. Wynn's sizable feet, getting tidbits from the cook, or out in the rose garden.

For Maisie, it was time to go upstairs anyway. She'd been putting it off all morning, even though the task was her own idea.

Two months earlier, they had returned from their honeymoon, a lovely word Maisie was sorry she would never use again. Maybe she and Jameson could take another trip in a few years and give it a different "moon" name. Perhaps a *wine moon* or a *warm bread moon*.

Mm, warm bread. Perhaps there was time for a snack before she went upstairs.

"Stop stalling," she muttered to herself. "*In delay there lies no plenty.*" Silently, she added, "*Twelfth Night,*" because her curious husband always asked her the origin.

Climbing the stairs, past the cheerful new wallpaper, she gained heart. When she and Jameson were on their wedding trip, Mrs. Williams and Mr. Wynn had seen to the freshening of the home, as the housekeeper called it. However, they'd left any changes in paint and wallpaper, rugs and furnishings, to the new bride. Maisie had entered her clean and sparkling new home, tired from their travels but eager to make Jonling Hall her own.

With Jameson's permission and approval, of course. He was only too glad to have his home redecorated, as everything was the same from the time his half brother, Tobias, lived there. She had learned one thing, Esmera hadn't liked it and had not changed a stick of furniture.

Nothing could have pleased Maisie more.

She had not changed too many things—new paint, drapes, and a pretty carpet in the drawing room, as well as a new sofa, in case Jameson and Esmera had behaved on it as she and he had done on Maggie's. The landscape painting remained over the fireplace. The dining room received modern wallpaper, and the stairwell, too.

Their bedroom, despite it containing Tobias Devere's furniture, suited them both. With new wallpaper and drapes, she was very happy with the room in which they made love and slept.

She emphatically did not want her own room. Purposefully, she had put her things into his bedroom and never left it. Even her collection of plays was on the shelf in their room, despite him offering her a shelf in the study. She preferred to keep her books close.

As to a room of her own, there were plenty of spaces in the house for her to be alone when she wished, either to read or sew and, often, to write letters, and for much of the year, there were the gardens to enjoy. The kittens loved them nearly as much as Maisie, and they would have a far better and longer life than in London.

Mrs. Williams remained delighted with her six furry charges, although the kittens loved Mr. Wynn excessively, following him around the house, indoors and out.

With the staff and the cats settled, Maisie and Jameson vowed not to go to London for the entire following year, unless called to for a wedding or a funeral.

At long last, that very day, Maisie was going to tackle "Esmera's bedroom." With her husband's blessing.

Their husband, she supposed she could call him.

In any case, she reminded herself with her fingers gripping the door handle, this was merely a room like any other. Indeed, it had been the room Esmera spent most of her time in. However, with the late Lady Turner so loathing the country, Maisie wondered if she'd actually spent more days and nights in residence in Jonling Hall than Esmera had during her brief marriage.

Slowly, she pushed it open. The door hinge creaked. She would have to remember to ask Mr. Wynn to get it oiled. The room, itself, wasn't creepy or dusty or maudlin. It was beautiful as Esmera had been. Mrs. Williams had made sure the maids cleaned it thoroughly and kept it aired out.

Maisie sniffed. It smelled like orange blossom water, as did all the bedding and towels in Jonling Hall. Since there was no bed in the room anymore, the aroma must be in the clean curtains and carpet. *Wonderful!*

Jameson had not minded when she'd asked to leave Esmera's room until last. Maisie had wanted to get the rest of the house redecorated for them to enjoy. She also was mindful of the unfavorable impression it would have made had she arrived home from their trip and appeared to sweep away his previous wife.

As a thoughtful gesture to his new one, however, Jameson had the four-poster bed Esmera had slept in removed and sent away while they were in Europe.

Opening the massive wardrobe, the gowns with Esmera's perfume clinging to them greeted her in an array of saturated colors. Mrs. Williams would be along any minute to help her pack them up.

Fingering the red silk and the gold satin, Maisie decided to send them to a charity in London, doubtful anyone could wear such ballgowns in the country. Even Esmera's day gowns would leave Sheffield. Maisie didn't want Jameson suddenly encountering one of his deceased wife's dresses on the local baker's wife and receiving a nasty shock if he recognized it. She closed the wardrobe.

With the bed gone, there was only a small reading table and two chairs, the wardrobe, a trunk, and a dresser. After the gowns, she and Mrs. Williams would take a cursory glance in the trunk, but Maisie had already arranged for its shipment to Inigo Maradona to give to his parents. Eying the hairbrush and silver mirror, she would put those into the trunk as well.

Hearing footsteps on the stairs, she assumed it was Mrs. Williams, until she recognized the booted footfalls.

Turning as Jameson entered, Maisie felt the same rush of pleasure whenever she saw her husband. It wasn't simply his handsome face. It was the joyful spirit in his eyes when he looked at her, the way his mouth already began to curve into a smile.

"Greetings, wife," he said, not yet having tired of greeting her as such. "Mrs. Williams will be up shortly."

"You came as a messenger?" Maisie teased.

"I would use any excuse no matter how trivial to see you. Besides, I didn't know if this chore would be difficult for you. I am offering to take over."

"And I assumed it would be hard for you, so I am happy to handle it."

He glanced around. "Honestly, the room does not affect me, except for how it will next be used. That excites me to no end."

After Maisie's recent discovery, the best purpose for this pretty, sunny room had dawned on her. She could still recall the relief when Jameson agreed.

"Jenny told me of the best crib maker in Yorkshire county, and I've already written to him. I would love to take a trip to his shop."

He took her in his arms. "Then we shall do so this week."

"And I think lighter-colored curtains and rug. Jenny also told me Simon is gifting us a rocking chair for the long sleepless nights with the wee one." She patted her stomach with the barest hint of a thickening. "So, we don't need to purchase one."

"I think he's simply trying to scare us," Jameson said.

Then he kissed her without preamble. She found his surprise kisses to be the best ones. Along with the long, drawn out kisses heralding their evening lovemaking. Along with the kisses he placed all over her body when they were lying naked. Along with the morning kisses before they got out of bed.

She sighed.

"A happy sigh, or do I need to come up with a joke?"

Romeo and Puck suddenly ran into the room, chasing after each other, and then stopped, perhaps realizing they were in a room where the door was normally closed to them.

"I'm exceedingly happy," she confessed. "But always ready for a joke."

"One man asked, 'How did you come out of that argument with your wife?' 'Just fine,' said the other. 'As usual, I apologized for being right.'"

"Not funny," she protested.

He brushed a curl off her forehead. "How about this one? One man said, 'I figured out how to manage my wife.' 'How?' asked the other, about to get married. 'I always let her have her way. A happy wife is the only type of wife to have.'"

She drew back. "That is *not* a joke."

"No, but it's common sense. I always want to make you happy."

"Then cease the jests about wives. I do not care for them."

He laughed at her tone. "Let me try again. Why is a fashionable woman like a thrifty housekeeper?"

She started to smile, already preferring the topic. "Why?"

"Because she makes a great bustle about a little waist."

Maisie snorted at his play on words, then covered her mouth at the unladylike noise. He drew her hand away and kissed her again.

When she drew back, Mrs. Williams was at the doorway, holding large burlap sacks for the gowns. Not something she wished her husband to witness.

"Go now, and let me get on with this. I have a nursery to create."

He went to the door, nodded to Mrs. Williams who entered the room, and then he looked back. His gaze locked momentarily with Maisie's.

"Let me know if you need help. *My heart is ever at your service.*"

Gasping as he left, she stared at the doorway where her wonderful husband had just quoted Shakespeare.

"Timon of Athens," he called back to her as he descended the stairs, delighted laughter in his voice.

At that moment, Maisie hoped she had a girl baby. She would name her Marion, teach her to read and write, and give her the everlasting joy and comfort her mother had given her.

And of course, they would make thistle blossom jelly together.

ABOUT THE AUTHOR

USA Today bestselling author Sydney Jane Baily writes historical romance set in Victorian England, late 19th-century America, the Middle Ages, the Georgian era, and the Regency period. She believes in happily-ever-after stories for an already-challenging world with engaging characters and attention to period detail.

Born and raised in California, she has traveled the world, spending a lot of exceedingly happy time in the U.K. where her extended family resides, eating fish and chips, drinking shandies, and snacking on Maltesers and Cadbury bars. Sydney currently lives in New England with her family—human, canine, and feline.

You can learn more about her books and contact her via her website at SydneyJaneBaily.com.